# SODA POP SOLDIER

## ALSO BY NICK COLE

### The Wasteland Saga

*The Road Is a River*

*The Savage Boy*

*The Old Man and the Wasteland*

# SODA POP SOLDIER

## Nick Cole

**HARPER** Voyager
*An Imprint of* HarperCollins*Publishers*

Harper Voyager and design is a trademark of HCP LLC.

HarperCollins books may be purchased for educational, business, or sales promotional use. For information, please e-mail the Special Markets Department at SPsales@harpercollins.com.

FIRST EDITION

Library of Congress Cataloging-in-Publication Data has been applied for.

ISBN 978-0-06-221022-7

14 15 16 17 18   OV/RRD   10 9 8 7 6 5 4 3 2

# Chapter 1

The war starts at 6 A.M., in-game time. By 6:45 we're losing Hamburger Hamlet as our entire line begins to disintegrate.

It isn't a total collapse. Pockets of resistance hold out in key positions, buying ColaCorp time, expensive time, to fall back and reorganize. On my right flank, Kiwi holds a high hill overlooking the Song Hua river basin. We call that hill WonderSoft Garage because of the small power station and vehicle spawn depot located there. WonderSoft had made the capture of that hill and power station a primary objective in the last three battles we'd fought at this end of the basin.

And it looked like they were gonna try for it again today.

Over BattleChat, Kiwi swears as he burns through the ammo that an air resupply Albatross barely managed to get through. In my mind, I can see empty lager cans parading around the workspace that is Kiwi's keyboard and monitor, as ambient in-game sound resounds in a metallic symphony of ammo brass expended in adult-sized doses. If the sound of auto rifles and explosions is a kind of music, and to some of us it is, then Kiwi is Beethoven.

Through graphically rendered feathery willow trees and the game-supposed heat waves of the day, I can barely make out what's going on up at the top of the hill in brief glimpses. Three fast-attack WonderSoft Goats, their version of a jeep, and a Thrasher light mech are burning. Thick oily smoke belches from the mech, and a moment later it explodes in a shower of sparks. More WonderSoft Goats and Thrashers climb the road to the bridge that leads to our side of the river.

WonderSoft infantry scramble from cover, racing to other cover, as Kiwi fights hard to keep them from crossing the choke point at the bridge and capturing WonderSoft Garage. It's about to get real intimate, real quick.

"Command, we're gettin' killed up here," shouts Kiwi over BattleChat. His transmission is broken and distorted by automatic weapons fire in the background. "I'm down to three grunts," he continues. "Request reinforcements or evac, A-S-A-P! If you've got fire support, I'll take it now, but you'd better drop it right on top of my position, your choice, Command."

Minutes earlier I'd requested Command point two transports of grunts our way as reinforcements. One of our dropships got jumped by a flight of WonderSoft Vampires as they'd approached the LZ. The other, piloted by RiotGuurl, had gotten away.

I hope.

RiotGuurl is as good a pilot as I've ever worked with. Losing the first transport hadn't been an easy choice for her, but when a WonderSoft Vampire caught your electronic scent, there weren't many options left for a transport squadron other than to split up and run like hell to get away from that wicked ground attack jet.

Since then RiotGuurl was maintaining radio silence. I know she's chasing every nook and cranny in the jungle-clad hills that surround the basin on all sides, flying her gunship way too close to the computer's representation of the ground, looking for a route back into Hamburger Hamlet so we can resupply and reinforce the river crossing. Maybe even help Kiwi.

"Be advised, Command, it's just me now. All my grunts are KIA." Kiwi again. "Two ammo packs left and multiple Softs inside the wire." Kiwi never gives up. Even when he's being overrun. Maybe it's an Australian thing. Once this war is over, I plan on taking some of my winnings and heading down under to spend some time in Gigaboo Flats at the Wonky Boomerang, Kiwi's favorite postbattle watering hole. But hopefully the Cola Wars will never end, or else how will I get paid?

"Kiwi, evac not possible at this time. Sorry about that, son." It's RangerSix, ColaCorp's tactical commander. The fact that he's overseeing our little firefight reinforces how crucial this battle really is for ColaCorp.

Using my targeting monocular, I scan the sloping hills and tall grass behind and above Hamburger Hamlet for our commander's avatar. RangerSix is the kind of guy who can change a battle with a basic rifle kit and some explosives. As usual I can't find his hiding place.

Across the river, WonderSoft artillery begins throwing everything they've got at us. Head down inside my command post, I crank my speakers to full ambient in-game sound, cutting off Catherine Wheel's seminal late-twentieth-century album *Ferment*. I'm waiting to hear RiotGuurl's turbines. She's Kiwi's only hope now.

"Sixty rounds left. How about fire support, RangerSix?" It's Kiwi.

"Negative at this time." I hear the quiet frustration in RangerSix's smoke-stained voice.

"Die in place again, huh?" grunts Kiwi.

Behind me, in the detailed squat bamboo and stone village that is the game designers' representation of a fictional Southeast Asian river basin village, a place we call Hamburger Hamlet as a nod to the often bloody struggles for online supremacy that take place there, our armor rolls through, retreating farther to the east. We've been holding this side of the river, waiting for our massive Charger IV battle tanks to cross the muddy brown shallows under heavy mortar fire. Now, it's time to bug out.

WonderSoft Garage has always been the key to control of the river crossing at Hamburger Hamlet. There's no bridge, but the river's shallow enough to get most vehicles across. Now that the overwatch Kiwi was providing at the garage is on the verge of being taken, the battle, at least here alongside the river, is lost for ColaCorp. Any of our units on the far side of the river aren't getting back to our lines without an airlift. The game day still promises more fighting. It's Saturday, and the network goes big on coverage for the weekend. But to lose good armor this early would spell disaster for whatever Command has in mind for us to do next. We've gotten the Chargers back to this side of the river. That's enough for now. We'll have to fight another battle somewhere else.

"Afraid so, son," says RangerSix to Kiwi over BattleChat regarding any kind of assistance. Or to be more specific, the complete lack thereof. "Sorry."

Kiwi doesn't reply.

The turbines of RiotGuurl's Albatross scream loudly as she coaxes the VTOL transport slash gunship into a tight bend south of my position. The fat hover jets that hang beneath the stubby wings of the wide-bodied OD green Albatross kick up a spray of water as she bleeds altitude and speed getting close to the surface of the river.

For a brief second there's hope.

But, as I swing my avatar's view around, locking her craft into my HUD, I don't need imaging software to tell me her ship's already down to 48 percent integrity. The Albatross is vomiting black oily smoke while blue flames climb from the turbines across the fuselage, licking at the pilot's canopy. Seconds later a dart-winged fast mover, camouflage shifting from sky gray to river brown as its onboard computer tracks position relative to target and adjusts the color scheme, comes into view. It's a WonderSoft Vampire and it vaults the bend farther down the river, rattling out short bursts from its forward-mounted 30 mm chain gun directly into the Albatross's burning fuselage.

The pilot's an amateur.

RiotGuurl's finished.

Any good pilot would just let her crash into the ground, but this jerk wants a special gun camera "kill" to put up on his web-wall. A professional player kill worth bragging about. Or at least he's hoping to brag about it.

"Not today," I mutter and order my air defense grunt to take out the Vampire, an easy kill at this range and altitude with a preoccupied pilot. The grunt, skinned in jungle camo and battered light body armor, leaps out from behind the barn at the far end of Hamburger Hamlet and scrambles to shoulder the ground-to-air HammerClaw missile.

With in-game ambient sound cranked up to full, I hear an unseen WonderSoft sniper's Barret3000 go off like the sudden snap of a dead branch. A moment later my grunt is flung backward from the impact of the supersonic round.

That means WonderSoft has snipers in the hills on our side of the river. Things are actually worse than they seem.

"C'mon you lazy . . . ," growls RiotGuurl over BattleChat as her Albatross loses an engine and begins to list badly to starboard. I know she's scrambling to maintain some kind of altitude in order to get the replacement platoon she's carrying out the door and somewhat near our position alongside the river. Parachutes puff to life just beyond the flaming fuselage, but the falling stick of badly needed grunts and players will be scattered all along the river at best. With our line currently collapsing, they'll be less than combat effective. They probably won't even be able to link up with any friendlies.

I hit E on my keyboard and then Spacebar, making my avatar jump up from behind the sandbags I'm using as the command post I'd set up back when I thought there might be some kind of contest for Hamburger Hamlet. But that's not happening today.

I race for the air defense grunt's gear, knowing the sniper sees me. A good sniper will wait for me to reach the dead grunt. It'll take two point five seconds to exchange my rifle kit for the shoulder-fired HammerClaw Air Defense System the downed grunt carried. That'll be all the time the sniper needs to blow my avatar's head off. My hope is that a good sniper, and I hope this sniper is good, is waiting for another grunt to appear and pick up the valuable Air Defense gear. My other hope is that he's not expecting a real live player. Or at least that's what I tell myself as I reach the grunt's prone body.

ColaCorp SOP insists live-player avatars look just like the AI-controlled grunts. Hypermuscled, digital depictions of front-line real-world combat troops. Dirty green jungle-stripe fatigues, dull green and grease black tiger-striped face and arm camo. Even the same gear with the rare exception of a shotgun or a favorite sidearm. It's good policy. The enemy expects an AI grunt's reaction to any given circumstance. So we all look like grunts; that way the expectations are lower. Except a live player can do the unexpected.

RangerSix is probably behind that smart idea.

I pause at the kit and roll left a heartbeat later. A spray of dirt blossoms on-screen as the Barret's round explodes in the mud just beyond the dead grunt's body.

Where my avatar's head should have been.

Now the WonderSoft sniper will need to pull the slide back and chamber another massive round, a serious drawback to using the Barret3000.

I exchange kits with a tap on the keyboard, raise the shoulder-fired missile, and select *Shotgun Mode,* firing on the fly, not even waiting for the high-pitched tone indicating lock. The micro missiles that scatter away from the launcher don't have far to go as the Albatross and Vampire streak straight over the top of Hamburger Hamlet. They sidewinder skyward and punch right into the bottom of the frost-gray SkyCamo of the WonderSoft Vampire.

*Kaboom.* No Vampire. Musta hit an armed weapon or maybe even the fuel tank.

Meanwhile, RiotGuurl's finished.

"Lateral's gone . . . I'm going in," she says just before the Albatross smashes itself into the cliff wall below WonderSoft Garage above the river.

I know RangerSix sees it happen. Seconds later he's broadcasting an areawide alert. "Albatross Two-Six is down. Repeat, Albatross Two-Six is out of action. All units, we are leaving this AO! Be advised we are evacuating the river. Fall back to rally points appearing on your HUDs now."

A moment later, a yellow triangle indicating a rally point has been established a kilometer to our rear appears on my avatar's CommandPad. The tanks rumble away dustily into the foothills behind Hamburger Hamlet, unbothered by the snipers. Across the river I can see WonderSoft grunts swarming into their slate-gray troop carriers. A missile streaks away from one of them, crosses the river, and smashes into a nearby barn, turning everything into sudden flying, flaming matchsticks. Casualty reports flood in from my platoon. I order my two heavy-machine-gun units to open fire on the WonderSoft transports as they approach the river crossing. Smoking tails of depleted uranium rounds streak low over the river at hypersonic speeds as plumes of water blossom in the shallows and on the far bank. My gunners are just finding their range as the first WonderSoft transports wallow into the muddy brown water.

On the hill above my position, WonderSoft Garage, the rattle of gunfire and brass has stopped. Kiwi's out of assault rifle ammo. The fight up there is over.

"Kiwi, what's your status?" I say over BattleChat as I retrieve my rifle kit.

"Not good, mate. Not good at all. It's a real knife and gun show up here."

"I can hold the Hamlet for a few more minutes if you can get out," I tell him.

"Negative. Perfect, not happening. It's too hot, hot, hot to leave." I hear the *pop pop pop* of his sidearm as he spits out the repeated word.

"Be advised." It's RangerSix again. I can tell he's pointing this message at me and me alone. "We are leaving this AO now, Perfect-Question! Get your platoon moving and cover those tanks. Watch for antiarmor mixed in with snipers above your position."

"What about Kiwi?"

RangerSix says nothing.

"No worries here, mate," Kiwi breaks in. "I'm havin' a barbecue and I've invited all the WonderSerfs. Main course is a whole lotta thermite." Seconds later, "See ya, Perfect."

The entire jungle hilltop around WonderSoft Garage blossoms in rosy red, flaming destruction. The explosions billow and rise above the soft feathery jungle haze and the sleepy yellow-brown river. Several smaller, secondary explosions accompany the blast, indicating WonderSoft's APCs, probably just arrived to establish control of the captured objective, have also been invited to Kiwi's barbecue.

Kiwi loves his explosives.

"G'day, mate," I whisper, watching the apocalyptic ending of ColaCorp's hold on WonderSoft Garage. Then my squad is up and moving into the hills, low and slow, watching for snipers.

# Chapter 2

"My grunts were getting chewed up the whole way back to the evac point. I lost twelve." I'm telling Sancerré about my bad day.

"Oh, where did you lose them? Go to the last place you'd look. Whatever it is, it's usually there, in the last place you'd look."

My girlfriend does not understand my job.

"You're not listening," I say.

"Yes, I am. You said you lost your little grunts."

"Yes, I did say that, but you don't know what I mean by grunts. If you did, you would know I cannot go back and 'find them' in the last place I would look for them. They're dead. KIA."

She pauses from packing her camera bag. I notice there's a little black dress and heels inside.

"I understand. You don't need to get testy with me; it's not like I'm two years old," she says as she snaps up some memory sticks from the floor. "They're something to do with your game. Just go find them, or better yet, get some new ones."

"First off, Sancerré, grunts are computer-controlled AI bots assigned to each player. They look like basic versions of our avatars. Like real modern combat troops. Once they get 'killed' they're dead. They don't respawn. Second off, it's not a game. It was, when I was paying to play like all the subscribers, but now I'm a professional and if you'd get your head out of your viewfinder, you'd realize the 'game' I'm playing is paying the rent right now."

"We don't use viewfinders anymore; SoftEyes shows exactly how the shot might be composed."

She's a photographer.

"I understand that because what's important to you is important to me," I say. "But that doesn't always seem to be the case in reverse."

"Okay, okay, enough. Tell me about your bad day playing war. What happened to all your grunts?"

"They got killed. Happy?"

"People got killed?"

"No, my grunts got killed, and every grunt under my command is my responsibility and gets deducted from my total score, which gets deducted from the ColaCorp victory point total, which gets deducted from my weekly bonus."

"You shouldn't let that happen." Her tone indicates she understands the seriousness of the loss. Or at least that we won't be getting as much money as we need in next week's paycheck. "Who killed all your grunts?"

"Listen, there are real players fighting me online . . . fighting my team, ColaCorp. Got that?" I feel a rant coming on. I feel an argument in the air. Like an afternoon storm coming straight at you.

"Yeah, duh! I wasn't born yesterday," she snaps.

And . . . I love her.

"Goon."

"You're a goon."

"I love you."

"I love you too." She sighs and sits down next to me. "I'm sorry I haven't been listening. It's just that this is a really big spread for *Vanity*. And being an assistant for fashion's greatest eye, in his very own opinion, is . . . very . . . let's just say it has its problems." She sighs again, and there is enough in it that I know the world is bigger than me and my problems. I know I'm not here just for me. That . . . I want to rescue her.

"I'm sorry," I say. "I feel bad for just coming in here to vent. It was a bad day all across the board. We were fighting for advertising space at Madison Square Garden and Channel Two. It was kind of a big day."

"Is that why they pay you? Because if you and your friends win your little games, then they get to own those places?"

"Well, they don't get to own them, but they get the right to pay to advertise in them. Plus LiveNet broadcasts the best parts of the action with lots of product placement." It's surprising to me that Sancerré, a trained commercial photographer, doesn't understand advertising-gaming rights. But fashion seems to be its own little world. Hence the photo shoot last year in which she'd had to hide under a model dressed as an undead Marie Antoinette carrying a light saber as the dust children of Mogadishu ate red apples on a dirty street full of cheap PrismBoard advertising. I think it was an ad for jeans.

"I guess today was pretty important then," she offers.

"Yeah, it was. But forget about it. How long do I get you for?"

"I'm afraid that's it, soldier boy. I've got to be there early. Miss Thing threatened not to show up over shoes and they want me in just in case she actually makes good and doesn't show." She shoulders her bag and checks her makeup in the mirror one last time.

"Is she really that bad?"

"Worse. She actually will show. She will get what she wants and then she'll play the martyr as everyone grovels for her forgiveness. It's disgusting."

"I guess I might just chill tonight," I say with a stretch and a yawn. "I'm pretty wiped. If you're back by midnight we can go watch the big PrismBoard at Madison Square Garden change over to WonderSoft."

"I wouldn't count on it. Mario made us clear our schedules. He wants to buy us all drinks at Burnished."

"Do I need to worry? I mean, I know you love those things. I'm sorry I don't have enough. I wish I had more. I'd spend it all on you . . . honest." I would.

"I know you would. You don't have to worry about those things. Everything will be okay. It won't always be like this."

But somehow I do worry, and I imagine it being much worse.

Later after she's gone, I bring up my compilations. I'm feeling very 'Nam. I mix a scotch and SevenPlus, ColaCorp's new not-cola and light a smoke just as this great remix from the 2030s of "White Rabbit" by the band that first did it comes on. Outside, the late winter sun drops below the horizon. New York locked in winter is even more depressing than getting pwned by Wonder-Soft. I want jungles and golden sunsets. I want a hot yellow sky and murky haze and gurgling brown rivers. I light some incense, crank up the humidity control, put on an army surplus T-shirt and 'Nam out.

I settle into the warm glow of the scotch, dragging absently at my smoke. I think about WonderSoft Garage and Kiwi. He's near the end of a bad streak of getting killed. ColaCorp doesn't like that kind of thing, and it's only a matter of time until he gets reduced from professional status back to overqualified amateur. He needs a win. In truth, the whole team needs a win. We all do.

WonderSoft had come into its own in the past six months of online warfare, dominating most of the battlefields for advertising supremacy. Eastern Highlands was my first campaign as a pro player-officer and already we'd lost some major advertising venues in and around New York. Losing everything to Wonder-Soft is probably going to get me booted back to freelance, which will cut down on any future campaign actions. Worrying about Kiwi only reminds me that his situation is only slightly worse than mine, and everybody else's at ColaCorp for that matter.

My 'Nam set gets psychedelic, cascading over remixed hits almost a century old. I mix another drink and log in to the bunker, the gathering place for ColaCorp professionals after battles. Senior commanders generally don't drop by after a loss, but after a win they come in and hand out bonuses and slap our backs over the feeds. Today's beating at Eastern Highlands and the loss of Madison Square Garden and Channel Two ensured we wouldn't be seeing them tonight.

It sucks to lose.

Kiwi's avatar, large and hulking, shirt off and showing curling tribal tats, leans against the bar talking to JollyBoy, an intel specialist, and Fever, a great medic who's managed to revive me on the battlefield more than a few times, including one time I swore I was really down for the count. I double-click them and bring up all three of their feeds. Kiwi looks even more frightening in real life than his avatar. Huge, hulking, tattoo overdose, a leering lecherous grin, almost drooling into the monitor. His eyes are the only feature that tell you he's a friend and not foe. His eyes say, *I'm kind; you can trust me, mate.*

"Perfect, Perfect, PerfectQuestion. Did ya make it back to the rally, mate?" he asks me.

"Cheers, Kiwi. It was touch and go, lost a lot of grunts. But, yeah, we got picked up at the rice paddies just as WonderSoft started dropping their artillery all over us."

"We lost three slicks at the LZ," JollyBoy announces happily. The joker he is never fades, even when he's delivering the worst of news. Losing three Albatrosses made me glad I was on one of the slicks that got out of there. What a cheap way to get it. It's one thing to be out there fighting, making a bad choice, getting caught in the cross fire, whatever, and losing your day's winnings and bonuses. But catching a slick and feeling safe as you hear the turbines spool up and thinking you've just escaped one bad day of gaming and that you're gonna get paid and make it to the next fight only to have it explode a moment later—well, that's another thing. A bad thing.

"Any players?" asks Fever. Fever cares little about the fighting. I don't think I've ever even seen him running around with his weapon out. He only carries his med packs, boosts, and revival pads. He cares more about us than the battles.

"Yeah," JollyBoy says with a smirk. "ShogunSmile and War-Child . . ."

"These laughin' newboys with their haiku tags. Serves 'em . . ." Kiwi's drunk, but just drunk enough to catch himself at the beginning of a lecture on tag choice. His discipline isn't long for this world.

"What're you listening to, PerfectQuestion?" asks Fever, catching the music in my background.

"Lemme see . . . 'Vietnam' by this reggae guy, Jimmy Cliff."

"Sounds good. . . . feed me."

"Me too," says Kiwi. I patch them into my music, inviting JollyBoy also.

"No thanks, PerfectQuestioney. The Harlequin likes his industrial trance calliope mixes."

JollyBoy is weird.

We play music for a while and watch funny clips from the day's battle, usually something we or our grunts did that was dumb. We talk about what went wrong and what we should have done, all the while each choosing a song, not realizing we're saying something about ourselves, the day, and maybe life. Finally Kiwi plays "Waltzing Matilda," mumbles something about the long ride to the Wonky Boomerang and logs off without further good-byes. JollyBoy has long since faded into other conversations. Fever smiles and says, "Keep your head down, Perfect," and is gone. I scan the cantina for RiotGuurl.

Why?

Because it was her first battle as a professional. That entitles her entrance into the bunker. I tell my empty apartment it wasn't her fault that we lost and put on "Black Metallic" by Catherine Wheel. Another drink and I force myself to think about Sancerré and a relationship that's coming apart at the seams. But my guitar-driven thoughts keep returning to RiotGuurl.

Who is she?

Where is she?

And why do I care?

# Chapter 3

At twenty to midnight I wake, still sitting, still holding the remnants of a watery glass of amber scotch on my stomach.

This is my life. Digital death, destruction, and some computerized mayhem by day, long lonely nights with too much scotch and too little of the woman I loved.

Love? Loved?

Love.

Too much of some, and too little of something else.

"Do I love what I do?" I ask myself as I throw on my trench, a vintage leather piece purchased as a reward after promotion to professional, and hit the streets for the short walk to Madison Square Garden. I guess I do, otherwise why else be out on a dark winter night, dirty green glowing frost clinging to the sidewalks, just to see the fruits of my defeat?

Just before midnight, across the street from where I stand in the shadows, the giant PrismBoard goes dark. It had been showing a blond construction worker slaving away in a hot suit setting up a thousand reflector assemblies. Slowly, dawn's first rays hit the fragile plantlike assemblies, which then burst into life like so many exploding crystals. Around the construction worker, Mars begins to turn green as plants grow, cities rise, and the construction worker begins to age into a handsome silver fox. His hot suit is suddenly gone and now his tanned skin shows through a brilliant white cotton shirt and khaki trousers as an equally beautiful little girl, presumably his granddaughter, grasps his hand and holds up a cola. He smiles and drinks. Then the ColaCorp logo emerges.

The ColaCorp ad runs two or three more times while I wait and then, at just the moment the Martian colonist begins to age for the fourth time, the PrismBoard goes dark. Now, only the blue lights of the tall towers that disappear into the cloud cover below Upper New York remain. Upper New York blocks out the night sky. Strange, eerie lights move back and forth up there, above the cloud bottoms. The dark feels more sinister as those faraway lights provide the only illumination down here in the dark remains of a mostly forgotten old New York.

I feel that preconcert moment before the main act comes on. When it's dark and you feel like something important is about to happen. Or at least you did, when you were young and a band seemed like it might be something more than it was.

The WonderSoft logo appears on the PrismBoard as French horns, mournful, tiresome, noble nonetheless, begin to serenade the nearby streets with the coming of WonderSoft's endless barrage of SoftLife products. In front of me, in the middle of the street, a bum in silhouette passes by while techno-Gregorian chants promise both of us hope in a bubble.

What does that bum want from life? Glory days remembered, youth retained, a friend long gone, never returning, suddenly appearing. WonderSoft wants him to have the latest SoftEye. He passes on, oblivious to the expensive marketing of WonderSoft's next gen product, my defeat, their victory.

"Two sides of the same coin," says a voice from the shadows behind me. I turn and see a tall and very thin man. Shadows abound all around us as the light from the PrismBoard shifts, and for a moment all I can see is a long coat, a wide flat hat, and a SoftEye gently pulsing purple in the left eye of the stranger. Then I can see all the images of WonderSoft's ad playing out across him and the light-turned-bone-white alley he stands in.

"I say, two sides of the same coin, isn't it?" he repeats. His voice reminds me of some English actor from one of the period piece dramas Sancerré watches only for the outfits, or so I suspect. Like a violin playing Mozart. With malice.

"I don't follow . . . ," I mumble.

"One's defeat, another's victory. Your loss, someone's gain." Now WonderSoft's Voice of the Ages begins to sell product above and behind me on the giant shining PrismBoard.

"SOFTLIFE, IT'S NOT JUST A DREAM ANYMORE . . ."

"Who cares, though? We were tired of the old, give us the new," continues the thin man from the shifting shadows. "A new liberator has come to save us from the shackles of ColaCorp, or U-Home, or UberVodka, or TarMart, or, yes, even someday, WonderSoft." Golden light erupts across the street as the PrismBoard gyrates wildly to the exciting new life WonderSoft promises. From the shadows the thin man steps forward and I can see him clearly now as the light display floods his face with a thousand sudden images.

"DREAMS, LIFE, LOVE, SEX, FRIENDS, FAMILY, POWER, SOFTLIFE OFFERS ALL THIS AND . . . ," intones WonderSoft's Voice of the Ages.

"Death to the tyrant, hail the new Caesar!" shouts the thin man above it all and throws his long arms sickeningly wide. In the golden light of the PrismBoard I see that he is not so much a thin man, but more a bony man. A man whose skin is so tightly stretched, it shows all the bones in his face.

A man made of bones.

"Faustus Mercator, commenter on things past, things to come, and . . ." He laughs. "All things in general, really. Butcher, baker, and of late, kingmaker. At your service." He removes his hat—doffing it, I think they used to say in old bound books—and makes a slight bow, never once taking his SoftEye off me. The skin of his skull is dry and tight and, as I said, bony. Every ridge, protrusion, and scar is seen beneath the shaved, dark stubble of his bulbous head.

A character. Out here on a night like this. I wonder if he's just a fan, or even a reporter blogging on the changing of the marquee. I've started getting a lot of e-mail for PerfectQuestion, and not all of it can be classified as fan mail. Many times there's an undercurrent of disgust, rage, or sometimes something worse. For a moment I stare at him contemplating what he's capable of. Hoping for the best, I shudder and wrap the trench tighter around my body. I don't have much body fat or warmth to spare. Borderline poverty does that to you. I smile, nicelike, testing him. His response will let me know if I should fight . . . or flee. His agile build and height, three inches above my six feet makes a good argument for flight. He smiles back, immediately, beamingly.

"Picking up your check tomorrow, I s'pose?" he asks, drawing out the last word.

He knows I'm a professional. Maybe the only people down here at this time of night are the winners and the losers. Since I know who the losers are when I look in the mirror, that must make him one of the winners.

WonderSoft. But which one? BangDead, Unhappy Camper, OneShot, CaptainCarnage, maybe even Enigmatrix. Wonder-Soft had been recruiting the best for much of the past year. Their national battlefield advertising wins reflected as much.

"SOFTLIFE, A NEW WAY, A NEW HOPE, A NEW TO-MORROW . . ."

"No bonuses I'm afraid, though." He continues on, his smile a sudden row of large white headstones erupting between thin lips. "At least not with . . . your present company."

"Do I know you?" I ask.

I'm not a fighter. I don't mistake my online capacity for rapacious violence with my real-life code of nonviolence, which isn't so much a code but more of an excuse for not being the toughest guy in the world and all the problems that comes with. I don't make that mistake.

"I know a lot of things, PerfectQuestion. A lot of things." He also knows my online tag. Great, what else does he know?

"Monday morning, after tonight's match, you'll show up at Forty-Seventh and Broadway, ColaCorp's once proud headquarters," Bony Man continues. "And you'll be shown to the seventy-fourth-floor meeting room. Checks will be handed out, and poor old RangerSix will discuss what went wrong and how things might get better. In the end you'll leave and prepare for Tuesday night's big match in the Eastern Highlands. Forget Sunday night, later today, tonight in fact now that yesterday's dead and buried. Sunday night's just small change, just a bunch of brush-fire skirmishes to be stamped out. Tuesday's the real big game. We all know that, PerfectQuestion. Big things are afoot, heavy lifters moving in, all kinds of nasty tanks and antipersonnel plat-forms. Should be a real—what did your pal Kiwi call it?—a real 'knife and gun show,' I believe. But while you're sitting there, PerfectQuestion, listening to all those really nifty big plans of RangerSix's, and when you leave that ever so small, I mean tall, building, ask yourself . . ."

Big pause. He beams, holding his breath. Like the suspense is supposed to kill me.

"Are you happy, PerfectQuestion?"

"What?"

"Are . . . you . . . happy, PerfectQuestion? You know, a feeling of joy, optimism, ecstatic belief. Are you happy?"

"All right, I'll ask myself if I'm happy, OneShot, or Unhappy Camper, or Enigmatrix, or whatever your name is. And if I'm not, what's it to you?"

"Tsk tsk and pshaw," says Bony Man.

Someone read a little too much Dickens.

"I'm no such animal, PerfectQuestion. You're the killer, online. You would know those worthies if you met them in real life. They're killers, like you, online of course. Not me. I haven't the skills for such pursuits. I have only the highest respect for people like yourself who can keep track of so much, all the while pointing and shooting, managing the little lifelike dolls you call grunts, dodging the bullets of the enemy, once again, online of course. No, my fingers get all crossed up and, to be honest, they've got minds of their own. You wouldn't believe the things they've done, the trouble they've gotten me into." He held up one long spiderlike hand in front of his face. Images from the PrismBoard slither across its length.

"My brain gets so discombobulated with all that hectic killing, online. No, no, I'm made for other pursuits. I have talents better used in the real world. But as for you, young PerfectQuestion, you young golden boy, you young Pericles, this is your day, your battle, and you would easily defeat an amateur like me, online of course. I even wonder how much of a challenge Enigmatrix herself would actually be for you. You're quite a killer, online of course." Again he smiles, leaning in at me. I clutch the sawed-off broomstick I always carry in the deep right pocket of my trench. It isn't much, but it just might have to do.

"Which brings me to my original command, or request, if you prefer. Ask yourself, tomorrow on the seventy-fourth floor: Am I, PerfectQuestion, happy?" His polished patent leather shoes grind roughly on the pavement as he spins away from me, turning to leave. It makes me think of stone crypts being opened. He's leaving now, still talking talk and leaving.

"Ask yourself, PerfectQuestion," he throws over his shoulder, "are there meeting rooms higher than the seventy-fourth? Who's getting the bonuses? Where is Sancerré? Where will she be tonight? And don't forget to ask yourself the most important question"—he turns at the edge of the shadows deep in the alley, almost enveloped, almost swallowed whole by the darkness that brought him—"Am I happy?" Then he's gone.

"SOFTLIFE STARTS TODAY, INSIDE YOU."

# Chapter 4

The Sunday Night Game starts and I'm tasked with clearing out a small village of WonderSoft insurgents as the battle lines attempt to coalesce. The insurgents are players who've volunteered, by paying their monthly WarWorld Live subscription, to fight for WonderSoft. The insurgents crossed the Song Hua River downstream and have been ambushing ColaCorp units using a small village up in the jungle highlands as a base.

I haven't lost any troops because I like to play it safe, and all my grunts are fairly leveled up. They don't make many of the mistakes the basic AI-controlled grunts often do. So we take the village and neutralize five insurgents. I check my bonus pay on all five as soon as WhippySFX, the last WonderSoft insurgent, goes down in a hail of gunfire near the village's central raised hut. At twenty per, I make a cool hundred. Not everything I need, but every bit helps.

"PerfectQuestion, this is Six; what's your status?" I switch from my CommandPad to BattleChat and reply.

"We're finished here, whaddya got for us next?"

There's a pause. I wonder if the connection's dropped, or if we're even being jammed by WonderSoft's electronic warfare units. Then, "PerfectQuestion," says RangerSix in his signature matter-of-fact drawl, "I need you to order your unit to link up with ShogunSmile four clicks west of your position. Give him command authority . . ."

I've been fired.

Then, "I need you to log in to OpsDeck for a briefing, Question. We've had a superlab opportunity open up for us, and I need you to take command of the operation. I'm countin' on you, son. Get this done quick and clean."

Not fired.

I order my unit to pack up and move out to ShogunSmile's AO. Three minutes later I'm in the OpsDeck screen and going through the briefing on the superlab.

"Scouts have discovered a hidden complex up-country in the mountains near the city of Song Hua," begins the briefing program avatar, a military admin type. The high-res photos show a small complex nestled beneath a mountain that's more a giant oblong piece of rock erupting from the jungle than anything else. Stunted trees cling to one of its misty sides. The other side is a sheer rock face above the complex.

"Satellite imagery," continues the briefing, "indicates the complex is a laboratory-class facility where dangerous and illegal superscience research has recently been conducted."

WonderSoft will want this, but ColaCorp needs this. Whatever it is. These labs can provide bonus game-changing tech. No doubt WonderSoft will go for it, even if it's just to deny us the asset.

The briefing camera, mounted on a recon drone, overflies the facility revealing a night-vision look at what we're going into. It's an open perimeter and a jumble of squat buildings in two adjacent locations. One location has the distinct look of a dropship landing pad, but slightly different from any I've seen before. The other looks too industrial to be anything but a lab. There's a construction crane on the far side of the lab complex. The complex is mostly composed of octagonal interconnected modules that lead to a main multistoried building. The briefing asks me to choose which type of unit I'll request to take into the superlab.

I tell it to give me the light infantry template.

The briefing hesitates, then takes me to the unit loadout screen. I try to activate my personal unit, Delta Company, but it won't let me. "All main force ColaCorp units engaged at this time," it tells me in its calm, computer voice. The only option available is to pull unknown players from the ColaCorp Special Forces reserve unit.

Great. I have to use amateurs. I stare at the facility map again. There'll be three maps. There're always three maps. I'm probably looking at the first one. So what's the game?

Death match? Domination? Infection?

I check the ColaCorp Special Forces reserve roster. Currently there are over a hundred thousand plus ColaCorp fanplayers waiting, worldwide, to join the network televised fight.

"Isolate veteran-status players and above."

"Done," replies the briefing avatar.

"Isolate light infantry skill sets."

"Done."

I want to tell the avatar to remove the ones with poor social skills and negative sportsmanship reviews, but sometimes those ratings are just the results of complaints filed by sore losers. Sometimes being good at online combat doesn't necessarily make you great at being human.

"Isolate kill counts ten thousand and above." Sure it's WarWorld Live kills, the home game played on console with other amateurs, but ten thousand kills means they're serious about the game and they've got some skills. That's when I started getting noticed by professional teams.

"What's my pool?" I ask.

"47,754 players meet your requirements," replies the avatar.

"Isolate on-target percentage. Above 50 percent."

I don't even ask how many that leaves. I just want shooters now. "All right, fill all five squads from those requirements."

A moment later the avatar sends invites to all players fitting my requirements. The first fifty to respond and log in to the OpsDeck are going in-game during prime time with me to take the superlab.

Within seconds the rosters are full.

"Please choose tactical insertion method," the avatar tells me.

I check the map again.

I check my options. I've only got one. Dropship. In the map, I set the spinning holograph of the LZ marker down on the landing pad. There are three back-blast fences that surround the site. We can use those for cover before going into the main complex.

WonderSoft, on the other hand, can go in any number of ways. They've always got options because they've always got money.

Next I choose my weapons. I select my standard loadout for close-quarter matches like this. I take a gray and graphite black-striped Colt M4X assault rifle with extended banana clips and holographic tactical sights. Three dots, predator style. For my sidearm I take a nickel-plated long-barrel .45 loaded with hollow points. I also take five grenades: three flash-bangs, two smoke. I take my personal avatar skin, which is okayed by ColaCorp for tactical instance maps like this. ColaCorp jungle-pattern camo cargo pants and green tank top T-shirt. Jungle boots. Shaved head and a camo pattern I call SnakeFace. My guy even has stubble. Like me. Except the avatar skin is based on some action hero from the last century. Guy named Schwarzenegger. I'm big on last-century stuff. Things were better then.

"Going live in fifteen seconds . . . ," says the briefing avatar as it begins the countdown to tactical map insertion.

I switch to BattleChat. Before saying anything, I bring up the unit roster. Most of the player IDs have been set to the default position by the network. Can't be showing all kinds of disgusting images to the entire world. I check the names. They are the usual assortment of half-thought-through, misspelled crud that marks amateurs. Some outright obscene name choices, almost half, have been changed by the network to "Player" then a random number.

That'll teach 'em to take this seriously. It's their one shot at going online to fight in front of the whole world and no one will ever know who they are because the network changed their tag and used a placeholder name instead.

On-screen I see the red-lit interior of the dropship Albatross. I pan right and look out through the cockpit canopy. We're cutting through a thick miasma of dark blue and black clouds. Rain assaults the windshield. I try to get a look at the facility from the air, but all I catch are tiny twinkling lights and shadowy buildings.

Moments later we're down on the landing pad and rushing from the Albatross. Players head away from the dropship and go prone in a circular perimeter.

So far so good, and I didn't even need to tell them to do that.

The dropship's engines spool up and the craft lifts off and away from us, cutting its lights and retracting its landing gears as it disappears into the rain and clouds above.

*King of the Hill* appears across my screen.

I hate this type of match. Means we've got to secure the access point to the next map and hold it for three minutes. A King of the Hill match always turns into a shooting gallery for the side that doesn't want to hold the access point.

"Listen up," I say over BattleChat. "Name's PerfectQuestion and this is the op . . ."

Meanwhile I'm selecting the streak rewards I'll receive after each kill plateau.

"We've got to secure the entrance into this lab. That's Map One. WonderSoft will try and do the same thing. Your first job, always, is to kill WonderSoft. Next, identify the entrance to the lab. Last, we'll hold that entrance for three minutes. This is a movement to contact for now, squad tactics. I hope you took weapons you can run and gun with, 'cause we ain't fightin' no defense. Okay?" No one replies. "All right, now's your chance to show ColaCorp something."

In the dim blue light of the storm, a wild collection of jungle combat warriors rises from the tall grass near the LZ. I use my CommandPad to organize five squads of ten. Sure, we're all wearing the same faded ColaCorp jungle green so that we look like a team and are only slightly different than WonderSoft's standard digital gray jungle-camo pattern, but the similarity ends there. Some avatars have shaved heads. Some are wearing boonie hats. One guy even has a K-pot from World War Two. It's all stuff they've either bought through WarWorld's online store or earned as achievements. I couldn't care less how they look. I'm just hoping they've leveled up their weapons. I'd hate to be going into this with someone using the basic unmodded AK-2000 you start WarWorld Live with. But I quickly notice many of the weapons are skinned with high-tech paint jobs and scoped with state-of-the-art targeting systems. That bodes well for impending current events.

The network feed goes hot. Right now the game director is cutting in to watch the action. This superlab objective is critical, but not to today's battle. That's happening, win or lose, somewhere else. But the tech the lab might yield could be a game changer later, if ColaCorp pays to develop it, in the strategic outcome of the ColaCorp campaign against WonderSoft for Eastern Highlands. But we have to get it first.

I break the first three squads off into a group and form a wedge. The other two squads I put in reserve behind the main body and order them not to move until I tell them where the action is. With First Squad on the left flank, Second leading the tip of the wedge, and Third Squad on the right, we move out from the LZ, heading through the wet mud and dark for the dimly outlined facility. Low-hanging mist shrouds the tops of the high mountains. Over ambient I hear nothing but the slap of rain as it sluices down from the tops of buildings and into the muddy streets below.

"Move forward," I say over BattleChat. "Watch for targets; call 'em as you get 'em."

"Lock and load, rock and roll!" screams some hillbilly named SonnyJim over the chat. Another player, LilStreet, opens up his feed. Hard-core drum and bass rap starts pouring out across BattleChat. The first spoken lines are about murdering hoes who cheat and being pushed down by white "so-sigh-et-tee" while someone chants "Monee- Monee- Monee" over and over. I cut his feed.

It's so far so good as we move beyond the back-blast fences and onto the main street of the complex. The pouring rain begins to let up as a small breeze shifts the grass and some hanging industrial heavy tow chains nearby. They creak and jingle while our boots suck at the wet mud. It's only a matter of time before we engage WonderSoft and then all bets are off on whether I can keep everyone under control long enough to find and hold the access point.

"Hey, Question?" says a player tagged AwesomeSauce15. A girl's voice. Sounds young. I can hear the bubblegum snap in the background of her mic. "Sign over here says this is a bioweapon research facility. Weyland-Yutani. Never heard of 'em."

Smart. She's looking for clues. That's the other half of this type of match: solve the puzzle. Most people think WarWorld's all about shooting at one another. It is. But smart players use everything they can learn about the map to then shoot each other.

"Noted," I whisper over the chat. "Tighten up, Third."

We move farther down the main street of the complex. There are a few abandoned construction vehicles on the street. Their wheels are sunk in the mud.

"No sign of any Softies," whispers Bronco24, point man for Second Squad. We pass the first two buildings guarding either side of the small muddy street leading up to the main hub of the complex.

That's when it goes down.

"Comin' in from above," says AwesomeSauce15 as she cuts loose with three short bursts from her HK Mini submachine gun. I check the sky and see nothing but cloud cover, then, drifting down through the mist, I see WonderSoft troops with night-gray parachutes blossoming above their avatars. They must have had the *Base Jump* option and gone off the top of the rock that overlooks this place. Bullets begin to strike at the wet mud all around us.

"First Squad, take that alley on the left. Third, go to the right. Secure both ends of the alley and set up a base of fire. Second, on me!"

I actually hear someone say, "What squad am I in?" But it's too late for that.

"Squads Four and Five, hold the entrance to the landing pad. Stand by, I'll advise you shortly on where to concentrate your fire."

I go wide right behind the building. I check my Command-Pad as we hustle into the dim wet alley. I've already lost two out of Second. The kid playing hard-core gangsta rap got it first. Probably for the best.

The firefight begins in earnest as WonderSoft gets onto most of the roof of the main complex. It's not the worst scenario. I can handle that as long as we control the ground. Sometimes coming in the boring old way, out of a dropship and then in on foot, is the best way. I can control my troops and keep the unit cohesive for a time before it gets all "tag with guns." WonderSoft's arrival had some surprise value in it, but they didn't get much out of it. Now they're strung out all over the rooftops. We, on the other hand are still together, which allows us to work together.

"Who's got sniper rifles?" I say over the chat.

Bucklebee and IrishRogue tell me they're each carrying. "Good," I say. "Fall back and circle wide through the jungle. Get up on to that construction crane at the far end of the facility and get us some cover fire going. Anyone with a heavy, watch the road ahead."

I scan the other side of the street and see Third Squad already moving into the other buildings and engaging targets.

So they're useless to me.

"First and Second, bound up the left side of the street and try to sweep this end of the complex. Watch the rooftops. Second Squad, moving now. Follow me."

I push out into the muddy alleyway running alongside the main street. I take a couple of shots at a WonderSoft grunt on a nearby platform and hit him in the legs. He goes forward off the roof and falls into the mud farther down the street with a wet splat. Most of Second has followed me, and while someone uses a couple of grenades on a nearby roof, I check the dead Wonder-Soft player in the mud and realize we're facing a Special Teams unit. The guy's wearing a grinning skeleton motorcycle mask over his avatar's face. WonderSoft must've spent some dough to get this unit involved in the fight, which sucks because it means, yes, they're amateurs, but they've also trained together.

"Question," says AwesomeSauce over BattleChat, "I can see a couple of guys from Third on the other side of the road. They're about even with us."

So maybe they are useful, jury's still out.

The gunfire from both sides is deafening.

Ahead, there's a small street and then what looks to be some kind of garage or hangar across the way. I check the Command-Pad and see that Third Squad is down to half strength.

"Okay, First," I call out over BattleChat. "Poppin' smoke. Get ready to move up the street. We'll cover you from here." I scroll my mouse and right-click a smoke grenade. I toss it out into the main street to cover First's movement. WonderSoft begins to fire into the thick, erupting smoke. Everyone with me begins to unload on the rooftops.

I get a head shot on one.

Now I have two. I need one more for my first streak reward.

"AwesomeSauce," I call out over the chat. "Check that garage across the road and tell me if it's clear."

I watch as her avatar, a lithe, young, impossibly perfect-figured female soldier wearing standard-issue fatigues, oversize boots, and a cocked jungle hat with a black feather in it dashes across the road and into the hangar. A second later I hear the tight *braaap* of her lethal HK Mini.

"Clear now," she says breathlessly over the chat.

"Good work. Get ready to move into that hangar, Second, as soon as First says they're in position."

I check the CommandPad and see Third's now completely decimated. I've lost two with Second Squad, and First hasn't lost anyone.

"Four and Five, stand by to move up," I say over the chat.

"Covering," screams someone from First. Then, "Suppressive fire on that two-story at our one o'clock." Someone's got leadership skills. I make a mental note to watch the replay and find out who took charge of First.

"Move, Second, into the hangar!"

The gunfire from First is cacophonic, but we still lose a guy,

Player9000177, as we cross the street firing and race for the low dark mouth of the hangar entrance. Once we're inside, I tell what's left of Second to watch the exits.

I bring up my CommandPad, watching as my avatar exchanges the smoking M4X for the battered CommandPad with the nicked and camouflaged edges. Game designers like to make things look frontline authentic. The satellite feed shows me where my squads are and any known WonderSoft positions that have recently fired weapons or been observed by any of my troops. WonderSoft appears strung out across the complex. We're concentrated in three areas—First on the street, Second with me in the hangar, and the rest back at the LZ. Good. Now it's time to find the "hill" and try to be king of it for at least three minutes.

Even though WonderSoft is firing on the hangar, I'm able to stand back and use my tactical monocular to scan parts of the complex. If I happen to land on the King of the Hill entrance, I should get an intel analysis timer. But it doesn't happen.

I need my first streak reward.

*Baaanngg!* Suddenly my screen turns a blinding white as ambient sound dissolves in a high-pitched whine.

Someone's just flash-banged us.

My first thought is that WonderSoft is trying to take the hangar.

Seconds later my screen shows me shifting, distorted double images of my surroundings. Someone fires wildly as tracers blur across my vision. I hit Z and throw my avatar to the floor of the hangar, watching my screen throw wild ghost images everywhere.

"Boycott TarMart because of their racialist policies!" screams someone on my team. When my on-screen vision returns, I can see that the someone is SGTSmokeLoveWeed, and he's preparing to pop another flash-bang and blind us all. I set my three-pronged aiming reticle over his chest and ventilate him with a short burst from my M4X. His avatar's body sprays blood spatter across the wall of the hangar, ragdolling from each impact, jerking in time to some grotesquely hip dance. He's dead and out of the game before he even hits the wall.

Great!

Third Squad was useless to begin with, and now I get a bonus round of "let's take this very public opportunity to make a personal statement at the expense of my online job."

Don't people ever get tired of protesting? Not everything's a March on Selma moment.

AwesomeSauce is hit, but she's not dead.

"What're we gonna do, Question?" she asks me over the chat.

*Yeah,* I ask myself. *What are we gonna do?*

One of Second Squad took a *Medic* perk and he's throwing out medical packs emblazoned with the red-and-white ColaCorp logo. In the dim little hangar, AwesomeSauce's health starts to return.

Surprise, surprise, terminating SGT-whatever has rewarded me with the kill I need to start my first streak reward. The refs were on that one. Good call.

Now I have access to extra equipment, supplies, air strikes, and a whole host of options depending on which streaks I've selected to unlock each time I reach a kill tier.

I activate my first streak. A moment later the gritty voice of the unseen game announcer calls out, *"Drone Recon,* inbound."

I scan the overcast skies and see the shadowy outline of the spindly recon drone circling the complex. I check my CommandPad.

*Recon Drone Intel package available.*

I click on it.

Two reports.

I can see everyone on the battlefield. WonderSoft is concentrated around a small area west of our position on the street. The main building separates us. They're moving toward it. The rest of the Softies are on the buildings all around us. I distribute the report to my squads, and seconds later I hear our two snipers begin to fire from the distant construction crane. I watch as a Softie blinks out of play on my CommandPad.

The other report reveals the entire tactical map, where the King of the Hill zones are and also other possible intel locations. I spot a King of the Hill zone at an entrance to the main building just ahead of us, a loading dock. But there's another entrance on the other side of the facility right where that smaller group of Softies is heading. Back near the landing pad there's another small secondary intel site, simply titled Sulaco Uplink.

I don't have time for that. We've either got to crack that King of the Hill zone at the end of the street or somehow stop WonderSoft from starting the clock on theirs.

"Listen up, Fourth . . . I need you to double-time it to the location I'm marking on your HUDs now. That's the King of the Hill zone WonderSoft's gonna try and use. I need you to stage here." I draw a red circle behind some smaller buildings near the WonderSoft door. "Fifth, I need you to move to this location and put some fire onto that target. Once you're in position, open up on 'em. Fourth, as soon as Fifth Squad works the target over, move in and finish off any survivors. You shouldn't have much resistance between here and there, but that doesn't mean there isn't a Softie out there running *Stealth* perks, so watch the shadows."

"Question." It's AwesomeSauce. "We can't take that zone at the loading dock with just what's left of First and Second."

"Have to," I reply.

I watch the map as both the fourth and fifth squads move out to intercept WonderSoft. In five minutes it should all go down.

"All right, First, we're gonna need you to keep all the Softies heads down for a minute. We're moving all the way up the street to the loading dock. Once we get there, we'll hack it and start the zone. Try and keep them off us."

"Roger that, Question," says a guy named BubbasChoice.

"Well, AwesomeSauce, we've gotta take the hill, that's the name of the game. You with me?"

"I'll go first." Her tone is bored. Flat. Condemning.

"Anyone got a streak goin' yet?" I ask over BattleChat.

"I got *Death from Above*," says one of the snipers. "Three kills already."

*And you haven't activated it yet,* I'm thinking. "Could you go ahead and use it?" I ask him.

"Sure 'nuff."

A moment later I hear a low-flying aircraft high above the battlefield.

"Air strike, inbound," warns the game announcer.

"We need to hit the entrance now," I shout over BattleChat. "Go! Go! Go! Everyone take the hill. Snipers, do what you can to give us some cover."

I rush out into the street, beating AwesomeSauce. Hoping at least one person will follow me, I head toward an abandoned cargo truck canted in the middle of the muddy street, firing short bursts at where I think WonderSoft might be. I reach the truck and pin my avatar against the side. Bullets are flying everywhere, smacking into the side of the truck on galvanized, crushed soda can notes. I can hear the loud, distant cracks of our snipers' rifles. I lean out from one side of the truck and watch as most of Second Squad rushes up the muddy street around me, heading for the loading dock. Three of them get hit instantly. I draw a bead on one of the WonderSoft shooters and double-tap him in the chest.

I need four more kills for my next streak.

What's left of Second is with me on the truck.

"Keep firing, First, until we reach the door," I call out over the chat.

"Hey, Question, truck's on fire," notes AwesomeSauce.

She's right. In seconds it'll explode.

"Get away!"

Everyone sprints toward the loading dock.

The truck explodes behind us.

Casualties.

Above us, a small close-air-support aircraft is making missile strikes on the Softies near us—*Death from Above*. One rocket goes straight down into a building ahead of us, and a second later the entire building explodes, sending a shock wave of debris and flame out at us. My avatar is knocked back and onto the muddy street. I take 50 percent health damage.

I'm up and moving just steps away from the shadows of the loading dock. I make it to the loading dock. A small sign near the security door welcomes everyone to Hadley's Hope.

First Squad is firing from behind a concrete wall down the street.

I hack the lock, watching as my avatar inserts his high-tech hacking tool into the computer lock and starts the operation. Fifteen seconds later, the game announces, "King of the Hill starts now."

The clock starts, and we've got three minutes to go.

"*Enemy Drive-by*, inbound!" yells the in-game streaks' menacing announcer.

"Take cover!" I call out needlessly.

Down the street, a low-riding flat windowless APC with thick ceramic tires and a small swivel-mounted Hauser minigun turret races toward us.

I've never seen an APC like that on a streak.

I briefly wonder if it's some kind of new WonderSoft vehicle, just as I hear *Bluuuuuurrrr*; it's the gun erupting in a loud, high-pitched sound as it sends hundreds of miniballs ripping into what remains of Second Squad—except for me, AwesomeSauce, and another guy. And seconds later, that guy's heavy machine gun—wielding avatar disappears in a shimmering haze of lead as his body receives hundreds of hits almost instantly. Awesome-Sauce switches out her HK Mini for the RPG on her back. She fires fast and skips the RPG off the muddy road with a small splash and right into the undercarriage of the APC. It explodes upward and lands on its side with a metal-rending crash as it begins to burn.

"That worked" she yells over BattleChat as if I need to be told.

The King of the Hill clock is already up thirty seconds. Two and half minutes to go.

For the next two minutes it's a shooting gallery and we're the ducks. WonderSoft's elite unit keeps us pinned down behind the narrow confines of the loading dock, making sure they keep up the fire while they reload. We take sporadic shots and I get two of them.

I need one more kill to activate my next streak.

I check the CommandPad and see that Fourth Squad is engaging the WonderSoft unit on the other side of the facility. WonderSoft has started the clock on their King of the Hill zone. For some reason, Fifth never ended up where I told them to and they're moving in way too soon and too close on WonderSoft.

"*Enemy Gunship,* inbound," warns the game announcer.

If they drop it in on us, we're finished. I hear the approaching engines of the gunship. It's an HK. A hunter-killer. It streaks over the darkened sky and begins to hover above WonderSoft's zone. Its auto cannons roar to life and I watch on the Command-Pad as both fourth and fifth squads are wiped out.

One minute.

I spot a distant Softie shifting position and drop my sights over him, squeezing off a quick burst. I hit him, and he keeps running. I track a second longer, lead him, then fire again. This time he goes down, and I've got my last kill.

And my next streak reward.

I call in an *Auto Gun Drop* and just after the game announcer says, *"Auto Gun* package, inbound," a dropship streaks underneath the gray canopy of the storm and drops a parachute containing the *Auto Gun* package off its back cargo deck. It lands near the beacon I've tossed onto the floor of the loading dock. I only have to crawl out onto the platform a little way to unlock and activate the package. Once I do, I watch as the sides of the crate flop down and the gun unpacks itself. Within seconds, its targeting lasers activate, cutting through the gun smoke and gloom as it begins spitting out short staccato bursts of hot lead at any WonderSofties within range. I get six more kills in the space of a minute.

"Thirty seconds!" calls out AwesomeSauce over the chat.

I'm down to nine players from both surviving squads, including the two snipers at the far end of the complex.

WonderSoft cracks their zone and advances to the second map just after our timer hits zero.

We get the King of the Hill bonus as the loading dock's main door slides open, revealing a shadowy, wide, low-ceilinged hallway where overhead lights flicker on and off at random intervals.

"RangerSix, this is PerfectQuestion," I say as I call in our status to Command.

"Six here; go ahead."

"Command, we need reinforcements. I'm down to nine total, including myself."

"I know, I've been watching the network feed, son. Heckuva a job. Bad break on Third Squad, though . . . but I was hoping you'd get the main door open, at low cost, and you did. I'm authorizing you one of our fan SF units. I think they'll do the job considering where you're at."

Where I'm at?

"Where am I at, exactly?"

Long pause. Hairs rising on the back of my neck.

"You didn't read that sign at the front gate, the one that said property of Weyland-Yutani Corporation?"

"Saw it. Didn't mean anything."

"And the big identifier on the face of the main building," continues RangerSix. "LV-426. C'mon, Question, you've never seen the greatest sci-fi combat film ever made? *Aliens*."

I pause. On-screen my avatar crouches on the platform as the eight other surviving players reload their weapons. My avatar is holding one hand to his headset, indicating I'm in communication with another element. Over ambient sound I hear the high-pitched whine of an Albatross's engines powering into its braking hover. I turn. The Albatross rotates above the street. In front of the loading dock. it hovers above the mud.

"Everybody wants to play Space Marine, Question, but this is where it all started . . . Colonial Marines," says RangerSix over the chat with a wheezy laugh.

Some fan units go beyond just training together like old gaming clans hoping to get picked up for a network battle. Some take the next step and modify their avatars to effect a cosplay element. I guess these were that sort. I've even heard of fan units who go on vacation together and try to live like their characters in real life. That's a little much for me.

Colonial Marines.

Their armor and camo is similar to ours with only slightly different touches. It reminds me of images I'd looked at of soldiers from the Vietnam War. But spacier. They have helmet-mounted small lights attached. I can't see how that will be any use in online combat. The trick is to not attract attention to yourself so you can shoot first. Headlights seem to be the opposite of that.

"Are these guys somehow . . . relevant to this map?" I ask RangerSix.

He laughs briefly. "Yeah, they're real relevant, Perfect. Listen, this is how I see it. I just did a little checking. This is some sort of advertising stunt for the network. The map, that is. I just talked to a guy over at programming who told me they're debuting a trailer for the *Aliens* reboot after the match tonight. Really, you never saw *Aliens*?"

"No, never. Is it good?"

He laughs again.

"You need to watch it, son. Listen up, this map will somehow relate to the movie. Whether it's original source material or something from the reboot, I don't know. But the bioweapon you're looking for is most likely an alien. So watch out, there might be a whole lot of them inside the main building. If there are . . . well, your team's in big trouble."

"An alien?"

"Roger that, Perfect. An alien. If, and I'm just guessing here, we can get that tech unlock, if we can get the alien as a combat unit or something, that could be a game changer for us. So, if you can get it, get it. If you can't, make sure WonderSoft doesn't. The last thing we need right now is a bunch of those crazy things running around my battlefield, playing for the wrong team."

"One question, Six? What does this alien look like?"

Again he laughs. I don't think I've ever even heard him laugh once. Or express emotion. Anything. "I really can't believe it, Question," says RangerSix, still laughing. "Look like? It looks like a cross between a gorilla and a shark and a scorpion. You'll know it when you see it, son. Six out."

Two new squads of Colonial Marines come up the loading dock ramp.

"What's the mission, sir?" asks a player tagged MarineSgt-Apone.

"We've cleared the first map. King of the Hill," I tell him. "Now we enter the second map. No idea what match it might be, but we're all about to find out. This is a superlab op, so the endgame is to retrieve the tech and get out. You guys down?"

"Straight up, Question," says MarineSgtApone, a black burly commando-type avatar chewing a short stubby cigar.

"Listen up, Marines," he says over BattleChat. "We got to go in and clear us some Softies out. So you know the drill; watch the corners and clear the shadows. We've done this on our own mods. WarWorld's level design might be a little different, maybe even a lot different probably, and the AI on the aliens is most likely gonna be insane, can't tell. But in the end they're just big bad bugs, and we're probably the best suited for this one 'cause we be the bug stompers. Who'd a thought?"

Everyone cheers. This must be like the Super Bowl for them.

"All right, let's squad up and move in," I announce over the chat. At the lead of First Squad, I head into the alien-infested remains of a place called Hadley's Hope. LV-426.

# Chapter 5

"So, Apone," I whisper over the chat as we proceed slowly down the dimly lit passageway leading into the belly of the main building, "what exactly are these aliens?"

There's a pause. *Wait for it,* I tell myself.

"Never seen the movie, sir?"

"*Aliens?*"

"Yeah. Never seen it?"

"No. So go ahead and tell me what we're walking into."

Pause.

"Well, sir . . . I don't know. Uh . . . Never know with the WarWorld programmers. Somethin' trickylike no doubt. But uh . . . basically an alien is like a tiger that's been crossed with a spider and a T. rex."

"Huh . . ." I think about that. "Not a gorilla, shark, scorpion?"

Pause.

"Yeah," says Apone. "Those too."

"They don't have weapons? Guns or explosives or laser beams or anything like that?"

"Uh . . . no. They are the weapon, sir."

"I don't understand . . ."

"You should just watch the movie, sir."

"It's a little late for that."

We arrive at a massive security door. The numbers 01 are stamped in a large space-age font across the door's surface.

"We open that door, sir," whispers Apone over the chat, "be ready 'cause I got a feelin' it's on real properlike."

"I read you five by five on that, Sergeant," says one of the other marines.

Everyone takes up a position across the wide hallway. The overhead lights flicker intermittently and without pattern as gun-toting avatars cling to the sides of the hall, kneel, or lie on their bellies. Two heavy gunners take up the center position; one is a big male avatar, the other a short, curvy, tough-looking Hispanic chick. Apone advances to the door controls.

"Ready, sir?" he asks over the chat.

"Do it."

The doors part and slide open.

There is a moment.

A whole entire moment of stunned surprise.

The door opens onto a wide multilevel room. It looks like some sort of administrative complex: clean, sterile; soft blues and plastic whites. Partitioned spaces surround the perimeter of the room. Part office, part medical lab.

But that's not the surprise.

We're the surprise. And so are they.

WonderSoft.

Us.

Fully armed for bear, loaded with heavy weapons and explosives and separated by thirty meters of flimsy space-age office cubicles.

WonderSoft's elite SF unit has just entered the far side of the sprawling office space. They're still in a patrol column on the walkway that surrounds the room and leads to the lower level of administrative desks.

"Let's rock!" screams one of the heavy gunners, and it is indeed on. There's no time for the CommandPad. It's old-school run and gun. In seconds, both sides are pouring into the room, firing at everyone. Heavy gunners are cutting the place to shreds, their weapon fire echoing brutally through my fragile speakers. I lob flash-bangs and slide behind a row of cubicles for cover. Paperwork and computers are exploding all around me. Several marines are already down. I hear the distinct *brraaap* of AwesomeSauce's sub Mini doling out a short, unhealthy supply of bullets. I pop cover and engage a death-masked Softie with a burst that punches into his neck and head. His avatar goes down spraying fire, dropping a grenade. A half second later, the cubicle he disappears into splinters from an explosion.

Within seconds, both sides are behind cover and firing at each other from opposite sides of the room. I'm crawling toward one of the walls, hoping to start a flanking action, when I pass a row of active computer monitors showing various security cam feeds of different locations around the complex.

That's when I see the alien.

Aliens.

Yes. It is all those things.

Gorilla.

Shark.

Scorpion.

Tiger.

Spider.

And T. rex.

On the monitors I see views of the outside of the facility. Others of some unknown part of the lab. I also see some sort of dimly lit maintenance area, and another monitor shows the hall we just came down. Or one very much like it.

Aliens are racing down it. Aliens are filling every shot. Aliens are coming for us.

All around my position, WonderSoft SF, Colonial Marines, and what remains of my squads are shooting at anything that moves, like there's a moonlight madness special on ammo. A Colonial Marine lunges past me, auto rifle firing short bursts at some unseen foe. He goes down, slumped over another cubicle.

*Team Fortress Death Match* appears across my screen.

The second map has started.

In a Team Fortress Death match, both sides attempt to construct a defended position while trying to destroy the other team's defended position. This should be very interesting, what with all the gorilla, spider, tiger, shark, scorpion, aliens running amok. Oh yeah . . . T. rex, can't forget the T. rex part.

I check my CommandPad for tactical updates.

"Hey, Apone, listen up. Those things are right outside, and my guess is, they're coming in after us. It's a TFD match. We've got to find a position and fortify before those things get in here."

"Yeah, I saw that, sir," he says between bursts of auto-rifle fire. "Real cute of WarWorld."

The Hispanic female gunner chick is advancing through the field of desk debris, raking WonderSoft's positions with short bursts of her very large, heavy-caliber machine gun.

"We gotta get outta here now!" shouts someone over the chat.

On my CommandPad tactical display, I find two air shaft vents leading away from the room. One is on WonderSoft's side; the other, on ours. That'll lead somewhere. We can't defend this room unless WonderSoft's willing to stop shooting at us—which I don't think is an option right now.

A quick look at the roster on my CommandPad tells me I'm down to just nine players again.

"Apone," I call out over BattleChat. "Rally everyone . . . here." I mark the access hatch nearest our position. "I'm popping smoke . . . should give us some cover."

"Roger that," says someone whose chat gets overrun by a staccato burst of sharp-edged weapon fire. I'm not sure if it's Apone. Maybe he's dead.

I hear a loud hammering sound beyond the gunfire erupting against the doors and walls. Thunderous. Sharp. Growing and turning into a thousand grasshoppers smacking into a windshield at high speed. A quick check of the security door we came through and I see why. It's denting inward. Those things are flinging themselves into it.

"Covering fire!" yells the Hispanic chick over BattleChat. MarinePFCVasquez. An immense amount of weapons fire resounds across the cavernous room as her weapon switches into overcycle mode. She must be running the *Rapid Fire Freak* perk.

I pop smoke and shout "We are leaving!" over the chat.

By the time we make the access hatch, I hear the door metal tearing apart. There's too much smoke to see anything else, and there's nothing to block the access hatch with.

Eight of us make it into the ducting.

I'm glad to see little AwesomeSauce along with the rest of the survivors, all marines.

"Follow me," I hear MarinePvtWierzbowski shout frantically over the chat. He must be at the head of our dwindling column inside the large air duct. Behind us we can hear screeching—animal alien screeching.

MarinePFCVasquez's gun falls silent back in the main room. I check the CommandPad to see who's left. Vasquez is KIA.

I have to admit; I'm a little tense right now.

"Keep following the duct. It should lead to an area we can fortify," shouts Apone over the in-game screeching of distant aliens and our echoing passage along the galvanized metal ducting. I hear automatic gunfire ahead of us. Behind us again. Off in the distance . . . then, not at all.

If WonderSoft gets taken out by the aliens, does that mean we get a default win? I'm guessing not.

"Wierzbowski!" someone screams over the chat. "They got Wierzbowski!"

"LOL . . . just like in the movie," someone else says, laughing.

"Take the left fork," shouts Apone over the chat and automatic weapons fire. Pistol shots. Behind us, on ambient, I can hear scrabbling claws and a leathery slithering against the outside of the ductwork all around us. WarWorld has gone all in on this map. The muscles in my neck feel like iron bands. I open and close my jaw to shake out the tension, then blink twice and look at the screen again.

We pass a torn-out section of the ductwork. It gapes outward, covered in dark inky blood and rising steam.

"Keep moving, Marines!" says someone not Apone.

I chance a look behind me and see an alien scrabble around a corner in the ducting. An alien. I cut loose with the M4X and hit it multiple times. Acid and tentacles explode in steam and blood. More of them are scrabbling behind the dying thrashing shrieking thing, to get over it, to get at me. To get at us.

"Anyone holding a 'nade?" I shout over the chat.

"Last one," says MarinePvtFrost. "After that, we're down to just the magazines we got left and some witty banter." He laughs over the chat.

"Use it behind us, now!" I tell him.

The corridor's tight, but he gets it behind us and destroys the ducting and some of the aliens.

"Something ahead . . . ," says MarineCorpsmanDietrich. Her voice is frantic. "I think it's an opening!"

"Check it first," warns Apone.

"Like we got a lotta choices right now, Sarge," adds Frost.

After a moment Dietrich calls out "All clear" over the chat and we're in. Then, "Hey, we're in Operations!"

I crawl through the last of the ducting and drop down into a small room with two doors. The marines are already opening them, guns aimed outward.

"If this is anything like our mods," says Apone, "then we only need to seal the two doors that lead into Medical. Those and the duct we just came through."

"Yo, heads up, there's a materials station here!" calls out someone named MarinePvtDrake.

"Good, grab it and start sealing these doors, Marines," orders Apone.

I walk out into Operations and find desks, displays, and transparent walls. The marines are already welding steel plates across the two main doors to the section. I see AwesomeSauce bent over a nearby display. Its light turns her avatar's face a soft blue.

"We've got feeds on most of the facility," she says as I approach. "They're everywhere. The aliens, that is. WonderSoft is probably in the living quarters section but I can't get in there. So . . . if they made it, they're there." She snaps her bubble gum. "What now, Question?" I check my CommandPad.

We're down to AwesomeSauce, Apone, Drake, Dietrich, Frost, and a guy named Crowe whom I haven't heard from much.

That makes seven of us.

The goal of the TFD match is to destroy the other team's defenses before they destroy yours. With the aliens surrounding everything, that means if teams don't have a fortress, then they don't have much of a chance at survival. WonderSoft is on the other side of the station. Between us and them, there are . . . a whole lot of those things. I watch the monitor as one of the aliens drags the body of a Softie avatar down a dimly lit grated corridor.

"Can we hurt them from here?" I ask AwesomeSauce. "Using the computer system?"

She's silent for a moment.

"Nah, doesn't look like it."

I'm thinking.

"Listen," I say over the chat. "Obviously you guys are fans of the movie. I've never seen it." I pause, waiting for the various shouts of incredulity to pass. Then, "Does anyone have an idea how we can hurt WonderSoft? I mean, anything from the movie."

No one says anything.

"In the movie, the atmosphere processor blows the whole place up," offers Apone. "We could blow ourselves up. Not much use in that, I guess."

"Yeah, kinda defeats the purpose, Sarge," says Frost.

"I don't suppose anyone's got a *Bunker Buster* streak? We could drop it on the living quarter section and take them out or at least expose them to the aliens."

"I got a *Special Delivery*," says Drake. "But we need to be out in the open for that. We could use the weapons package option it comes with, though. That'd be real nice right about now."

And I've got *Hang in There, Lil' Buddy*. My final streak. A dropship escort for two minutes. But we're inside. What's it going to do, fire through the windows?

"I haven't seen this old movie either," says AwesomeSauce. "Why do they blow up this atmosphere thing?"

"Oh, they don't mean to," says Dietrich. "Just happens after a really awesome firefight when they get ambushed by warriors . . . those things. The aliens. They damage it when they walk into the nest."

"The nest?" I ask.

"Yeah, that's where the alien queen makes her nest."

"What if . . . ," I'm thinking out loud. "What if that's map number three? What if this map TDF match has an inherent destruction feature? The aliens. They destroy your fortress, forcing you to find and move into the third map before that happens. It's probably a matter of time before . . ."

There's a dull thump on one of the doors. Everyone swivels, guns pointing at the door, watching the dent that's just appeared there. Then another.

"They're here," whispers Apone.

"Yeah . . . matter of time," says Frost. "We better do something fast 'cause if they get in here, it's gonna be a real short meet and greet."

"I think this isn't the game," I say. Everybody's still watching the door. It's dimpling inward even more. Everyone's slowly backing away, putting desks and displays between themselves and the rapidly deforming door. "We've got to get out to that atmosphere processor. That's where the next map is. The aliens will destroy both fortresses in a matter of time. We don't need to wipe out WonderSoft, the aliens will do it for us. Drake, have you unlocked the vehicle upgrade on that *Special Delivery*?"

"Played for three years . . . what do you think?"

"Good, call it in and drop it right outside those windows there." I point out into the dark landscape of wind and rain. I can see shadows moving out there among the rocks and debris. There's nothing human avatar–shaped about them.

"Uh, we can't get through those windows with just rifles and no explosives, genius. That's a transparent wall. Guns are useless. We need, at least, a 30 mm chain gun or explosives," says Dietrich.

Seams are beginning to appear in the door leading to Medical.

"Hang on . . . ," I say, activating my third streak. "It's about to get real hairy for a couple of seconds."

A seam in the door's thick welded-plate metal rips open like a shirt. One of the aliens sticks its shiny black bullet-shaped head in. Its grinning jaws snap open as another set of smaller teeth shoot out, dripping thick saliva.

I fire a quick burst and the thing's head explodes, its jaws still snapping as the body goes limp.

"I think 'hairy' might be an understatement, Question," whispers AwesomeSauce.

"Yeah . . . we're, like, done," adds Drake. "I got sixty rounds left and . . ."

"Call in that vehicle now, Drake. Do it! Select the APC!" I shout over the chat. Meanwhile I'm dialing in my last streak. I set the spinning red target hologram on the door the aliens are about to come through.

"Ready, everyone . . . you know the drill. Conserve your ammo. Check your targets. Everyone stay frosty and we'll get through this," says Apone over the metallic pounding and concussive thuds. The door is coming apart.

"*Escort Gunship,* inbound," announces the game.

"Heads down, everyone!" I yell over the chat.

The aliens are crawling through, tails whipping, teeth gnashing, claws reaching, opening and closing. Drake begins to fire.

I turn to see the dropship lowering beneath storm-leaden clouds and the darkness outside, swiveling as it hovers beyond the large windows. Guns extend, centering on the spinning red targeting reticle I've placed over the door the aliens are coming through.

"Get down!"

The dropship's 30 mm cannons whir to life, smashing the explosive-resistant window to shards, sending a hazy stream of ball ammunition right into the splitting door. Aliens explode, ejecting yellow acid and greenish guts everywhere.

"Drake, call that APC in now!"

"Done."

The spinning guns of the gunship wind down for a moment, waiting for a new batch of targets.

I shout, "Move now! Everyone through the window and out to the APC." Aliens are still climbing through the Swiss-cheesed metal opening that was the door to Medical. The guns of the Albatross spool up again as AwesomeSauce and Crowe clear the smashed window. More aliens explode. Even more are coming through.

"Something's got me!" shrieks Drake over the chat. I look over to see an alien coming through the floor. I fire a short burst into the dark hole beneath his feet and the thing explodes down there in the dark. Drake's avatar screams. Nice touch, WarWorld.

"I'm down to 25 percent," notes Drake over the chat.

The whining death pitch of the dropship's guns recedes.

"C'mon, we are leaving, Marines!" says Apone.

It's a small fall out through the shards of the window and into the mud and rain. I take 2 percent damage. Rain falls across my HUD as my avatar gets to his feet. Ahead of me the others are already scrambling toward the APC. It's an identical version of the APC used in the *Drive-by* streak earlier. Above us the hovering dropship swivels, its chain guns dispensing a blurring barrage of death in a wide arc at multiple closing targets all around us. Over in-game ambient sound, I can hear the dying screeches of the prehistoric-like aliens mixed with the howling wind and splashing rain.

An alien comes charging and thrashing out of the dark, tackling Drake's limping avatar. The other marines and AwesomeSauce are firing at a swarm of aliens trying to cut them off from reaching the APC. I close with the one on top of Drake and execute the hand-to-hand kill option by clicking both mouse buttons at once. I can't chance shooting the thing, it's all over Drake. A quick cut-scene plays out as my avatar reaches one hand out and grabs the thrashing head of the alien. My long-barrel .45 comes into frame against the skull of the alien and fires, putting a hot bullet through the elongated skull. Its jaws snap shut, then open, going slack in death.

I get Drake up and we're moving. We barely make the red emergency-lit interior of the APC as the vehicle's autoturret fires madly at the swarming aliens. The dropship above us turns, engaging multiple unseen targets. Like I said, we barely make it.

We're moving fast over dark terrain. AwesomeSauce is driving. I check the CommandPad and mark the location of the distant atmosphere processor.

"ETA in five," she shouts over the chat and the rumbling drone of the APC.

"You think there'll be more of those things out there?" I ask Apone.

"Can't say, sir. Can't say that at all. But my guess is that most of the aliens are probably based around Hadley's Hope. The only thing we're for sure guaranteed to find at the atmo' processor is the queen."

The queen is probably what we need to defeat to gain the tech option.

Dietrich's running the *Medic* perk so we get our health back. The APC also contains a full-reload supply point. We can't swap out our weapons, but we're totally rearmed. Magazines and 'nades.

The APC pulls up in front of the massive sloping pyramid that is the atmosphere processor. Outside it looks like we've traveled to another world. The jungle and the mountains are gone. Here, there is only twisted rock and fast-shifting clouds of purple blue and shadows that almost seem to streak across the low sky. Small red and white lights twinkle and blink from the superstructure of the plant, signaling in the gloom of the storm.

"In there," says Apone over the chat. "'bout nine levels down we should find the nest . . . and the queen."

We move in. Tactical formation.

The place is crawling with aliens.

The marines seem to know where the access stairs leading down are.

"We've run this mod on our own, several times. 'Cept this is way better," says Drake calmly over the chat as he cuts down three warriors with a burst from his auto rifle.

At level five, strange growths, almost like the bone structure of some ancient dinosaur, cover the tight passages and narrow descents. At level six, things move from intense to insane, as aliens start crawling along the walls and ceilings, leaping in at us. But we stay tight and figure the shifting AI out. In time we're working as a team, cutting them down as they come at us in sporadic waves. We're calling out targets, burning through ammo just to keep them back. At level eight we find nothing. Just a wan red light and darkness covering the entire empty level.

"We made it," says AwesomeSauce. I don't hear the bubble gum.

"Yeah . . . ," says Drake, his voice high pitched and triumphant. He's cruising on a cocktail of success and gunfire. "Sometimes things turn out way different than you thought they would. In the movie we all . . ."

"Sulaco Uplink, established," interrupts the game announcer abruptly. "*Orbital Strike,* imminent."

" . . . died," finishes a much subdued Drake. Then, "Man, *Orbital Strike*'s like game over for all of us. Both sides."

*So that's what that was,* I think, remembering the intel point back on the first map.

RangerSix told me that if I couldn't get the tech, then I was to make sure WonderSoft didn't get it either. I guess the WonderSoft commander had the same orders.

"One minute to *Orbital Strike,*" says the gravel-voiced game announcer.

"Those cheaters," swears AwesomeSauce, her voice petulant, bitter.

"Yeah," says Frost. "Losers gotta lose."

We're done. Nothing survives an *Orbital Strike*. The only reason you use it is to make sure the other team doesn't win. No matter how good they are. Or how hard they played.

"Listen up, Marines," says Apone over the chat quietly. "We made it this far. Let's go down there and finish this thing now. Who cares what happens after that."

Silence.

"Straight up," says Crowe. "Let's do it to it."

We rush. We rush the stairs to level nine and find the shadow of a massive alien queen looming like some otherworld prehistoric nightmare in the mist, surrounded by large elongated eggs. She hisses, then roars, her jaws opening and snapping shut.

"You guys did great tonight," I say over the chat just before it all goes down. "Good job."

"Hey, Question," says Dietrich. "You're no Gorman . . . thanks, everybody, that was the best game of my life."

I didn't get that Gorman remark, but everyone agrees in their own way. It reminds me for a moment that games are supposed to be fun. Just fun. That's all. We were terrified all the way. Nervous. Laughing. Solving the riddle of the game together. Y'know . . . fun.

Then . . .

"Marines!" yells Apone as we enter the ninth level.

We're firing, bullets smashing into the rushing, looming queen. Acid splashes everywhere, away from and into us. Her tail is whip-snaking up and then down upon us. Claws wide . . .

"Stand by for *Orbital Strike*," says the game flatly.

And the screen turns white . . . then gray, outlining everything in drifting ash. Slowly freezing. Dissolving. I'm looking into the jaws of the alien queen.

*Game Over* appears across my screen.

# Chapter 6

Sancerré doesn't come home from the shoot that weekend, or the club the crew was going to afterward, for that matter.

Sullen gray morning light reminds me I came home late, after standing outside Burnished, trying to catch a glimpse up at the candlelit club entrance that led to an interior I'd never see. I'd stood outside in the snow, listening to the sound drifting down from the floors above: clinking glasses, too loud bar chat, and a coy laugh that reminded me of another one I knew all too well. I came home and drank scotch and watched a replay of Sunday night's battle. I drank and tried to focus on the business of work. I lost myself in memorizing WonderSoft weapons charts, APC hard points, and everything else that might give me an advantage. If Cola-Corp ends up defeated in the Song Hua Eastern Highlands campaign, then we were finished for most of New York City's best advertising.

What then?

My paycheck, rent, Sancerré? All three seemed tied together. My only answer was to get better at killing WonderSoft, grunts and players.

In sleep, I dreamed hot dreams of sweaty candlelit battlefields of still, tall grass in the night. Billowing white clouds barely moved against the almost light blue of night beneath a bone china moon. In the dream the air felt warm and smelled of sandalwood. Kiwi was there, in the gunner's mount, and I drove the armored, in-game jeep we call a Mule. Both of us guzzled gallons of amber scotch and listened to a surreal mix of the opening march from "White Rabbit" on a small portable radio as phrases and words from across time and politics, Eastern chanting and wailing, things Sancerré had said, formed a soundtrack for our efforts to kill every one of our enemies.

WonderSoft.

Landlords.

Mario, the world's greatest fashion photographer, in his own, not very humble in the least, opinion.

Rich guys, kids I knew in high school, rock bands we hated, corporate America and the open source hackers who ruined everything for everybody. Everyone and anyone got it, and even when they should have stopped, they kept coming at us in waves. They kept closing in on us as Kiwi worked the revolving matte-black triangular twin barrels of the Hauser minigun atop the Mule. Kiwi shirtless, sweating, grinning, screaming over and over again, "It's beautiful, man, it's beautiful."

I dream of war . . .

. . . and wake to early, soft gray light, watery scotch, and the lock chime beeping softly as Sancerré comes through the door, mumbles a "sorry," and goes into the bedroom and closes the door behind her.

# Chapter 7

Downtown, at Forty-Seventh and Broadway I take the express elevator to the seventy-fourth floor. In the mirrored walls I see my cleanest khakis can't stand up to the shave I need. My whitest shirt, my only white shirt that might pass as acceptable for mainstream society, can't look clean enough against the gray-green pallor of my face. At least I had my Docs polished on the way over. And the caramel-colored leather trench, what can you say, it's the best; it goes with my entire wardrobe and it's full of surprises, like the aviator shades I find in the inside pocket along with a random matchstick.

Nervous?

Sure. Who wouldn't be after a couple of beatings like this weekend's, an assured dressing-down and impending bonus possible termination, rent due, girlfriend probably cheating, and oh, yeah . . . I'm hungover.

I don the aviators, bite the match, and try to convince corporate America I am the problem. An invisible Do Not

Disturb sign wraps itself around me. The suits in the elevator, bright boys of banking and finance and higher education and weekends in a place I've heard called the SkyVault, cease their inane chatter of ultramodels, back ends, deals, points mergers, options, and blah blah blah . . . Bang.

I am the problem!

Mayhem made to order.

I can tell they get the message when they shuffle out whispering to each other as the doors close behind them. I ride out the last stretch to the seventy-fourth alone. In the silence, the bony man, Faustus Mercator, asks me *Are there meeting rooms above the seventy-fourth?* and . . .

. . . *Are you happy?*

The large, polished mahogany conference table shines thickly as drop-down monitors, paper flat, slide from the ceiling. I can hear Kiwi bantering with JollyBoy. Outside the immense windows, gray morning wafts by in misty cloud banks. Soon all the screens are filled with the fifty-nine others who make up Cola-Corp's professional online army. Of late, an army beaten repeatedly by WonderSoft.

"Ladies and gentlemen," says RangerSix from the largest screen on the main wall. He's represented by neither avatar nor real-time image, just an old-school radio wave pulsing with the steady intonations of his speech.

"First off I want to start with the obligatory 'compliment sandwich,' which all my self-improvement books tell me I need to use when talking to nonmilitary personnel. S'posed to help me in corporate America. But, dammit to hell, kids . . . there's no time for corporate double talk. Everyone gave it their best and we still got beat, and we got beat badly. In the process we lost several assets we very much needed to take back the Song Hua river basin. Vampires got into both tank battalions, and now we're down to three. I repeat, three tanks. Three tanks ain't gonna support any kind of counterattack. So, in short, we're down to the Eightieth Infantry Brigade; two artillery companies, the 661 and the 663; and what's left of our air wing, which boils down to an attack squadron and the Albatross platoon."

"We've always got snide remarks . . . oh, and lots of sticks and stones," Kiwi offers cheerily.

"Not funny, son." RangerSix sounds like he wants to stomp on Kiwi. On my Petey, Kiwi messages me, "Too bad WonderSoft has rubber armor and we're made of glue."

"Right, sir, sorry," Kiwi says, chastened.

"You're a good soldier, Kiwi, but I would be remiss if I didn't let you know our next battle will determine whether you stay on professional status or not. Frankly, it might mean that for the rest of us also. The number crunchers at ColaCorp feel salaries, our salaries mainly, asset fees, and sponsorship could be better spent on more traditional advertising. So we have to do something right here, right now to prove them wrong. In short, boys and girls, we need a win and we need it Tuesday night. So here's our plan . . ."

I think about the plan.

I think about it as snow drifts in from the front that's making its way down onto Manhattan. High above, above the seventy-fourth floor, the bottom of Upper New York pokes through the clouds. Down here on the ground it's business as usual, as the few commuters who still live in the old city hurry through the fading afternoon light, hoping to get home before the storm hits.

I need to go home. I need to confront Sancerré about where she was all weekend and why she didn't come back last night. But the check ColaCorp gives me is way too small to pay the rent. So I head to Grand Central Station. I've got an hour to get there, and if I don't make it in time, I won't be able to earn any money tonight.

It's money we need, Sancerré and I, to have a relationship before we end said relationship. We are, as of midnight last night, officially ten days overdue on our rent.

Sancerré once told me that Grand Central Station used to be beautiful.

I hate the place.

It smells like bad patchouli and cheap disinfectant. Supposedly it once handled the entire commuting workforce of old New York. Now it's just a series of huddled stalls. Old hippies from the double "0"s hawking their incense candles, FreakBeads, and tie-dyed Blue Market SoftEyes. I could care less about sand candles and cheap monocles that reconstruct everyone naked.

Some people I don't want to see naked.

The only thing I'm hoping for right now is to buy into tonight's tournament and get on *Truth and Light*.

I hate *Darkness*. Only freaks play *Darkness*.

Right now around the world, *Darkness* fans, many more than those who make a habit of actually playing *Darkness,* are hurrying home to make sure their subscriber accounts have handshaked with the Black so they can watch the sick fantasies of others come to life.

I meet Iain near a stall where two old hippies are listening to *Pearl Jam Redux* as they try to sell SoftMat knockoffs that probably won't last out the year. They're stoned, so who cares if Iain lays a disk on me that carries a minimum two-year Education sentence, federal I might add, along with the obligatory sex offender rap for a take-home bonus. That's hard time if your log jibes with what the feds will be watching for tonight.

"What'd I get?" I ask him while thinking, *Please be* Light. *Please be* Light. I repeat it over and over to myself.

"You never know, bucko," says Iain. "You . . . never . . . know, so buy the ticket and take the ride."

I stare at Iain. He sports two SoftEyes, both anthracite gray.

I wonder what's going on behind those lenses. Does he care? Is he worried or scared, like I am? If some sicko used the disk he's just handed me in the last match, I'm now liable for any crimes he committed while logged in using the program contained on that disk. A routine stop, a minor altercation, and the cops run a cursory data surf on anything I'm carrying and I'm busted for sure. If so, who knows? With a good lawyer I could fight it, but good lawyers cost good money, and the only money I'm holding is a small supply of increasingly rare cash, the only form of currency the Black deals in. Iain does not accept MasterVisa.

"Are you in or out? It makes no difference to me?" says Iain, as if he's trying to push me.

Iain has always been one cold cat.

"I'm in." Even though I shouldn't be. *Please be* Light.

*Please be* Light.

"Then that's one large, my brother," he whispers. I hand Iain a grand. My last grand. The grand earmarked for half the rent.

*Please be* Light.

I'm home by five just as the storm hits the streets hard. I crank up the heat and find a note Sancerré has left for me.

*Back tonight. I promise. I'll explain. Sorry.*

> *Love,*
> *Goon*

It's Monday. She doesn't have any kind of shoot I remember her talking about. I've got four hours until I can crack the disk, so I pour a small scotch and fire up a little reggae. Soon I'm asleep and Kiwi and I are once again fighting our way across that nightmarish landscape, a battlefield of candles and sawgrass. Night winds drive unseen wooden wind chimes against each other.

We kill a hundred medieval knights conjured up from an Eiger nightmare. Kiwi works the twin Hauser, screaming, as the sound of our guns turn orchestral at some point. Gregorian darkness. The knights are lurching, off perspective, bullet-riddled charcoal sketches that remind me of Picasso's *Don Quixote*. They're too much for us and they refuse to die, swinging wide-bladed two-handed swords as we are overrun. The moon fades, the barrels melt down, and only the medieval chanting remains in the dark and the shadows that survive.

"It's beautiful, man . . . ," whispers the voice of an unseen Kiwi.

I wake, wonder where I am, remember, then mutter, "Please be *Light*."

# Chapter 8

At nine thirty I'm mostly sober, though I've filled a nice big tumbler of scotch and pulled out half a pack of smokes I've been meaning to throw away.

The stuff you're liable to see on the Black is often just too much for a sober mind.

I lock my disk in, run my cracking daemon on it, then my computer screen turns black.

Maybe my computer couldn't handle it.

*Abandon All Hope* . . . appears on-screen.

I hate this stuff.

I'm trying not to run the lights in the apartment to keep our electric bill down, and I know there's no one in the room with me, but already I have a case of the willies. The pervasive sense of dread that accompanies the Black is already making its way into my mind. My old speakers begin to thud out the beat of ancient tribal drums as hammers strike anvils, nailing out high ringing notes. I look at the clock.

9:33 P.M. New York time.

Across the world, weirdos with a taste for the twisted that can no longer be satiated by the SimDungeons they've constructed in secret are logging on to an illegal open source i.p.

Looking for thrills.

The words *open source* are enough to get federal data surfers interested in what you're doing, while at the same time dropping the AG's office an e-mail to start filing blanket charges. Open source just isn't done anymore. I know the reason why, all the reasons why. They teach them in history class. But it's the only way to make money tonight, right now. Money I need yesterday. Who cares if open source was once responsible for the deaths of tens of millions of lives and a worldwide global collapse, pandemic, and famine. I need rent money.

Please be *Light*.

On-screen, blood red fades to gray, becoming concrete, stone, then finally grit.

I'm wondering what kind of game we're playing tonight as I catch myself again repeating inside, *Please be* Light. *Please be* Light. *Please be* Light.

Will it be third world dueling crime syndicates in an open-world version of Kinshasa in the never-ending quagmire that is Greater Africa? Drugs. Hit missions. Gang warfare in the streets. Genocide.

Or . . .

Some over-the-top science fiction classic that's been rewritten for the Black and its particular take on lust, torture, and ultraviolence? There was a *Star Wars* tribute Black game that got busted and made the news last year because some Hollywood actor hadn't told the feds about his undeclared income from the game. He'd made an extra hundred thousand dollars playing a rapist C3PO who was fairly good at poker.

I stop.

Please be *Light*.

"Boys and girls, gents and ladies," begins a soft, malevolent voice through my vintage Grundig Sharp speakers. Vintage meaning old, but they still do the trick. "Saints and sickos, tramps and troublemakers, predators and prey . . . it's dyin' time . . . again."

Please be *Light*.

"Worldwide we are registering over fifty-five million subscribers for tonight's event," continues the announcer in his overstylized carny-of-the-damned tones. "And we ask ourselves, my fellow little perverts . . ."

Pause.

"Who will hack, slash, rape, and loot their way out of our little horror show tonight and for all the nights we play our game until everyone be dead or damned? Who's ruthless enough to backstab, steal, and cheat their way out of hell? Tonight, my lovelies, we begin . . . again, in"—the voice is musical, singsong, melodic, its cheery note a counterpoint to the death carnival I'm sure I'm about to find myself in—"the lost World of Wastehavens."

The music crescendos and then, after a short interlude of silence, returns to the wanderings of a mournful flute.

I have no idea what the World of Waste-whatever is.

"Behold the tower of the Razor Maiden, the Marrow Spike," continues the announcer.

My screen clouds over. Blue shadows resolve into swirling dust, and from somewhere nearby over ambient in-game sound, I hear a crack of dry thunder followed by the patter of rain falling mutely into ancient, thick dust. Water drops cascade and echo and I'm struck by the certainty that if Sancerré is truly gone, out of my life, I'll listen to the rain and think of her and it will be little consolation to a very lonely me.

On-screen a fat gibbous moon, swollen, corpulent, and odd, makes its way across the night as its light falls on a lonely desert. In the distance, a rising tower, more perversion or malignant growth than structure, stands out in the moonlit night. Its crazy architecture rises, feasible only in computer-rendered graphics, pushing away from a crumbling city that is slowly being consumed by the dunes of an endless desert. I let go of a fading hope I'd harbored for a simple AK and the clear-cut purpose of merely machine-gunning my way through this game until I'd earned enough money for rent.

Modern warfare is my specialty. Fantasy, not so much.

The spire is jagged and thorny, a black silhouette against the desert night, rising from the jumble of odd-angled ruins in an arid waste devoid of anything living, all made colder by the moon's pale light. Only the most morbid tourist would choose such a place for an online vacation.

A piano in minor chord ponderously strikes cryptic notes as the camera pulls focus. I'm scanning for landmarks, features, anything I can use later to navigate my way to some cash and prizes. I don't see any obvious enemies. Yet.

"Even now, pretty and not so pretty little things," continues the announcer abruptly, "you're awakening from your crypts, graves, tombs, and sewers . . ." On-screen the view switches to a collapsing graveyard in some courtyard near the the tower, forgotten and abandoned millennia untold. Gravestones with Gorey-like inscriptions denote fallen warriors. The sound of grinding stone caressing stone erupts across the ambient soundscape. A necrotic hand pushes from the earth. The piano continues to strike those minor chords, alternating now with other diminished chords that seem full of suffering and hollow all at once, turning the soundtrack into a march, into a call to nothing good.

I hate the undead.

They make me jittery. In most games, they just come at you in waves. Guns are basically useless. In fact, most things are useless against the undead. In the end it comes down to baseball bats and lead pipes. Which doesn't matter—the more of them you send back to death, the more of them appear. I always wonder, after games I've played that involve the undead, after killing a thousand, two thousand, what that does to my mind. It can't be good. One time I played a game where I had to kill fifty-seven-thousand-plus undead just to unlock an achievement. I can distinguish between reality and games, but . . . some people can't. What does killing fifty-seven thousand humanlike once humans do to players?

The undead are a hard way to spend a thousand bucks.

A hard way to make rent.

"Prisoners and fiends, victims and in-betweens . . . ," continues the game's unseen announcer. The rattling of chains, a tortured scream, a woman sobs. Everything happens fast and just moments before the game reveals my avatar, the unknown character I'll play as I attempt to beat this game, I see the tower above and hear the whimpering of a child.

"Razor Maiden, devourer of the innocent, eater of life, queen of hell, commands that you die tonight, or live trying."

In these online tournaments, and might I add, illegal open source online tournaments, the goal is to figure out the game and then beat it before all the other players find and beat you. You've got to start somewhere, and often that's a game in and of itself that must be beat before you can actually start beating the main game. Just like life. I'm guessing the game I'll be playing to start with is "escape." But from where and how, I don't know just yet. Along the way is where I'll really make money. Contests, treasure troves, even in-game bargains can lead to big cash and interesting prizes. Or so I've been told.

The intro is over and now my story, the story of my avatar, begins.

"Please be *Light*," I whisper once more in my empty and very dark apartment.

Gloomy clouds thicken on-screen, then a golden shaft of light, something my eyes are starving for, stabs down through the clouds.

In Olde English script, the word *Light* appears as I hear a distant trumpet play a fading call to arms.

"Noble Son"—it's a different voice than the game announcer, kindly, a sage or a king perhaps—"I am Callard the Wise of Rondor, and I'm here to help you. You must rescue a child of hope from the clutches of the diabolical Razor Maiden. Your training as a Samurai of the mysterious East has given you the *Focused Slash* ability and the *Iron Hurricane* attack. Armed only with your katana *Deathefeather,* you have journeyed many leagues into the southern deserts to reach a fabled lost city buried beneath shifting sands so that you can climb the jutting ruin of the Marrow Spike and confront evil itself."

Pause.

*Wait for it,* I tell myself.

"Alas, you have been captured by the nightmarish horde of the black witch Razor Maiden . . ."

There it is. Captured.

I hate games where you start off in the hole.

The question now is, How many of my fellow contestants are also captured? Whoever's not captured has a big advantage. Even worse, am I captured by one of my fellow players? Someone playing *Darkness*?

"The Black horde has taken your hand in payment for daring to approach their forgotten realm," continues Callard the Wise of Whatever. "But fear not, Samurai, there is hope! Somewhere within this ancient desert lies the Pool of Sorrows. If you can find it, maybe its restorative waters will return your lost hand, and then, once you've found your legendary blade *Deathefeather,* perhaps you might dispense the justice Razor Maiden so richly deserves."

I feel cheated.

Damn Iain.

A thousand bucks down the drain on a one-handed Samurai that's probably being tortured and raped from the get-go.

The picture on-screen dissolves as the voice of Callard reminds me to "find the child." What child, I'm not sure, but apparently a child must be found.

The screen changes from panorama to point of view. I'm inside the avatar's skin. The HUD comes online and I'm checking the layout. Vitals are down 50 percent. But who's exactly a million bucks after having their hand lopped off? My right clicks are enabled, so I scroll through a menu of available feats I can slave to the mouse and bind to the keyboard. I like the old-fashioned mouse, none of these reticle-cued, SoftEye enhancements everyone's trying to sell me these days.

With part of my mind on the screen that shows my surroundings, and the other scrolling through a submenu checking what skills I can employ, most of which are offline, I see the grotesque feet of a large monster shuffling toward me. My POV is only responding to the vaguest of movements, like I'm drugged or chained up or something. Over ambient, beyond the scrape of the jailer-monster's feet, I hear an agonized scream followed by repeated cries for mercy. Then the obligatory tormented scream punctuation as hot iron sears flesh. Again, the screaming.

*The Dungeon of Endless Despair* flashes across my screen.

The jailer nears my body and hauls me upright. I stare from the darkness of my snow-swamped apartment in midtown Manhattan, into the face of an Ogre on-screen. Protruding canines and bleeding gums compete for computer-rendered audacity with an oozing gash that was once an eye.

"Wot's yur name, maggot?" growls the Ogre through my DellTashi display, something I purchased on credit after being confirmed for professional status with ColaCorp.

A QuickMenu opens up asking me to type in my name.

"Loser" springs to mind along with "Thousand-Dollars-Down-the-Drain Guy."

I can't use PerfectQuestion. If ColaCorp knew I was gaming in the Black, I'd lose my pro status immediately.

What comes next comes from nowhere. It doesn't mean anything to me, and I can't remember ever hearing it before.

"Wu," I type in.

"Wu!" shrieks the Ogre and roars with laughter and flying spittle right in my face. My POV spins crazily about as the Ogre, easily well over seven feet tall, hurls my Samurai at a far wall. Ragdoll physics take over as the laws of the universe in this online world send me flying through the air. After a bone-rattling impact into a wall, I land on a thin pile of straw in the orange light of a nearby guttering wall torch. The damage deducts 2 percent from my Vitality and now I'm down to 48 percent.

I'm still searching all the Samurai's submenus. He has some awesome skills and devastating attacks. But all of them are offline, probably due to the missing hand and damage. I find one called *Serene Focus*. It's live, so I enable and drag it onto the right mouse button. I read the quick hint description of the skill as once again the Ogre lumbers toward me all grunts and wheezy laughs.

"I'll baste yur bones with yur own blood 'n' crack yur skull between me teeth, I will."

A very ogre thing to say.

Meanwhile back at the skill description, I read that *Serene Focus* allows the user to slow down in-game time while still moving at an intensely fast speed.

Yay, now I can watch the Ogre beat me to death in slow-mo.

I scan the jail cell. Torchlight and shadows, more alcove than cell, it opens into an undefined gloom beyond the flickering light. I do not see my Samurai sword, *Deathefeather,* anywhere nearby.

The guttering torch along the wall of my cell reveals nothing that would be useful right about now. The Ogre is almost on me again, grunting and laughing. I pan up and see the great sabers of his fangs rending his own scarred and bloody welt of a lip.

I have to admit, whoever wrote this software, even though they're stealing my thousand bucks, did a great job. It sucks to be me right now.

The Ogre's tumorous Adam's apple bobs up and down. The game's soundtrack cranks up to do or die with the bleating tribal horn of triumph every dark beast that ever walked the worlds of fantasy is known by.

Imagination.

I know what to do.

I right-click *Serene Focus,* and the blaring war drums and horns slow down as though drowned in a thick syrup of sugary sonic deadness. The edges of my screen distort to soft focus. From somewhere nearby, I can hear the delicate strings of the Japanese koto plucking out singular, poignant notes.

I don't know why, but I understand now.

It's as if the programmer wrote a quick cut-scene illustrating the point of *Serene Focus* and dropped it onto my mental deck for a frame or two.

*"The hands of the Samurai are like the legs of a crane in a shallow pond. Early morning, fog and mist, they do not disturb the water, or hesitate. They lift and descend and the water remains unmarked."*

Yeah, I understand how the crane walks through a shallow pond and doesn't disturb the mirrored surface of the water.

Creepy, huh?

I target the Ogre's bobbing throat and attack with my left mouse button. The Samurai's only hand reaches out from my POV. In this instant, I hope the developer spent good money on things other than great graphics and good physics. A well-built game will render an opponent's entire body, allocating damage based on anatomy and physiology. When computer games were first invented, all you could do was attack another player. It couldn't differentiate if you hit him in the legs, head, or chest. Hell, even a hit in the nuts or gouging out an eye were undefinable. Computers couldn't crunch that level of data. But games evolved. Eventually you could make head shots. That was at the beginning of the new millennium. Now, technology can target specific muscle groups. I hope whoever built this circus of pain paid enough for that level of design. Otherwise, I'm dead digital meat. And homeless.

On-screen the Samurai's hand reaches out. The represented on-screen digital world fixates on the great bobbing tumor that is the Ogre's throat, as the hand of the Samurai grasps . . .

. . . then crushes it a second later.

In a game like this, where players and watchers are looking for the sickest of not-so-cheap thrills, the likelihood was high that the designer went all-in for the best in blood and gore. My *Serene Focus* gamble pays off as the Ogre stumbles backward, gasping and reaching for its shattered throat. It stumbles, falls, then dies in the shadows beyond the cone of torchlight.

Now, I'm in the game.

If you count having one hand, 48 percent of your health left, and most of your options offlined, as "in the game," then yes, I am in the game.

I check my Samurai's inventory. I find only the robelike gi of the Samurai and a pair of wooden sandals. Both equipped. No lacquered armor or sword for that matter.

I move forward and hear *chock . . . chock . . . chock,* the wooden sound of his sandaled steps, echoing in the dark. Underneath that is the breeze-whipped guttering sound of a torch. And underneath it all, wandering rhythmic drums and the full chords of a baby grand piano play, striking out harsh tone clusters that cry doom, gloom, and the loneliness one finds beneath the earth in lost and forgotten places.

Music is important in games. A tempo change can mean an impending attack. A certain chord can indicate the state of affairs, good or bad. Even though I like to keep my own tracks going, I still keep ambient in-game sound and soundtracks in the groove just so I can check in on that level. Some gamers don't, and more often than not they pay for it.

I proceed forward, using my keyboard to move the Samurai into the darkness beyond the torchlight. The game factors time and vision in and adjusts my POV to the dim lighting. I see a great buttressed hall stretching away and above me as batlike architecture embraces high shadowy reaches, unconquered by the dim, barely tossed illumination thrown from small guttering torches along the wall. I stick to the shadows as much as I can.

I'd taken the Ogre by surprise. Now my *Serene Focus* is offline and waiting to recharge, which could take some time. Not if, but when I meet new enemies, they'll probably not be as vulnerable as the stupid Ogre who was probably just a "bot," controlled by the game's artificial intelligence. When I meet other contestants, other players, they'll be quicker to hack me to pieces and loot my body before any questions can be asked. In fact, I seriously doubt there'll be any kind of Q and A.

Right now, I need a weapon.

In the alcoves to my right and left, I see hulking creatures performing obscene acts on their unwilling and occasionally willing victims. I'm sure these are just appetizers for the weirdos who can no longer apply for a simple pornography permit, the mentally ill who've failed the psych test and proved themselves to be a danger to society. Open source Black games are their last resort to get any kind of fix—even if it means ten to fifteen years' hard Education if they get caught.

With just one hand I'm next to useless. I proceed forward despite the pleas for help, cries of agony, the delight of the deviant.

A menu option opens, letting me know I can tuck the Samurai's damaged left hand under his opposite arm to control the bleeding, but I'll be at a combat disadvantage. Still, it'll control the damage loss. I've already lost another 2 percent health.

I do. I curse Iain again. And I wonder where Sancerré is right now.

Then I stop. I've got to focus and make this thing pay, regardless. So I force myself to play the game and let go of all the other junk in my life.

If I've started in the dungeon, I reason, then the child I'll need to rescue is most likely at the top of the tower. That's the obvious path and the only goal I can think of right now. Somewhere, I'll probably find a staircase leading up from the dungeon and into or near the tower.

I need to go up.

Instead, all I find are rendered rough-hewn stone steps leading down into a faintly green iridescent well of darkness. Dripping water from fanged stalactites above provides a tympanic counterpoint to the lonely wooden *chock . . . chock . . . chock . . . chock* of my Samurai's cautious steps down through the mostly silent descent. The steps finally lead me to a natural cave. I move the Samurai close to the wall and, cleverly, the avatar turns sideways and hugs the rocky surface. Once again I'm amazed at the authorship of the game.

In the cavern, a long-legged dark figure, with slender thighs but misshapen by a large potbelly, prowls about. Fat arms and tiny hands caress a ropy bullwhip. Above this, a curiously odd-shaped head, covered by a leather mask, cranes itself side to side from the short stump of a neck. In my gut, I know it's another player.

I call him Creepy.

Probably *Darkness*.

Beyond Creepy, a natural bridge heaves itself over a gaping chasm. The other side is little more than a lone, distant torch and flickering shadows. I wait, back to the stone wall, hidden in the dark of the passage. Once again I scroll through the Samurai's submenu looking for some ability that might be of use. I find nothing. *Serene Focus,* which I could employ to push Creepy off the ledge after a quick rush, refuses to come back online as it slowly recharges.

My brain begins to tickle, and I wonder for a moment if I'm being watched. I check the stone staircase behind and above me. Nothing. I watch the stone ledge where Creepy seems to be patrolling, looking for something, even waiting for someone. A new submenu, which I'd been prowling, opens up the history of my Samurai. After I get past all the code of honor and devotion to the art of combat stuff, I catch a line that intrigues me.

*The Samurai, a master of balance and grace, employs these traits to deliver decisive death blows and evade enemies.*

I unpin the Samurai from the wall and walk forward. Creepy instantly stops pacing. The whip hangs limply from one studded-gloved hand.

I send him a message in text.

"HOLD, friend, let's talk."

I open up a chat channel and send him an invite. My quickly evolving plan, in short, is to do a little role-playing. If Creepy likes to play with his food, and if I can maneuver him into a position near enough the edge of the chasm, I might be able to push him over said edge, or even get myself onto the bridge and away from him. I might be able to evade him if I catch him off guard or lure him into a sense of complacency or even, perhaps, do something more lethal. The bullwhip is a weapon I could probably use with one hand. The Samurai were masters of every weapon, and if I am going to make my thousand bucks pay off, then I need to think like a Samurai and get a weapon.

Will Creepy go for it, and if he does, what does he want? Role playing involves me looking into his room, his world, wherever in the world that is, and him, even more frightening, looking into my world, my apartment.

I take a quick sip of scotch, consider lighting a cigarette, and wonder again where Sancerré is right now.

Shortly my worst fears are confirmed. A visual channel opens in the top left-hand side of my screen. Creepy in real life looks exactly like Creepy in the cave. He's cosplaying himself in the game. From behind the black mask I see two beady eyes alight with feverish intensity.

"Guten abend, mein freund."

Crud, a German.

"I don't . . . sprechen . . . English?"

For a moment Creepy's face seems to twist with frustration. Then, "Ja, my English is nicht sehr gut. But I make it for you." Red lips painted with lipstick smile awkwardly back at me. For a brief moment he seems nice, harmless, like a kid I knew in school who just wanted to make friends but didn't know how. I feel sorry for him and instantly I degrade Creepy's threat level. Maybe he's just playing for kicks, looking for a good time and, more important, a friend. I can use that against him. Maybe I can even get him to leave me alone, or help me.

"You vant to make vis der role playing or maybe you vant to vatch me do stuff?"

This is too easy . . .

. . . and I know it's too easy.

And nothing is ever too easy.

"Yeah," I say, "I like to watch." I feel a million tons of sludge oozing through my veins.

"Ja, really?" says Creepy flatly. *Watch out,* I hear my mind scream.

"Okay, I'm gonna lock my door so no one comes in, vait a second." He gets up from his keyboard as I wonder two things.

One, who is "no one"?

And two, wouldn't you lock your door before dressing up like a weirdo sadomasochist pervert to play an illegal Black game?

He gets up from his computer, turns his back, and goes to the far end of the room, receding into the fish-eye lens of the visual chat.

It's now or never. I run for the bridge. The head start I get on him now that he's away from his keyboard might give me just the edge I need to at least get onto the stone bridge. Maybe the bridge narrows enough that I can make him fall if he chases me or at least slow him down.

But from the moment I slew my POV toward the bridge to begin my dash, I know it's doomed. Ten steps out and, *crack*, the whip's sonic slash echoes over ambient. A POV-spinning second later and I'm facedown on the digitally rendered grit and gravel of the ledge. I slew my POV around and see Creepy pulling hard to haul me in. On-screen, the visual link's still active, and I see Creepy smiling, drooling, chuckling softly to himself as the glimmer of a crimson SoftEye burns malevolently inside the cheap shiny leather of the mask. He's got some kind of motion-recognition software running. He's pulling hard at an invisible whip, dictating the movements of his on-screen character.

He'd kept an eye on me the entire time.

No deception. No gain.

I send my cursor scrambling through the Samurai's submenus looking for anything to use. *Serene Focus* still refuses to activate, but it's crawling toward a full charge. Under a menu called *Posture* I find all kinds of things. *Sitting, Standing, Relaxed, Entertaining*, and even something called *Breakdancing*. But it's the combat postures listed there that intrigue me the most. Creepy's almost passing out from glee on visual, so I cut the link. Focusing on the *Posture* menu, I find a variety of weapon and martial arts stances for different combat situations. Some are online, but all the powerful attacks seem to require both hands. Some even require the Samurai's lost sword, *Deathefeather,* specifically. I quickly scroll through the martial arts, searching for anything to use in the next ten seconds. I find *Hopkido,* even something called *Hwa Rang Do,* but it's *Judo* that attracts me the most.

Creepy drags me upright. His avatar's grinning, sweating face thrusts itself into my monitor like a fiend. I can only imagine what's going on in Berlin, or wherever Creepy resides. This is probably like the Super Bowl for him. Creepy wraps his bullwhip around my neck and my screen suddenly hazes over in a red mist as a thudding heartbeat begins to pump slower and slower through my speakers.

He's strangling me.

My health meter drops quickly to 40 percent. I switch combat postures to *Judo,* even though Creepy's got me by the neck. Now his avatar begins to fumble at my clothes.

Man, the developer didn't slack on any of the options.

At 35 percent I execute a *Judo* attack. If I just thump him hand-to-hand style, I don't know how much good it'll do. I suspect not much. But sometimes good games build in finishing moves and cut-scene attacks.

I'm rewarded with both as once again the game dazzles me. The Samurai slams his head forward into Creepy's leather-clad face in front of my POV. Then the screen switches to a circling overhead view as the Samurai, now holding Creepy by the skin of his chest, falls backward in slow motion. The attack off-balances Creepy and he's flying through the air toward the lip of the chasm. He's still holding the bullwhip, and it trails away after him as he disappears over the edge.

My Vitality bar is now at 28 percent. The red mist has cleared. I move to the edge of the chasm peering into the darkness below and the lash of the whip comes flying out of the darkness and hits me again, deducting another 2 percent from my health. The labored breathing of the Samurai erupts on ambient. I'm down to precious little health, and being that this game is sadistic, chances are I'll pass out before zero. That way all the deviants get the thrill of knowing that, though their simulated victims are unconscious, they're still alive and watching from the other side of the screen at whatever comes next.

But I'm not done.

I'm still in the game, and my thousand bucks isn't gone, yet.

Below, I see Creepy. He hasn't fallen down into the blackness of the pit. He's on a rocky outcrop just below the ledge, winding up for another attack, his whip dancing out behind him in the pale green light from above. I target him, press Spacebar, and jump while moving forward, executing a flying kick. Once I'm airborne I realize the potential for catastrophic error. If I miss, or if Creepy moves, it's off into the dark pit beyond and below. With 26 percent Vitality left, I probably won't survive any kind of fall.

Slipping in the bathtub would probably kill this Samurai right about now.

Also, I'm jumping down almost twenty feet; even if I hit Creepy, I'll probably kill myself from residual damage. But who cares. I hate Creepy, I hate the world's greatest fashion photographer, and I hate WonderSoft. I focus my rage squarely onto Creepy's leather vest and plan on driving my foot right through his chest cavity.

*Serene Focus* comes online.

At the last second I quickly right-click it and a cut-scene of raindrops falling into a quiet garden superimposes itself over my fall into Creepy. I'm moving slowly. Syrupy. I hear the strings of an ancient era recall sorrows past.

All that *Serene Focus* jazz.

Time slows even further, and I plant my foot lightly into Creepy's chest, backing him just to the edge of the outcrop as his whip falls from his hand. I bounce off him, taking less than 1 percent of damage, and backflip onto the rocky outcrop in slow motion. For a single moment, maybe fifteen frames in the camera of life, I face Creepy on the outcrop, across the world.

Then I attack.

One click.

A quick roundhouse hot key spins my POV in a great circle as the Samurai grunts in satisfaction at the well-honed spinning kick connecting with Creepy's jaw. *Crunch*. It shatters as Creepy launches outward, backward, and then downward into the empty black void beyond us. I watch him go and he doesn't seem to stop until he disappears into the darkness way down there.

Wherever "there" is.

No one could have survived a fall like that in real life. I remind myself this isn't real life. It's a game. I pick up the fallen whip from the black dust of the outcrop.

Now, I have a weapon.

I turn to face the rock wall. *I'll climb back up onto the ledge above,* I'm thinking.

My screen begins to shake and the rock wall in front of my perspective begins to race past my eyes.

I'm falling!

I pan down and see the entire outcrop is sliding into the abyss after Creepy. Great!

The floor begins to tilt, threatening to dump me right into the avalanche, but I balance on the sliding rock with light taps on my direction keys. I spare a glance upward and already the green glow from above is a distant blob, and soon after that it's just a small pinpoint of sickly light. Then it's gone. The rock wall rushes by me in gray and sudden red hues as if passing indeterminate fires. The stone face of some fanged demon leers up at me as I fall toward it. I pass it and consider trying to get onto its jutting head, but it's gone too quickly and the rumbling rock carries me farther down into the dark.

At that moment the screen goes black and the game dies.

# Chapter 9

An hour later I'm standing in the dark, watching the storm roll in underneath Upper New York. Everything is darkness; outside on the streets below, no one. It feels like the night after the world ends. I'm nursing a scotch, confused and wondering what to do with myself. The Black went down for a reason. The only one I can think of is that the feds got close to someone important and the Black runners freaked out and went dark. Like the city.

And I'm out a thousand bucks?

If so, things can't be worse than they already are. It doesn't matter if I have half the rent. The landlord wants it all. If I don't have all, out I go.

My Petey's doomsday ringtone goes off.

Important message.

The Black will be back up in six minutes.

That should make me happy. But it doesn't. All it means is that my thousand isn't totally gone, yet. Maybe the game's been bugged now. Maybe whoever shut it down, the developer, the programmer, the Black runners themselves, got caught and they're flipping the red queen on their subscribers.

Us. Me.

Maybe.

What other choice do I have?

No message from Sancerré.

I finish my drink, make another, and sit back down at my desk. The Black goes live and the word *Begin* flashes across my screen. I can see my HUD. My hot keys, minimap, and Vitality and Stamina meters are all there. But the screen is completely dark.

I touch the movement direction keys. Side to side. I hear the shuffle of the Samurai's wooden sandals stepping and then echoing off something unseen and nearby, fading off into the distance.

My eyes accustom to the darkness of the screen and I realize nothing's wrong. At least not with my computer or the game itself. It's just really dark wherever I am in-game. I can't even make out shapes or outlines. It's pitch-black.

A complete absence of light.

Deep under the earth. Where the light don't go.

The bottom of the pit. The end of the fall.

Great.

In other words, I'm lost in the dark.

The words *Oubliette of Torment* appear across my screen in crimson gothic spike script.

What the hell is an *Oubliette*? I tell my Petey to look up the meaning of the word. It tells me it's a synonym for dungeon. From the French, meaning literally, "a forgotten place."

So I'm in the forgotten place of torment.

I pan upward. The darkness seems even deeper there.

So how did I survive the fall into the pit? Or did the game just place me in this zone at random? Or does the pit somehow lead to the Oubliette of Torment?

Over ambient in-game sound, a guitar plucks sardonically at discordant strings. Or at least that's what it feels like to me. I make sure the whip is equipped and start out into the thick darkness. A small musical loop begins cycling across the soundtrack. It's the music of flutes swirling downward on a sigh more than anything else. It begins to accompany the sarcastic guitar.

In time, my Samurai bumps into what I think is a wall. I turn right, trying to use the wall as a guide. The wall turns to the right, and I feel like I'm heading into a darkness even deeper than the one I've been in. Ahead, far off in the distance, I see some kind of light. Or a lessening of the dark.

The soundtrack seems to come and go. At times I'm concentrating so hard on finding my way through a maze made of darkness that I barely even notice when the music stops. Then, when I'm least expecting it, the guitar plucks an impulsive string with an odd twang, jolting me upright.

Am I getting lost? Have I made a bad choice and this is the game's way of telling me so?

And maybe I should lay off the scotch.

I arrive in the less dark area, and it takes me a vertigo-filled moment to figure out what's going on. The light reveals itself to be an odd-shaped square. Sides slant off in one direction; I know it's a shape of some sort, I just don't know which one. The square of light is bone white and crosshatched, as though there are bars somewhere high above, between the light source and the floor it's shining down on. I look up. I can see only an indeterminate spotlight and shadowy bars between it and my Samurai. I move forward into the lighted area and realize there are other squares at random intervals, leading off in another direction. There are solid walls of darkness between me and those islands of crosshatched black and white.

Could the light source be the moon, and in between it and me are high grates or grilles, open toward the game's version of night? The desert? The tower? The crosshatched squareish islands of light form a rambling hall leading off in a direction my in-game minimap refuses to identify. All the cardinal points on the minimap are noted with a question mark.

I'm either lost, or I've gone into a zone where east and west, south and north, don't have any meaning.

That can't be good.

A thought occurs to me as I try to reason out what's happening. What's happened. I don't like this. I don't like this for a lot of reasons. The main reason revolves around my thousand bucks. Maybe I've wasted my money, died in that fall into the pit, and now the game is wasting my time by sending me to its version of the afterlife.

Am I in the game's hell?

Can I escape?

Maybe there's no escape.

My fingers are paralyzed, hovering like claws over the keyboard and mouse. I feel like taking a drink from the nearby scotch, but I don't.

This is not supposed to happen. They can't rip me off like this.

Why can't they? It's an open source Black game. To myself I think, *What'd ya expect? A shooter channeling you down narrow lanes full of explosions and action just like some ride at Disney-Island or the latest game of* MegaWarrior? *The whole game on rails to keep you in the story and completing the game, so some big developer can give you a good time for your dough, at cost?*

This, that ain't.

This is an open source illegal online game, akin to gambling. Mom used to say, "The house always wins."

Well, Mom might have been right. Again.

I follow the crooked path of bar-covered light and in time I see them. Beautiful women. They're barely clothed in a variety of costumes ranging from slave girl to merchant princess to slutty elf, and they're all chained on either side of the hall. Cross-hatched light swims along their undulating bodies as they raise their shackled hands in supplication.

Obviously I'm distracted. The bodies are rendered perfectly. Each of them is, like I said, beautiful. Different. No two the same. They reach for me from the dark as I pass, and I know this has got to be some sort of trap.

Succubi?

But they're chained.

A raven-haired statuesque Amazonian in flimsy silk whispers "Please . . ." at me as I pass. Then I hear another voice. A man. Middle Eastern. "She's real and waiting, my friend. Just slay her and you can watch us beat her live via the feed."

"What?" I say into my mic.

"You heard me, my friend. Pick one. Chop off her head and you'll be invited into her real world. You'll see what she's doing. And what's being done to her. I promise you, it will all be very thrilling . . . and humiliating for her."

I stare at all the girls, computer-rendered models of real-life models. A programmer's promise of what they look like in the real world. What I'm seeing now is what I'll see when I join her feed. Each of them was that prettiest girl in school we all wanted to know. Guys like me had crushes on girls like these. Just crushes because guys like me would never say or do anything about a girl like that. They were epic; we were just . . . us.

Somehow their beauty took them away from high school and all the towns and cities they came from. Took them to the ends of the earth. And then some. Some girls became actresses. Ultramodels. Trophies of the rich. And some . . .

. . . end up in online brothels on the other side of the world. In the Middle East where their owners can get away with this stuff because women are still just a possession there. Always have been. Probably always will be.

If you have the dough, you can have them. But that's not my style.

I continue on, leaving the moaning beauties behind me, their bodies burned into the folds of my mind forever.

Light begins to illuminate more and more of the dungeon, and I can see cages and bars. Within the empty cages I find rusty manacles and chains. Broken furniture. There are long hallways leading off into other darknesses. I avoid those places.

There's no rhyme or reason to this dungeon. The cages and bars and cells cluster the debris-littered spaces between deserted hallways and gray silent passages. I weave through it all, carefully, ready for an attack that never comes, lost and getting more lost. This game world is nothing but a city of empty cages . . .

. . . until I find the man dressed in rags chained to the stone wall of a small cell.

"Hey there!" His voice is raspy and high. "Hey there, buddy. You wanna have some fun?"

Emphasis on fun.

Trap.

I approach the cage slowly. *Chock . . . Chock . . . Chock.*

"Samurai, huh?" asks the raggedy man.

I say nothing.

"Where's your sword?" He begins to laugh. Coughing and laughing, he shakes his manacled wrists in delight.

"Like I said, wanna have some fun? That is . . . if you're interested?"

"I'm looking," I say over my mic, "for the way back to the tower."

He laughs. "The tower. That's . . . now that's just odd." His avatar's face seems puzzled. Then, "Tower's a long way from here . . .

or maybe it's better to say it like this . . . you're beyond the tower now. Yeah, that's much better."

I'm in front of his cell. He's chained to the far wall. Images float across the back wall of the cell, around his body and above his head. Like an old projection movie screen with pictures running across its dirty face.

"Everybody's watchin', Wu. You got a big share right now. Over three hundred thousand subscribers just waitin' to see what you're gonna do next. They wanna see what you're gonna do down here. Congratulations, you've made it all the way down to the bottom. Fun, huh?"

"Is this . . ." I feel stupid saying this. "Is this hell?"

The raggedy man laughs, coming closer to the bars. "No, man, this ain't hell. More like heaven. Don't you get it? This is what the Black is really all about. Not all that fantasy stuff up there. Slayin' dragons and gittin' treasure. Down here's where the real action is. Trust me."

Treasure sounds good. Dragons, not so much.

"What if I wanna get back up there? Is there a way out?"

"Funny you should mention that," says the raggedy man. "Funny indeed."

Within the moving images flashing across the wall at the back of the cell, a man sits in the corner of a small room. It's almost a cell like the one in front of me. But it's covered in green padding. Like it's a drunk tank or something.

"So here's the game, Samurai. You a player? Well, we'll see. This one's called, 'The way out.' Just for you."

The man in the movie, in the padded cell, is thin. Bony thin. Gaunt. Drug addict gaunt. His tiny eyes dart in random directions every so often, as though he's seeing something I'm not.

"That there's Yuri," says the raggedy man from his place on the floor. "Yuri's a real class 'A' drug addict. Multiple convictions. His case file even states that he is quote unquote, incorrigible, but it says that in Russian, so it's the Russian word for 'incorrigible.' Never knew his father. Mother was a high-class prostitute until she got AIDS. Then she was just a low-class one. But she kept him in public school long enough for him to develop a nice drug problem. Then he became a criminal, 'cause even though drugs are legal, well, my friend, hell, they ain't free. Hence the crime. Anyway, he's a real waste of human life. His career highlight came when he beat an old lady into a coma for the thirty-eight dollars in her purse so he could score some meth. She lived another three years in an institution. She never regained consciousness. But what the hell. So be it. So here's the game."

Within the moving images, a metallic drawer slides away from the padded green wall of the cell. Yuri pushes himself upward and off the wall and staggers unsteadily toward the drawer. He snatches something unseen from it quickly, then retreats back to his corner. Kneeling down, his mouth slightly agape, I can see what he's holding.

It's a syringe.

"Yeah," says the raggedy man in the cell in front of me. "He's an old-school, hard-core junkie. Anything'll do. So we'll start him off with just a little taste o' the junk. Just something to get him going, y'know?"

Yuri, hands trembling, pulls back his sleeve, slaps a vein into shape, and spikes his way-too-thin arm. His shoulders slump at the end of the fix. He takes a shallow breath.

"Fun, huh?" asks the raggedy man in the cell beneath the images. "Wanna play?"

I say nothing. This is the Black's idea of fun. I've heard rumors. Apparently they're true. I'm pretty sure whatever the game is, I don't want a piece of it.

"You want out, don'tcha, Wu? Wanna get back in the game, said so yerself."

I do.

I've got to make this thousand bucks pay off. Strike that. I *need* to make it pay off. If Sancerré ever decides to come back, I have to have a place for her to come back to.

"Tell ya what," says the raggedy man. "He's an addict. So, y'know, anything'll do. Now, how 'bout we play for just a little bottle of hard liquor, nothing serious. A little old liter of bum liquor. We won't even give him a loaded revolver or nothing, I promise. We did that one time. It was hilarious. Ya ever see the video? It went viral."

"No."

Everyone's heard about these dark little games on the Internet. They're called "DIY Green Projects." Or "Taking out the Trash." Like it's a public service or something. Make someone kill themselves. The truth is some people get a thrill out of watching people die. They'd do it to anyone if they could. It's just that drug addicts are the easiest to do it to. No one will admit they like to watch people die. But then why do people always slow down at traffic accidents? What're they hoping to see? Blood. A body. The paramedics working hard. A person begging for their life. Death. Here on the Internet no one will know you saw it happen. The Internet's the place to see what you can't admit wanting to see. No more having to cruise the toll highways looking for a wreck. Now you can watch some death just like back in the days before the Meltdown when open source almost destroyed civilization. Back then there were lots of videos of stuff just like this.

A boy soldier shooting an infant in the head.

A dictator begging for his life.

Three thousand people dying as burning buildings collapsed into the street.

Except this is real. This is live. This is right now.

That's what the Black is. What it really is. It just hides under the guise of a game where you might win some stuff. It attracts competitive people who will do anything to win.

People like me.

"Fun, huh?" says the raggedy man.

He moves closer to the bars, his hair spiky and blond. He wears dirty boots and pants and a rumpled coat. I can see the manacles and the chains were just part of an act. They weren't restraining him at all. He leans in close. I can see his protruding, fanglike canines. They're sharpened to long points.

Vampire.

I hope the cell door is actually locked.

His manacles weren't.

"Don't worry about me, kid." He wipes his wrist across his mouth. "I just wanna make you a star. So go ahead and off this piece of trash, and I'll give you anything you want."

I'm not going to do that.

But I do want something.

I want to get out of here, wherever here is, and back into the game, wherever that is. I want to get to the top of the tower and along the way earn some money and maybe a couple of prizes.

So . . . I've got to play along.

"Anything I want?" I ask.

The caged Vampire smiles. "Yeah, anything."

"What if I want a way out of here?"

"Who would want to leave? We've got all kinds o' games and a huge Internet audience. You could make some really good dough down here. Have some fun while you're doing it. We got sex games, torture games, death games. We got this traffic cam hacked in Beijing. We can change the crossing signals and really hurt some people. You find that little game and you might win yourself a new house. You wanna new house, Wu?"

"No, I want out. I want back in the game."

"Well, now, let me think about that." The Vampire rubs his sleeve across his chin, his eyes searching. Whoever's running him forgot to turn off their EmoteWare. "Yeah," he mumbles.

"Yeah, there's a way. Why not. So here's what you gotta do. Yuri will take anything 'cause he's a drug addict. He don't know no better. There's stuff, hidden and guarded, all over the Cages; that's where you're at." He throws his sleeve wide encompassing our surroundings. "Each time you give Yuri a little something, I'll tell you a little bit about how to get out of the Oubliette. How to get remembered by the game again, is more like it. I can't get ya out. But there is a way out. If you can find out all you need to know before Yuri dies, then he lives. If Yuri dies, then you lose, and you might as well get comfortable down here. Deal?"

I make a deal with the Vampire.

I leave him grinning and coughing out his raspy laugh as I go in search of the things that will kill Yuri.

I feel like I need a hot shower after that conversation.

I wander the Cages, rattling barred doors and checking open, empty rooms. In a distant cell, beyond its creaking, rotted door, I find a once-human thing hunched over a low table, muttering. Its skin is dark and when it looks up, I'm confronted by two luminous green eyes. I ready the whip.

I'm down to 28 percent health and still combat disadvantaged by the missing hand.

I strike and watch as the whip passes straight through the thing. It grins, rising off the floor.

Creepy's whip must be normal. This monster probably requires some kind of special weapon to damage it. Slowly the thing begins to float toward my Samurai, its rotting arms following its torn fingers and scabby palms as it reaches out for me.

I back out of the cell and retreat into the moonlit area of cages and bars. I turn to see what it'll do. If it'll stay within the room or follow. The open door looks like a gaping dark void. A moment later the thing, eyes wide and glazed over while at the same time staring directly into my screen, floats out of the cell door, coming for me.

I run away, and the thing begins to cackle. A quick check behind me and I see it's following swiftly. I double-tap the forward key and hear the rapid staccato of the Samurai's wooden sandals over ambient. One wrong turn and this thing corners me. Game over. I've got nothing to attack it with. I know this as I run deeper and deeper into the senseless maze of cages.

Eventually, I do take that wrong turn. I turn down a blind alley of dark-stained stone walls and worn-out wooden doors. It's a short hall that dead-ends quickly. I can hear the maniacal cackle of the thing getting closer. I try all the doors. They're all locked except for one. I can hear my Samurai beginning to breathe heavily as he reaches the extent of his stamina and temporary exhaustion sets in.

The last door opens on a beautiful, barely clad woman strapped to a long wooden table with gutters and runnels. Three small men, Dwarves, stand around the table, holding bone saws and wicked knives. Their beards flame red; their eyes are dark, and their hair, short and cropped.

"Come to cut her up?" says one quickly. "Or come to just watch?" asks another. "Tell us where you want the first cut made."

Man, this game is twisted.

Greedy bulbous dwarven faces shine in the light of a lone torch as they stand around the whimpering woman. Sweat runs down their wide foreheads. Their hair shifts and writhes in the flickering light of the torch. They cluster about their nubile captive.

Just outside I can hear the cackle of the thing chasing me.

"The Wight Strangler's a coming," mutters one. The others seem not to care.

"Let's cut her . . . here?" whispers another and makes an incision along her oversize chest. Her breasts quiver with lifelike reality beneath what little clothing she wears. Blood begins to run down onto her ribs.

"Do you like that?" asks one of the Dwarves. "Hot stuff, huh?"

*No, I don't like that,* I'm thinking just as the Wight Strangler bursts through the cell door, its hair writhing, its green eyes burning, its necrotic hands already reaching for me. Apparently it strangles, that's its thing. Its lips snarl, sneering.

I use the whip's secondary grapple attack, targeting the lone torch on the wall. The whip snakes away from my POV with a solid sonic *craaack,* wrapping itself around the sconced torch as I hold down the left-click button. I pivot back toward the oncoming Wight Strangler and double-click the left mouse button again. The whip jerks the flaming torch into the oncoming Wight, striking it in the chest. Instantly the thing recoils in pain, on fire, the flames spreading across its grisly torso. It raises its bony head and wails, fleeing from the room in pain.

I follow it into the hall, picking up the still-burning torch as I leave the room. I equip it. Behind me I hear one of the Dwarves say, "Let's take off her pretty legs and see what she looks like then?"

"Yeah, but one at a time, I want to enjoy this," murmurs another. I slam the door behind me.

The Wight is whimpering mournfully in the dark passage outside, sobbing as it crawls away from me, leaning itself against one dirty stone wall. Smoke curls up in thin wisps from around its narrow abdomen and up over its hunched back. I follow it, standing over it for a second. Then I shove the burning torch into its back, holding it there. It screams, catching fire. It screams even more as the flames consume it whole and it burns, turning to ash quickly. Its screams reverberate through my speakers long after it's gone. After it's nothing but ash, it's still screaming bloody murder through my speakers.

Then I realize the screaming is actually coming from behind the door. The woman is screaming, filling my tiny snowbound apartment with bloody murder.

I loot the Wight's corpse and find only a small bottle. The quick description pops up when I hover my cursor over it. It's a bottle of NarcoDex. Twenty doses. Even I know NarcoDex is a powerful surgery-grade anesthesia. A lot of people party with it on just one dose. A lot of those people die. This will kill Yuri for sure. I have no doubt about that.

I stare at the bottle, listening to the woman scream as the Dwarves cut her. They're giggling, murmuring among themselves as they do it. They must be NPCs creating a tableau for any players that might happen down this way, something for the subscribers to watch between the games that are the main event, like kill Yuri, or change the traffic cam in Beijing. Maybe you can even make the cuts. I'm sure you can. It probably all looks very real. That's why the game went in on so much anatomy programming.

Make it look real. For the fans.

She's still screaming. Begging them to stop.

I hope they are NPCs. I at least hope she is.

Either way, I've had enough.

I cut into my music cloud and select a track to drown out the screaming.

"Mama Said Knock You Out."

I crank it to full . . .

"Don't call it a comeback."

. . . then I open the door and beat the living hell out of the three sadistic Dwarves with Creepy's whip. I'm left-clicking so hard my finger goes numb by the time the song ends.

When I'm finished, they're dead.

Or at least they're not moving.

Except for the last one. I've practically flayed that Dwarf alive. He grins up at me through blood-bubbling lips. Then whispers, "Look at her face." He giggles weakly. "Just look . . . at it."

They've dismembered her.

Her eyes are vacant. Staring upward.

I swivel away from my screen, clutch the sweating glass of scotch, and guzzle it in one go. I stand up, walk purposefully to the bottle, and reload. It's hitting me hard, softening the edges. I watch the snow fall across the night outside. Watching beyond its twirling, drifting flakes and into the blackness there.

I sit back down at the computer.

I've got to do this.

I loot the Dwarves' corpses and come away with a meat cleaver and a bottle of aspirin.

My fingers are like claws, stretched out over the keyboard. Hovering. Waiting to strike down at any key. Except I don't know which one to hit.

I don't know what to do next.

I find my way back through the warren of bars and cells called the Cages. I pass other shadowy passages to somewhere else, watching them diminish in perspective as they disappear off into the darkness.

I find the Vampire's cell.

I've equipped the meat cleaver instead of the whip.

I can't kill this Yuri, whoever he is, just to make rent.

"But you were thinking about it," I hear myself say.

I wasn't.

There's a way out and back into the game. The Vampire said so. He's probably being controlled by one of the Black runners, the people who organize and put on Black games.

The mafia.

"Did ya get somethin' for poor old Yuri?" The Vampire appears against the bars of his cell. His bloodless hands grip the bars tightly.

"Yeah," I say over my mic. "I got him something. But first, tell me about the way out of here."

The Vampire shakes his head. "Nah, nah, nah . . . that's not how it's done. You gotta give Yuri some stuff first. People wanna see that happen."

"What kind of people?"

"What kind do you think, Wu?"

I wait. I'm hoping he'll just talk, babble, ramble, or whatever. Give away some clue as to how to get out of here. I'm not counting on it, but I've got to give him the room to make a mistake. So I wait for him to say something. He does the same.

"The kind of people who've tried everything in the world to make themselves happy," I say, trying to provoke him into explaining everything in the world. Or why the world is the way it is, as he sees it. He seems the type. Whoever's behind the Vampire's mask seems the type. Maybe he'll get carried away and let something slip. "And they just can't," I continue when he doesn't jump at the bait. "And now they're hoping this'll do the trick. Hoping that watching someone cross over the line between life and death, taken by those that will instead of those that won't . . . they're thinking, 'Maybe this will make me happy?' Make them enjoy life just a little more. Those kind of people?"

"You're quite a philosopher," says the Vampire softly. "Maybe it's not that at all, player. Maybe it's just something less."

"Something less?"

"Yeah, something less. Maybe it's just, you know, human nature. See, *waaaaay back* . . . when the Internet used to be full of fun stuff like this, y'know before the Meltdown and all. Full of girls doing porn, kids getting hurt, people offing themselves, people hurting each other. You know . . . humanity. Back before the Meltdown, this was the Internet. Before all the rules and licensing, this was how it was . . . and it was great. But then the Meltdown came along . . ."

"Yeah, I know all that. I don't need . . . ," I interrupt.

"But see, you do . . . you do need a history lesson, player," shouts the Vampire. "See, you can't legislate 'good' behavior. You can't decide what's right and wrong. People still gonna be people. People still gonna do this stuff, man. Still gonna find a way to watch people get their kicks."

"It's sick," I say, goading him.

"Who're you to judge?" He explodes again. He's close to the cage, grabbing the bars intently. "People used to say bein' part of another race was wrong. Or engaging in certain types of recreational pleasure. Or lifestyles. But . . . really it was just 'cause the people sayin' it was wrong, were just filled with hate for the people that were doin' whatever the others said was wrong. They just made all that stuff up. There weren't any reasons. They just decided what you were doin' was wrong. That way they could discriminate against you. That's all. Just good old-fashioned, plain old hate. Lemme ask you, and don't be a smart guy about it, player. Lemme ask you this." He pauses, licks his lower lip, then wipes his sleeve across his mouth. "Is anything really wrong with anything?"

I stare at him.

"C'mon. Isn't that what the great society we've been building is all about? Getting rid of hate. So we got rid of the racism and cultural hate, and now, some guy wants to kill some losers and we gotta judge him and say that's wrong? What if it's hardwired into him? What if it's in his DNA and stuff? He can't help it. It's who he is. I don't know, but if you ask me, it's pretty hateful to prevent him from being who he is. Even if who he is . . . is a homicidal maniac." He laughs briefly. Like he was expecting me to get it, to join in. Then he stops.

We stare at each other through the bars.

"C'mon, man, some get their kicks one way, it's who they are. Others . . . this is them. Government says you can't log in on open source. Government used to say drugs were bad. Bein' gay was illegal. All kinds of stuff. Now drugs are legal, gay too. Ain't nothin' wrong with anything. It's all good. It's got to be. For you . . . and for me. Understand?"

It's getting late. My eyes are tired. The skin over my skull feels stretched too tight by unseen iron clamps.

"So whaddya got for poor old Yuri?" he says. "He just needs another taste of anything. Somthin' to get this party started. Hey, you might even have fun. Did you ever think about it that way?"

I didn't and I doubt it.

"I found somethin'," I say. "But . . ."

The Vampire looks worried for a second. I know he, as a Black runner, is interested in showing something, anything illegal, to his subscribers. That's why they pay to watch what shouldn't be seen, a player helping some random guy kill himself. Whoever gets a thrill . . . forget it. It's sick.

But that's not the game. Vampire Man thinks it is. But it's not the game I'm playing.

We're playing poker. We've been playing all along. He just doesn't know it.

"I found something . . . but . . . it'll kill him. That's for sure." That's my ante.

"Oh, man, that's great," squeals the Vampire. "Just great!"

"But listen . . . I can't do that . . . to . . ."

"Aw, man, you don't even know him," whines the Vampire. "Just do it and get it over with. I'll tell you the way out. Promise. C'mon, man, people want to see this thing happen. Either you'll do it or some other player will come along and do it instead. So why not do the inevitable and walk away with a niçe take-home prize? C'mon, man."

I wait.

"Listen, this just came in . . . I've got an offer from an anony-mous subscriber. He says he'll give you five grand if you do it right now. But he wants to know what you're holding. He thinks you're lying."

I wait.

Then, "I killed the Wight Strangler."

There's a pause. He's probably running the NPC monster database, checking the loot drop.

"Oh, momma, that's good, real good, man. Yuri won't know what hit him. He's so stupid I bet he takes the whole bottle in one go."

"I bet he does."

"Someone's just offered ten to watch you do it and cut everyone's feed. They want it all for themselves. Fun, huh?" says the Vampire, his eyes gleaming, his narrow face pressed between the bars of the cage.

I wait.

"C'mon, man, you can't just pass up ten large and easy for a private show. It's just Yuri. Remember the grandma he beat into a coma. She died, man. You want morals . . . I got morals for ya . . . this is it . . . you're dispensing justice for her. For her family. Do it, man!"

"Okay . . . tell me about the way out."

The Vampire watches me for a long moment.

"*Alll rriiight,* I'll give you a piece to show you I'm not lying, then we do this thing. But not the most important piece. And I tell you right now . . . if you don't have the most important piece, it ain't even worth trying. So don't even think about it. Got me?"

I do. More than you know, Vampire Man.

Using my menus, I've taken all the doses of the asprin to increase my health, except two. Hopefully that will help Yuri get some rest. I can't save him. He's on the other side of the world. But you never know, maybe a little rest and a moment of clarity, and maybe he might not ever pick up another drug.

I hear myself ask, *Who're you kidding exactly?*

Right now it's all I can do for the guy.

"You got to go through the Hook Pit. That's it, now give over the NarcoDex and let's watch Yuri party, man." The Vampire is almost joyful. Almost. "This is gonna be great!"

"Sure thing, here ya go."

I right-click on the Vampire and drop the aspirin in his inventory.

"All right . . . now we're gonna see . . . hey!" he screams. "Hey, come back here!" But I've already turned away. I'm walking farther into the Cages, looking for the Hook Pit.

I find it thirty minutes later. It's two o'clock in the morning. I've had to fight a few monsters. Some Goblin jailers and a couple of mephitic Scamps. Nothing serious. Also nothing to loot.

They come at me out of the shadows of a wide dingy sanctum between four large holding cells. The Goblin jailers have short scimitars; the mephitic Scamps, small shields and spears. Two and two.

Four versus one.

I bat aside the nearest Goblin's scimitar and strike quickly with a focused attack. I bury the cleaver in the Goblin's skull and the thing falls to its knobby knees. The other Goblin swipes at me and misses as I back off quickly. The Scamps circle for a better position, their long demonic ears twitching, their tongues lolling.

I take a chance and engage the last Goblin, who nicks me for 5 percent damage. I change my stance to *Judo* and grapple with him, picking him up over my head. His scimitar flails away above me as a necklace of various bloodstained teeth dangles down in front of my POV. I toss him at one of the Scamps and he crushes the thing, impaling himself on its spear.

I equip the dwarven cleaver again as the other Goblin comes in swinging his curved little scimitar. I take a quick cut at his wildly dancing form and slash his throat. The Goblin jerks backward clutching at the cut, green blood seeping through his deformed fingers. Then he's dead.

The last Scamp rears back with his spear, preparing to hurl it right into my back. It's all I can do to hit *Serene Focus* and slow time. I sidestep the hurtling dart, charge in under the Scamp's extended arm and splayed claw, and slam the cleaver into his ribs, where it breaks off and shatters.

The thing falls to the stone floor amid the debris of smashed furniture and rusting manacles.

It's crawling away from me as I pull out the whip.

"Noss," it pants as its black guts slither out onto the dirty floor, falling behind it in a bloody wake as it drags itself away from me. "Noss . . ."

"What is Noss?" I ask it.

"Noss graba chucka you. Killa yuh s'pose. Killa yuh s'pose."

The thing's eyes flutter.

Again, I am amazed at the detail of the game. The Scamps even have their own gutter-speak language. The NPC AI thinks it's actually dying. Crazy.

"Tell me where the Hook Pit is!"

"Noss . . . Noss tellee yuh."

I hit it with the whip and it screams a pain-filled "Ayeeeee!" One claw reaches for the ceiling.

"Tellee me!"

"Tellee me?" it repeats, panting.

"Tellee me."

"Huks . . ." It coughs wetly. "Huks. . . ." Then it points. I follow its bony, scaly arm. It points off into a darkness beyond us. "Huks," it pants one last time and then dies.

The cleaver is useless. When I inventory it, a note pops up telling me it's "unusable."

I follow the direction of the dying Scamp's arm. I pass silent cells set in crumbling walls. It feels lonelier here in this part of the dungeon, if that's possible. Warped wooden doors seem skewed and somehow too small for their frames. The stone floor is patterned in that crosshatched moonlight of a never seen moon. High above there must be bars of some sort.

Somewhere.

The compass on my minimap still reads directionless. Four little question marks at the four cardinal points.

Weird.

Over ambient sound, the guitar twangs and spiraling flute phrases have surrendered to an open white noise that seems to rise and echo. Cascading over itself, it falls away as if down into a chasm or out into a void where sound never returns.

The music is empty and depressing at going on three o'clock in the morning here in New York City, but I'm heartened by the change. It means I'm entering a new zone. Shortly the Cages end and I'm standing at the edge of a wide pit, looking out into a forest of hanging thick-linked chains that fall into an unseen nether. Different lengths, all the chains end in wide, scythelike hooks. I cannot see the other side of the pit.

# Chapter 10

I hear the Vampire behind me.

"So . . . you really want to leave?"

I don't say anything. I just stand there watching the open pit, the hanging chains, wondering how I'm going to get across and back into the game.

The Vampire had said, "remembered by the game."

"Look at your avatar," he says, sidling up next to me. "You'll never make it with just one hand. Then there're the girls. They ain't gonna help matters."

"Just tell me how to make it back. You said there was something I needed to know?"

"Nah, that's not part of the deal. You give me that Narco-Dex and I'll tell you." He pauses. "Doesn't mean you'll make it back into the game, but I'll tell you how."

"What's down there?" I see nothing but darkness below the length of the scythe-tipped chains.

"Nothing," he whispers. Close to me now. "That's the game's version of the Recycle Bin. Anything goes down in there, it's gone. For good. That means you. This is the bottom of the game and . . . if you can understand this, it's where the game really begins. At the end. The bottom. This is where everyone really wants to be."

I open my inventory. My cursor hovers over the NarcoDex.

"You know that, right?" asks the Vampire. "You know that this is where 90 percent of the players in the world are trying to make it into. They know about this place. They know this is where the fun is, man. The Oubliette of Torment. This is where you can do anything you want to almost anybody. And some-times, they want you to do it. People just wanna watch it happen. Some people even want to be part of it, even if it means they're the victim. This is it, man. Freedom of choice."

"Even if it means the freedom to destroy yourself," I say, let-ting it hang between us.

He doesn't respond.

I select the NarcoDex.

"What happened to Yuri?" I ask, thinking of the kid whose mom sold herself and got AIDS. A kid whose life I'll never know. A kid who found some kind of escape from his life in drugs. I found games. We're the same, in a way, but different.

"Awwwww, man, that's bogus," whines the Vampire. "We had to give him the aspirin. Had to! That's the game."

"And?"

"Well . . . he just . . . he just fell asleep. But trust me, once we fling that metal drawer open and he finds the NarcoDex, it is game on." The Vampire starts to laugh, standing with the tips of his feet just barely over the edge of the yawning abyss. He spits into it.

I'd seen spitting in one of the character action submenus.

"Game on . . . ," he mumbles almost to himself.

I toss the NarcoDex into the abyss.

The Vampire watches it go. For a second I wonder if he can fly, if he'll chase it. But he doesn't. So I guess he can't.

"Dumb, man. Dumb," is all he says.

He turns and walks off into the darkness behind me, back to the Cages. Back to the "fun."

I've figured out where the nearest hanging chain is.

I think.

I hope.

I step back a few paces. Then I double-tap the W key and race toward the edge of the abyss and the sucking darkness below, focusing on the dangling, reasonless chain, centering my POV slightly above the horizon of the lip of the pit. At the last second I hit Spacebar and jump. My Samurai's good hand thrusts itself out into my screen, open, ready to grasp the chain, and suddenly the chain goes from distant to near, all at once.

The timing is crucial. In the nanosecond of hang time between leap and chain, I realize that.

I left-click and my hand grasps the forged iron chain, its links slipping through my fingers until I unexpectedly stop. I look down and see the Samurai's wooden sandals resting on the top of the wide blade at the end of the chain.

What next?

My Samurai's hand grips the iron chain.

I try the movement keys. I tap right once and the chain gives a slight move in that direction. As though my avatar is shifting his weight to get the chain to swing. As it comes back to center, it stops. I double-tap right again and the chain moves a little bit more. As it swings back to center, I tap left and the arc of the swing increases slightly.

After a few minutes, I've gotten the hang of it and the chain is swinging in wide arcs out over the abyss, nearing other chains.

Now or never.

I left-click at the top of an arcing swing to the right and sail across the void toward another chain I'm aiming at. Again, far rushes to near in the brief moment of flight and I barely grab the next chain, realizing the timing of the grab is even narrower than I'd thought.

Repeat.

Repeat.

Repeat . . .

I'm making good progress through the forest of chains, keeping my mind off the numbing sobriety of what the slightest misstep or failure to catch the next chain means. Soon I've lost sight of the edge of the abyss and the Cages where I started. Around me is darkness. Wherever I am, some indeterminate light source shines down from above. I can see the glint of light off distant links of iron chains.

Sometimes the chains are far apart. Sometimes they cluster like stands of trees. It's nearing four o'clock in the morning, New York City time. I'm wondering if there's an end to this when I see a tight cluster of bound and twisted chains ahead. Twisted into a giant hive. Almost like a bird's nest made of iron linked chains instead of twigs and sticks. I adjust my swings to get closer to it.

Maybe this is the way out.

Though I have a feeling it isn't. The nest of chains feels too dark and too ominous to be anything good. But then after tonight, after Yuri and the butchering Dwarves and the women in chains, I'm wondering if there's anything good in this game.

Is anything wrong with anything?

The Vampire.

Yeah, I think about the ten grand someone would've paid to . . . and then I finish the thought . . . to kill Yuri. I forget about it and concentrate on my swings and grabs.

I don't look at the darkness below. Recycle Bin was probably the wrong term. Looking down into the blackness, it feels more like the literal meaning of the word *delete* than anything else.

Deleted.

One missed grab and I'm deleted.

I'm near the nest of chains when she crawls out from within it. She's long legged, another programmer's fantasy of the perfect girl rendered in mythic proportions. She has a belt of silver coins across shapely hips. A too-small bikini top made of the same polished glimmering coins covers an impossible chest. Above her cat's-eye makeup, two short twirling horns rise to sharp points above her falling blood-red hair. Her feet are thick bird-of-prey claws. Her arms are wings with strange claw hands that erupt from the pinions.

She cries out, birdlike, after she catches the movement of the chain I'm resting on as it barely swings side to side in the darkness. A second later she begins to slowly beat her wings, running, then launching herself out into the void toward me.

Her wings sound like leather flapping in the wind.

Two others, one blond, the other brunette, similar and yet each stunningly different beauties in spite of their claws and crow feather wings, follow her out of their nest and circle the darkness around me. They make close passes, their leathery wings beating, flaunting their bodies and whispering.

"You're going the wrong way," says one, which one I can't tell. The other two echo, "Yes, the wrong way." They hover out over the darkness, their wings beating, beaconing.

I wonder if I am going the wrong way.

Then they begin to sing.

A lullaby.

It's haunting . . . it's beautiful.

In New York it's past four o'clock in the morning.

For a moment my avatar's POV suddenly blinks. Like the Samurai is getting sleepy. Which is weird, because I really am tired, and I'm starting to feel it. I think about another scotch.

The Harpies are drifting closer.

"Harpies," it occurs to me, seems right. I didn't even think about it, but that's what they're called. Except why the song?

That's like Sirens. The two are different. But both . . . both had bad intentions for heroes. In stories.

The Samurai's eyes close again and when they open, the Harpies are closer. Singing their lullaby. Beautiful . . . and drifting closer. Their skin glows softly under the mysterious light, making them erotic visions of sweat and myth. Their voices, deep and husky, blend in a trancelike harmony, and even though their words are somehow lost, or unimportant, I know it's a lullaby they're singing.

I think about opening my apartment window for some cold, fresh air, but if I do, I'll never get the apartment warm again. I think I'm even out of the masking tape I'd need to reseal the windows around the frame.

I'm not focusing on the screen and when I force myself to, they're even closer.

Do something.

What?

I tap the keys, getting the chain going using momentum and direction.

The Samurai's eyes close again.

This time, in the darkness behind my avatar's closed-eye POV, my screen reveals a scarlet and velvet vision of one of the Harpies, the blonde. She's languishing on a bed of crushed velvet, surrounded by rich cabalistic tapestries. Her flesh is nubile. Her lips full and pouting. She blows me a kiss . . .

. . . and then the eyes of the Samurai are open and I realize that I've almost actually fallen asleep in the real world. I felt, for a moment, like I was there with her. In that bedroom.

The chain swings out and away from them. I aim for another chain to leap onto and it's a bad aim, but I make it. Barely.

*Get away from them,* is all I can think. *Get away from their song.* I use the momentum of the next swing and launch out toward another chain farther away from their nest.

They follow, their song slithering softly through my speakers. Their voices pleasantly scratchy and warm . . .

. . . and my eyes close.

No, the Samurai's eyes closed. I'm still looking at the screen. I shake my head and blink to make sure.

On-screen all three of the Harpies are writhing and revealed. Each different. Each stunning.

The Samurai's eyes open, and I catch the oncoming chain at the last second. I can hear the leathery slap of their wings, beating as they get closer and closer to me.

I tap the other direction keys and get the chain moving in a wide spinning circle, coming back on the three relentless Harpies, and faster than I can focus, I land the blade beneath my avatar's feet right in the belly of the brunette.

Her eyes widen in terror at that last onrushing instant before I connect.

The other two scream and circle frantically.

I leap away from the spinning, Harpy-impaled chain, flying off into another cluster of chains.

Risky.

The other two follow.

I miss with the next pass, but on the try after that, I stick another blade right through the chest of the blonde. I pan my POV down, seeing her head cast back, blond hair flying out in the wake of our flight, drooling a thin trickle of blood as we swing through the darkness.

The last one, the redhead, is tricky. She keeps dodging my attempts to run the swinging chain's blade into her. But at least their song has stopped. They all must've needed to be alive for that kind of attack. But now she's making close passes with wicked curved little daggers in each of her claw hands. I dodge her attacks and almost lose my grip.

I can't get her lined up for an attack with the chain blade, and in the end I juggle the inventory window, hot key my whip, and just as I get the momentum going to the maximum peak of the chain's arc, I let go of the chain, hot key the whip, and grapple her around the neck with its secondary attack. In midair, with just seconds before I fly past a cluster of chains, I sling the whip and the strangling Harpy into a hanging chain, aiming for the blade. I don't even have time to see what happens as I slew my POV back to watch the Samurai's hand just get hold of another chain.

When I look back, searching for the Harpy, I see she's missed the chain and blade. Alone in the darkness, she's fluttering around wildly, clutching at the whip wrapped around her slender neck. I hear her gagging as her wings cease to beat. Then she drops, spinning off into the darkness below.

Deleted.

I'm hanging there in the darkness.

I can see the nest, and I think about searching it. There should be some kind of loot drop. But there could be more trouble.

I don't have the health or the alertness to do much else tonight. It's going on 4:30. I'm actually hoping the game will shut down for the night when a small message appears at the top of my screen.

Shut down in five minutes.

I look around.

Where's the exit? Where is . . . anything besides these chains? I don't know.

I see a line of chains leading off into the darkness. The intervals between chains are wide. Each will be an extremely hard jump.

That feels like something worth investigating.

I make a few jumps and land on the first chain. Now that I've got the hang of it, the jumps aren't all that hard, but they take longer and longer to get the momentum up to reach the next chain. When I'm at the extent of my highest possible arc and momentum, I leap and barely catch the last chain I can see in the distant darkness. Holding on, it careens off into nothingness with my Samurai clutching the last possible link I could have caught. I begin to swing the chain again, gaining momentum, looking for the next chain. But it isn't there.

"I won't tell you the last part": that's what the Vampire had said. Without it, I wouldn't make it.

I look back along the way of chains. I can barely tell if I'm lined up along their path off into nothing. I can see the vague outline of the last one I'd jumped from.

The Vampire said I'd never make it out if I didn't know the last part.

What's the last part?

One minute to shut down for the night.

4:30 A.M. New York time.

The storm has stopped outside my window.

I get the chain going as fast as I can. The momentum brings me up a tall mountain suddenly going vertical, then down into a valley and then rising again, climbing the arc to the next mountain. At the top of the next arc, as high as I can imagine the swing will possibly go, with as much momentum as I can possibly extract, I let go and fly off into . . .

What other choice did I have? If there's something out there to grab on to, then . . .

There is nothing.

My Samurai flies forward into a nothing-colored darkness.

Then I take 10 percent more damage as I tumble forward, my POV rolling end over end across the screen.

Thirty seconds to shutdown.

I'm standing. But on what I can't tell. Everything is pitch-black.

I take a few steps forward.

Stars begin to swirl at my feet.

I take a few more.

The stars swirl and coalesce and then I'm sucked down into their whirlpool.

Ten seconds.

Blinding white light.

Five seconds.

I see a desert.

# Chapter 11

Whistling winter wind is slipping through a crack in the tape that surrounds my windows, windows that look out onto an empty snow-covered Thirty-Third Street. I don't need to look out and know that Thirty-Third Street is blanketed in snow, empty, and quiet out there. Instead, I lie here on my couch and just know that it is. I fell asleep here in the last moments of night. I woke up here this morning.

The morning sky is bright, too bright, and my eyes ache. Reaching up to shield them from the glare, I discover I'm still holding a tumbler of scotch. Nearby, a series of mostly unsmoked cigarettes litter our old coffee table. The few that I'd managed to ignite sometime in the night have turned into long ashy fingers.

I'd gotten pretty drunk.

After the game went down, the power went out as the storm slammed into the city. The world outside my windows turned gray tweed, like a grainy black-and-white photograph Sancerré once showed me when we were first getting to know each other. Later, thunder rolled through the long canyons of the desolate city in the moments after sudden flashes of lightning. The storm was directly over the city and it mixed well with my Sancerré-infused melancholy and the frustration of a thousand dollars disappearing into a dark abyss called the Black.

I'd tucked the character disk I'd gotten from Iain back into my trench, inside a secret compartment I'd cut and sewn myself. Then I drank and watched the storm. Sancerré didn't call, and the storm passed.

The morning felt bright and clear and the opposite of everything in life. To the east I could see chromatic blue sky. The streets below were empty now that city services had moved up onto monolithic arches of the Grand Concourse of Upper New York spanning the old city below. It was quiet down here and I sat watching the snow-covered street, waiting for the coffee to brew.

I've been drinking too much lately.

I had to find Iain this morning and find out when the game was going back up. Hopefully not tonight. Tonight I had a fight in Eastern Highlands for ColaCorp's few remaining sponsorship venues. A loss tonight might mean the end of my career as a professional.

If it came down to it, I'd probably have to write off the thousand bucks I'd spent on the Black.

I turned on my computer and got an e-mail from RiotGuurl.

"Hey," she wrote. "We're gonna kick butt tonight! Meet you in loadout at five thirty. I won't let you down this time.—RiotGuurl"

She was taking her first defeat hard.

I felt responsible, but I didn't know why I should.

Maybe she was one of the few innocent people left in my life. That seemed like something valuable to me right now, like it was something worth holding on to or even protecting. I'd never met her, I didn't even know her real name, but somehow I knew she was good. Call it a hunch.

I had to find Iain and quick.

I hit the streets twenty minutes later, still nursing my thermos of coffee. I always carry a thermos of coffee, scotch plaid. I stuff the smokes inside the trench to get me through the hangover, and as I catch one of the last, and very few, old subway trains for Grand Central, I try to phone Sancerré.

"Hello," she answers sleepily.

At that moment, I know it's over. I'd suspected it for a long time. Now, I knew it. She'd slept somewhere else, with someone else. The fact that I was having to call my own live-in partner and act like I was some nimrod coworker calling in because she was late for work made me feel lame. And wounded.

I'm over it.

I hang up.

I take a slug from my thermos, which I squeeze back into one of the trench's deep pockets, pull out the rumpled soft pack of smokes, and light up. You're not supposed to smoke on the subway, but since they're free to ride, the transit authority doesn't patrol them anymore. I light the cigarette, sit down in one of the few remaining orange plastic seats, and blow a big cloud of smoke at the completely empty car.

I wonder what the subway was like back when they used to be crowded.

At Grand Central I find the old hippy couple's kiosk.

There's no sign of Iain. Either he'll show to reschedule all his contacts and let us know when the game's going to resume, or he'll take our money and run. I stand around for a moment. The massive hall is quiet as late-morning winter light throws long dusty shafts across the high walls, leaving the side tunnels in darkness. Sancerré once told me that there was a lot more to Grand Central than people knew. Levels, apartments, hidden corridors. She said she'd once attended a party at Grand Central around a swimming pool filled with alligators.

Now it's empty and quiet.

I imagine someone's making her breakfast right now. Or maybe they're both getting dressed. Guilty, ashamed, Sancerré is probably dreading facing me. Why do I care if she feels guilty? Or maybe they're happy, giggling, excited about what they've done and what it means. A secret I'm not part of.

A small Asian boy who'd been sitting on nearby steps at one end of the main hall gets up and walks purposefully toward me. I know he's going to hit me up for something.

But he doesn't.

"You Wu?" he asks.

"What?" I say after a confused pause in which I try to blend game reality with real reality while wearing a hangover. I fail. "What?" I say again.

"I said, are you Wu?"

I look around. Too weird.

"You're not Wu," he pauses, his hard look turning to one of disappointment. "Guess not; sorry, chump." I stand there watching him walk back to his spot on the steps. Maybe a quicker guy, like some avatar built for the entertainments, would've realized sooner that a contact attempt just went down. But I'm not some hard-boiled gumshoe or a high-flying financier of international intrigue. I'm hungover, and the innate gothic gloom of the old station and the blueness of an all-night storm binge leave me feeling slow and numb. Before I can walk over to the kid, Iain, in designer combat boots, expensive jeans, and that butterscotch leather coat he always wears, walks around the side of the kiosk. The hippy couple, who I thought had been awake, begin to snore in unison behind their mirrored blue faux SoftEyes. The kid remains sitting on the nearby steps.

"Yo, there you are," says a smiling Iain, revealing an Iain I've never met before. Friendly Iain. "You know, I don't even know your name." Yesterday he couldn't have cared if I'd been mugged and beaten ten steps from him, now he wants to be my new best friend?

"It's Meatball McGillacutty, what the hell do you care?" I don't feel like playing games right now. I'm out a thousand bucks, soon to be homeless, and my girlfriend's sleeping with someone else—ex-girlfriend, that is. My regular job, which I love, is going over the hill and into history just like Custer's Seventh. So I'm not telling some scumbag Black dealer my real name. He can go straight to hell.

Which is exactly what he doesn't do. Instead he pulls out a very real-looking Glock subcompact ten mil—I've seen them in various games I've played—and sticks it right under my chin.

"You don't wanna tell me your name, fine," whispers Iain close and coldly. That's the Iain I'm familiar with. "But politeness goes a long way in business and you . . . you ain't being polite."

His eyelids hang at half-mast like some prehistoric predator lizard. He's been here before, and I'm pretty sure he's been on both sides of the outcome. The side where he doesn't pull the trigger, and the side where he does.

I glance over at the Asian kid still sitting on the steps.

"John Saxon," I lie. I don't know why I lie. I got that one from the Asian kid. He reminds me of Bruce Lee, and I'm a big fan of *Enter the Dragon*. It's stupid of me to lie. But like I said, I'd had enough for one day.

Iain tilts his pistol away from my chin, almost pointing it at his own face.

"*Laissez les bons temps rouler*, Chumpchange; that's more like it." He tucks his pistol behind his back under his coat like some two-bit entertainment thug and looks at me all combed-straight-back blond hair and bright one-chipped-tooth smile. Except that his eyes are still souless, incapable of any real warmth or affection.

"I'm really, really, sorry, John," he begins in a sincere tone that again doesn't match the eyes. "I'm really sorry about your game going down an hour in. Listen, man, no one saw it coming, it just happened. And sorry about the gun; it's just that I've had to run around pacifying all you angry game geeks and a few others. Listen, I'm gonna do you a solid; let me give you a brand-new character disk. I got a new stack last night, new characters and everything. The game's going to reset after midnight tonight and then everyone's logging back in. Cool?"

No, it isn't cool. Why does he want my character disk? I kinda like the Samurai. I wasn't married to the idea of running him and maybe I can get a better start, but the truth is I didn't want to give it to Iain.

I've had enough of having things taken from me.

"You know," I say, like it's all a big hassle and I'm slightly afraid of offending him, which I am, "I'm not going home till late and, truth is . . . I like the Samurai; I'll just keep him. Thanks anyway."

For a moment his eyes flash intense superheated anger, and then an invisible hand seems to restrain him, correct him. Like he's remembering something from his court-ordered anger management classes, which I'm sure have played a big part in his rehabilitation from the various crimes he's been convicted of. Or someone just sent him a text on one of his SoftEyes. Or whispered in his ear.

"Okay, that's cool, my brother. We're all cool." His hands were suddenly up as he backs off a few steps.

But it isn't cool. Alarms are going off. Time to get out. I glance over my shoulder at the Asian kid, who is still sitting, still looking at his shoes. When I turn back to Iain, I swear I catch him looking over my shoulder, off to the left and into the shadows of a tunnel that leads down to the empty rattling trains.

"All right, gotta go," I say.

Iain's mouth, unlike his lizard eyes, wishes me good luck. But the congeniality of the moment before the gun has disappeared. Almost as if it hadn't ever been there.

I turn and walk away, hoping to make it out into the brutal cold before Iain puts two in my back. As I walk past the kid I mumble, "Follow me in five." I hope Iain doesn't hear.

I'm not clever enough to come up with anything else.

Outside in the snow, with barely a car passing on the ice-swollen streets, I wait under a raised track in the shadows of what looks to be a long-abandoned diner. Literally, people don't come down to this part of town anymore. High above, on the Grand Concourse of Upper New York, I can see a train of slip cars hanging beneath the road, winding its way underneath the cityscape above. Someday I want to be rich enough to live up there and ride that car every day.

I wonder if "up there" is where Sancerré spent the night.

Maybe.

"You Wu or not?" comes the voice from below as I stare rubelike, up at Upper New York. The kid, who at first look seems oddly, if not expensively dressed, stares up at me with disgust. His short pants are a new temperature-converting material made by NikeAtlantis that I'd seen hitting the streets of late. The shoes, thin-skinned runners, obviously also temperature dominant, were HyperGear friendly, which meant the kid's parents, or whoever, had the money for him to delve into CompuWear.

"Yeah, I'm Wu." First karate-kickin' John Saxon, now the enigmatic Samurai Wu. *What's next?* I ask myself and then think about lighting a cigarette. Instead I fish out my plaid thermos and, cool character that I am, pat the secret pouch where my Black disk is hidden.

"Yeah, my grandfather says to give you this, chump." He hands me a slip of paper. You don't see that much these days, paper, though the "grandfather" would explain that little mystery.

"Okay, so cool," says the kid. "See ya around, chump." Then he's off on a FlexyBoard he pulls from one of his pockets, hovering out across the deserted snowbound streets of Forty-Second. He disappears down an alley a few blocks later.

Unfolding the note I read, "Don't give up the Samurai."

# Chapter 12

The war starts up again at 6:30 that night.

I'd met RiotGuurl an hour earlier in loadout. Our avatars now stare at each other as we text back and forth in-game. For some reason she'd rejected a visual link and after bugging her once or twice about it, I let it go. I don't need this, whatever it is, along with everything else. I need to focus tonight.

I equip my grunts with an infantry loadout for two squads. The remaining two I mix with sniper and antiarmor teams. Our mission tonight, as outlined by RangerSix on Monday morning, is to hit the airfield in the plains beyond Wonder-Soft Garage. Way behind enemy lines. Meanwhile, the main body of our force and WonderSoft will be converging head-on in the hotly contested rice paddies of Eastern Highlands.

RiotGuurl and myself are tasked with striking the airfield, which, curiously, no one has ever bothered to name. Fever is going in with us, riding medic. Kiwi is attached to the main force and leading a full infantry company of heavily armed grunts near the main action. Command is hoping he'll be able to raise his kill count and avoid any personal deaths by being near enough the action to make a difference. RangerSix likes Kiwi; it's the number crunchers at ColaCorp who have problems with his stats. Even though his frequent deaths were often accompanied by high enemy kill counts as he ended up being the guy who covered our butts in what had been five weeks of continuous retreat, the accountants focus on the numbers they choose to focus on. They've scoped the numbers the way they want to see them, and that way does not portray Kiwi in a good light. If we lose Eastern Highlands tonight, then we're down to Song Hua Harbor, our home base. If we lose that, we're faced with elimination from WarWorld, and it's the effective end of professional online gaming for me.

"How come you didn't show up at the bunker the other night?" I text RiotGuurl.

On-screen, my grunts are shuffling up the cargo ramp, over-loaded with weapons and special gear, and into RiotGuurl's matte-black special ops Albatross. Everywhere tanks and troops are organizing inside the loadout hangar. Below the stubby wings, near the squat VTOL engines of the Albatross, RiotGuurl's crew is busy loading drone gun packages on the weapon mounts.

"Didn't feel like it," she texts back. "Getting 'ganked' by that Vampire was humiliating. I will tonight, after we knock out the airfield. Promise." She adds a leering emoticon that dies laughing, then explodes.

"I got hammered," I text. Lame, but I'm looking for any kind of opening with her. Maybe she's a party girl.

She doesn't reply.

"JollyBoy's painted the target," she writes back.

She's probably just received the intel specialist's survey report.

"Says there's a lot of infantry, no AA," she continues. "Good for me. Bad 4 u."

I find it hard to believe WonderSoft isn't protecting that airfield with at least a few antiaircraft guns. We'd lost most of our air power early on, but they still had AA units and it would be stupid of them not to put 'em on the airfield. What else were they going to do with them?

"I don't know about that," I reply. "They might have them hidden and ready to bring out once the server goes hot. Has he marked an LZ?"

I wait as my platoon finishes loading itself onto the spec ops Albatross. Thirty-nine killer grunts armed to the digital teeth with state-of-the-art modern weaponry, ready to take the airfield. My plan is to have my infantry set up a perimeter while my snipers and antiarmor stay under cover, ready to take care of the expected enemy counterattack that will show up once we take control of the airfield. After dropping us off at the LZ, RiotGuurl will fly a figure eight across the airfield and deploy all the drone gun packages. If we can hold the airfield for an hour, it'll be ours. Then we can start producing reinforcements locally, right in WonderSoft's unprotected supply lines. That could stop WonderSoft cold tonight. That is, if everything works as planned. It could be the break ColaCorp is hoping for.

But then I remind myself, it's always a great plan, until you meet the enemy.

"Yeah, he found an LZ," she texts back. "Sending it to you now . . . listen, my life's complicated. I shoulda been there that night but I had to work after the battle. You seem like a nice guy . . . you're a good gamer . . ."

Fever's avatar appears in loadout and pings us with tie-dyed emoticons crooning some old-school song about only needing love.

"It's just that . . . ," continues RiotGuurl in text, "I don't have any room for a new friend. I hope that's cool?"

Man, everybody's so concerned about their cool rating lately.

"Yeah," I send back. "My life's no picnic, either, right now. Maybe later."

In my mind I'm writing her off.

Writing her off as what, I don't know.

I'm just trying to get to know a fellow coworker and suddenly I feel like some creepy stalker. Whatever. Let it go. And just as I'm about to finish the official write-off, she writes back, "Maybe?," followed by a winking emoticon.

At five till game launch we're airborne, in hover mode, waiting for the gate to open. On visual, I watch the pregame show as Doc Childs and Monty Guzman prepare to call play by play and color commentary for tonight's battle.

"That's right, Monty," says Doc. "Tonight's match could determine the fate of ColaCorp. Consistent beatings for two months have changed the face of the team. Earlier, when I talked with RangerSix, the team's veteran tactical commander, he had this to say." Now RangerSix's avatar, in full dress uniform with Cola-Corp's red-and-white-striped dress beret appears in a small pop-up. He's standing in front of a Charger IV tank's swivel-mounted rocket racks.

"Frankly we're going for broke tonight. Everybody knows the game; there're not going to be a lot of surprises," lies RangerSix. "The battle will probably take place, as we all know, right smack-dab in the middle of the rice paddies. Their intel knows our troops hold the high ground. That's our only advantage, Doc, and we're not going to give it up. WonderSoft's got a great commander in GeneralKong, and a great team with professionals like Enigmatrix and Captain-Carnage. Add to that their numbers, which my intel is putting at three to one." Again RangerSix purposely lies. Estimates are as high as five to one as of five thirty. "And it's going to be a real knockdown drag out fight tonight, that's for sure," finishes RangerSix.

"It's going to be a slaughterhouse!" erupts a gleeful Monty Guzman.

"No two ways about it, boys," continues RangerSix. "But we've got a few tricks up our sleeves and everyone's going to fight real hard and give 'em hell. Frankly, WonderSoft's going to be fighting for every pixelated inch of that battlefield tonight, and who knows, maybe we can turn 'em back."

Now it's back to just Doc and Monty. "Tough words from a tough man," continues Doc Childs. "But a series of bad breaks and, to be brutally honest, Monty, bad intel, and this team is facing elimination." Doc smiles, full bright, then seems slightly concerned for our impending and, as far as everybody is concerned, assured doom.

"Cheers, mate." It's Kiwi, and he's holding a FostersLunar, a not cheap and very large low-earth-orbit microbrew he's got a line on.

"Are you drunk?" I ask.

He burps loudly then hunches over his computer, his enormous face getting twisted by a funhouse effect he keeps on his camera. "Nope, just thirsty."

"Well, get it while you can. You're gonna be real busy tonight."

Now the gates are going up and the Albatrosses and other attack aircraft are moving forward. Below, ground troops and vehicles flood through the loadout server, disappearing into blinding white light. Less than a second later, the transition to in-game takes effect.

"Kill 'em all!" screams Kiwi.

The first hour is maneuver and dodge for our spec ops Albatross as we slip away from ColaCorp's main force digging in around the fog-shrouded hills above the rice paddies. I listen in on the BattleChat channels. If we're expecting an immediate assault, then we're wrong. WonderSoft hangs back beyond direct fire range, on the slope below the paddies. Our forces, holding the ridgeline above the large shallow ponds of rice, are centered around a sharp green hump of a jungle-cloaked hill, lying in wait. WonderSoft has to cross the rice paddies to get at the hill. They still haven't crossed into range by the time RiotGuurl transports our little platoon of grunts through the high-resolution canyons of green and mathematically generated lava rock above a soft brown gurgling river well away from the impending action.

For a brief moment, we track a lone Vampire on a scouting mission, far off to the west. The Albatross has exchanged its mini-guns and missile launchers for a spiffy sensor package that can cloak us from most electronic detection. As long as we keep it low and slow, it can also passively detect anything that's throwing up enough of an EM signature. We hide once we spot the streaking Vampire, RiotGuurl bringing the Albatross in nice and tight under a beautifully immense banyan tree that hangs over the shallows of the muddy river. She shuts down everything, drops the three landing skids, and settles us gently into the water. The Vampire passes, but it's crystal clear to everyone that it's looking for us.

When it's safe, we power up and move on, leaving the tranquil little stream. If this were a fishing game or maybe a fantasy crawl, this would've been a perfect little spot to relax and enjoy the programmer's art. But like so much of WarWorld, no one will ever fight here. There are vast tracts of unused space within the digital boundaries of WarWorld that might never even witness our digitally rendered passing shadows on this pixel bright day of physics-processed jungle haze.

We race forward toward the airfield, now five minutes out.

"I've got the LZ on radar," says RiotGuurl over BattleChat.

I do a quick check of the BattleChat channels back at the main action.

The battle is on at the paddies. WonderSoft tries to cross with armor, using their light Wolverine mechs, armed with brutal coax chain guns to sweep the brush just above the paddies. Our side remains silent.

Then RangerSix, in a quiet, understated voice, gives the first command.

"Fire for effect," we hear him say to the gun batteries behind the hill.

Our artillery begins to pound the advancing enemy with high-explosive rounds. The first strike, as I watch Kiwi's battle-cam channel, manages to take out two of the twelve Wolverines. Seconds later, another one of our gun batteries opens up with white phosphorus. Burning hot white rounds impact the water and earth berms, not destroying any mechs. Instead, the white phosphorus ignites the tall waving grass inside the paddies. Some of the unquenchable phosphorus finds its way onto a few of the mechs, smoldering as they advance through the smoke and fire beginning to build within the paddies. After a minute, the battlefield is drifting thick clouds of white mixed with intermittent oily black ropes of smoke.

Another gun battery opens up with SMAFF rounds. SMAFF rounds are ColaCorp's secret weapon, the result of our one superlab capture at the beginning of the Eastern Highlands campaign against WonderSoft. Other corporate armies also have secret weapons. Money, time, and in-game resources such as captured superlabs and supply points allow each side to develop a special weapon. Some teams develop better rifles, specialized grenades, or even a new kind of tank such as the Bull. A relativistic supercannon mounted onto a main battle tank, the Bull renders almost all physical defenses invalid as it has the effect of pulverizing acres of terrain. ColaCorp, on the other hand, managed to capture a weapons lab back at Jihad City or what the designers of WarWorld called Karkand, and we got SMAFF technology. SMAFF is basically a combination of intense IR obscuring smoke and electronic numbing microparticles that can cloak an area in a haze both visual infrared and electronic for hours if the winds are right.

Now SMAFF rounds are falling onto the paddies, and within moments the entire area is obscured in a cream sauce of distortion. On Kiwi's battlecam, I see him glance left and right, checking his company's position, then his troops are up and moving. He orders them to form tight squad-based formations, and armed with thermite charges, they move into the smoke to search out the temporarily blind mechs and destroy them by hand.

I watch as Kiwi low-crawls toward the vicious snub-nosed beast that is WonderSoft's Wolverine light battle mech. The gunner is spraying wildly in all directions as the SMAFF begins to disorient his targeting and order receiving capability; he's probably a grunt. A round or two manages to splash wetly into the muddy water near Kiwi. Stopping, Kiwi raises his AK-2000, aims through the iron sights, and drops the grunt with a brutal burst of short barking gunfire. The coax gun continues to swivel on its turret as the grunt ragdolls backward. Kiwi leaps up and scrambles forward. He exchanges his assault rifle for thermite and plants it on one leg of the mech. His green-and-black-gloved fingers come into view as he enters the arming code, and the bomb is soon counting down to Independence Day. Kiwi hustles back into the soupy gloom of SMAFF and seconds later . . .

"Visual on the LZ," says RiotGuurl over chat. "Seems nice and cold."

*Ka-blaaam!* The first thermite charge explodes on Kiwi's battlecam. Half a second later, a connoisseur of destruction can detect the *ka-voosh* of the Wolverine's fuel tank igniting in a secondary explosion.

We're off to a good start.

"Ten seconds to insertion." RiotGuurl's door gunners open up with the swing-mounted fifty-caliber machine guns, firing short controlled bursts into the hangars and control tower surrounding WonderSoft's airfield. I kill Kiwi's cam just as he knifes a WonderSoft infantry trooper in the back. I bring up the Albatross's camera and replace Kiwi's channel with its visual feed.

I start my 'Nam Battle Surf playlist with "Somebody to Love," by a band once called Jefferson Airplane. Inside the Albatross, the ground lurches upward off to our right as RiotGuurl brings the gunship into a tight turn. Small-arms fire starts coming up at us. WonderSoft's rear echelon troops are scattering across the airfield, leaving three bat-winged gray SkyCamo heavy bombers queued up on the taxi apron.

"Looks good," calls out RiotGuurl. "Stand by for insertion." She toggles the attitude thrusters, bringing us in behind a small copse of trees near the north end of the field. Nearby, empty concrete squares serve as landing pads for WonderSoft's own absent version of the Albatross, the Whale hunter-killer gunship, just like ours, only lumpier and more heavily armed.

JollyBoy's marked LZ shows up in a candy-cane-striped box on our individual HUDs. This is JollyBoy's hilariously funny, at least to himself, trademark tactical highlighter.

"Go, go, go!" screams RiotGuurl over BattleChat. We're down a second later as the rear cargo door flops open into a grassy field. The grunts hustle down the back ramp as the door gunners rake the airfield with suppressive fire. Most of the enemy troops disappear into a small refinery on the far side of the airfield beyond a high wire fence. An alarm Klaxon can be heard dimly above the Albatross's whining hover jets and whispering turbines now set to idle as we disembark.

Fever and I are the last out, and already the platoon has formed a half circle facing the most likely enemy positions. An occasional round zips through the trees at us, but that's most likely the scattered WonderSoft support grunts taking random shots while waiting for orders from above. "Above," in all likelihood, should be freaking out with incoming sitreps about our incursion into WonderSoft's unprotected rear.

I squawk my own sitrep to Command as RiotGuurl pushes the throttle forward and lifts off above the tree line of the copse.

"Good hunting, Perfect, I'll start . . ." She's cut short by the most urgent of modulated tones, rapid and emphatic. An anti-missile alert is screaming relentlessly inside her cockpit.

Damn JollyBoy to hell!

"Incoming missile, three o'clock," yells one of her grunts in the background of her comm channel. I hear RiotGuurl sigh as she works frantically on her keyboard to yank the now fat and stupidly vulnerable Albatross out of the streaking missile's way. Two seconds later, a small missile trailing white smoke darts like some wispy sidewinder across the airfield and into the side of RiotGuurl's Albatross.

I hear the engines of the Albatross strain to gain altitude, as well as the slight *pump pump pump* of her afterburners as she tries to raise the nose and engage them, but nothing's happening for her.

It's at that moment that WonderSoft springs its trap.

Faintly, far off there's a *thump*. Then another. Then another.

"Incoming!" I call out over BattleChat. I open a channel to RiotGuurl, at the same time slewing back to my command menu for the platoon. I direct the platoon into the thick copse of trees for protection. Fever follows them, staying in their center. Above us, RiotGuurl's door gunners jump out of the struggling Albatross, sprouting parachutes at a ridiculously low altitude; that's one of the benefits of fighting in a computer world as opposed to the real one.

One of them has managed to disconnect his swing fifty cal and takes it with him.

"Get out, you're not gonna make it!" I shout to RiotGuurl over the chat.

"Almost . . . ," she replies, then both hover engines die and the Albatross hangs for just a moment before pitching off to its right and into a death roll. Even she knows it's lost, and a moment later as the first mortar rounds start coming down on us, I watch her little avatar body fall from the burning wreck of the spiraling Albatross as the white flower of a parachute, thankfully, blooms behind her.

WonderSoft isn't freaking out.

They aren't panicking.

They had a plan, and as usual, they're many steps ahead of us. Even though now, at this crucial point, one step is more than enough. We didn't surprise them, they surprised us. Mortars fall directly on top of us, on their own base, right where we'd landed.

The small copse of trees shudders with each impact of the light artillery rounds, designed to kill personnel, not vehicles. Exploding foliage is disintegrating with each burst, spreading shrapnel and mayhem throughout my task force. I drop to the ground, hitting Z on my keyboard, and wait for the barrage to end. At the center of the airfield, the spec ops Albatross, spinning, slams into the ground hard and explodes.

At least that'll prevent the bombers from using the runway to take off for now. A minor victory, if any, for what will now probably be a massacre.

I flash an urgent sitrep to RangerSix who, true to form, knows what and what not to sweat.

"What's your current situation and plan right now, son?" says RangerSix across the CommandNet.

"Albatross down, ambushed at the LZ. No casualties yet, stand by for numbers shortly," I say, fearing the worst.

"Are you combat effective, son?" He wants to know if I have enough grunts to take the field and finish the mission. If not, extraction really isn't an option.

"We're good to go, sir." What other choice do I have? We have to take the field.

"HOO-ah, son. Now get out there and complete the mission, Six Out."

The artillery begins to lighten up. Getting us into the trees had been quick thinking, and it was a good thing we came in near enough to get under cover. Maybe JollyBoy was thinking after all.

I radio RiotGuurl.

"What's your status, girl?"

"Came down on the far side of the field past the fence. I'm on top of the refinery."

I'm not sure if that's good news.

"Afraid I've got bad news, though," she says over BattleChat. Yay!

"You've got a motorized battalion moving up the road. Looks like they're staging down at WonderSoft Garage so we didn't see 'em on the way in. They're makin' bacon to get to you, so get ready quick."

It just keeps getting worse and worse.

I set my platoon up around the copse, fanning out two antiarmor squads to circle the airfield and stay below line of sight, in a small trench that encompasses the field. It'll be their job to take care of the vehicles. The sniper teams move out toward the hangars, deploying antipersonnel mines behind them once they've reached their positions. The two remaining infantry squads, along with Fever and me, will slug it out here and now for the airfield, using the copse and its minimal protection as a firebase.

In the distance I can hear enemy vehicles approaching, switching gears as they gain the plateau where the airfield is.

An hour later, fighting hard, we've killed the first motorized company that's tried to dislodge us. I'm down to one sniper team at the far end of the runway, an antiarmor grunt running amok with a man-portable Genscher antiarmor system, and Fever, along with less than a squad of infantry grunts still holding the shot-to-hell copse.

Tracer rounds are coming at us from every direction, smacking into the few remaining leaves of the splintered trees in the copse. Our mobile barriers are giving us just enough room to move around and shoot back. RiotGuurl from her vantage point has watched the companies of the motorized battalion, no small expense for WonderSoft, come barreling onto the runway, hoping the smoking wreckage of the Albatross is all that remains of our ill-fated surprise attack. What hasn't perished in the crash has probably been knocked down by their artillery, or so they could be thinking.

They're a little surprised when my snipers knock out their vehicle commanders sitting in the turrets and right seats of the smaller vehicles. My snipers also manage to get one actual live player commanding the cleanup team. His dog tags are added to my combat knife with a small trumpeting noise made in-game for terminating a live player. He wasn't a professional, just an amateur looking to impress WonderSoft with free combat support.

It wasn't much, but it felt good to be making it hard on WonderSoft in some small way.

When their second assault goes down, I have the fifty cal that survived the crash set up as my primary gun. It covers the airfield, raking the incoming light-skinned vehicles with high-explosive armor-piercing rounds. Moments later, antiarmor snake trails spool out from various points of "my" airfield. One light mech explodes in a shower of sparks, and a few other AT rounds punch explosive holes in WonderSoft's fast-attack gun-laden Mules, the standard get-about battle utility vehicle, or the modern jeep.

Next, stunned and dismounted infantry, now leaderless, are regrouping while assaulting pell-mell into our kill zone. Within minutes, thanks to RiotGuurl's above-the-battle sitreps, we know another infantry battalion is staging itself on the far side of the refinery.

"Command," I call out over the net. "Be advised, we are expecting another assault on the airfield in minutes. Request artillery support on standby."

"Negative, artillery unavailable at this time." It's the automated fire control voice. Our big guns have probably been knocked out back at the paddies.

"Kiwi, how goes it?" I open a pop-up showing Kiwi's POV channel. He usually keeps it unlocked.

"We're falling back onto the hill." His HUD doesn't jibe with that. He's still among the smoking mechs down in the SMAFF-shrouded paddies. There are bodies everywhere, WonderSoft's and ColaCorp's.

"Did you say 'we'?" I ask.

"Oh yeah," he laughs. "We, as in our army, are engaging in a retrograde action, designed to allow the enemy to advance into a trap, heh, heh."

"You mean 'they,' the rest of the team, is retreating?"

"Looks that way, mate."

"But you're not?"

"No, not right now, Perfect. No, I've decided to die in position again."

"Dude, that's not an option for you this time."

"Word *option*'s a funny thing, Perfect. Sometimes you got 'em, sometimes you don't, mate. Know what I mean?"

"PerfectQuestion!" It's RiotGuurl. "Whale gunship just arrived and landed near the refinery. Enigmatrix just got out. Damn!"

"Hold on, Kiwi . . . What do you mean, how do you know it's her?"

"No time to explain. It's her! Her avatar never wears a helmet, plus she's carrying Enigmatrix's favorite weapon."

"MagForce shotgun?"

"Yeah. Stupid weapon, but she makes it work."

With the highest in-game kills and the top-ranked spot in the league, Enigmatrix could have carried a water pistol and she'd still be the deadliest soldier in the game. She moves fast, smart, and accurately. She uses cover, grunts, anything, to get close to her enemies, all the while pumping out uranium-depleted slug after slug from her MagForce shotgun. Generally shotguns are an ineffective weapon for the battlefield, but her skills combined with an overwhelmingly rapid command intuitiveness often get her close enough to start shredding groups of grunts and players alike with that vicious hand cannon of death. There was always a moment, everyone claimed in the chat rooms, when you thought you could take her, once you saw her carrying that relic of a weapon. After that, it went mostly downhill for everyone who'd made the mistake of thinking they could take her.

Now, she's here for me.

"Kiwi," I say over his feed. "Enigmatrix is here! You've got to get off that battlefield alive today!"

"I understand, mate. But my grunts and players have all been killed and the rest of ColaCorp is back up on the hill. Wonder-Soft is almost out of the paddies. One more push and I'm behind enemy lines. Plus I can't move from behind these burnin' tanks without getting picked off, so I guess it's time for my standard grand exit."

In Kiwi's hand, I could see him switching out his AK-2000 for a thermite package. "I'll scatter these around. We'll see how it goes."

"Kiwi . . ."

"It's just a game, mate. Forget about it. We'll always be pals. But today, I gotta go. Forget about me and kill Enigmatrix. I hate that Sheila. At least something good'll come out of today. Every time she looks at her almost perfect record, she'll know that one of the good guys ruined it just a little. And in my own way, mate, I'll think of that as one from me."

On the other side of the field, through the far side of the wire fence and into the refinery, I can see WonderSoft infantry moving in small groups. One group, dust-gray camo and battered armor, heavily armed with Colt 7.62 high-powered, compact urban assault rifles moves in, while another group, down in the grass or behind a wall, covers them. It's good, calculated planning on Enigmatrix's part, and it's probably going to get me killed.

"RiotGuurl?" I call out.

"Yeah, Question?"

"I have a plan."

"Yeah, me too. What's yours?"

"I want you to steal that Whale that just landed."

"Wow, same brain, me too. I'm already on it. Just the two door gunners right now, but I think I can get it. Then I'll come in and pull you and the rest of the unit out from behind the copse. Then we get the hell out of here."

"No. I want you to steal that gunship, get back to the paddies, and pull Kiwi off the field. If we don't get to him before he gets killed, he's out of ColaCorp. Roger?"

Silence over the chat. Simulated bullets rip up the computer-generated earth and zip through the air all around us.

"Roger?" I repeat.

Silence. "All right, if I can get there in time."

"You've got to. If he gets killed, that's it for him on pro status. You know how much that means."

"All right, PerfectQuestion. Same brain," she croons uncharacteristically.

Now I have to deal with Enigmatrix.

Already, my few remaining wounded and digitally gory bleeding grunts are getting chewed up heroically as WonderSoft and

Enigmatrix begin their final assault, hoping to overrun our position inside the copse. Fever is doing his best to revive my downed grunts, often dodging bright hails of gunfire to get to a grunt that's been dropped in an exposed position.

"Cover me, I'm going to get one," he's said several times over BattleChat.

"Covering," I reply and then open up with short bursts from the AK-2000 spec ops mod rifle I've picked up. I'm engaging targets at 150 meters plus, or so my digital imaging scope tells me. I switch to thermal and scan the grass looking for any low crawlers trying to use the terrain to get in close enough. I fire a nice long burst, just something to make WonderSoft grunts get their heads down. Then Fever reaches our downed grunt, grabs him, and drags him back behind cover. Out come the shock paddles and hopefully we have another rifle back in the game. When he's not doing that, he crawls about distributing medical packs behind fighting positions, reinforcing our health meters.

If only real battles were fought so easily . . .

Across the airfield, I see Enigmatrix with her grunts as they take up positions behind the burning Albatross, using it for cover. A few of them pop out from the sides, firing short, loud bursts that ring out over ambient in-game sound.

"Get that fifty working on the downed Albatross," I order my grunt platoon sergeant, highlighting the wreckage as a focus point for my remaining combat effective units.

That done, I flip the selector on my rifle to single shot and scope the corners of the wreckage, hoping Engimatrix will use her grunts to look around the sides of the burning gunship.

*BANG!* One pokes his head out from behind the wreckage, and I take him down with a head shot. Seconds later, a grunt medic races out from behind cover, pulling out his revival paddles. I fire two rounds, catching him leg and torso, and he's down too.

Smoke grenades come up from over the top of the wreckage, spiraling out toward our position, bouncing, rolling, and tumbling in front of us. Puffy white billows of smoke erupt, obscuring what is no doubt their impending attack.

I wait, scanning for shadows in the constantly moving smoke that's enveloping our position. To my left, I hear *CrackBoom;* a shotgun rings out once and then again twice in rapid succession. The fifty cal stops its mechanical sewing machine of death. Two more grunts go offline on my HUD roster. I flip the selector switch to auto and unload a full magazine into the smoke, working the gun from right to left. Quickly I slap in another magazine and empty that to the right and to the rear. And as I'm unloading, the leaping Enigmatrix, her avatar with crimson hair the color of arterial bleeding and body skinned in a tight gray CamoSkin suit and wearing thick combat boots, descends upon me, as if leaping through the blossoming smoke.

Winged Death.

I raise my rifle, not bothering to stop the deadly stream of automatic gunfire coming from its barrel, and just as she falls into my scope and the cone of hot-leaded death spitting out of its barrel, a *ka-chunk* reverberates through my speakers and lands in my soul.

I'm out of ammo.

She smiles. One-handed, she points her shotgun at me, pushing it into my chest.

BOOM.

A reverberating, metallic echo of thunder erupts across my speakers. On-screen she's still smiling at me.

Her avatar is smiling.

Smiling Death.

Shotgun smile.

I pound my keyboard in frustration.

My vitals whine critically as I struggle with the mouse to

slew my bloody-mist vision left and right. Looking for Fever. Looking for help. I'm on the ground, on my back, looking up at the billowing smoke and the blue sky beyond.

She's off to finish the rest of my grunts.

I click my attack button and hear my avatar yell, "Medic, I'm hit."

I left click again, "Medic!"

Third time. "I'm hit!" screams my avatar, screams me.

Smoke.

Time.

Fever.

"I gotcha, buddy. Clear!" yells his avatar above me.

My screen heaves and shudders. I'm too far gone this time.

"Clear." He hits me with the paddles again, and again I heave.

My vitals are too far gone. The whining shock paddles whistle as they build up another charge. I'm less than three seconds from online death.

"Stay away from the light," laughs Fever weirdly over Battle-Chat. "Third time'll do it, buddy. Always does."

"Clear!" And the slamming shock of resuscitation revives my character. I'm back in the game.

"Follow me," says Fever. Staying close to him, we move as rhythmic blasts from Enigmatrix's shotgun and my HUD roster tell a tale of defeat as she methodically works her way through what remains of my task force.

We're out of the smoke and running for the far side of the airfield. A Goat, one of WonderSoft's fast-attack dune buggies, has been left off in the high grass, probably driven in by one of the motorized companies that attacked us earlier. It's abandoned. Seconds later, we're in. I'm driving. Fever works the mounted minigun as we come around our burning Albatross, tires squealing on the wide aircraft runway. He rakes Enigmatrix's grunts, dropping more than a few as blood sprays away from them in bright misty smears.

Then there's this thing called payback.

It starts with Enigmatrix smiling and leaping in to shoot me in the chest as she laughs. Maybe it's just me transposing that onto her. Maybe she wasn't laughing from the other side of her screen. Or maybe being the top player in the game gives you the right to modify your avatar to one of a laughing shotgun-wielding sociopath. Or maybe everybody else has found some hidden command menu that lets them personalize their avatars with that particular taunt. Maybe. But whatever it is, her grinning, leaping, laughing avatar runs out of the smoke on the tarmac of the runway, right in front of me. All my grunts are dead and she's reloading.

And I'm driving.

She doesn't even look up as I run her down and tally up an in-game player kill.

Payback.

# Chapter 13

I stand up and stretch. The muscles in the back of my neck ache. My fingers feel cramped and my index finger seems beaten to numbness by all the mouse clicks. I walk to the window and look out at the night. Snow falls through orange cones of light from the few remaining streetlights that still work down in this part of town. I think about turning on the television and watching the postgame show but I don't. I like the quiet. My building has always been quiet. Not that many people live here. But lately it's gotten a lot more quiet. I never see any of the neighbors I didn't really ever know.

There's nothing in the fridge except a wedge of Brie cheese. Sancerré's favorite. The lonely cheese inside the empty appliance looks like a photograph of noble poverty. Like something Sancerré would have shown me at a gallery back when . . .

I'm still thinking about the battle as I stand with the refrigerator door open, the only light source in the tiny kitchen. There's a small hum as the appliance clicks into over-drive to compensate for the waste of my artistic contemplations. I'm thinking about Enigmatrix and why ColaCorp keeps losing and why JollyBoy picked such a bad LZ. It was a poor choice.

I'm starving and the cheese looks good. The first night she ever came to my apartment I'd served her Brie and sliced green apples. We'd had wine. She'd said Brie was her favorite forever from then on.

Forever.

I close the door on the cheese and wander through the apartment. I sit down on our bed in the dark, on her side. I notice the things she kept there.

Hand lotion.

A book.

Some nail polish.

They're all gone.

If I open her closet will I find nothing? Maybe a couple of hangers? Some random unwanted thing?

I don't open her closet.

It's dark and cool and quiet in here and it's just the break my eyes need for a few minutes.

Those minutes in between worlds.

And I don't really want to turn on the light because I might see how much of Sancerré's stuff is actually gone. So I just sit in the darkness and think about WonderSoft.

They're always a step or two ahead of us. It's like playing against a gaming clan that's all on mic and communicating. Running their plans, calling out targets, reacting with extreme force and numbers to all your old tricks. There's nothing you can do but lose when the game's against you like that.

I'd say they were cheating, but that's next to impossible with the way WarWorld runs its online security.

And maybe WonderSoft is just better than us.

Than me.

I think about the cheese in the fridge.

I listen to the quiet.

Maybe Sancerré will come back. So I'll just hang on to the cheese in case she does.

# Chapter 14

At midnight I'm logging back into the Black.

I'm beat.

The fatigue of fighting my way back to our lines in WarWorld hits me as I wait for World of Wastehavens to dump all its gothic gloom into my computer.

It's the moments in between, the silence of load screens, that really gets to me. Makes me question what I'm really doing here and wonder if life, real life, is somehow passing me by. Real life. Real love.

I consider pouring myself a shot of something for whatever madness happens next, but I'm too tired to do it, so I sit in the dark listening to the computer click and hum its rattling way toward game start. It's the only noise in our apartment.

My apartment now.

I guess Sancerré's really gone.

*Abandon All Hope* . . . appears on the screen, and the game begins. I ready myself for whatever happens next, thinking of that desert I'd glimpsed in the last moments of the last session . . . and of Sancerré. My fingers hover lightly over the direction keys. Ready. Waiting.

The scene my computer shows me is one of an endless sea of beautifully designed, sand-sculpted dunes of light and shadow, completely still and yet undulating into the shimmering horizon.

A desert.

Not the depthless black pit I'd been in, forgotten by the game. The Oubliette.

Instead . . .

Overhead the glaring white sun stares directly into my Samurai's eyes as I pan upward and out over an endless worn-out sky. Its blazing mirror is an image of angry silver rage. Faded blue skies surrender to the sand that covers the horizon in every direction. On-screen, the word *Begin* briefly appears in gothic spike script, then disappears.

There is nothing to do but move my Samurai forward, and I do. For an hour I head deeper and deeper into the trackless waste, nothing on ambient except the *scrunch scrunch scrunch* of my Samurai's wooden shoes as they grind their way up and down sandy dunes seemingly without end. The occasional cry of an unseen buzzard, a lonesome flute track, and a subtle discordant hand drum compose the musical score of the game.

I have no weapons. Just the few martial arts attacks that I can select under the *Posture* menu. I leave the Samurai in *Judo* mode and continue on. Off in the distance, a sprinkling of worn desert palms rises from the shimmering heat, and I know this is something because the soundtrack adds a guitar, barely electrified. It begins to strum some lost late-1970s reminiscent riff. Like something from the Eagles' "Hotel California," its urgency rising by degrees. It cascades, then the mix repeats.

That tells me this oasis is something worth investigating.

Even though there is something in the music that reminds me of a warning. A caution.

I think of water and that reminds me to glance at my health indicator, which I haven't looked at for some time. I'm down to 20 percent, barely above passing out. I have a feeling the blistering in-game heat of the desert is probably making it difficult to heal. Still, I trudge on toward the tall palm clusters, hoping for an oasis. Maybe if there's shade, I can hang out and heal up.

I've wasted my thousand bucks.

It takes me another half hour of skirling desert winds, lone flute, drum, and disembodied guitar music punctuated by the occasional cry of some an unseen buzzard to get to the oasis. The Troll that guards the oasis is large, mean, and ugly.

You know, a Troll.

He lumbers about the far side of the oasis, muttering and grumbling, unaware that I'm watching him from the top of a tall dune near a shimmering, shallow pool of crystal-clear water.

Above me the sun seems to have barely moved. My health meter hasn't managed to rise in the least. Instead, it's slipped to 19 percent.

Yes, this definitely has been a well-spent thousand bucks.

I low-crawl my Samurai along the top of the rising dune, slithering through its almost pure white sand. Below, the oasis is a pool of clear water, underneath which I can see the emerald-and-gold-colored flagstone paving of some lost and ancient civilization. Sand lies along the bottom of the pool in sporadic drifts. The paving stones beneath the water are covered in inky black pictoglyphs. Near the pool the Troll, black and warty, with oily hair and large misshapen features, walks tall and dangly armed into a red-and-white-striped large tent on the far side of the oasis.

At one thirty in the morning, real-world New York City time,

I'm too tired to figure out how to defeat the Troll. Even if I do, what about the in-game "rescue the kid" quest I have to complete to earn any kind of return on my thousand? Forget all the bonus prizes and cash awards that are supposed to be scattered throughout most Black games. I have yet to find even one reward. Instead, I've managed to spend most of my time in some sort of lost and found bin. Now, I'm out in the desert with no sign of the tower on any of the horizons. I am well and truly lost. I was supposed to be fighting my way to the top of a tower full of horrors, and hopefully, prizes. Instead I'm still somewhere that feels a lot like nowhere.

Did the server mess up and dump me out here? Is this all just some big con job? If it is, there's no one I can complain to, being that it's a crime to even participate in a Black game. Oh, and I'll forget about addressing my concerns to Iain, due to the fact that he carries a gun as part of his customer service policy.

I'd envisioned more, at least something other than what I'd gotten so far, a whole lot of nothing. No prizes. No loot. No money. Every *Darkness* character I'd managed to eliminate I would have gotten a one-hundred-dollar bonus paid into my online account. Twenty down and I could've quit just on that. So far, no one and nothing, and Creepy must not be dead because there's no bonus in my account. It's one thirty in the morning and I'm very tired.

Frustrated too.

I add up the two thousand that's due in rent, the empty checking account, and tonight's defeat in WarWorld, and this is it. This is all I've got. I either do something here and now or I start finding boxes for my stuff.

Thanks, Sancerré.

I move forward silently after unequipping the Samurai's shoes. I make no sound as I descend the sandy dune and make my way toward the edge of the pool and enter. Delicate bells dancing slightly at the mere thought of a breeze play across ambient sound as I enter the crystal-clear water of the desert pool.

I listen and hear nothing else.

I cross the pool, studying the green-and-gold pictoglyph-covered flagstones along its bottom where the drifting sand hasn't collected in long fingers. The soundtrack introduces a woman crooning Middle Eastern–inspired throaty wails of passion and desperation. I listen beyond the low soundtrack and hear only my robed legs moving through the pool, and even a light desert breeze passing gently through the fronds of the tall palms that surround the oasis.

I've formed a vague plan on how to take out the Troll, and I reason out the method of my approach once again as I stand in the pool, hoping the Troll won't suddenly appear. I need to sell myself before I commit to any plan. At 19 percent health, one misstep, and I'm dead.

Trolls are creatures of the dark, serving evil, doing generally despicable things. It's daylight right now, so maybe he's weaker, maybe he's even resting inside his tent. Who knows what midnight party he has planned? But I'm betting, if he's resting, I can either get by him or set a trap and get the jump on him. Whatever I do, I have to start doing something quickly. The server has reset me way off the beaten path. Somewhere the game is progressing and all kinds of loot and prizes are being handed out as players climb the tower. Or at least try to. Meanwhile, I'm facing an enemy I have neither the health nor body parts, nor even weapons for that matter, to fight.

I move closer to the edge of the pool, near the red-and-white-striped tent as the breeze carries the coughing snore of the Troll out over the sand and water. Stepping from the pool, I spot the Troll's wicked-looking gigantic scimitar stuck into the sand near the tent.

The weapon is far too large for me to use with one hand, but

I take it anyway. I don't have much else. I see a miniature representation of the gigantic scimitar in my inventory screen and it's grayed out. I can't use it. It most definitely will need two hands to wield and I only have the one, but I keep it anyway. At least the Troll won't get it. Besides, I've got a plan.

In *Crouch* mode, I slip softly across the sands toward the tent, and just outside the front of it, I find two stakes at the ends of long ropes connecting them to the tent. With a quick bit of submenu juggling, I manage to anchor the loose ropes between the two tent pegs just outside the entrance to the tent, along the well-worn path down to the pool. I drop the large, shiny, scroll-worked scimitar and, using my mouse cursor, manage to sink the hilt of the scimitar a short distance back from the trip rope, angling the wide wicked blade so that it points upward toward the gently moving flaps.

Then, I circumvent my trap and enter the tent.

The Troll is sleeping on a large pile of shining silver coins sprinkled with intermittent bits of gold. His face is protected by one large hairy arm as his swollen belly rises and falls in halting rhythms. The Troll's armor is better than what I'd normally expect to find in most games. Usually, in the few other fantasy games I've played, the average Troll is wearing leather, gruesomely constructed from the hides of humans. Maybe it'll have an occasional scrap of some random piece of armor or a gold earring or tooth set among a cavalcade of rotting friends. But this Troll is wearing fine scale mail constructed with delicate circled plates, each carved with runes. In all likelihood, this Troll is a boss. A major NPC that players usually find at the end of a zone, guarding a fantastic weapon or treasure, loot of some sort. There is no way I should have started this game anywhere near him.

Yet another reminder of how I'm getting cheated out of my thousand bucks. If Iain weren't an armed psychopath, I most definitely would express my customer dissatisfaction.

The Troll is probably one bad dude. My simple trap may not even kill him. I scan the tent for something else I can use against him. Maybe I can find a one-handed weapon I can at least cut his throat with, or maybe even use to blind him. Nothing. There are a few chests, but rattling though one of them or picking a lock would probably alert the Troll. I eventually do want to alert the Troll to my presence. That way I can lead him to the trap. One of the chests might contain something useful. If I work quickly, I can get whatever I find equipped and then use it on the Troll before he attacks. If he wakes up and finds me looting his stuff, I'll just run and lead him back to the trap.

It seems like a good plan. But doesn't it always seem like a good plan? It's later on that you learn, not so much.

There are three chests half buried among the piles of silver coins. Through the fabric of the tent, I can see the lowering sun turning an afternoon bloody red. It's still bright out, but in-game late afternoon seems to be happening. Soon, nightfall. My guess is, that's when the Troll wakes up. I examine the three chests.

Chest number one is composed of pale wood and a blackened grimy lock. Chest number two is more of a delicate sandalwood box. I could smash it open with my hand, but the noise no doubt would awaken yon grumpy über-Troll. The third chest is large, large enough for a good sword. Its wood is highly polished mahogany, its lock a shimmering silver. Along the sides, ornately carved runes pulse rhythmically.

I really don't have much choice. The third chest is no doubt trapped with magic runes. The first chest is probably locked and mechanically trapped. I target the second box and deliver a judo chop with my attack button, disintegrating the top of the box.

Almost instantly, the Troll is bellowing and rising up from his pile of silver coins. Even though he has no scimitar to cut my few remaining health points to shreds, he raises a large bronze buckler strapped to his other arm, which I hadn't noticed earlier, it being thrown off to the other side of the coin pile. My only hope now is the box. Inside are the shattered remains of a crystal decanter. I move my mouse over it and a QuickNote lets me know that it was some kind of perfume. Incense of Mermaid. Useless, shattered, and a poor choice. My only choice. The Troll's great shield slams into my side and I'm airborne. I watch the Troll recede away from me as I fly through the air, through the flaps of the tent, as I pass into the pool with a splash. The Troll is moving, and as he hits the flap of the tent, all bellows and indignation with added threats of grinding bones promised, the taut rope arrests his stride and down he goes cleanly on his own wicked blade. He's grinning, smiling as the scimitar pierces his throat and comes out the top of his warty wide forehead.

Silence.

I'm down to 3 percent Vitality. I should be passing out, fading into death. But I'm not. My health is rising. I stand still, not wanting to jeopardize the healing process. Near the edge of the pool, a thin line of dark blood streams down from the Troll's gigantic misshapen head, dyeing the pixilated sand a deep crimson. I wait. My health continues to climb through the forties, the fifties, and surprise, surprise, my hand is growing back.

At 100 percent health, the blazing red sun melts into the dunes, leaving the oasis bathed in the long cool shadows of early evening.

My hand has grown back.

Torchlight flickers to life near the Troll's tent, and still the desert flute gives counterpoint to the steady beat of the soft drums over the game's soundtrack.

I exit the pool and enter the tent. I left-click the pile of silver and am rewarded with a QuickNote from the game:

Congratulations on defeating the guardian of the Pool of Sorrows, the Desert Troll Khalabash. His corruption of the pool is ended. Six hundred e-bucks have been deposited to account #98402374727-111122338. Please note this account and enter your password for confirmation.

Yes!

I think of two things at once. First, how did I defeat an über-boss without being in the game in any reasonable starting position? Second, what should my password be?

Sancerré?

I still care for her. If I had a moment to catch my breath and get some sleep, maybe we could sort this thing out between us. Maybe I can make enough money tonight to keep her. Maybe enough to keep her away from that whoever it is she's with. Maybe.

I enter her name.

Next I turn to the chests. The one with the runes is definitely going to be tricky. Maybe it'll even outright damage me. But I have the Pool of Sorrows behind me and all the free healing I can ask for. Still, maybe I should wait.

I check the mechanical one with the grimy black lock.

Just a touch and it springs open.

A full-sized view of the chest's bottom fills my screen. Over the top of the chest, I see flashing golden text.

*Choose Now 10, 9, 8...*

The countdown is accompanied by a loud dull *gong* ringing out across ambient. In the bottom of the chest lies an ornate double-bladed axe and a slowly revolving holograph of one of the LuxIsland resorts.

I spend 7 through 2 of the countdown considering LuxIsland. These are the ultimate in actual real-time getaways. I could lose myself in every indulgence from an Undersea Hotel suite beneath the floating island to survival contests that dot the tropical paradise above. Fight a giant on a rope bridge and win a night with one of their repudiated world-class courtesans. Just the thing to forget Sancerré. Rope climb a dangerous cliff to get to the best restaurant this side of the Grand Concourse of Upper New York. Anything and everything I could earn for a week in paradise on earth. But at the end of that week, what? My stuff in boxes. Sancerré gone and my professional status most likely finished. At *1* I click the axe and am rewarded with the grinding sound of forged metal being sharpened on a spinning stone.

"The *Axe of Skaarwulfe* is yours, brave warrior!" reports the game. I heft the axe and check its rating, noting its severe edge and a silver skull worked into the haft.

Now for the chest with the pulsing runes.

I move forward, bracing myself for what will most likely be an explosion of computer-generated death. I position myself so that if the chest does actually explode, it'll blast me back toward, and hopefully into, the Pool of Sorrows.

I touch the lock and wait.

The lid slowly rises, filling my screen with a pink background light. Over ambient, the tribal drums stop, and only the crooning of the desert woman continues. Low, humming monastically, as if she's in a trance.

"Hang on," I mutter to the dark room and my Samurai.

As the pink misty light fades, I find that the chest contains an Escher-like maze of fractal open-ended paths. My mouse cursor literally becomes a mouse on the screen. I need to move it through the maze to unlock whatever is beneath this layer of security. I move the mouse across ribbons and paths, looking for the end to the maze. Some stairs lead down, then up, and occasionally I pass the little cartoon mouse through a door and the screen tumbles onto its side. There seems to be no solution to this maze. Again, the maze cants over onto its side and I find myself titling my head to keep up with the on-screen madness.

Then I realize that sliding the Escher-scape onto its side is the key. It isn't a maze so much as a tumbler in a lock. On the fourth perspective-shifting turn, a ding rings out loudly over ambient and now the maze itself, the stairs and platforms, all of it, begin to turn like some ancient lunatic grandfather clock. My bewildered little mouse wipes sweat from his brow as I race him forward into the tick-tock madness. A missed turn or a badly timed leap from a sliding stair will send him scrabbling into the machinery of the maze. Twice he narrowly avoids being squished by the coglike turning platforms and grinding gearlike stairs. I have no doubt that if that happens, whatever deadly surprise the chest is trapped with will present itself momentarily. Slowly, the plucky little mouse manages to avoid getting crushed or pinched, and again the maze turns. Again and again until on the fourth turn, the ringing *Ding* is followed by a loud *Baaawawawaoooooongggg*, signaling another "tumbler" has unlocked. Two tumblers down, how many to go? I scan the Escher-scape for some clue and find none. Time is passing and how long this game will go tonight I have no idea, but I need to get this chest open fast so I can get what's inside and get moving back to the tower. Wherever that is. I still have to complete the quest and get a return on my thousand. So far all I've managed is this lousy axe. Oh yeah, and the six hundred e-bucks.

Now the maze begins to whirlpool as stairs and rooms come together, then part in concentric rings. I stare at the screen looking for a pattern, waiting. Obviously this has gone Mario on me and I'm going to need to make the mouse perform a series of jumps and hops to get to the center of the whirlpool.

A missed step or jump and what happens next? No doubt nothing good. And what if this is the trap? What if the tumblers never unlock? What if this chest is designed to keep me waiting and playing while the game moves on and the other contestants grow powerful enough to come looking for me and earn their kill bonus on my distracted hide?

What if . . . everything bad happens to me?

Forget about it. Play the game you're playing.

The spinning whirlpool of flipping staircases and platforms is beginning to pick up speed. *Now or never,* I think to myself and dodge the plucky little cartoon mouse into the maelstrom. Hop, jump, skip, roll a few times, and the little mouse almost tumbles, or skids, into the rendered oblivion below. Again the view tumbles to the side, and now the platforms and surfaces begin to secrete an oily sheen and instantly my mouse is sliding toward a rotating edge.

Back in my room, my eyes and skull ache with fatigue. The concentration required is beginning to take its toll. I bend forward, craning my neck close to the screen, willing every ounce of focus onto the mouse as I slip and slide toward the center of the whirlpool. Now there is no stopping, no resting, no waiting; the little guy has to make it, and as he nears the center of the whirlpool for one last jump, the badly timed leap has him grasping a ledge that is rapidly spinning him toward a vertical descent. Viscous, clear sludge, oily and bright, races down, dripping onto the head of my gasping mouse. The muscles in my neck feel like taut iron cables coated in rust. I can feel their connection to my eyeballs screaming blue murder.

Then a descending ledge below my mouse cantilevers itself into position and swings upward. I drop and bounce off this rising ledge and rocket skyward. The mouse lands on a narrow beam that seesaws upward and away from him. I race him up the rapidly rising slope and, with a final strained leap, make it into the whirlpool at the center. At last, *click;* it's the final tumbler. After a *ding* and a *Baaaawawawawaoooong,* the screen mists over and the depths of the chest are revealed.

*Complimentary dinner at Seinfeld's* floats in cold blue letters across the screen.

Then a crunchy bite from an apple can be heard over ambient, as a hollow bass voice like a gong proclaims, "Warrior needs food, badly!" Then more words appear. *To redeem this complimentary meal, present self at eatery after nine thirty and simply say "Gauntlet" to Tony.*

All that for some lousy meal.

I'd never even heard of the place.

Generally I preferred places like Chilibee's or California Pizza Fixin's. Anything high-class is usually beyond me. Sancerré liked the cool spots and hip eateries. Me, meat on the street is good enough. The only problem is that most vendors have mortgaged everything they have to get up onto the Grand Concourse, and with the latest batch of winter storms, the few that remain find it a little too much to brave the icy New York streets to sell hot dogs or somesuch. But a free meal is a free meal. Or maybe I could trade it out.

Closing the chest with my Samurai's hand, I survey my in-game surroundings. The light from outside the tent has faded to a dusky blue. I search the tent once more before going outside and find something I'd missed, a large, freestanding mirror hidden underneath a sheet. I pull back the sheet and confront myself.

Or at least the self of my Samurai.

He's of medium height, more Anglo that Asian, though his burning coal-black eyes seem to hold some trace of the East in them. Behind him, I can see the flapping tent as the first night winds begin to blow across the desert sands. Palm fronds rustle above me on ambient sound, and once again, I have to admit to myself, the level of detail in this game is amazing.

Unnerving at times.

Smoke begins to cloud the mirror. It swirls softly beneath the silvery surface then resolves into the sanguine face of an old man, kind eyes sparkling, whiskery and a gap-toothed smile. He's bald other than small bristles of white hair on the sides of his close-shaven head.

"I'm Callard the Wise; come and hear my wisdom." He speaks in a genial, almost wry manner.

I open a voice link. "Who are you?" I ask.

"I am Callard, sage, imminent philosopher, and wandering nonplayer character. I must tell you, Wu the Samurai, that even now, dark forces are pursuing you, thirsting for your untimely demise."

"I've barely played this game," I almost shout back through the screen. "The one player I've met, I can only hope is dead. Otherwise I'm in big trouble. Anybody who can survive a fall like that . . ."

"Alas, ChemicalFairy, the player you threw into the abyss, did perish. He expired after losing a contest of 'Is This Poison?' inside the Gorgon's Jest within the very same Oubliette of Torment you fell into. But that is no longer important, wandering and enigmatic Samurai. I must warn you that Plague, a special buy-in character, has recently purchased a place in the game with the sole and consuming purpose of eliminating you."

"What . . ." I'm beginning to wonder when I might get a break. "Who or what is Plague and how did they buy in, and why do they want to kill me?"

"Ah, the tale of Plague is one that goes back many centuries, wandering Samurai. To begin . . ."

"Hold up a sec, Callard! I want to know why someone bought in just for the pleasure of eliminating me, an unknown player. Or is it some kind of special buy-in for bounty hunter players and I've been randomly assigned?"

"No, Samurai. This participant requested you personally and even now is riding toward your location. The client paid a high price, unusual but not unheard of in Black games, for the privilege of tracking you down and killing you."

The mirror swirls with smoke and now the dim image of a horseback rider is seen descending between two dunes. The black horse lathers and froths, its eyes rolling and wild, as it makes its way up the near dune filling the mirror. The dark horse and cloaked rider stop. A bloated and swollen moon, corpulently leering, its detail rendered by in-game graphics, hangs over the rider's shoulder. The rider carries no visible weapons, and his face is covered in tattered dirty gray rags. He wears a dusty, weathered, wide-brimmed hat.

"Don't I have a right to complain? I mean, come on, Callard, this isn't fair. I bought in and I've had nothing but trouble since this game started."

The mirror clears as Plague fades from view, returning to the smiling face of the wizened Callard.

"Oh, simple Samurai. I would caution you that there are forces beyond your comprehension at work here. I might suggest that you get moving and get back to the tower."

"Still, this isn't fair. I mean, this is like the worst Black game I've ever played. I'm getting nothing but the short end of the stick."

"You could fill out a complaint form," says Callard dryly. "But we don't really have a complaint department as this is a highly illegal enterprise and we don't really feel anyone will do much complaining to the authorities. But if it's any consolation, I'm helping you. I warned you about Plague and the skeletons, didn't I?"

"Skeletons?!"

"Oh my . . . I forgot about the skeletons."

The flap in the tent parts and in shambles a wobbly skeleton holding a scimitar and bronze shield. The shiny surface of the bronze shield reflects the flickering torchlight within the tent. I equip my axe and swing, missing the skeleton by a yard as the clever thing nimbly hops backward and rattles its grinning teeth at me. Apparently the AI is set to "pretty good."

The skeleton takes a cautious swipe at my exposed position and rewards me with a slice that costs me 15 percent health.

"Oh, at least I didn't forget to tell you about this," says Callard the Sage from the mirror. "There's an underground passage beneath the Pool of Sorrows. If you can get it open before Plague arrives, you may be able to get back to the tower rather swiftly."

I raise the axe and swing again, cutting down from above my head, directly onto the skeleton's chalky skull, or at least that's my intention. Instead, the skeleton raises its battered bronze shield and deflects the blow, even though its force brings him down on one bony knee. He cuts wickedly with his jagged scimitar at my legs, but a light touch on the keyboard gives me a nice little hop, timed to miss the blade.

"I'm telling you now, wayward Samurai. Open the gate to the Halls of the Damned and you'll get back to the tower. Once there, we may meet again. Also, I may try to contact you in real life."

"Wait? Aren't you an NPC?!"

I capitalize on the skeleton being low and missing with his attack. I crash the axe downward onto the kneeling skeleton. The shield collapses like cheap aluminum. It does little to deflect the axe's true course, which ends in a fine powdery spray of the skeleton's disintegrating skull.

"No time, Samurai, all will be explained. Hurry to the gate and get gone before your mortal enemy, Plague, arrives."

# Chapter 15

In the moonlight, clickety-clack skeletons, with scimitars and spears, always shields, close in a circle about the oasis. If they weren't out to kill my Samurai, the whole scene might be strangely beautiful. The moonlit dunes, the bone-white skeletons hobbling down them and across the sands and into the night-made indigo of the Pool of Sorrows, water softly rippling in the moonlight. I grab one of the torches from outside the tent and wade the Samurai into the pool, looking for the gate Callard mentioned. The gate to the Halls of the Damned; it would lead back to the tower, the Marrow Spike.

Painted figures, typical tomb burial scenes I've seen in other games, decorate the submerged green-and-gold paving stones. I move to the center of the pool as the first of the skeletons reaches the water's edge. I look down into the clear water, searching for some sign or clue as to how to unlock the hidden gate. An approaching skeleton makes little noise as its slender shinbones barely disturb the waters of the pool.

Instead, its chattering teeth and mumbling bony rattle tell me of its approach.

All I can see beneath the water are depictions of tiny inky figures harvesting, planting, living, and dying. Their painted skin is ochre and their hair black. They all wear white linen kilts except for one.

That's my first clue.

I try to fix the spot in my mind where I've seen the one figure different from the others, but the skeleton is on me, chattering and slicing through the air, making windy passes with its rusty weapon. I retaliate in full force with a sideways swipe of the axe and hear the satisfying crunch of a skelie's rib cage. The blow from the silver-skulled axe sends the skeleton soaring off onto the sandy banks outside the pool as though an unusual amount of force has acted in coercion with my swing. Either that or the Samurai has an extremely high strength rating.

I've shifted position with the force of my attack and now I scramble to recover the lost pictoglyph, the one different from all the rest. The ripples of my frantic wake are obscuring the shifting pictoglyphs beneath my Samurai's feet.

Two more skeletons enter the Pool of Sorrows.

At last I find the figure I'm looking for. The difference is only marginally noticeable from the hundreds of others. It's a figure wearing a gold tiara, a woman rather than a man, a queen rather than a peasant or a priest. Her eyes are thin slits, like a serpent's.

A skeleton jabs my backside with his spear, reducing my health by 10 percent. The water of the Pool of Sorrows is restoring some of my lost health points but not as quickly as I'd like. Another skeleton circles behind me, making small back-and-forth movements with a rusty bronze scimitar.

I study the Queen figure, as I choose to call the tiara-wearing serpent-eyed woman. She points toward a different portion of the pool. The circling scimitar skelie blocks me from getting there.

Now, spear skelie jabs again and I sidestep and chop down quickly at the haft of its spear. The blow drives the spear down onto the sandstone pavement below the water, disintegrating the Queen figure and a large surrounding portion of the submerged mural.

Now I either know where the Queen was pointing, or I don't.

I execute a spinning attack, using the axe's relativistic force in combination with my backward spin, and land a blow directly onto the spear skelie's shield. The blow splinters the shield and smashes the skeleton in two.

Now, scimitar skelie is on me, chopping from above, ravaging my dwindling health bar.

Just when I'd gotten it back up again. Oh well.

If it worked once, it'll work again. I execute another spinning attack and send that skeleton off into the far end of the pool with a splash.

I race to where I hope the Queen was pointing and scan the pictoglyph-covered flagstones beneath the shifting water as I move in circles. Behind me, the skeleton I'd cut in two drag-crawls its way toward me through the water, muttering revenge and death through chattery teeth. He's using his broken spear for leverage.

Now the paving stones tell a different story. One of judgment and suffering as the Queen, now attired in a reaper's cloak, hews her way through an army of cowering peasants. Below them opens a yawning dark chasm as the peasants and sometimes just their body parts disappear into a black sun that is an abyss.

The skeletons, all of them now, have reached the pool. Nearby thundering hooves, drumlike and hollow on the desert sands, tell me of Plague's approach.

The pool is as good as any place to fight. Its healing effects might mitigate some of the damage received, and the axe seems to be a formidable weapon. But this Plague player, whoever it is, that's the unknown variable.

A leaping black Arabian crashes into the pool. Plague, coal-dust-gray cloak and rags, draws an antiquated blunderbuss and fires at me. At my Samurai. The weapon's more hand cannon than pistol. A spray of water from its near miss erupts in a plume at my feet. Then Plague on horseback tries to run me down. I dodge and issue a quick swipe at the nightmare's flank, barely missing. Around me the motley collection of skelies are closing in—grinning, rattling, and chattering. Weapons ready.

I hear a slight sucking noise over ambient.

Beneath my feet, where Plague's smoking blunderbuss ball barely missed me, a small whirlpool has formed, sucking the water of the Pool of Sorrows into its event horizon.

To where?

At the far end of the pool, the black rider, Plague, coughs and mutters to himself as he reloads the blunderbuss. The skelies close. There is no time and no choice other than the one I make. I raise the axe high over my head, mark the spot where the whirlpool drains beneath my feet, and slam the *Axe of Skaarwulfe* down onto the paved stones where all the little pictoglyph people had gone to hell.

The crash is deafening, and everything on ambient gives way.

Plague's coughing, the rattling bones of the skelies, the tribal drums, the flute, and the keening moan of the desert woman.

I fall into darkness.

Again.

I fall, bumping and sliding along the edges of a widening pit. A spiral stairway just beyond the reach of my Samurai's fingertips winds its way upward and down into the darkness as I fall past it.

I open a menu under *Actions* and scroll quickly for something I'd seen before.

*Free Climb.*

It was disabled when I'd first seen it, but that was back when the Samurai had only one hand. Now it's active. I click it and the Samurai's fingers splay outward, the axe either returning to inventory or dropping off into the darkness. Sooner than I expect, the Samurai's fingers find purchase, and a quick assault of rapid damage shotguns my health bar. But the Samurai's fall stops. In the dark of the pit, the Samurai hangs precariously from the jutting lip of a carved and leering demon, similar, vaguely, to the one I'd seen on my last fall from the ledge where I'd fought Creepy.

I look up. The hole above me is raining paving tiles and water from the pool. A lone skeleton tumbles past me, falling off into the blackness below. I see Plague's dark outline against the moonlit night above. He stands among the burnt matchstick silhouettes of the skeletons and the night and the moon.

Part of the stone staircase spirals down through the demon's head, out one eye, in through the other and out the mouth just below my handhold. My movement keys bring the Samurai liquidly up onto the rotting stone staircase that spirals through the demon's head. Again, I check above and see Plague, torch in hand, being followed by a collection of ancient bony warriors, descending the staircase, which must have begun right below where I'd stood in the Pool of Sorrows.

I could fight them on the stairs one at a time, maybe two, but they'd have the advantage of numbers and attacking from above. Not the best position to defend.

I start down the staircase, into the unknown.

The stairs weave down into the pit, dancing sharply inward then darting out crazily over dizzying drops into misty nothingness. There are flickering shadows at every turn as lonely drips and mournful disembodied moans resound over ambient. The torchlight of my pursuers makes me nervous. At times I see it high above, winding down along the precarious rocky stairway. At others, not at all. I experience a sense of vertigo as I move downward quicker than I probably should, occasionally striking out at shadows I suspect of being something more.

At last I reach the bottom. Above me, I hear the thump of Plague's hobnailed boots and an occasional wet gurgling cough coming down the well after me. Behind those sounds, I hear the clickety-clack of the skelies, their bony feet scurrying down the stony staircase. In front of me a wide hall stretches off into misty nether. A sickly green iridescence washes the darkness all about me. I can see the outlines of canted tombstones and crosses standing out against the gloom, leading off into nothing. The ambient soundtrack begins with an abrupt twang from an electrified bass guitar. It's disturbing and lonely. Then it's joined by runs of descending minor scales from a Hammond B3 organ.

This hall does not bode well for my Samurai if the ambient soundtrack is any indicator.

I move forward, equipping the axe from inventory. I move cautiously, one step at a time. There's danger here, a trap of some sort, but from where and how, I don't know. In the back of my head a voice screams for me to move faster and get as far away as I can from Plague and the skelies, but now, with my spider sense on overdrive, I have to find the trap first. Otherwise . . .

It comes quickly, maybe thirty feet down the hall with no end in sight. From the walls and the floor, hands, necrosis dark, oozing green, patches of white bone underneath, erupt like an explosion.

Everywhere bony hands are reaching for me.

The simulated undead crawl from beneath the programmer's vision of a rocky and forgotten tomb tunnel. I run forward fast, moving quickly, hoping the end of the passage lies somewhere shortly ahead. A zombie, gap toothed and grinning through green patches of ragged flesh, rises up, shambling and abrupt. I crush its head with one terrific blow of the axe. Already two more shamble after me, moaning like burning paper scraps consumed in a fire. I step back, raise the axe, then smash it down on the first, almost cutting it in two. The other swipes at me for a paltry amount of damage. He gets it next with a twirling blow from my axe. Beyond these, the hall stretches out over ground that's becomes like a sea of waving grass. Except it's not waving grass. There's no breeze down here.

Fields of the rising hands of the undead. Crawling out of the earth. Not waving. Clutching.

The *Axe of Skaarwulfe* glows a soft, bloody red, casting a thin light like a cone of hell in a gray shadowy nightmare. Behind me zombies shamble forward. Ahead, they wait, moving slightly, as if sensing my approach.

I have no other choice.

I go forward swinging, slashing, hacking my way through the Halls of the Damned.

By dawn, the wan New York winter light begins to suggest itself into the room Sancerré and I once shared, as the game announces shutdown. I receive an e-mail on my Petey telling me when the game will resume next. But even as the unseen game masters tidy up the business of a black-market game, I am still crunching my way through zombies. For close to five hours, the sounds of brittle broken bones and wet gurgling slaps have resounded across my room as the *Axe of Skaarwulfe* weaves destruction in wide, sickening arcs across and along the Halls of the Damned. For the past hour I'd seen a massive foundation rising off in the distance of the cavernous hall. Maybe the tower, I hoped.

By no means have I killed all the zombies. There are too many of them. Fifty-seven thousand, maybe more, maybe less. I've lost count. It's unreal. It's insane. It's the dream of a madman with a penchant for masochism and a degree in game design. In-game, behind me, off in the distance, I hear Plague's unholy band pursuing me. But they too have to fight the zombies. The blunderbuss resounds in deafening cannonades that echo off the walls of the murky chamber. Sprays of lead shot find purchase in thick, wet, pulpy decomposing flesh that sounds all too real over ambient.

I ignore it and continue to cut a path of destruction toward the foundation of the tower. Soon, within the last moments of the game, I reach a rising platform of rickety wooden stairs and a giant iron door leading into the foundation of the massive stone edifice.

Then the game thanks me for not dying and hopes that I will next time. The screen goes dark, leaving only a jack-in-the-box laughing in sickly long loops on my monitor. I turn my computer off, stand, and immediately feel slightly sick. My spine and skull ache. Blood courses into areas it seems unfamiliar with. My right index finger refuses to bend. Too many, far too many, clicks of the mouse.

I stumble for the couch and crash down into it, telling myself I need pancakes and milk and bacon and light, or life? I'm deciding which when I realize I'm sleeping, or dead.

I couldn't have gotten up even if I'd tried.

In my dreams, I've never left the Halls of the Damned. Sancerré is there and so is Iain. Both keep telling me it's great to be there and that sooner rather than later I'll understand why. I keep trying to use my axe to slay milling zombies that are some-how a threat to Sancerré, but I can't lift it from the ground. So I drag it behind me through crowds of lingering zombies holding martini glasses. Except all the zombies are really actors, extras, waiting for the director to call "action" and then, I'm convinced, they're really going to get me. In the dream I'm sure of it. Even Kiwi is a zombie. He says, "Cheers, mate," and then the beer he's just drunk drains out through his ragged throat. The bony man, Faustus Mercator, is there too. He's grinning, talking to zombies, nodding at me through cigarette smoke and real live jazz somewhere far off.

# Chapter 16

It's not really sleep. Not with battlefield dreams of automatic weapons and other nightmares that clutch and grasp from inside gray-green shadows. Then it's white morning light and too many cigarettes as I lie, almost catatonic, on the sofa. Sancerré's sofa. A sofa someone will probably soon come and take away.

What will be left of us then?

Out on the streets it'll be cold. Winter hasn't even fully invested the city yet. Up on the Grand Concourse, on the protected walkways, they're just taking down the last of the New Year's Eve decorations around New Times Square. But it costs money to get up there, and down here the streets of the world's once most populous city remain quiet, locked beneath a deep blanket of snow.

I check my Petey and there's no message from Sancerré.

I've got six hundred e-bucks sitting in an account and a free dinner at someplace called Seinfeld's. But getting off the couch is more than I can handle. I want scotch, some food. I need to transfer that six hundred into my account before the next automatic and final rent demand hits in three days.

Meanwhile, the fridge holds nothing besides the cheese that passes for even the vaguest notion of sustenance, and the bottle of scotch is way over there, across the room.

I doze, and when I wake to the pulse of my Petey, I notice a lit cigarette still dangling from my lips. How did I start smoking again?

It's an anonymous text. Probably some spammer has managed to penetrate my feeble FreeWare defenses.

*Tonight Only. Elite Membership. The Chasseur's Inn.*

"Really, tonight only!" I exclaim sarcastically. I hate spam. I'm supposed to believe that tonight only, I'll be allowed into only the most coveted of nightspots, the Elite Lounge, where celebrities go to disappear, a place about which little is known other than the obligatory "what is not known" teaser. My hatred of spam almost drives me into a fury that would have surely sent me across the room for scotch. And ice, if I was truly committed. Instead I manage to flop one leg down onto the floor where it refuses further service.

Game hangover is real. I don't need to see the public service ads to know about it. I'm living it.

My Petey double pulses. Must be important. It's a message that, whoever sent it, manages to answer all my social avatar's questions and ensure the necessity of an Emphatic Message.

*Be there tonight, PerfectQuestion* reads the message.

Underneath, in a font best reserved for fifteenth-century cartographers, *Faustus Mercator. Your new pal.*

I'm up, and my head throbs from the sudden change in altitude. I grab the scotch bottle and carry it to the fridge where I find one ice cube. Outside, the city is smothered in ice. Inside my fridge, not so much. I pour two fingers, think better of it and use the whole fist. It's hot, and it vanquishes game hangover in a round.

Things are getting weirder and weirder.

I bring up my music app and crank out some "White Rabbit." I'm going deep old school, way back to the days of the early minutes of Second Grunge. The Cobains let go and drag the melody down to the basement. I think about Faustus Mercator and wonder, not if he is dangerous, but how dangerous he is. Probably very. Very dangerous. Muy dangeroso. The guy radiates creepy menace in a way JollyBoy aspires to.

Under the influence of my morning scotch, a line by Warren Cosmo, lead singer of the Cobains, keeps running through my mind: "He be dangerous so I holla, 'cause it's not just another hookah-smoking caterpil-lah." I'm Alice. So the caterpillar could be . . . I don't know what. WonderSoft collectively . . . or Enigmatrix. And the bony man, Faustus Mercator, he's definitely the Cheshire cat. The seventeen-minute musical interlude complete with ancient Hammond B3 organ à la the Doors sets in, and I wonder if I'm Alice, or is Sancerré? And what is RiotGuurl?

RiotGuurl. Her life's complicated? Mine's a SoftChip diagram with a Marto-Chinese instruction manual. First off, I'm about to get kicked out of our . . . my apartment, and my only hope to save myself from indigence is to finish, and not just finish but beat, an illegal online game that may or may not resume, not just anytime soon, but ever. Second, my girlfriend has definitely gone off the radar and for all intents and purposes is sleeping with someone else. Add bonus points for the fact that she refuses to go gently, in my mind, into that good night of lost loves. My real job, the one where ColaCorp is being handed its lunch every round, is just a few battles away from no longer being an actual job. Finally, there's this creepy guy, Faustus Mercator, and he wants me to present said pass to the fully enhanced gorilla hormone-juiced goon squad that call themselves doormen at the most exclusive club in Upper New York City, the Chasseur's Inn, and waltz right in for . . . what?

"What" is the question, PerfectQuestion.

Add that said doormen slash gorilla goons have been known to deliver a courtesy beating for mere brazen attempts to inquire about entry membership into aforementioned exclusive club. And on top of that, a gentle hint to a coworker for possible "more" . . . has been rebuffed. I mean, let's call it as it lies. I've been rebuffed. Nothing new there, and yet . . . the sting. No, sting's not the right word. The . . . matter . . . the matter . . . I need more scotch . . . the matter (ahhhh) remains unresolved.

I drift under the embrace of warm smoky scotch and imagine the possibilities of RiotGuurl. Things are afoot. Strange doings. And soon my drifting turns to sleep. Peaceful, necessary, perfectly undisturbed sleep with bonus heavy snoring and some drool.

There are no dreams of war unrequited, or even love unrequited for that matter. When I wake a few hours later, I'm not hungover, and outside my window gentle sleet is falling thickly across Gotham.

I wonder if it will ever stop. I wonder if it's been snowing my entire life and any change, any sun remembered, is just a dream, a fantasy I once had. I dress and hit the silent streets. Above, or so the view from my doorstep tells me, the city lights up there are coming on, pulsing beneath the clouds that separate old New York from Upper New York above. I'm headed there, and my one serviceable gray suit and white button-down had better cut the mustard for both Seinfeld's and the Chasseur's Inn. I've done what I can to my hair and gone with restrained messy. I need a shave, and the razor I don't find reminds me that Sancerré had been leaving long before she ever left. I wonder how long. Which moments were real? Which were mine to remember?

The SkyBus at 30 Rock is the best place to go up for me. As long as possible, I want to stay off the grid, and the farther I have to walk to get to a station, the less anyone who might be watching knows about where I actually live.

30 Rock smells of urine and burnt-out energy-efficient light tubes. I avoid a collection of bums singing in the lobby around a portable barbecue the Port Authority guards won't leave the safety-glass secure elevator transit zone to put out. I pay the forty bucks to get up to the Grand Concourse. I guess I'm dressed okay, not well, but well enough, because the security guy is more interested in wrinkling his nose at the bums than grading my ability to stay up on the concourse. I receive my pass and head to the boarding staircase for the next SkyBus headed uptown. Literally.

I have until six a.m. tomorrow up there. Then my pass expires. Then I'm an illegal.

The bus is clean and nice, with subdued lighting, chrome fixtures, and massive soft recliners emblazoned with the Upper New York logo. Within a minute, under the pressure of acceleration, the brand-new shuttle bus climbs upward along the rail that leads to Upper New York. We're almost vertical as my seat gently adjusts itself so that I'm sitting upright as we climb straight into the sky.

I already feel the difference the concourse brings out in a person. It's as if you're leaving whatever you were below, behind you. You're someone else now, and the acceleration is freeing you from that other guy who slips off your back and into the vents at the rear of the bus and down into the icy gutters of New York.

It's only a seven-minute trip, but the bus dispenses a limited amount of cocktails. I settle on a another scotch, no mixer, and by the time I use my Petey and get a scan for the bill, the drink comes and I've got four minutes to finish it.

Then again, do I need to finish it now? I could take it with me. Drinking on the Grand Concourse in the middle of a snow-swept night, headed for a great meal, then the most exclusive club above town, would be . . . something to remember.

The drink makes it with me past security, and I step out onto the wide curving concourse. Snow cascades horizontally through the blue light thrown up from the floors of the immense walkway. It should be icy cold high up, but the environmental systems here are state of the art, and any cold is kept at bay by silent superconductors, exchanging cold air for stable energy, in turn heating the terraces, supplying power, and holding the Grand Concourse to its four arched anchors over old New York. After all the hurricanes and floods of the past, this was once considered the greatest engineering project of all time, an entire city built in the clouds.

Until the SkyVault.

Miles above, in low earth orbit, another city, this one built in space, rides shotgun over the planet Earth, exchanging goods with intersystem freighters returning from Mars. There are echelons of reality, and then there are echelons beyond reality. And then there is the SkyVault. Tonight, as I make my way to the edge of the Grand Concourse, which winds itself like a broad flat river through the serpentine mesh of upraised spider legs and wraith fingers that are the high towers of Upper New York, tonight the Grand Concourse is enough for me. The Grand Concourse is a ceiling for old New York that I've stared at for a long time, but really, it's just one of the global anchors for the Sky-Vault. It's a floor I've only been to once before. I've remembered that day ever since as one of the best of my life. It was unreal, and my mind kept rejecting the memory and the dream of the boy I once was the last time I was here, the one time when my family spent an entire day here in Upper New York. Or at least my mind wanted to reject it. I guess deep down I didn't. Instead I dreamed about it. I used to draw pictures of it as a kid every day after our first visit. A fantastic city made of arches, hovering over the remains of old New York. Finally, seventeen years later I've returned. Seventeen years after my family attended a one-day company picnic up here, I'm back. I'd always imagined I'd get back up here a lot sooner than I did.

I remember everything about that day.

I remember later, as a teenager, forcing myself to forget how amazing everything had been to a nine-year-old boy. It was too hard to live with in the town we were from, and to know that all this, the bright fingers that clutched at the sky floating above, was here and that this was every day for some people, while for others it was just a moment. A day at PlanetDisney. A day to be held for just a moment in your hand, and then forever in your mind.

Trying to forget that day was my way of rebelling.

Once I became a teenager, I chose to forget everything about that day as much as possible.

I sip scotch and my mind reels, rejecting everything rising above me now, on this night, twinkling like jewels set in impossible strands of luminescent pearls. I try to look down, over the edge of the concourse, but the city where I live is mostly dark. Only a layer of floating mist and clouds cover my city, down there.

The sights above that surround me, the sloping concourse, the rising levels, the myriad of lights that thrum and pulse behind a thousand windows beckon me with taunts and temptations of a life I've never known but always wanted to. Everything is up, up, and away, and if there is anything worth having, it is indeed up here. Of below, nothing remains worth remembering.

I drain the last of my plastic tumbler, rattling cubes of scotch water.

If I'd wondered where Sancerré went, now being in the greatest city in the world, I knew. Her trail led here. Looking back, thinking about her large brown eyes and bookish beauty and ambition to see the entire world, I'd known it all along. The problem was I'd blinded myself, like that rebellious teenager so long ago who tried to forget the best day ever.

\* \* \*

Over thick slices of steaming corned beef piled atop the soft rye bread that I chew, I realize I haven't had a decent meal in . . . ever. My meal at Seinfeld's is turning out to be truly epic. I wash it all down with an "I drink your Milkshake. I drink it down!" milkshake full of dark chocolate and peanut butter ice cream. But the real rock star of the whole meal is a side of rich Maytag Blue Cheese—covered fries. I've managed to eat three pickle trays while waiting for my meal and I know, at some point, I'll regret the whole attack on the Seinfeld's menu. But how many times am I going to eat on the Grand Concourse gratis?

At one point, as I pick up a crispy hot french fry dripping with Maytag Blue Cheese dressing, a highbrow waiter, heretofore unseen, appears bearing a silver plate. On it is a card with a single digit number.

The number 9.

"Would 'sir,'"—he says "sir" loosely—"care for anything else?" The emphasis on "else" implies that while my credit is unlimited for tonight, the love certainly isn't.

"Yes." In fact I would care for something else. "I'll have the Kramer's Mackinaw Peach Cheesecake. Two slices. Oh, and a café latte port to wash it down. Please." My emphasis is on the "wash it down" as I reference their most expensive after-dinner drink, which consists of a fifty-year port, steamed organic Kobe milk, and what little of the Jamaican Blue Mountain coffee that's still manufactured on what's left of above-water Jamaica.

I can be obnoxious also, when pressed.

The waiter executes a perfect about-face.

"Hey, Chauncey."

"Sir?" Again with the loosely.

"What do I do with this?" I ask, picking up the stiff card with the number 9 printed on it.

A moment's hesitation as Chauncey considers what he'd like to actually tell me to do with it. He doesn't though. I've noticed service on the Grand Concourse is excellent. The people who work here are grateful for the jobs they have. Joblessness is an excellent reminder that colony ships are populated with those who can't pay their taxes and will spend the next two hundred in slow freight sleepers heading for the "promise" of Alpha Centauri.

"Sir should dial the number on the phone behind you, sir." Again, loosely with the "sir."

"Thanks." Then I'm alone with the card. Thick cardstock. Actual paper, not Buckycards like every wannabe mem-broker deals out like cheap Thai candy.

The meal has refreshed my brain, invigorated my constitution, and given me a new unwarranted self-confidence. A confidence that's lately been shattered by all the beatings in Eastern Highlands, massacred by the sickness of the Black, and shot in the skull, right between the eyes I might add, by Sancerré.

I dismiss her and everything else plaguing me.

Sometimes your outlook, what you choose to let get to you, can be simply turned off. Studies have been done by people who do studies indicating that gamers have an incredible ability to turn off outside influences like bad days, debts, and wayward girlfriends and lose themselves in a task; that is, killing ogres, machine-gunning Third Reich zombies, solving puzzles. The problem is, the problems are still there, waiting for you, when the game's done. Then they come back with a vengeance, especially after an extended game binge. When you're tired, at your weakest, after you've taken a solid beating online.

But tonight, with a pile of corned beef in my belly and the sugar from the "I drink your Milkshake. I drink it down!" milkshake dancing across my cerebellum, I make the choice to turn all of it off. Maybe I'm not me anymore. Maybe I'm not some guy who has everything to lose anymore.

Maybe I've got nothing to lose.

I mean, yeah, it can get worse, but thinking about it constantly isn't going to help me. Instead, I need to see where things are going. Step out on a dead of winter night. Go places. Maybe some strange doings might tap a cash river into my parched accounts. Sancerré is gone. I'll just keep telling myself that.

I dial the number. Number 9.

It rings.

"Wu, I presume," says the voice on the other end of the line.

"You got me." I look around, trying to see who might be calling me from another booth. Maybe another diner seated in one of the other red leather banquettes.

"No, my friend. You have me. It is I who would like to be in your debt. I've enjoyed your progress thus far and I'm interested in making it a little more interesting for you, and for me."

"And you are?"

"Ah, Mr. Wu. My name is not important. Just as your real name isn't important. I've paid a great deal of money to ensure that you received my invite to tonight's dinner. Naturally, with anyone engaging in a Black game for profit, anonymity is priceless, or at least high priced. A game rife with torture and graphic content, unashamedly illegal open source software well below the regulation standards of our fine governments, the best I could hope for was to communicate with you under the guise of your character. So, Mr. Wu, it is in all our best interests to keep everything, most things rather, nonspecific."

"I agree." I suck the last of my "I drink your Milkshake. I drink it down!" milkshake's thick peanut-buttery milk shake goodness.

"So let us decide." His voice reminds me of a lawyer or a banker, a successful one. "Right here and right now, to remain merely Mr. Wu and Myself. No names. We won't be conversing further. This is a onetime offer with rewards that you'll just have to imagine. In the event you accomplish a certain task for me over the course of the game, there will be one more call. From here, whenever you wish. I won't respond. I won't even say anything. You'll just dial the number 9 and name your reward."

"You mean I can always come here and dial 9 and I'll get you?" I ask.

A pause.

"It's better to say that only I possess the number 9. For you it's a onetime call," says the voice on the other end.

"Why?"

"Like I said, so that you can name your reward. Whatever it is that you want."

That stops me in my tracks. It's not every day someone offers you whatever you want. In fact, are there ever any days like that?

"Yes, Mr. Wu," he says softly. "Whatever . . . you . . . want. Are we clear on that matter?"

In so many ways, yes. In one way, no. I can think of a lot that I want. I can't think of why anyone would make that happen for any service I'd consider actually doing.

"So . . . I just come back any time, dial 9, name my wish . . . sort of a genie in a Jewish delicatessen circa 1990."

"Effectively, yes. But first you will need to do that little favor for me on your way to the top of the tower." I catch myself checking out the other patrons, a glitzy cross section of mem brokers and ultramodels. Mentioning the Black makes gamers nervous. This guy knows the plot, knows about the tower. He's either another player looking for an alliance or, worse, a pervert looking for a little private entertainment.

"Listen, it's just a game. I'm just a player. That's all. I play it because there's money in it, not because I like this sick fantasy you creeps find so fascinating . . ."

"I find the Black detestable, Mr. Wu." He pauses. I feel him composing himself on the other end of the line. "But in my state of being, knowledge of it is necessary. I purchased your meal tonight and planted the reward with the purveyors of the game.

Besting the Troll and the trapped chest at the Pool of Sorrows was no small feat. Not every player could have accomplished that with such simple finesse. Many, in fact, could not have. I am in need of a thinker, not a 'run and gunner' as many gamers like to think of themselves. So you are not 'just a player.' You may in fact be the kind of player that I need. I need a thinker to perform a task for me, in-game. If you perform this task, successfully, then come back here to the restaurant, have another complimentary meal and then dial the number 9. I will not say anything. All you have to do then is name your wish. In the event you don't perform your task, you might not have the credit report to get back into Seinfeld's, so you dialing 9 will be a moot point at that point."

I sigh.

"What's the job?"

"Kill Morgax." There's a pause. "In-game, of course." Then the line goes dead and I'm left holding muffled ether. I have my orders. My two slices of Kramer's Mackinaw Peach Cheesecake arrive.

# Chapter 17

I survive the bouncers.

They don't kill me, beat me, or kick my teeth in. Don't get me wrong, it's still a frightening experience. Human beings just shy of full gorilla strength, hypertrained in the latest hand-to-hand combat techniques with more ways to maim, wound, and kill than the programmers of online worlds can imagine, are frightening. Especially when they're standing right in front of you. But I pass. I'm on the list. I wonder if Sancerré will be here.

I'm sick that way.

There've been a lot of coincidences lately, I wouldn't be surprised.

In the main room I find a low hanging ceiling with polished oak beams, trench tables, and überboobed courtesans in stockings and lace serving the elite. It's someone's vision of a seventeenth-century gentlemen's club, but with models for serving wenches who drew the line at showing too much flesh just so they could step over it. I hear passing bits of dialogue that seem straight out of one of Sancerré's period piece entertainments: dukes and duchesses, that sort of thing, all of it delivered in Olde English and nonsensical cockney by epically hot women. I can't even imagine where to get a drink, but I know I need one. Regardless of the pass, I'm out of my element. A drink will do me wonders, or so I delude myself.

A slender, top-heavy brunette in pale lace approaches me, smiling hungrily through full lips and perfect teeth.

"Wouldst thou care for a foot rub, sire?" she lilts in a purr, emphasis on "rub."

I say something.

I think I ask her what her name is.

"Tatiana," she tells me. Tatiana. Is that her real name? . . . and do I care? I command my mind to think of something witty to say, but my brain refuses and screams for chemicals like booze and nicotine to hide behind.

"Perhaps sire feels the need for something . . . other?" she suggests, coquettish emphasis on "need."

"Scotch," I whisper though clenched teeth.

"Of course, sire." She snaps her fingers crisply, and with the voice of a bawd, cries, "Hastings, one scotch for the master."

Her hands rest atop shapely hips beneath a slender waist. Long legs end in perilous heels and dainty feet. These are the things I focus on to prevent myself from looking at her immense chest, long neck, perfect teeth, beautiful face. Et cetera, et cetera.

If I am uncomfortable, it shows.

She, on the other hand, is used to being admired, on display, desired.

Hastings, a liveried butler type, appears with scotch in a cut-crystal decanter and a matching glass atop a silver platter. Hastings pours and I grab for it as the tray wavers from my clumsy assault.

And the scotch is gone.

I'd planned to sip. Deftly, smoothly. Like some spy in a Soft-Play, but I guzzle like a man found recently crawling across the desert.

I feel a little more solid. Something witty will come. I'm almost sure of it.

I look into her eyes with every intention of playing it cool. Her long lashes flutter almost imperceptibly, and I wonder how they flutter in other moments, passionate ones, and before I know it, I'm gone. But there is Hastings nearby with the decanter. Every ounce of my will is required to tear myself from the temptress and raise one finger, indicating my desire for Hastings to fill my empty glass again.

"Excellent, sire," murmurs Hastings and turns away once his service is done.

"Come, sire, sit by the fire," she whimpers. "I'll sing you a song and caress your aching head." I'm pretty sure, at that point, I die. I know I smoke and drink a little too much, and lately, a lot too much, but I must have passed out, because whatever happened next is fuzzy. Images of her astride me in the public room, rubbing my temples and skull with long delicate fingers, surface through her perfume and other charms. She sings, no . . . she whispers me a song. A song from long ago.

"Anything you want, you got it, anything at all, baby."

After the corned beef, the scotch, the winter, nights of war and stress, the Black and . . . Sancerré . . . I'm not there anymore. I'm here. I'm fading into those fingers, that skin, her hair, and everything seems to wash down the drains of life and I'm left with nothing worth calling my own.

Everything fades.

From Sancerré's gentle laugh to the sound of the wind against our taped-up windows in the night. It's all gone now. We'll never lie in each other arms and listen to the moaning of the wind in the night.

For a moment I hear JollyBoy's laugh, far off within the ruckus of period courtesans and present revelers. His laugh seems too real and it almost jerks me out of my moment. Almost. For a moment I open my eyes. I see the spinning microcosm of the public room of the Chasseur's Inn. I look for what I know will be a laughing JollyBoy, his head jerking spasmodically to something only he finds funny. It's too real. But my eyes find nothing except the dark pools of Tatiana's and they drive me back under, making me question if I'd actually ever opened my eyes. If I'd actually ever been awake. Or if all of life was just this dream.

I'm gone.

"Anything you want, you got it."

Baby.


Maybe it's not sex. What's sex? Maybe it's all a metaphor for another thing. But this elevator screaming high above the atmosphere is too plush, too warm, too quiet for the outside cold that's frosting the glass.

Space.

Actual space.

In that dream, we leave Upper New York. Above is the Sky-Vault in orbit, tethered by the diamond strand of a space elevator cable, falling straight down upon us.

My muscles don't work. From my legs to my jaws, all refuse the commands my mind issues as Tatiana stands above me, the stars behind her, though they don't get any closer or grow larger, they just twinkle and wink. Above us, I can see the ships docking into something bright and shiny I've only heard about, read about, watched live feeds of. But there it is.

The SkyVault.

For a moment, a scramjet falls away, like it's dying. Dead. Then outside our windows, it's twisting and turning as it angles toward Tokyo, Sydney, the Bankgok Biomass. Engines ignite, and it's burning slow and bright at first like a torch. It's hard going to get up to cruise velocity. But for a brief moment, I take my eyes off the rocket's flame and glance at the gossamer lace that restrains Tatiana's body. It's growing even more unfettered as gravity begins to lighten its covetous embrace. We decelerate as we approach the dock at SkyVault. And when I look back at the scramjet, it's already burning hard and furious, diving through the atmosphere for its destination. A quick run to drop off the smart products made on Mars and then pick up more SoftLife gear for the burgeoning colonies, enticements for all to come up.

And again I fade.

And when I wake, here I am.

Light and airy. Twelve miles high, riding shotgun above New York City. It's just me, a white leather couch, Tatiana murmuring in my ear, and the opulence of the spinning suite in space, and . . . Bony Man.

I raise my hand as if to shield myself from something unclean. No, as a greeting. Again, my muscles barely work.

"There you are, my boy." His eyes shine brightly, almost luminously, within his clean-shaven bony head. He hobbles forward, assisted by a cane, with a limp I hadn't noticed before. He removes a toothpick from between large clenched teeth as he approaches. Hovering, he jabs me not too delicately in the arm with it.

From far away I feel a soft stab, and my mind, reacting more to the visual than the source, emits a long slow yelp that seems to escape my mouth even though I tried so desperately to keep it between clenched teeth.

"A little too much, I suspect." He leans close, inspecting me. I'm experiencing, if that's the right word, the not-too-clean aspects of his breath. "A little too much, Tatiana, but good work nonetheless. Maybe you should pop off, my little vixen. Too much and you'll kill us all."

I have no idea what they're talking about, but at the mention of death, I too am aware of how impossibly slow my heart rate is and how syrupy my mind has become.

Suddenly I know I should be afraid, even though I'm not. I should be, but I can't be.

For a year I watch Tatiana rise, every curve and fall, flanks dropping then rising as she leaves the room on long legs and high heels. There are some women who you watch walk out of your life and you feel nothing. And then there are some who make you feel like you've been branded with a hot iron. Tatiana was the latter, and I felt gratefully sick for the scar she'd left. Even though it hurt, still I was grateful.

Bony Man takes a seat not too far away, and for a while we watch the earth spin from view outside a clear wide window of dark and starlight. A few minutes later it reappears. After three turns, he says something. My mind is less slack than my jaw. I'm clear now. Or at least, clearer.

"Thus we arrive at the present state of affairs," says Bony Man. For a moment, I swear I'm almost thinking the same thing. He nods toward the earth.

"So much wonderful loot down there." He sighs happily. "My goal is to get all of it, PerfectQuestion. How about you? Do you love, I mean really love money?"

I love Sancerré, I think, but that's not right. I don't anymore. Whoever could, after having been touched by Tatiana? Still, I loved Sancerré. Once.

I wasn't sure what was "what," and "when" seemed more than confusing.

Why do I feel like that's a lie? Why am I thinking about Riot-Guurl and her "right now's not a good time" text?

And . . .

. . . why does that make me feel like an idiot for even trying?

"Money, money, money," says Faustus Mercator, the bony

man, with a big smacking lip pause. "Money." He turns his leer to full, eyes hysterically wide, and gazes into my blankness.

Note to self . . . if I ever doubt for a second what Faustus Mercator is really up to, I want myself to remember this little nugget from the personal thoughts of Faustus Mercator.

"I love money."

He smiles, and it's a really unpleasant vision of teeth and canines and want. Like a wolf in the night.

"Love it, I do. Plain and simple," he says. "And that, my dear PerfectQuestion, is what this is really all about. It's what your game is all about. All games are about money. Money. Call me bald." He laughs at his own pun as he rubs his hairless scalp. I murmur something. "Or bold, but that's what I really want. I just want all the money in the world; is that so wrong? So here's my little plan. Ready? Okay. Among other things, I am manipulating the market of game warfare advertising, in an attempt to control a large bulk of the available advertising revenue. By doing so, I can influence the masses to buy the products I want them to buy. To take the journeys I want them to take. And you, PerfectQuestion, are a very small part of my plan, whether you like it or not."

He leans closer.

"You're a good soldier, online of course. And my team needs good soldiers, all the time. Right now, you're doing the good soldier bit for hard-luck little old ColaCorp. They should be out of business within the next two weeks, by the by, WarWorld-wise. But don't worry, fear not, there's a plan, a solution to your mounting problems dear, dear PerfectQuestion. And here it is, that moment your mother and father warned you about. Paths diverging in the forest and all that. Y'know, the choice between right and wrong. Did you ever get that speech, from your parents or college professors or anyone, did you, PerfectQuestion?"

I nod helplessly, not remembering if I ever actually did.

"You know the one: Do the right thing, son. Never lie cheat or steal, son. Don't turn your back on a friend, betray a commitment, steal, murder, desire. Try to get ahead. Ambition. All that jazz. Well, PerfectQuestion, I'm here to tell you . . . they were all wrong. Wrong, wrong, wrong, wrong, wrong. Doing all that stuff is great. The rewards are limitless once you embrace unrestricted greed. Forget morality. I say pshaw. It's all really just made up to prevent you from getting ahead. And, bonus round, having fun doing it.

"Look at your former filly, the estimable Sancerré. Why, she's really moving up in the world. Last I heard, she's in Europe hanging off the arm of that what's his name. Word is, she's even going to get some big breaks in her career. The sky's the limit, and all she had to do was turn her back on being loyal to a flawed concept. Fidelity. I'm sorry if that hurts dear, dear boy, but it's the truth. You were both going through the motions. Yes, one morning she woke up, in someone else's bed I might add, and sorry but it's true, she just woke up and made the decision to get hers. She was tired of waiting. And now, my PerfectQuestion, I'm offering you that most premium of chances. The one people really do try to summon the devil for. And I'm not even asking for your soul. All I want is for you to come and work for old Faustus Mercator. All that money that I want, some of it could be yours. And some of all, well, I'm guessing that's a lot. So what do you say? Why don't you come and get yours?"

*Really?* I think to myself. Really. There's never an easy way, is there? All I'm trying to do is be the best at what I do, professional gaming, and make the rent each month. After that, maybe find a little place to call my own in life. Someone you can love is a bonus. But here I am high above the earth, rent unpaid, desperately due. Sancerré gone and to top it all off, there's a world-dominating, apparently mad villain offering me the chance to be a flunkie in his grand scheme to take over the world. The only thing missing from this is the smoking nuclear missile in the background and, oh yeah, the large digital countdown clock.

I expect you to die, Mr. Bond.

I try to stand.

My mom and dad taught me a lot of things, and maybe they missed a few of the finer points, like how to be really successful or how to have enough in a world economy that's making a clear Grand Canyon–sized delineation between the haves and the have-nots. But they did teach me the difference between right and wrong. Walking out on your team, on a friend . . . I never saw my dad do that. Even though he never made it this high, except for one day, and he was kind enough to share that day with his family, he was still a good man. Like I said, I tried to take a stand. I tried to stand up.

But the couch is too damned comfortable.

"Ah, Tatiana," croons Faustus. "Without her in the room, those Soft pheromones just seem to vanish in a haze. But they do linger, don't they. Why, I could just toss you out of an airlock right now and there wouldn't be a thing you could do about it. Isn't that a scream?"

He leans down next to me. Looks into my eyes.

"But I can't, because security's so darn tight up here what with all the passcodes for airlocks and security feeds. So no, I can't kill you right here and now in the SkyVault. But down on the streets of forgotten old New York, why anything, and I mean anything, can happen. Maybe I'm getting ahead of myself. I do that. So what's it gonna be, PerfectQuestion?" he asks me. "Will you . . . help me . . . steal . . . all the money in the world?"

I'm not sure what I did. But this is what he said next.

"I see by the shake of your drug-addled head that you're really not thinking very clearly right now. Or are you shaking your head for yes? As in, yes, you will help me ruin the world economy and make more than a few bucks for yourself in the process."

Faustus Mercator stares at me intently.

"No means no. Okay, so it's a no then. Right, no . . . Okay, shake your head if you're shaking it for 'no.' That means you don't want to work for me and assist in my plan to take all the world's money."

I was shaking my head then. I am almost sure of it.

"Fine then." Faustus snaps his fingers, and from somewhere, a softly glowing Tatiana enters. Hip, leg, heel, hip, leg, heel.

"All right, I'm really very disappointed," says Mercator, rising. "Now I'm going to have to kill you."

# Chapter 18

I've been here before.

The morning sun on my apartment floor reminds me of better days. Sunnier days. But the white light is too wintry to be anything other than the cold morning New York seems to be caught in the permanent grip of.

The first thought I have as I fade from the dream of the night before is that if it ever stops being winter, things might get better.

What is "better"?

Sancerré.

ColaCorp winning, at least once.

Getting up there, where I was last night.

Knowing which way is actually up.

I'm not dead, yet. I'm still wearing my cheap gray suit from last night. How I got back, if I ever really was up there, is something I'm not altogether clear on.

It's morning and I'm alive. In my apartment. It's all too weird, and frankly, it must have been the scotch and the stress and maybe even the corned beef. Faustus Mercator probably isn't even real. Come on, he really wants to steal all the world's money, and because I, a lowly gamer, won't help him, he's going to kill me? Please.

Down here, underneath Upper New York, where I live and will probably live for the rest of my life, the streets are generally very quiet. But for some reason, there's a lot going on outside this morning. Getting up, even though there really isn't much of a reason to until this evening when ColaCorp fights the last of its last stands, isn't really necessary. But, like I said, New York streets are quiet, so it's rare if anything ever goes on at this time of the morning. I stand up and amazingly, I'm not really all that hungover. In fact, I feel normal. Maybe slightly dull headed.

Out on the street, after pulling back the curtain, I see a dozen men dressed in matte-black SmartArmor, carrying a large amount of matte-black, boxy, no-nonsense, state-of-the-art automatic weaponry. One of them glances up at me. I can see his pulsing purple SoftEye.

He waves, trying to be friendly.

I've got good eyes. At this distance I can tell he's saying something out the side of his mouth. Several of them turn to watch me, each wearing a pulsing purple SoftEye.

Two questions leap to the front of the queue.

Why is a small private army staging an attack outside my apartment building?

And the second question is . . .

. . . why is one of these jackbooted thugs shouldering an antiarmor rocket and aiming it directly at me?

I fling myself away from the window, manage a fluid turn in which I grab my trench, and head straight for the door to the stairwell. I hear the aviator shades hit the floor but there's no time to scoop them up. With the door open and my body not moving as fast as my mind thinks it should right about now, I launch myself down the rickety stairs. I hear glass break just before I reach the next landing, and then brick, wood, and plaster scatter across the landing above, spilling debris and dust down onto me.

Then I hear the explosion.

Another two landings along my descent, and I hear the front door explode as someone puts a shotgun to it and destroys the lock with a special lock-breaker slug, no doubt.

On the bottom floor, their capture team chases me out the back door as I crash into the slimy, ice-laden alley. I find my feet, let go of common sense, and sprint as hard as I can. Within minutes, I'm three blocks away, and no SmartArmor-wearing thug is going to catch me as I race through alleyways and abandoned buildings.

My landlord, on the other hand, is going to evict me.

For the rest of the day, I ride the rattling subway system, wearing last night's suit and parsing the details, trying to figure out my next move. Which, when I really think about it, would be novel since I haven't really made any moves.

So Faustus Mercator is real.

He really wants me dead.

Why didn't he just space me last night?

Tatiana slithers into my head, and for a good hour I circle the city and think about her. Obviously, not that she needed it, she was wearing some sort of designer hyperpheromone that drugged me to the eyeballs. Still, she can't be all bad. Not with those looks.

Four hours later, it's two o'clock and I am devouring my third platform gyro. I have a really great metabolism, one of my parents' choices when they ordered me.

My biggest problem, other than the fact that a sociopath wants me dead, is that I have to be online somewhere as Perfect-Question and fighting for ColaCorp later this evening. I check my Petey, waiting for a message from the Black. There's still that to consider.

I kill the next four hours looking for an Internet café I can hide out in. I'm fairly sure once I log on as PerfectQuestion, Faustus Mercator will hunt me down and kill me, accidentally of course, after the night's battle has ended. Most Internet cafés are too vulnerable. Two thugs, the scenario might be imagined, irate over a game of *Bang*, a simple online first-person shooter that most teens and gang members play, in which players hunt each other down with shotguns, get into an argument. Eventually, the two hotheads exchange gunfire over the obligatory allegation of cheating or outright screen-looking and, oops, I get killed in the cross fire. Or they make it look like a robbery gone bad. Or even a thrill kill by a bunch of chain junkies looking for the next high.

If Faustus Mercator wants me dead, I'll probably be dead in the next few hours.

I think about calling him and arranging a truce or something. Maybe all my morals and standards bravado was just the scotch. Dodging his hit squads on the streets above, and thinking about the no doubt burning remains of my apartment, is enough to make me seriously think about switching sides.

But that's not me.

If I do that, I won't just be letting me down. I like RangerSix. Though we've never exchanged a personal word, he's the kind of guy you want to earn the respect of. Letting him down, as well as Kiwi, and especially RiotGuurl—it just wouldn't be the same. Then I'd just be some mercenary looking for the next buck.

That there's a traitor on the team already seems likely. How else could WonderSoft always be just a step or two ahead of us. But who?

I thought about JollyBoy and the trap at the LZ back at WonderSoft's airfield.

I can't fall asleep in the subway, and I find myself thinking about the past. Way back, when I thought ColaCorp could win this war. Lately it's just been one long retreat. So why not switch sides?

Again, the faces of friends pass outside in the darkness, along tunnels beneath the city. Even my parents. Something deep down, something the gene engineers didn't intend, something inside me, tells me that I don't like guys like Faustus Mercator.

I don't like guys who think they can just run amok while the rest of us let them. The photographer Sancerré ran off with, he's probably a lot like that. Maybe that's why I felt the way I did about Sancerré. Not that she chose someone else over me . . .

. . . but that she chose someone who would just use her. Tell her everything she wanted to hear. Give her the big break she was always working so hard for, then cast her aside one day because he didn't really, actually, love her. Like I did. Do. That innocent, wide-eyed, taking-in-the-whole world look in her eyes would die a little that day. Maybe the guy on the street wouldn't notice, or the next guy who came along, but if you knew her, if you knew it had been there once and that it was gone now, that was what broke my heart about her the most. That the good inside her would die someday.

If I couldn't stick it to the wonderful Mario, the world's greatest photographer, at least in his own opinion, then maybe I could just stick it to a world-dominating madman like Faustus Mercator.

Just once for all the little guys in life. Guys like me.

I call RangerSix and plead rats in my building.

He arranges for me to get access to a terminal inside Cola-Corp corporate headquarters in order to be able to participate in tonight's battle.

Everywhere, or so it seems to me, people inform on my passage through the city to ColaCorp headquarters, remarking on my journey, a little too interested in which way I'm going to get to ColaCorp.

Or maybe I'm just paranoid.

Later, I get through lobby security at ColaCorp and manage my way onto an elevator that's playing something forgotten over the speakers. The workday has ended, and now I have an entire floor to myself. In the back of my head, I'm already wondering if somehow I'm betraying my team, turning my back on RangerSix and the rest.

Why aren't I telling them about Faustus Mercator?

Outside, the snow begins to fall into the early New York night. Every so often, I hear an announcement for the next shuttle departing for the concourse above. Most of the executives must live up there. Finally the last shuttle departs for the night, and I sit in the offices of ColaCorp amid a dense quiet that feels almost comforting. Other than security, I am alone in the building.

I find a break room and use their expensive coffeemaker to brew up a truly wonderful cup of coffee.

Cream and sugar.

Silence.

Night outside.

I webcam my apartment building from a nearby city camera. It's gone. When I go onto the city services site, I find a note posted indicating the building had been scheduled for demo months ago and that it's uninhabited as of today.

All my stuff is gone.

Except for my trench, the Black disk, and my sawed-off broom handle. All gone.

Even the things Sancerré left behind.

It's hard to believe I was on the Grand Concourse just last night. Up there where things are different, better even. Or at least it was one of those nights that seemed that way.

I'm in loadout, adjusting my grunt's tactical settings and weapon kits when RiotGuurl pings me. Not in the mood, I almost ignore her. I can only take so much in one day.

"Hey!?," she texts.

"What?"

She sends me an invite to live chat with her avatar.

"Hey, I just wanted to say I'm sorry," she says in the form of her in-game, mirrored-sunglasses-wearing combat pilot avatar. Her hair is a red spike. Her avatar always wears a smirk.

"Nothing to be sorry about," I reply.

"No, I was severely not cool. I threw up a wall once I sensed you being . . . kind . . . to me. Sorry, it's . . . that was wrong of me."

"Forget it. I was just grasping at straws. My personal life is crashing like a South African hard drive. I had no business inviting anyone into it right now. It's me who should be sorry. So I am. I am sorry. I apologize."

"Hey . . ." She pauses. Then, "Sounds bad. What's going on?"

"I can't get into it right now. Let's win one tonight and then have a drink in the bunker."

"It's a date," she says, and then her avatar makes a pistol with one hand and fires.

The conversation ends as RangerSix broadcasts our assignments.

"Kids, tonight's a retreat. And it's no treat. ColaCorp has ponied up enough assets to buy us a carrier relief force if we can make it back to Song Hua City on the other side of the bridge. That's it. They want us to hold Song Hua Harbor, this side of the bridge, tonight. We get all our field assets off the map and onto the carrier group, we get to fight next week, but we're looking at a death match if that's the case. Effectively, that's it for us in the league. Last week was our must win. As of now, WonderSoft corporate is asking to be declared the winner of Eastern Highlands. This gives them the AtomMall advertising for the next quarter. In short, we lost."

"So what's the purpose of tonight?" asks Kiwi over the ether.

"Good question, son. And I don't have an answer for you. Other than that they weren't declared the winners in the last match, as the league felt their victory wasn't dynamic enough. You made 'em pay with a lot of tanks, and we got our artillery out of there. Thus, Song Hua Harbor tonight. Their assault begins at in-game twilight and should last well into the night. The town's lit up like a Christmas tree and the league wants us to put on a big firefight for the viewers."

"So when WonderSoft rolls all over us, it'll look like a victory parade," cuts in RiotGuurl. "Worth showing, huh?"

"That's the thinking," answers RangerSix.

"That sucks," she says.

RangerSix doesn't respond. But his silence seems like some kind of agreement.

"So here's the plan," continues RangerSix. "WonderSoft will prep with arty and then come down hard on the only road out of the highlands and into the port. RiotGuurl, you're on station at Song Hua. There's an airbase there and I want you on CAP and ready to fly close air support."

A 3-D map of the city appears on-screen. Three main avenues run north-south down to the harbor. Smaller side streets cut across the dense urban areas. The bridge leading to Song Hua City waits on the far side of the map.

"Our amphibs will be loading and artillery has priority, so we'll have them loaded by the time I expect to see the first ground units. Armor goes next. Don't plan on any stand-up fights, 'cause they won't be there to back you up. Stick and move. It's an infantry battle, so take lots of body armor and antitank. Finally, Kiwi, since you like explosives so much, I want you to demo the easternmost and westernmost north-south avenues. I suggest bringing down the buildings I've highlighted on your map. Hopefully this will channel WonderSoft into our little shooting gallery down the main street. If they want a big game, they might take the bait and try to push on through regardless of resistance. If we can get into some good fighting positions we should slow 'em down in time to get off the beach. In no way, shape, or form can they reach and cross the Song Hua Bridge. That is an immediate victory condition for WonderSoft tonight. No ifs, ands, or buts about that one. That's it, kids; you have your section briefings and code files. See you in the streets."

# Chapter 19

**W**onderSoft artillery comes in high, whistling through the twilight overhead, ranging in on the harbor where our heavy armor and artillery are waiting to load back onto the amphibs. Near the outskirts of a Southeast Asian cityscape lit up like a Christmas tree, the rest of us are dug in. I've set up around a construction site near the main road leading to the highlands, the direction in which WonderSoft should be coming from with all the armor they've got. Every so often Kiwi calls out "Timber!" over BattleChat as a series of shape charges ignite and explode, signaling the demise of another digital building as it crashes down into the streets, blocking the other two large roads that lead down to the harbor.

My grunts are spaced out across the construction site, dug in behind Dumpsters and tractors, with heavy-machine-gun teams covering the most likely WonderSoft avenues of approach. I have a mortar team set up to the rear of a factory about two clicks behind our position. Going over the map for the last time, I believe, or at least it appears to me, that

I'm going to meet the tip of WonderSoft's spear. If they come in motorized columns with tactical air support, as they usually do, then they'll be coming right through this construction site. Once they get past it, they'll be in the outlying suburbs, and it'll be house-to-house fighting for them to get to the harbor. RangerSix has indicated that if I can tie them up here, we'll make this the focal point of the battle. But first I've got to get them to commit to wiping me out.

I'm on top of the half-built building, exposed girders and open framework, surrounded by sandbags and sniper teams.

"Any sign of 'em?" It's RiotGuurl. I can hear the Albatross's turbines straining in the background of her mic. She's high above us, orbiting the battlefield, ready to drop ordnance on target.

"Nothing yet. Any sign of the scouts?" WonderSoft recon should be out in the heavy forest beyond the construction site gathering intel, trying to find the best approach into Song Hua. "I'm surprised they're not here by now. Nothin' on IR. So if they're coming in, might be on foot-running stealth camo."

"The beach is chaos right now," reports RiotGuurl. "A few of the first WonderSoft artillery rounds sank one of our transports right alongside the pier, and they had to demo it to get it out of the way. Other than that, most of their shots are going long. Way out into the water. Everybody's getting mixed up about what to do."

I switch to night vision and scan the forest road that leads off into the highlands, where WonderSoft will approach from. Nothing.

"Warning." It's ShogunSmile over BattleChat. His voice is calm. "Flash, Flash. Flash. They ain't comin' in on foot. It's a full-scale airborne invasion. I've got a flight of six, wait . . . now ten, Universe class WonderSoft transports inbound from the coast, coming in from the east."

"Are you real sure about that, son?" asks RangerSix, immediately overriding the sudden eruption of chatter.

"Fifteen seconds out. Low and slow," says ShogunSmile. "Any antiair online?"

"All units stand by to shift sectors." RangerSix's message comes in marked "Urgent Priority" on my HUD.

"Cargo doors open . . . I'm seein' the first 'chutes," says someone over BattleChat.

Moments later, I hear the huge transports thunder across the night dark sky above. The Universe isn't a VTOL aircraft like the Albatross, so it keeps moving. It's only used for transporting heavy armor and troops, and in this case, dropping lots of WonderSoft grunts and players all over us.

"We've got enemy everywhere," screams someone across BattleChat.

"Repeat," says RangerSix tonelessly. "WonderSoft is inside the perimeter. Leave your grunts with orders to defend your sectors and try to clear out the airborne units before the main body arrives. We are still expecting an armored attack from the east."

A missile arches upward from the paper-lantern-strung streets of Song Hua and cuts a departing Universe in half with a loud explosion. The monster air transport twirls off into another section of the city and explodes with a loud, grinding *Craaash*.

I order my grunts to hold the perimeter and set off into the narrow streets of Song Hua, looking for enemy paratroopers.

I run into three WonderSoft paratroopers a block away from the construction site. Two are setting up antipersonnel mines along a series of small storefronts, while one constructs a barricade in front of a McBucks Coffee. In the middle of the street, an air-drop crate rests next to an armored ballistic case for a WonderSoft heavy machine gun. Most likely a PRK 46 firing 7.62 ammo. The paratroopers look like ordinary grunts, but the fact that they've air-dropped means they're elite paratroop grunts with better weapons and enhanced combat AI.

I duck back around the corner of the building and key in a sitrep. As soon as I get the "acknowledged" from Command on my HUD, I head into a narrow wet alley running down the back of the storefronts they're fortifying.

I find the back door to the storefront they're in front of and lock-pick it using the *Door Cracker* minigame. Completing the minigame, I'm rewarded—*click*—as the door pops open ever so silently. I bring out my assault rifle and push open the door. It's dark inside. I switch to night vision, activating the target laser on the rifle.

Over ambient I hear a nearby crash. The inside of the building is being cannibalized for barrier materials by the paratroopers. They've probably been ordered to fortify and defend inside our perimeter. I proceed through a shadowy stockroom in the back of the building, searching for the front of the store. I'd opted for no silencer in the loadout, instead preferring uranium-depleted armor-piercing rounds because I figured it'd be that kind of out-loud fight. Instead it's the game of quiet assassination.

Right now, the silencer would have been a better choice.

Outside, I hear the high-pitched turbocharger of an approaching Mule from down the street. Moments later, it races up and skids to a halt right outside the front of the building I'm creeping through. The sounds of work stop, and I hear boots thumping against dry concrete over ambient as the grunts report to whoever's driving the Mule.

The sound of the boots is closer than I'd expected.

If the Mule had been one of ours, the shooting would've already started. It must've been air-dropped by WonderSoft.

Over ambient I hear, "Troopers 267 and 268, load that PRK onto my Mule." In-game orders are being given by a WonderSoft player to grunts.

I sling my weapon and bring out shape charges. Quickly I plant them on the wall nearest the vehicle, guessing at its position. I set the directional dial toward the vehicle and adjust the gain to direct the explosion into a concentrated cone. I up the yield to max and arm it with a fifteen-second fuse. The counter clicks over to fourteen and I run to the rear of the store, unslinging my rifle and crouching low.

*Flash!* erupts brightly in my HUD, indicating I've got a priority message from Command. "All available personnel rally on the television tower. WonderSoft has a spotter team on top and they're directing fire down on our units located at the harbor. We just lost a landing craft with three tanks on board!"

The fuse counter in my HUD hits nine.

"RangerSix, we cannot penetrate the lobby to the tower at this time." It's Kiwi. "There're three enemy heavy-machine-gun teams and loads of paratroopers defending the first- and second-floor lobbies." I hear the rattle of automatic gunfire in the background of Kiwi's link, then an explosion and shattering glass. "They're lobbing grenades at us from the roof," continues Kiwi. I hear more explosions, then a steady stream of automatic heavy gunfire stepping all over the last of Kiwi's transmission.

The fuse counter in my HUD hits 4. I'm hoping the Wonder-Soft grunts have just loaded the weapons resupply crate. I might catch all of them if they have. I think about the player in the driver's seat of the Mule. What's his first move going to be after the explosion?

Over BattleChat I hear, "I can't hit the tower. They've got two AA teams with Scorpions on the roof." In the background, the high-pitched torment of RiotGuurl's engines strain to dodge out of the way of an incoming missile, as her AA alarm screams urgently.

The fuse counter hits 1.

The explosion rips open the wall, sending simulated concrete and debris out into the street.

Immediately, I get three grunt kills in my HUD as tiny dollar symbols fall into my bounty account. I open up, full auto, with armor-piercing rounds, unloading an entire clip through the smoking hole. I get another grunt kill, maybe the Mule gunner or another paratrooper I hadn't spotted. I lob a grenade out into the street, slap another magazine into my rifle, and advance through the smoking hole in the wall.

At that moment, the Hauser minigun in the Mule's turret spools to life. To my right, the building begins to disintegrate as three thousand miniballs per second erupt from its spinning snub-nosed matte-gray triangular barrels. I run through the hole, unloading my rifle at where I hope the gunner is.

It's a race.

There's no skill in it.

With four rounds left, I switch to semiauto and target the gunner who's bringing the short twin barrels of the Hauser to bear on me, as a shimmering wave of miniball ammo reduces the wall of the building on my right to Swiss cheese. Closing in on me.

I aim on the fly and tag the gunner with three rounds that leave smoking holes in his avatar's chest. The last one has to count so I put it in his head.

CaptainCarnage lies slumped in the Mule's turret.

*IN-GAME Player Kill!* flashes across my screen.

In the corner of my HUD I see the network feed symbol go live, as somewhere a director is cutting together the footage for a highlight reel.

CaptainCarnage's dog tags appear on my combat knife.

"JollyBoy to RiotGuurl," I hear over BattleChat. "If you're up for a bit of harebrained madness, I've got a plan to get to the top of the tower and take out those cursed Scorpions."

I check the buildings along the street and remember the antipersonnel mines. If they'd armed them, I'd be dead now. But they hadn't.

"I'm in, JollyBoy; whatcha got planned?" says RiotGuurl.

"Oh, something wacky, something blue. Something only I know how to do. Meet me at this loc for pick up ASAP."

"Roger that, there in thirty seconds."

I don't trust JollyBoy. If anyone's a double agent working for Faustus Mercator, then it's him. If he takes out our best pilot this early in the game, then it's game over.

"Feed me that loc, Jolly," I say over BattleChat. "I want in too."

"PerfectQuestioney, I just knew you were insane."

"Takes one to know one, Jolly."

"So true, PerfectQuestion, so very true."

The coordinates appear on my HUD. I pull the dead grunt out of the driver's seat and hope the Mule will start after the explosion and all the bullets I hit it with. When it does, smoking and rattling at 36 percent integrity, I aim it toward JollyBoy's pickup.

The location is a small park near a simulated business complex. RiotGuurl's Albatross is already hovering over the waving manicured grass and bending willowy trees, loading ramp down. I drive the Mule up to the ramp, grab the machine-gun case from the vehicle's inventory slot and put it in the Albatross's inventory.

"All aboard the death choo choo," croons JollyBoy's slender, black beret–wearing avatar. A couple of micro Uzis dangle from straps around either shoulder. His face is camoed in black and white greasepaint like an operatic clown I'd once seen in a commercial for pasta or something.

"Let's go make ourselves some madness, RiotGuurl."

JollyBoy is calling the shots now. I'm just along for the ride. I hope I haven't made a mistake. If he's the traitor, he'll get two player kills instead of one.

Then there's another voice inside my head that's hoping he hasn't really betrayed us.

The Albatross picks up speed, but we aren't gaining altitude. We're flying nap-of-the-earth just over the tops of the buildings, dodging digital satellite dishes and sudden jutting apartment complexes.

"What's the plan?" I ask.

JollyBoy's avatar appears from the shadows of the cargo bay. Red emergency lights make him seem sinister and even more insane. If that's possible.

"No plan, PerfectQuestioney. Just show up." He pulls out his trademark neon green, dual-long-barrel .45s, complete with obnoxiously long silencers, and waves them in circles near his head. "Wave our guns around," he says with a grin exaggerated by greasepaint. "Y'know, show 'em we really mean business."

I was expecting more. Or at least something.

The engines whine dangerously close to maximum as the Albatross heels over into a tight turn. I check the cockpit and watch as RiotGuurl flies us straight down the paper-lantern-lit main street of Song Hua Harbor. In the distance I see a space-age television station, a glass spire, rising up above the city. I think it's based on some famous building from the Bangkok BioMass.

"It's really brilliant and rather simple! You see, PerfectQuestioney, we're gonna fly straight up the side of that thing and when chickie-poo up there says 'jump,' well, we jump. Hopefully just seconds, maybe even just a smidge of a second really, after we jump out, we land on the roof and start, you know . . . shooting everyone up there."

One of his pistols clicks and a flag with the word *Bang!* pops out from the barrel.

Humor.

"Fun, huh?" His perma-grinning avatar raises his eyebrows at me knowingly.

"Lobby in sight," says RiotGuurl over BattleChat. "Hang on! Going vertical in five, four, three . . ."

Even RiotGuurl sounds stressed. This plan is insane. But there's no getting through the lobby on the ground floor, that's for sure. If Kiwi and all his explosives can't manage that, I doubt the rest of us are going to do any better. Ahead of us, out the cockpit window, the TV tower races toward us at breakneck speed. Hundreds of ColaCorp bodies litter the entrance as WonderSoft machine guns rake the surrounding buildings. Bright green tracer rounds zip past the Albatross's cockpit as our opponents train their cross fire on us. One head shot on RiotGuurl through the canopy and that's the end of this little trip. On a positive note, we might take out the lobby defenses in what I can only imagine will be a spectacular highlight reel crash for the postgame show.

Suddenly we're vertical, and the Albatross's engines kick in hard. Already RiotGuurl is punching the afterburners in short bursts, causing the gunship to emit a series of soft *bump bumps* above the roar of the engines.

"What're you going to do about the AA once you drop us?" I scream at RiotGuurl over the noise of the straining engines.

"Don't worry about it," she says distractedly. "Get ready . . . here we go . . . jump!"

I hit E on the keyboard and instantly our avatars exit the Albatross in midair. I tap 9 and my chute deploys. The Albatross screams away into a loop, attempting to deny the AA grunts enough time to acquire and fire. I bring out my assault rifle and start shooting at the AA teams, but the wind is stiff and it takes all my fingers moving on the keyboard just to get me drifting down onto the roof of the TV tower, much less take a shot.

JollyBoy, drifting above me, holds out his pistols and waits.

Briefly I wonder who he'll fire at. Me or them?

The Albatross tops the loop high above us and heads down beneath the skyline of the city as an AA grunt fires his shoulder-mounted antiair Scorpion missile launcher, even though the concrete roof is exploding all around him as my bullets tear through the air between me and him. The antiair missile pops out of its long shoulder-mounted tube, deploys its navigation fins, and ignites, streaking right past me, sidewinding off toward Riot-Guurl's diving Albatross.

I'm dimly aware of the dry *click* my rifle makes when the magazine reads empty. The air-dropped machine-gun case smacks into the roof below. RiotGuurl must have had her grunts throw it off the cargo deck after us. As we fall, we continue to course correct our drifting parachutes, gliding down toward the roof of the TV tower.

If we miss the building, then it's all been for nothing.

The AA grunts pull out small black submachine guns and prepare to repel our assault. At the top of the tower, on a raised platform, a WonderSoft artillery spotter, using a handheld spotting monocular, is pointing toward us. Most likely, he's calling in reinforcements from the lobby to get up to the roof ASAP.

I hit the edge of the roof, almost missing it altogether, and reload my rifle as the AA grunts take aim. Above me, four soft whispering puffs emit as JollyBoy fires his two pistols, taking out all four Softies with kill shots in the forehead. Gently he slides to the ground and disconnects from his parachute seamlessly.

"Oh," he mumbles as if completely surprised. "I expected that to go far worse."

"RiotGuurl. What's your status?" I call out over BattleChat.

A second later she responds. "Airborne and on station, ready to drop some ordnance wherever you want it." She'd dodged the Scorpion antiair missile.

"How did you do that?"

"Honestly, Perfect, I don't even know."

"Ah, beauty and humility," says JollyBoy. "Two virtues I despise in everyone. On that note, let's go make WonderSoft regret their decision to take the TV tower away from us, whaddya say?" He raises a pistol and shoots the still-gesticulating spotter at the far end of the roof. "Whaddya say, PerfectQuestioney, old friend, old pal, old buddy?"

I enter the building first through the roof access. JollyBoy follows with his pistols out as I lead the way down the stairwell, with the heavy machine gun using its robo-assist sling. Below, I can hear WonderSoft grunts climbing the stairs up toward us. When they're three flights below, we crouch, waiting and ready. JollyBoy pops two grenades and rolls them down onto the landings below, bouncing them off the far wall. Then they wander down onto the next set of stairs. Moments later, an explosion plunges the entire stairwell into darkness.

I surge forward, swinging the machine gun around toward the landing below as I cut loose on two Softies stumbling about in the darkness. The rapid camera flash effect of the firing muzzle from the heavy machine gun gives me brief sudden glimpses of their demise. When I stop firing, the stairwell returns to darkness. Two shotgun blasts illuminate the smoke and gray walls as two more grunts, one with sergeant stripes, both with shotguns, surge up the stairwell below. I fire down at them, hitting the sergeant, flinging him back against the wall as rendered blood-spatter ink blots the clean gray concrete stairwell around his body.

The other grunt fires another blast from his shotgun, spraying me in the legs. The blast is ill-aimed and I'm hit with 23 percent damage. My screen fogs crimson as the shaky cam cuts in, simulating damage taken.

I've got to take this guy out before he can fire again.

I reply with a short burst into his chest. He ragdolls back down into the darkness of the stairwell.

Red emergency lights come on in, bathing everything in black ink and red blood.

"Scary, huh?" says JollyBoy.

"I'll watch the stairs. Radio in and tell RangerSix we're securing the tower from above."

"Roger, chief!" JollyBoy's avatar snaps to attention with a salute and falls over making a spring-gone-haywire sound in-game.

Great. If he's not actually a double agent, he might just be merely nuts. Which is worse? But I have to give him credit; so far his plan has worked. Or had it worked too well? That's the question.

"Kiwi?" I call over BattleChat. "Kiwi, we're coming down the stairwell. When we get to the lobby just above the ground floor, I'll let you know. We could use an update on the situation down there."

I get nothing in reply.

"Are you getting anything from the other players, Jolly?"

"Nothing. I don't even have access to my intel satellite. The game must factor in all the signal distortion from the television tower and cut down on our comm and intel access."

That was a surprisingly sober assessment for JollyBoy. Nothing funny about that.

"All right," I say. "We'll clear the stairwell until we get to the floors just above the lobby, then we'll see what we can do from there."

"Aye, aye, Captain. Commence mit der shootin'!" roars JollyBoy.

Over the next hour, we fight our way down the stairwell as wave after wave of WonderSoft grunts come up after us. After the first few assaults, the PRK is out of ammo so I loot one of the WonderSoft shotguns off a dead grunt and wade into the next wave.

# Chapter 20

Jolly, you ever heard of someone named Faustus Mercator?"

We're five floors above the lobby. Bodies litter the twenty floors above us. JollyBoy's avatar slides two clips out of his pistols and replaces them with two new ones in the dim emergency lighting of the stairwell.

"Faustus Mercator. Hmmmmmmmmmmm. Nope! Now, Jedediah Whirlygoogle, on the other hand, I do know, regardless of what my shrink tries to intimate about her actual place in reality."

My avatar is steadily reloading twelve stubby shells into the barrel of a looted WonderSoft Intimidator twelve-gauge assault shotgun. I've been scavenging ammo off WonderSoft grunts. My health is down to 54 percent.

"Honestly, PerfectQuestioney," JollyBoy says, sighing, "I never figured you for the fictionalized friend type. But it's always nice to know one's not alone in the world of imaginary buddies. Whirlygoogle's a talking duck."

"Seriously, Jolly. It's a guy who's been stalking me in the real world. I think he might have something to do with what's going on. Why ColaCorp is losing so much. Unrealistically so much."

"Faustus Mercator sounds made up," says JollyBoy. "If you'd told me Bill Johannsen or Scott Wilmsby . . . well maybe not Wilmsby . . . but Johannsen, definitely. Yes, if Scott or Bill Johannsen is somehow after you, out to kill you, stalking you like a hunted animal, well, I might take that a little more seriously. Someone with that sort of name is obviously a serial killer. But Mercator sounds a little too fake. And Faustus—reaching a bit there, don't you think?"

The game is minutes from shutting down. Tonight's match will be over, and the winner will surely be WonderSoft. They've overwhelmed us with an airborne assault and captured the key victory point, the TV tower, thus owning the map and battle of Song Hua Harbor.

We need a game changer in the next few minutes to even earn a draw and fight next Saturday night.

I can't stop thinking about Mercator, about how he's influenced the game for his own ends. Even though I've managed to survive the entire night fighting inside WarWorld, I still have to go out into the dark streets when it's all done. Out there is a man named Faustus Mercator and he's trying to kill me. Why? Because I won't play ball with him and whomever it is he represents. On top of that, someone on our side has made WonderSoft's victories much easier than they should've been.

Someone is a double agent.

JollyBoy had scouted the LZ at WonderSoft Garage, and we'd been ambushed right there.

"Listen, PerfectQuestioney, as much as I would love to swap Dickensian-themed enemies with you, we do have to take out the lobby. I'm guessing we've got about five minutes before the league shuts down the match. In fact, I don't know why it's still going on. That airborne assault did the trick. We're finished. But maybe it happened too early in the night? Maybe they wanted a real big finish type of battle? I don't know and I can't figure out why, but it seems as though WonderSoft has won."

"Seems like it," I mumble.

"On that note," whispers JollyBoy. "Let's go kill everyone in the lobby anyways. Why the heck not? Is it too much of an understatement if I ask, 'What have we got to lose?'"

"All right," I agree. "I'm in."

"Okay then. What have you got in the way of killing everybody supplies?"

"Ummm . . . this shotgun and a grenade," I say.

"I've got this much left." His avatar twirls each pistol on a long finger.

"Grim."

"Seemingly, PerfectQuestioney. Seemingly. But I do have another plan. Well, not so much of a plan, more of a desire."

"Desire to do what?"

"Kill everyone."

"Goes without saying, Jolly."

"It does and I never tire of it, PerfectQuestioney. Never, ever."

"All right then."

"What if I throw a bag of feral cats in there and the cats kill all three machine-gun teams and whoever else is down in there?"

In the silence of the red-lit stairwell I look at JollyBoy's green-haired, grinning avatar.

"JollyBoy?"

"Yes?"

"Do you have a bag of feral cats?"

His grin turns into a frown. His avatar runs really nice EmoteWare. I wonder if he has a dedicated graphics card running the BodyFace Scanning Bar.

"No, I don't," he mumbles. "But I should. I really should."

"Well, then we can't actually do that, can we, Jolly? Cats killing everyone just isn't an option for us right now."

A moment later his grin returns. Not evil. Not sinister. Not amusement or even knowing authority. Just glee.

"I do have these, on the other hand. Or to be more correct . . . correct-er . . . in the other hand."

His avatar produces three antiair Scorpion missiles from his inventory. Each is powerful enough to take out an armored Albatross.

"Did you bring the launcher?"

"Oh, boring old PerfectQuestioney, always with your fuddy-duddy ideas about just shooting things at people conventionally. This . . . will be much, much more fun."

"Yeah, fun."

"Laugh out loud, even I don't believe you mean that, Perfect-Question. No, really, seriously, old pal, old buddy, old Perfect-Question . . . all we have to do is arm these things and throw them like grenades. Sort of."

Theoretically what he's proposing is possible. There's a complex minigame for demo ordnance geeks in which they can ignite the rocket in the round after a five-second delay. But what's the use of that? The thing will just shoot off any random direction and explode. Also, if you fail the *Demo Ordnance* minigame, the thing explodes in your face. Killing you and your closest friends.

"All right," I say, "you do it."

"I'll do one and Duck-It to the second. You've got to do the other."

Duck-It Tape is a cross-team sponsor. Everyone, every corporate online army, carries Duck-It. Duck-It even gives you a bonus if you use it and it makes the highlight reel.

"I've never done one before," I say, referencing the *Scorpion* minigame.

"Phewww," exclaims JollyBoy. "Me neither. Now I won't feel so bad if I mess up and blow us both to smithereens."

"How does the minigame work?"

"I'm looking it up now on the wiki. I've got four monitors running. Should be a sec . . . got it. How do you feel about . . . trivia?"

"I've always found it too trivial to have feelings about."

I can be silly too.

"It's a *Themed Trivia* minigame. Answer five questions and you unlock a tumbler. Two tumblers and you can arm the round with a final question. One minute from start to finish."

"Themed?" Are we talking funny anecdotes referencing famous algebraic equations?

"Categories . . . ," says JollyBoy reading the wiki over the chat. "Modern Warfare, Space Exploration, Chinese History, and Sitcoms. Count me out for Chinese History, but I watch sitcoms constantly."

Does he watch Chinese sitcoms?

"All right," I say, formulating a plan on the fly. "Let's get down the stairs as close to the lobby as we can. We'll arm them on the last landing and then toss them through the door to the lobby.

"It'll be just like those cats I was talking about, Questioney. Ready?"

"Not really, but that never stopped me. I like your plan, Jolly. You're a good gamer. Despite all the antics."

"What antics? I take gaming more seriously than any other aspect of my life. That's one of the reasons why I didn't become an organ replacement surgeon."

We head down the last few steps and stop at the double doors leading into the massive WonderSoft-guarded lobby. I arm the remaining grenade and land it near the double doors. Seconds after the smoke from the explosion clears, we can see the doors crumpled and bent, hanging off their hinges. Since WonderSoft hasn't come charging through, it probably means they're waiting for us to do the honors. Of course, all of them have every laser sight they've got trained on the bent and smoking doors. There's just enough space to get the Scorpions through if we can arm them without blowing ourselves up.

"Ready?" I whisper over the chat.

"Nope. But let's try it anyways," squeals JollyBoy.

"Go."

I open the minigame panel on my Scorpion. Two tumblers left to right appear inside a silhouette of the missile. At the far right, an arming switch waits.

"Oh, darn, I got Chinese History," announces JollyBoy. I block him out and start the game.

Sitcoms.

Great. I've watched a lot of them. But they hadn't left a huge impression on me. Modern Warfare would've been more my thing.

Question One: Complete the name of this sitcom: "*Carmichael and the . . . ?*"

Badger.

Correct.

Fifty-five seconds.

According to Freen's theory of sitcoms, what must happen if a message is left for one of the characters by their employer supervisor?

a. The message must be misunderstood.

b. The message will be lost and lack of vital information will alter the course of events.

c. Another character must intercept the message and use it to own their advantage, at which point they will fail miserably as their plans blow up (much like this missile will if you miss this question) in their face, thus causing a confrontation with the intended recipient in which the recipient must then forgive the saboteur for trying to do the wrong thing.

    d.   All of the above.

There was no time to think.

I had seen all three happen in every one of my favorite sitcoms, from *Ripper and the Maid,* to *The Chillingsworths.* I answer d.

Correct.

Forty-two seconds.

Which of these is not a sitcom?

    a.   *Buster and the Browns*
    b.   *My Pal Killdor*
    c.   *Doctor Nurse*

Those sound like really old sitcoms. I have no idea what they were about. They all sound like sitcoms. But I know doctor shows are usually serious and rarely funny. I choose c and wait for the explosion.

Correct.

The first tumbler clicks, and now the second round of questions start with just thirty-one seconds to go.

Question: President Wong had how many daughters in the sitcom *Wongs on the Right*?

Two. I had a crush on the older one. Years later, she ended up dead after a shootout at a food collective on Mars where she was serving out a transportation sentence. Quite a fall for a fictional conservative president's daughter.

Second question: What's the title of the song used for the opening credits of *Chumley*?

Easy. I nailed it again with "Makin' Our Way." That song

always made me want to drink beer. I immediately thought of a McBucks Ultra Lager. Chumley's favorite. I probably had an easy lawsuit for subliminal programming battery, but no lawyer would take it these days.

Third question and nineteen seconds to go. What was Wordsworth's catchphrase in *My Butler*?

    a.   How sweet it is.
    b.   Ha cha cha.
    c.   Really, Shogun.

I loved that show too. Wow, I had no life as a kid. No wonder I'm a game geek. No wonder RiotGuurl or any other woman won't have anything serious to do with me. They probably saw my wasted life from a million miles away. I answer c. and say it to myself in the same droll way the butler used to answer the spoiled little Shogun Yamamoto.

"Reaally, Shogun."

Remember the time when the Shogun changed the bathroom scale to make his wife heavier so she would lose weight? That one killed me.

With eight seconds to go, I reach the arming switch.

A pop-up question appears.

Would you like a KillaKola?

It was ColaCorp's mainline product. Interestingly, they have high-end cola actually called Mainliner. I almost hit yes and prepared to throw the Scorpion through the blasted doors and into the lobby below.

I stop, barely landing my finger on the Y key with the slightest pressure. Not enough to depress.

The Scorpion was a WonderSoft weapon. Why would it ask me about a ColaCorp product? Could the answer be no?

Four seconds to go.

I hit no and my avatar's camo glove flicks the arming switch. I get a green light, showing the weapon is armed.

Back in-game, I lob the rocket through the broken doors and slew my POV over to JollyBoy.

He's gone. Behind me on ambient I hear, "Up here, Perfect-Questioney. I was only kidding; I love Chinese history. The moon colony, tennis champion Chow Wong, that sort of stuff. You might want to get down. In case they throw those things back through the door at us. They could . . ."

He'd left that part out.

A sudden hissing sound turns stereophonic *whoosh,* as the rocket engines within the missiles ignite and go careening across the lobby beyond the blasted doors. First, one explodes, we hear that, and as the building trembles from the force of the internal explosion, once again the emergency lights in the stairwell go out. Then the second one blows up with a tremendous *craacka-boom,* and there's a secondary shattering, as though first a wall had collapsed, followed by a sheet of disintegrating glass.

We raise our weapons and kick our way through the broken double doors at the bottom of the stairs.

The lobby, done up in polished gray marble and anthracite blue, looks like a war zone. One WonderSoft grunt crawls across the floor, his twin reflected in the digital polish and mirrored depth of the surface. JollyBoy puts one of his last bullets into the grunt's back and he stops moving. The rest of the lobby defenders are dead.

"Kiwi? Do you read me?"

"Loud and clear, mate. What's your status?"

"Lobby secure. Building cleared."

"Good, we're going to need it, WonderSoft broke through the line an hour ago with motorized infantry and light armor. We can't hold them much longer. I'll tell everyone to fall back across the bridge."

Down the street, I see our grunts and the rest of our remaining players leaving their fighting positions, running toward the bridge that leads into Song Hua City. In the distance, burning columns of oily smoke tell the tale of exploding WonderSoft personnel carriers.

"That's tonight's game, folks," says the announcer as they cut the live network feed.

The game shuts down, as suddenly the league's musical theme of triumphant horns begins to blare beneath the bleating voice of the announcer for tonight's match.

"What a game; can you believe it, Dale? Looks like ColaCorp pulled one over on the big WonderSoft machine and forced a sudden death round. We're getting word from the commissioner that tonight's game saw WonderSoft fail to achieve certain victory conditions, and due to the efforts of some outstanding team leaders in JollyBoy and Kiwi, with a two-hundred grunt kill streak by ShogunSmile, ColaCorp has earned the right to play another day. Tune in Saturday night when the boys and girls in blue will try again to shut down the red-and-white heroes of ColaCorp. It's going to be an exciting night with some big prizes for the players and also you viewers at home. Plus, this sudden death final match Saturday is going to be really different. There could be a big surprise if either team options the roll. The only clue we can give you for now is 'TimeWarp,' folks. Good night, everybody; this is Don Keckle saying . . . good-bye and keep on fightin'!"

# Chapter 21

I leave ColaCorp. Not because I want to, but because I have to. The Black is just an hour away from going live and I need a machine I can log in with. ColaCorp's IceStorm firewall won't let me get anywhere near a Black nebulae server.

I'm tired, I'm hungry, and I'm homeless.

The Asian kid with the skateboard is waiting outside. His HyperGear glows a soft neon blue as sheets of sleet begin to drive down onto the city.

Will winter ever end?

"Grandpa says you need to log on to Black, chump." He holds his FlexyBoard across his chest as though prepared to defend himself with it. "S'pose to take you to a terminal. You ready? Or are you gonna ask lots of stupid chump questions?"

I'm out of options. Our . . . I mean my apartment, is now . . . not. Along with everything else I own, my computer is most likely ground down to a fine powdery dust.

Any reputable café where I might actually get onto a terminal in less than an hour after the obligatory security background checks isn't going to be usable for tonight's Black tournament. Every public terminal is a public place to get whacked by Mercator and his RPG-toting merc tacticals.

"So do we take the board?" I ask.

The boy's almond eyes find new depths of contempt for me.

Out of the storm above, a high-end charcoal-dusted armored limo signals its arrival with an automated broadcast for pedestrians to clear the area. Its neon blue parking lights arch and swivel through the sleet and off the side of the building as it settles onto the street, adjacent to the curb. I'm impressed.

"Get in," orders the kid.

Limos cost upward of three grand an hour. They're never free. Someone will want something in exchange for all this impressive impression making.

The gray interior cycles from loading red to soft neon green as the driver accelerates back up onto the invisible sky lane above the street.

"Where are we going?" I ask. "Grandpa's house?"

"Airport."

"Grandpa's house is at the airport?"

"No. Plane at airport. Here's your boarding card. You've already been prescreened, so don't make a fuss and act the newb, otherwise you're going to miss your flight while you sit through medical. Got it?"

I give the kid a dismissive shake of my very tired head. It's hard being lectured by a fourteen-year-old boy. After staring out the window for a few seconds at nothing but swirling snow, I clear my throat and try to delve.

"At this point, I might raise a whole bunch of questions about where am I going, and why for that matter. But I think I'll just cut to the chase and ask, What's going on?"

The kid is playing a game on his very high-dollar version of my Petey.

"Listen, you PerfectQuestion, right?" he asks without looking up from some type of lunar colony game. I don't know which one.

"Right," I answer. After all, he did pick me up in front of ColaCorp. Why lie?

"Also, you Wu in very illegal game, right?"

I nod, hoping that if there are any federal livewire devices, they might neglect visual or atmospheric recordings and fail to detect my affirmative nod.

On-screen, the kid shoots down a Chinese lunar bomber. He's awarded fifty thousand points and the exclamation, *Most Indelicate!*

"You have fifty-three minutes left until Black game goes live. You need terminal. Trade jet is refueling for flight to Eastern markets for tomorrow's opening bell. We get you a terminal on the plane more than good enough to run Black game because no trader wants his location being accessed or screened. In fact, perfect for Black. Also, gets you out of city. In case you haven't noticed, people trying to kill you, chump."

Trade jets are the ultimate office for brokers of all types who want to be airborne over markets at opening bell all over the world. Airlines that operate them are secretive, ultrasecure, and very expensive. The kid's right; it's actually a great place to lie low and log on to the Black. If you have that kind of money. The "lots" kind.

"We got you cabin 67C, upper deck. That two stories above main wing so you won't be able to see much of Tokyo tomorrow."

"The cost for those rooms is. . . . I don't even know how much, but, but it's got to be . . ."

"Three million per seat or .05 percent of trading gross per trip. Most brokers pay the three million. It's cheaper."

"Just so I can play a game to make rent."

The boy returns to his game. Why wasn't he in school, instead of wandering around Grand Central that morning? What is he doing out on the streets of New York at nine twenty in the evening in the middle of a blizzard?

"Listen." The boy stops, seems to argue with himself for a moment, then continues. "Grandpa not grandpa. Maybe he like great-grandpa or even great-great-grandpa. Maybe even great-great-great. I just call him Grandpa. He greatest game designer ever known. He go way back. You ever heard of CD-ROM? No. I thought not. Me neither. Grandpa all time talk about old games and old ways. Sometimes I think Grandpa stuck in past. But all the same, I love him. Grandpa say feed the cat. I feed the cat. Grandpa say pick up bag of money from man in high tower. I pick up bag of money from man in high tower. Grandpa say, stay and talk awhile. I stay and talk awhile about old games he love so much. Grandpa say take chump to airport and put him on trade jet. I take you to airport and put you on trade jet. Grandpa didn't say anything about answer stupid chump questions. So I'm not gonna."

The boy turns toward the window and the storm, and five minutes of deep silence later we're settling into the approach flow for the executive terminal at Steinbrenner. Curbside, the kid kicks me out. Before the door closes, he blurts out into the howling wind after me, "Hey, chump!" I turn back.

"Listen, seat is hacked, so don't act stupid. Act like you actually bought it." The door shuts, and the armored limo lifts away from the curb.

Hacked?

Hulking men with the latest in armor and smart weapons guard the fortified entrance to Steinbrenner International. A thin man dressed in a well-cut suit steps forward, smiling.

"Mr. Saxon, we've been expecting you. I'm sorry but there

isn't much time for the lounge, we're just moments from push back. Any luggage we can assist you with tonight?"

I shake my head.

"Our scans indicate you're carrying a baton." I guess my sawed-off broomstick has a fancy French name. "Would you like to check that?" Meaning I'd need to check that.

I pull my only weapon from my trench and hand it over. When he sees that it's a baton in name only, he pulls a face but recovers quickly because he's a professional.

Next, I'm whisked through the curving glass and steel-arched post-retro terminal. Vintage lithographs from past airlines I've never heard of dangle from cables in the ceiling. At the gate, I hand a smiling model wearing a powder blue air hostess outfit, complete with pillbox hat and long white gloves, the hacked boarding card the kid gave me. Her translucent SoftEye scans it, entering all the information on it into the Lufthansa system.

"So glad you could make it tonight, Mr. Saxon." She flaw-lessly fades a flirty wink and turns to another model behind her. "Please escort Mr. Saxon to his suite."

The second model pivots, her long legs turning as her perfect heart-shaped face smiles for me to follow along. "Right this way, Mr. Saxon," she says as if happily surprised. We begin to walk down to the jetway leading to the massive trade jet's main door. "We have you down for a prime steak hamburger topped with Stilton cheese and a port reduction sauce after takeoff," she says over her shoulder, eyes riveted on mine. "This will be accompa-nied by the chef's signature duck-fat fries. I recommend the '32 Takehashi zinfandel. Can we offer you anything else to accom-pany your meal, Mr. Saxon?"

Mr. Saxon?

Who's that guy?

Apparently, I'm that guy for now.

Someone's paying and it surely isn't going to be me.

"What do you have in the way of scotch?"

Her eyes murmur a seductive respect before she names a brand that makes top-shelf malt look and taste like gutter liquor.

"I'll have a bottle of that. And some ice."

"Of course. My name's Candy if you'll be needing anything else."

Is there a suggestion of something off menu? Suddenly I feel like a rube just arrived at PlanetDisney. That won't work on board a trade jet. I need to be an international spy. The kid in the limo told me that acting like all this wasn't the norm was a great way of letting everybody know I didn't belong here.

Hacked.

Another model, pixie-cut blond hair, long-legged and lithesome, leads me down a connecting ramp that jogs to the left as a large glass wall opens up onto the massive Krupp Skyliner, the largest plane ever built. It's a bat winger with eight massive scramjet engines. The fuselage rises up from the hull where the two wings jut way off to the sides. At the rear, two tail fins climb impossibly upward. Its exterior is highly polished shiny metal with a white stripe running above the third tier of windows. Within the white stripe, the name of the airline shimmers in powder blue script. *Lufthansa*. The entire plane is graceful and terrifying all at once.

On board, we pass a lounge where jazz burbles away under the soft tinkling of glass and ice.

"Is this your first trip with us, Mr. Saxon?" asks model number three.

"No, I've done this before," I lie. "It's been awhile though. Any changes?"

"None to speak of." She presses a button for the elevator that will take us up to the executive deck. When the kid's grandpa hacks, he really hacks. Only very high rollers make it to the executive deck. Or so I'd once read in a trashy celebrity blog.

"After takeoff, we'll serve dinner. You can take it in your room if you like, or join us in the dining salon. There's going be a beautiful moon out tonight as we head west over the continent. Once we get up to speed, most passengers sleep until we arrive over Tokyo. Then the trading starts. Then it's on to Thailand, Cairo, and Paris where we'll be landing."

The elevator door opens on the plush white carpet of the executive level. Another model, rich auburn hair in tight, little coils that peek out from beneath her tiny pillbox hat, skin creamy and rosy but only slightly more beautiful than the others, greets me with a cut-crystal tumbler of amber scotch.

"We took the liberty of pouring your first drink, Mr. Saxon. The rest of the bottle will be waiting in your stateroom." Her voice is a husky purr.

I take the glass, nod to her, and taste the smoothest scotch in the world. The fire starts slow and warm and finishes nicely on an oaky note that smells like fall and burning leaves and the earth on a cold day.

Red disappears down a mahogany-paneled corridor all amber swirls and chocolate whorls. Blondy leads me in the opposite direction down the dimly lit corridor until we arrive at suite 67C. She punches in a code, and the crash door scissors away. Inside, I'm greeted by a large mahogany desk with a high-backed leather chair and a small seating area of two vintage brown leather cigar chairs with a chessboard between them. The chess pieces are ornate. Martian Colonists versus Corporate Raiders. The rest of the suite looks like a rich person's library.

"Through there," she says, indicating another smaller door, "is the bedroom." There isn't a way she could have said that and not sounded suggestive.

Then again, maybe it's the scotch.

"In the event of an emergency," she continues, "we will notify you of what to do. In the event of a crash, don't do anything. The cabin will fill with SafetyFoam moments before impact, after the suite has jettisoned itself from the fuselage. But don't worry, that's never happened." She laughs lightly. "A crash I mean." Almost a coy giggle. "Anything else I can offer you for now, Mr. Saxon?" I know the scotch is working when I think about making a crack regarding their turndown service.

Instead I bring myself back to the business at hand, the reason I'm actually here. "The terminal?" I ask, trying to make it sound like an afterthought. Nonchalant.

"We've already keyed in your bio-profile to the desk. Place your palm on the top, like this, and it will activate for you and you only. This is a state-of-the-art microframe from Bang and Olafssen. The display uses a nano-coral technology and I can assure you, the color is dynamic and very lifelike. Very easy on the eyes for long hours of trading. But it really comes into its own if you decide to watch your favorite entertainment. I love *Lavender and Croquet,* that BBC show. Every time I watch it on one of these, it's like I'm actually living in London back in the 1990s. Its processing power and bandwidth are capable of running twenty million individual applications, while handling data at a rate of forty to the tenth power luminal. All our passengers find this more than adequate for their needs."

There wasn't a look on my face. There was no leer at her obvious beauty. No pleasant buzz from the scotch. No stunned amazement that I was going into the Black on a scramjet hurtling at almost the edge of outer space.

I'm blank.

Because it's all too much.

"I'll take that burger now, if you don't mind," I mumble.

"Certainly. I'll be back with your burger shortly, Mr. Saxon," I hear her say from far away. The door silently slips shut behind her.

I check my Petey. I have eighteen minutes until the Black

goes live. I have to eat now because I can't have them in here serving me the burger while I'm in the Black. Plus I'm really hungry. I throw my trench onto one of the cigar leather chairs, use the nickel-brushed restroom and the softest white towel I've ever touched in my entire life, down the scotch, think about another and then think better of it. I probably need to go easy on the scotch until the Black ends tonight.

When I come back into the salon, the blonde is setting up my meal on the now cleared chessboard. Large starched white napkin, silver silverware, logoed tableware that looks expensive because it is. She turns and offers the bottle of zin for my inspection.

"Shall I pour?"

I nod. She could have asked me to light myself on fire and I probably would've just nodded to that too.

"I'm going to keep my eye on you." She leans close, suddenly the professional company line gone. "I can tell you have all kinds of appetites." She tugs at the top button of my shirt and bites her full lip as if trying to stop herself from something she desperately wants to do.

Then I have the dumbest thought ever. Honestly.

*Maybe she really likes guys who like hamburgers.*

When the door slides shut behind her without her giving a backward glance—she's fully confident that I'm watching her legs walk themselves out the door—I throw myself at the burger with seven minutes to go.

Have you ever eaten a burger that was so good, so really good in fact that you had no idea it was the best burger you'd ever eaten until the last bite, in which all the burger-cheese-sauce essence distilled itself down into the last perfect bite of cheeseburger? Unmarred by produce. Have you? Well, every bite of this burger was like that perfect last bite. Not just the last bit. The whole thing. Every bite. It was so good, I almost forgot the zin and ate the entire thing, groaning to myself each time the heady Stilton surrendered to the brash zin. Each flavor draped the grilled medium-rare burger with taste and succulence. Oh, and then there were the duck-fat fries.

Unbelievable. Hot. Salty. Crisp. How french fries should be. But better. The best. Ever.

I finish everything just as the three-minute warning sounds on my Petey. I remove the Black disk from my trench and boot up the desk, still chasing the flavor of the burger across my mouth. I down the last of my first glass of zin in one gulp as *Abandon All Hope, Ye Who Enter* resolves across the desk. The zin perfects the burger experience as it washes over my taste buds, reminding them just how great the burger had been. I sit down at the desk. Yellow lights flash outside my window as the Skyliner taxis toward the main runway. I hear nothing outside. No engines. No wheels. No chatter. A pulse of steady acceleration and we're lumbering, then running, then shooting down the runway for takeoff. A moment of lightness, and we're airborne.

On-screen, my Samurai stands before a steel door emblazoned with a raised skull and crossbones. Behind me, in-game, the zombies of the Halls of the Damned shamble their broken bone-chime dance up the crumbling platform after me. A blunderbuss resounds distantly as I remember Plague, my mortal enemy, is closing in. I reach for the iron door and open it.

# Chapter 22

The Krupp Skyliner is still climbing through the cloud cover over the East Coast as the taste of the burger fades and the zin finds its place inside my head.

For a moment I am just here.

What am I playing for tonight? I might be aboard the world's most elite airborne trading brokerage, surrounded by the beautiful and wealthy, but I'm still broke. Hard to imagine after a burger like that. But I am. So that's what I'm playing for. Money.

Also . . . someone's trying to kill me.

Inside the Black, I enter the room behind the skull-crossed iron door.

Wan blue light filters down through the crumbling latticework of a broken ceiling, ceilings, above. Dusty stone sarcophagi litter a vaulted cathedral. Will there be more of the undead? Vampires even?

Plague will be here soon, and I still need to get to the top of the tower and rescue the child. That's where the real prize money is. The real goal of this weird game. My goal all along and even more so, now.

I check my character and item stats. My biggest concern is the battered *Axe of Skaarwulfe*. It's down to 20 percent effectiveness. I'd used it exclusively for seven hours of solid undead killing in the last session. It didn't have much left in it after all the blood and dismemberment. I'd need another weapon, soon. If I can find the Samurai's blade, then I might do some serious business. After that, my next concern is health. I'm down to 54 percent.

I move forward, the *chock . . . chock . . . chock* of the Samurai's wooden sandals the only sounds within the crypt over ambient. I examine some of the bas-relief sarcophagi as I pass. Intricate scroll-worked bats and fanged cartoonish demons, cobwebbed and dusty, cover their sides. Carved into the lids are runes, a horned script full of winged flourishes, stamped in black slate. Obviously something important lies within.

If one lid comes off, do all the lids come off? Some sort of trap. Are all the sarcophagi trapped? Can I handle whatever's in even one of them? And what about all of them at once? There are nineteen sarcophagi. Nineteen seems like a lot for just the Samurai. Just me. If what lies within each isn't boss level, then it, or they, must surely be just below the highest NPC monster rank. The whole dark cathedral gloom of the place seems to telegraph something important. At the far end of the crumbling space, a wide stone stairway leads up toward a mist-shrouded landing and deep shadows beyond.

I reach the stairway, leaving all nineteen sarcophagi untouched. I haven't made up my mind as to what to do next. I know I need to move fast or face Plague with a weapon that doesn't seem to have much left in it. Inside at least one of the sarcophagi, there might be a weapon I can use. But nothing is for free. Nothing's ever free.

And why is Plague so hot to kill me?

Then there's Morgax.

Whoever it was on the other end of the red phone at Seinfeld's wants him dead. After that . . . I can ask for anything. "Anything" covers a lot of rent and so much more. *Anything* is really a big word when you think about it.

And then there are other things beyond the power of the word *anything*.

Could the nameless voice get Sancerré back? Save ColaCorp from losing Song Hua Harbor and pro-team status? That's a lot to ask. Maybe he just meant five million dollars or so.

Would I ask for any of those other things instead of a big pile of money?

I move the Samurai up the crumbling gray stone steps. Thick strands of cobweb stretch across recessed shadows in dark places. A figure steps away from the wall, out of the dark and into the dim blue light. It's a bearded old man wearing dusty gray robes.

"Hail, Samurai. I'm Callard the wandering philosopher and imminent nonplayer character."

I enable voice on the desk and see the active mic button illuminate inside the desktop display. Fancy.

"Hail," I reply. Role-playing.

"I believe you met my grandson earlier. How was your burger?"

"So you're Grandpa?"

"Something like that," begins Callard in his creaky old man's voice. "I'm more like the boy's great-great-grandfather. But why waste the time of the young on such meaningless details."

"I guess . . . ," I begin, trying to wrap my head around who Callard is and what he really knows about me. In the end, I'm not sure of anything. But it's too late, and Plague is too near for anything else but honesty. " . . . I'm in your debt for getting me out of New York. But . . . I'm not sure what you want out of me."

"Follow me." Callard turns and walks up the squat stairs

within the tomb. At the top, a massive circular door lies sunken into the ancient rotting wall. Leering fanged ogres in stonework relief hold dusty chains across it.

"Beyond that door"—Callard points to the large circular barrier—"lies the crypt of Kal Tum, the Ogre warlord of the Gaash Mountains. Servant of the Dark Prince."

I check the rows of waiting sarcophagi, below and behind us. Anticipating Plague.

"Great," I murmur, almost to myself. "In-game lore manufactured by some hack writer to add depth and texture. In the end, it all breaks down to getting the loot to get better loot. Right?"

"Often true enough, Samurai," replies the world-weary sage. "But this world is something more. Something I've worked on my entire life. Do you read books? I mean, have you ever read a book?"

"Of course . . ."

"I mean a real book. An actual book with paper pages and binding. Have you?

I pause. Remembering. Trying to remember.

"Yeah . . . once. My mom had one she'd kept. It was called *Stuart Little*. I read it over and over one summer when I was a kid."

Callard smiles. It makes his face come alive. Like there's real joy being displayed by all that EmoteWare. "That's a beautiful book," he says. Then, "Children don't read much anymore, but this lore, as you call it, was once the stuff of books I wrote when I was young man. Books about mighty kingdoms of elves and men, and epic battles between the dark and the light, and mysterious wanderers who journeyed to lost places and fought evil beasts, rescued maidens, and gained fabulous treasures. Many, many tales. I've lived in this world my entire life, Samurai."

He seems lost, remembering, in his fantastic past.

"So how do I fit into all this?" I ask, bringing him back, too aware of Plague's impending arrival.

"You are Wu the Samurai. An ancient and fated hero who . . ."

"No, I mean me, the guy at the keyboard who seems caught between a madman bent on ruling the world through advertisement, and an in-game hunter named Plague. Me, Callard or Grandpa or whatever your name is. Listen, I'm grateful for the help, but what's your angle? Why help me?"

"I know you, PerfectQuestion. I've watched you play. You possess skill, which is important, but you also possess honor and a love for the art of the game. I've been holding the Samurai back for a very long time. It's been difficult to hide him from these thugs. Wealthy patrons have begged for his code. But . . . I didn't feel any of them were truly worthy enough to do what must be done. Until you came along, PerfectQuestion. Though you don't know it yet, you too are noble. As noble as the Samurai is.

"My angle is . . ." Callard sighs. "Well, I'll need to tell you my story. We have a few moments until your nemesis shows up. I've dropped an entire legion of undead Centurions of the East in his path. All of them are from my book *The Thousand Dead*. It'll take a bit of time for Plague to chew through them. But I suspect he will soon enough."

"Who is he and why does he want me dead? Or my character dead?"

"I don't know. In the novels, Plague is a despicable assassin. He was the nemesis of my greatest hero. Many times they fought. When that hero went down, it was Plague who'd finally destroyed him. Although he too lost his life."

"And you don't know who bought his code?"

"Private bidder. Plus, it's a Black game. Identity is a treasure worth guarding. I knew something was up once I authorized you to take Wu into the game. The game started slowing down, and we realized we were under attack from an unknown entity. That was the interruption. Then, while you were in the Oubliette, a private bid came in and . . . well, I had no choice. The decision was out of my hands. Plague went after you. I hacked into the server, hoping you'd look in the mirror. Then I warned you, remember?"

"So, no idea then?"

"None as to his real identity. It seems he merely wants to kill you just as he did the Samurai in my books. I imagine he could be some deranged fan of one of my novels. If he can't play Wu, well, then he may be trying to be the arbiter of Wu's demise."

"So what's your angle, for the umpteenth time?"

"Ah, yes. Well, I need you to save the child, PerfectQuestion. Money: none. Prizes: what you find along the way. I control very little of the game now. These thugs who run the game are running a very aggressive virusware to keep me out of the system. But if you rescue the child: gratitude much, my friend."

"I don't follow."

"Long story short, PerfectQuestion. Way back at the beginning of the century, I was a writer. I wrote a lot of fantasy books. Books about this world. Fans by the millions. For a while I was a rock star. But that seldom lasts. Games, I always played them. The things I could tell you. These games, these things you play, they have a history. I was a child at the beginning of that history. One of my earliest memories is playing Pong at a house with a tennis court. That had to be the 1970s. The '80s came and there were arcade games. A quarter from your dad after dinner for the Pac-Man machine in the lobby when your family went out to a restaurant. Your only thought, as you ate fajitas or potato skins, was the machine, the game, and what you might do within its confines. If I say too much more, I might turn our time into a mere history lesson. But in time, games turned into worlds, and eventually after the writing, I began to build this world in secret. I hired the best programmers rock-star money could buy, layering texture and detail with each fresh million in royalties into my own little living world. In the end, years after I was no longer a rock star, I'd used up almost all the money that remained from my novels in bringing them to life. Then I began borrowing, hedging, refinancing the engines and optimizing the graphics as an army of designers was reduced to a simple platoon. Finally, in the end it was just me. And the debt. In hindsight, I can say this: it became a bit of an obsession.

"But there were some even more obsessed than I was with this world. In time the collectors, fans, and others wanted my living world after they'd found out I'd been building it all along. They'd pay me money to run their favorite character from the books. Some just wanted a taste from their long-gone youth. Others, a new experience. In the end, I borrowed unrepayable amounts of money to protect it for just another year. I wasn't really thinking. I was just . . . I don't know, honestly, what I was doing, what my goal was. Like I said, I was obsessed. And the money I borrowed, I borrowed from the worst kind of people."

"The Black?"

"Exactly. Now they use my world to run their contests and provide a place for the sick and twisted fantasies of their customers. It's totally corrupted now."

"So how does saving the child at the top of the tower change the fact that you owe the mob a grip of money?"

"The child at the top of the tower holds a doomsday file. Whoever rescues her can execute the file and crash the world. The whole thing, down to its runtime code, will disappear if that file enters the main stream of the nebulae server. These thugs who call themselves the Black, they don't know that. No one does but you and me. Whoever rescues that child can crash the world, or do whatever they want with it. The Black . . . they think it's just a big prize. A million dollars. But I've stolen most of the money, changed the code, and inserted a worm that will go live should the winner of the contest choose to execute the file, which I'm hoping they'll do out of anger at being cheated out of their million bucks. Most players would do it, or at least I hope they would, but I can't absolutely count on them to do it. But you, PerfectQuestion, you've got a chance to win and if you do, I want you to destroy my game."

"But you'll destroy your life's work!"

"I can live with that."

I thought about the world. I thought about people who destroyed things, fragile things that were little more than hope and someone else's dreams. I thought about Sancerré.

"I understand," I mumble. I did.

"Somehow I knew you would, PerfectQuestion. You truly are a noble Samurai at heart."

"I seriously doubt that," I say with a snort. "What am I gonna do against an army of deranged gamers, the Black mafia, and Plague?" I can hear myself whining and I don't like it. I didn't sign up for this. I'd signed up to get rich, quick.

Callard laughs. A chuckle really. Then he speaks. "Well, it's about to get very difficult indeed."

"My axe hasn't got much left in it; anything you can do about that, Callard?"

"About that, I actually can do something."

Callard walks over to a dusty cobwebbed urn lying within a deep shadow near the wall, and reaching in, he pulls out a cloth-wrapped item.

"I hid *Deathefeather* here when they made me cripple the Samurai. Once I managed to drop you into the Oubliette, it was easy for me to rig the randomizer algorithm so that the end gate would transport you to the desert and the Pool of Sorrows. From there, all you had to do was kill the Troll and survive the Halls of the Damned. Then it's a straight line to the crypt of Kal Tum. With the sword now, you'll be quite formidable. Take it and enter the crypt. On the other side, you will find the courtyard of the Marrow Spike. At the top, the child and the doomsday file."

"Are you sure, Callard? Are you sure you really want to destroy this world? It's a beautiful MMO and it sounds like you've spent a very long life working on it."

"This . . . this abomination isn't what I wrote about. These aren't my stories anymore. If it can't be the way I wrote it to be, then I'd rather burn it to the ground."

Seems a little extreme. But I owe him one. I wasn't getting murdered, "accidentally," in an Internet café back in New York. So the least I could do for him was destroy his hijacked life's work.

A resounding *craaack* echoes across the empty burial cathedral. Shattering stone rumbles distantly as the ring of metal being struck repeatedly punctuates a rising bass grumble of impending doom.

"It's Plague. He'll be through the wall shortly. Hurry now, into the crypt." Callard hands my Samurai the cloth-wrapped sword. It appears in my inventory.

"I'll hold them for a bit while you get the chains off the door," vows an overdramatic Callard. "It'll be my 'you shall not pass' moment." He pauses as if I should know the reference.

"All right, then," he mutters to himself, realizing I haven't gotten it. "I'll . . . do something about Plague."

I turn the Samurai to the Ogre warlord's crypt and break the chains with the *Axe of Skaarwulfe*. Behind me, I can hear the rattle of Plague's skeletal soldiers entering the expanse of the shadowy vault, then the wheezing cough that seems a constant companion of my Samurai's mortal enemy.

"How did you find out my professional tag, Callard?"

"Oh, I am all over the Internet. There's a lot more to this old man than meets the eye."

I roll the stone door to the inner crypt aside and turn as I hear the raspy grinding of lids being pushed up and away from sarcophagi. I watch as bat-winged vampires rise like wraiths from their sleep. Each is impossibly tall, each a pale, bloodless thing.

"All's fair, Plague . . . ," I say to myself as I enter the tomb of the Ogre warlord, leaving my mortal enemy to deal with the vampires.

# Chapter 23

Equipping the sword brings up a new menu of special attacks. Skills and abilities in other menus, previously grayed out, also come online.

"As long as the sword is equipped, I can chat with you," says Callard out of the ether, his voice as though from the bottom of a garbage can. The face of the sage wavers dimly in the reflection of the flat of the sword's shining blade. "But I can't be of much help right now. The administrators are watching. Wu, you've got to get to the top of the tower and rescue the child. Once you do, activate the doomsday file and destroy this world. I can't offer you anything other than what I've hacked for you already. But maybe you're the kind of player who might just accept the gratitude of an old writer as payment enough. Maybe. I don't know anymore. But you're my only hope . . ." He chuckles to himself as if remembering some lost memory. "Samurai."

"What's between me and the kid?" I ask.

"Merely hell, Samurai. Merely hell," he replies and disappears.

Behind me, the vampires are whirling about Plague and his remaining skeletal warriors. I hear the bang of deflected attacks rebounding heavily off their shields. The massive sculpted crypt behind and below me is littered with dusty bone fragments and rusty, broken weapons as nightmare battles nightmare. I'm standing in front of the gargantuan bronze shield-door, embossed with those fanged and horny runes spiraling from the outer edge in to the center. As I stare at the runes, they suddenly rearrange themselves into readable words.

Cringe, slave, and know you are both feeble and without honor. Within lies the still mighty Kal Tum, warlord of the Ogre tribes of Gaash, breaker of the Walls of Far Kattir, murderer, beast-slayer, man-eater, and eternal foe of Kurm the Venomous.

Inspecting *Deathefeather*'s stats, I find as I'd suspected I would, that one of its minor abilities allows the wielder to read forgotten runes and ancient languages.

Sword drawn and held back with one hand, ready to strike, I tap once on the giant bronze shield-door. I hear a hollow ring that echoes out past the barrier in front of me and seems to carry off into hidden spaces beyond the door. As I move close to the shield-door, a small menu opens, asking me if I'm sure I want to move the shield. I want to. The hands of the Samurai push the edge and center of the shield, as his straining grunt erupts across ambient. The massive rune-worked bronze shield slowly slides aside. Beyond is a dark corridor filled with shadows and patches of sickly yellow light.

I hear Plague's blunderbuss fire and fire again. Vampires are moaning in some kind of torment, hurling curses, as they swirl into dying piles of ash and dust.

I don't have much time left before I'll be face-to-face with Plague.

I enter the crypt, hearing the squish of wet mud instead of the dry *chock* of the Samurai's sandals. Dim alcoves set at intervals along the walls lead off into foggy distances. I swivel the POV of the Samurai and inspect the darknesses within the alcoves. *Deathefeather* doesn't give off any light like the *Axe of Skaarwulfe* did. Down dark narrow side passages, the fog-shrouded skeletons of tall Ogre warriors dressed in tattered and rusting armor, axes and spears crossing their chests, wait. Their giant-browed skulls and broken fanged teeth seem to scowl at me across the distances. I'm sure it's only a matter of time before these things come back to life. Or undeath.

I continue forward, ignoring the side passages. There's always Plague to consider, so I keep moving. I know I'm not ready to confront him yet. As I bring up *Deathefeather's* menu, one ability catches my eye. *Harvest.* If everything, if all these undead Ogres, come at me at once, as I thought might happen back in the Vampire's vault, then this ability seems just right. If I have to deal with the Ogre Prince Kal Whatever, and what I assume is some sort of ceremonial guard, then I'll punch *Harvest* and see what happens.

A brief description of *Harvest* reads, "When the Samurai is surrounded and outnumbered, he becomes as the reaper's sickle in the fall of great harvest at summer's end." Beyond that, what happens next is anybody's guess. But it seems to be his most powerful ability.

I've passed nine alcoves of waiting undead Ogre warriors when the trap springs. There's a sudden, impulsive *twaaang* over ambient sound. Then I hear a slow sandy grinding, building, bone knuckles cracking in anticipation of some impending battle.

All of it, all around me.

Ahead of me. Behind me.

The Ogre skeletons, eyeless sockets filled with yellow malignant hate, shamble from their waiting places, down their passages toward me. I take a quick cut with *Deathefeather* at the nearest one and watch as the thick bony arm of the Ogre comes off with a simple clean cut, dropping the spear it carried in its hand. Instantly the wide battle-axe in its other hand comes over its shoulder, cutting a murderous arc right down on top of me. I leap back as the axe sinks with a wet pulp into the marshy floor. A quick dash forward followed by a slash, and *Deathefeather* takes the other arm. The dying warrior leans forward, wicked greenish fangs wide and open, and attacks with a savage bite, nailing me for 10 percent damage. The snapping jaw cracks loudly, startling me.

I'm down to 44 percent Vitality. I cut wide with the blade, this time aiming for the neck and removing the Ogre's skull from his corpse. It remains standing for just a moment, then collapses into a pile of bones and old rotten armor.

The eight behind me crowd forward as more of them surge out of the alcoves ahead. Time for *Harvest*. I punch the hot key and watch as the frame rate of my POV begins to under-crank, producing a slow motion effect. No lonely Japanese guitar this time. Instead there's only silence, as superimposed red autumn maple leaves drift down across the screen, falling toward the ground. The sound of wind, soft like a reed flute, plays barely, then picks up and the Samurai charges forward. I aim him at the nearest rising monster, two slashing swords and an ogreish raspy roar waiting for me. Taiko drums explode across the soundtrack like the steady rolling gallop of some powerful elephant running me down. The Ogres, all of them moving far too slowly, raise their weapons, opening their overpronounced, underbitten fangs wide in roars of groaning hate-rage as I drive forward, raising *Deathefeather* with both hands. The Taiko drums thunder an urgent cadence as my blade becomes a sweeping scythe, a blur, three times its length. I drive through the closing wall of creatures, slicing heads and torsos, armor and axes, anything that stands in my way.

My Samurai charges forward, deeper into the maelstrom of ancient rotting Ogre warriors, and the drums continue to thunder louder and louder, as if at any moment the world's heart must burst and surely end. The speakers inside the Skyliner suite roar out with startling clarity and I wonder, briefly, if I should turn down the volume. But I know these suites are designed for total privacy. Traders of millions, billions, and, yes, sometimes even trillions need that level of privacy. So I enjoy the battle overture while fighting for my online life. After all, how many times am I going to get the chance to game in total luxury at thirty-five thousand feet?

Ahead, ancient Ogres heedlessly gather too close and thick, as if hoping to bury me with their numbers

As if butter can stop a blowtorch.

The passage opens into a wide chamber as I cut through the last of the dying, disintegrating giants. The drums crescendo suddenly and stop with a harsh slap in the moment after I've crossed into the circular chamber and driven the tip of the blade into the skull of the largest Ogre, a seated giant, twice the size of the others. Gleaming golden armor and two wicked axes remain motionless as the giant's misshapen head explodes in chalky green dust. The body falls back onto the throne it's started up from.

"Kal Tum, I presume."

How much time do I have until Plague clears the vampires and races up through the last of the Ogres?

The room seemingly ends here, going nowhere else. I move forward, searching the throne. On the left-hand side there's a knob. I right-click it and am asked if I'd like to open the treasure room.

Indeed, I would like that very much.

A panel behind the throne slides away, revealing a pile of gleaming gold coins and ingots beyond. I move into the hidden room and click on the gold. I'm rewarded with two thousand dollars waiting in a coded private account. I enter the password I'll need to retrieve it.

Where were you a week ago?

Then again, when I think about it, if I'd had it then, I'd have paid a month's rent on a now vacant lot.

I decide to let the timing be perfect.

The blast of Plague's blunderbuss fills the once Ogre-overrun passage I've just come through. I hear more Ogre skeletons rushing through the darkness with their grinding bone-chime walk and leathery whispery howls.

A ladder leads upward to a high ceiling in the treasure room. I climb it, and when I reach the ceiling, a recessed stone seems to be some kind of trapdoor. It's the only possible exit I can find. Clicking on it does nothing. I glance below, not fully expecting to see Plague. But there he is, reloading his hand cannons. The skeletons have not survived.

Maybe it's time to face him.

As he loads his pistols, he spits out a wet cough, emitting green flecked wisps of glowing smoke. Probably some sort of personal poison attack, hence the name Plague. Before I attack him I should know what it does. Otherwise . . . I roll over my weapon choices menu and select *Bare Hands*. I place them over the inset slab in the ceiling.

The word *Push* flares in gray across the screen. I tap the mouse and the gray begins to change to blue. Plague fires his hand cannons and grazes me. My health drops to 25 percent. A red mist sprays out along the edges of the desk in the suite as blood drops spatter my screen. I furiously tap the mouse as the blue letters of *Push* change to green then red and finally flames erupt around them. The slab moves aside as blinding sunlight floods my screen. My vision blurs out. I climb up into the sunlight as Plague fires again. Over ambient, a smoking ball whistles loudly past me and shoots off into the bright blinding dazzle I'm climbing into.

I'm blind.

When my screen clears, showing me a washed-out and faded image at first, I'm standing on a stone terrace that juts out from a gargantuan wall, curving away in both directions toward the horizon. The wall is made up of massive blocks of sun-faded stone. Below, a dazzling blue-and-silver palazzo, tiled to look like a postmodern version of a river, separates me from another massive wall. Beyond that, I see the leaning pile that is the tower.

The Marrow Spike.

In the palazzo, live players—they have to be—fight to the death in the shadows of two huge doors that form the gate that probably leads into the tower courtyard.

I'm down to 25 percent health. I have no idea how I'm going to get past the players slaughtering other players below and into the courtyard of the tower beyond.

Much less climb it.

Much less rescue the child.

In the polished reflection of *Deathefeather,* I can see the face of Callard wavering, as though he's underwater. The chat icon is live.

"It's a battle royale, Samurai," he begins. "I suggest you find another player and take him out quickly, then loot his corpse. You may find a healing potion or something to assist you in your quest, or at least keep you alive a little longer. Then enter the courtyard and climb the tower."

"Just like that," I say.

"Yes," he replies, ignoring my sarcasm. "Something just like that."

I scan the portico below the wall. The bodies of fantastic creatures lie torn to pieces, hacked apart or smoking amid spreading pools of blood. Beyond the mangled and dying, other players are still locked in a fight to the death, trading blows with fantastic weapons.

A Minotaur, muscles like iron bands rippling, holds aloft a demonic-looking blue-skinned dark Elf maiden. She's flailing wildly at him with two dripping daggers. Seconds later, the Minotaur rips her in two and, tossing her aside, grabs a massive spear sticking from the ground nearby. He hurls it through the back of a silver-haired warrior in full blood-spattered plate, wielding a flaming claymore, who's just finished disemboweling some sort of half man, half snake. A net and trident fall from the snake man's claws.

Near the gate, the classic Wizard type waves wildly with his staff at a small fierce Goblin with wide dangling ears. The Goblin's using a short sword and battered shield embossed with a red fist. He leaps in at the Wizard, cutting at his robes. The Wizard goes down on one knee as he throws sparking, exploding powder directly into the Goblin's narrow eyes. The armored Goblin stumbles backward, slipping in a pool of slick blood and guts. The Wizard raises his hands and shoots a dark blast of ozone-crackling energy at the Goblin, exploding him into a spray of guts and armor.

The Minotaur wrenches the ironwood spear from the back of the dying silver-haired warrior and heaves it once more. This time it hits the Wizard and lifts him off the ground, pinning him to the brass-bound oaken gates of the inner courtyard with a resounding *thuunnk* above the chaos of *bang* and *clang*, sword and shield.

I check the open trapdoor and see that Plague's almost to the top of the ladder, climbing with one hand as he trains his blunderbuss on the opening for a kill shot.

I scroll through the Samurai's menus, looking for something useful. I find nothing. In the *Innate Powers* menu, I notice the Samurai can assume selected defensive postures.

I check the battle in the palazzo and watch as a top-knotted half Orc, wielding two broken swords and bleeding thick gobs of black blood that's seeping through his ornate bronze chain armor, falls back on one knee. A shaven-headed monk rushes him with a twirling staff, planting it, then leaping forward with a flying kick. The half Orc gives ground and cuts the leg off the monk with one savage swipe of a broken blade. Dripping bloody spray decorates the palazzo's river of tile. The half Orc follows this with the other blade, jamming what remains of it straight into the middle of the robed body of the monk. A second later he's bent over and looting the dead monk's inventory.

Now's the time.

I leap from the terrace on the massive wall, landing in a defensive posture. Immediately, a Witch Doctor in full juju mask lunges ferociously at me hoping for the death blow as he circles his shrunken-headed mace above and throws a purple-silver powder across the space between us.

I click a hot key and draw *Deathefeather.* I go all in with my first attack. At 25 percent health, how many attacks can I expect? Not many. So it'll have to be everything up front. I let the Witch Doctor have it with the Samurai's power attack, *Focused Strike,* and cut him in half. I quickly check his inventory and take everything, barely noticing the thirty-five hundred dollars I pocket.

In the Black, it's winner take all.

He doesn't have any healing potions. I head toward the wounded half Orc who's desperately parrying a blow from a one-winged, badly bleeding Balrog who seems to have been everybody's whipping boy. He's covered in cuts and scars, but he's still the scariest-looking thing in the fight. The Balrog heaves a huge flaming sword back over his shoulder, preparing to bring it down onto the half Orc warrior.

I'm running straight for the back of the half Orc, the demon rising above him.

A rangy Elven Knight in scroll-worked armor, carrying a long sword and shield, charges me from the side, trying to cut me off, or just cut me down. I roll to the right and run, not daring to start parrying with so little health. I move forward through a knot of engaged warriors, cutting the head off an unsuspecting lizard man as I pass. I have no time to check his inventory. The Elven Knight's rushing, closing fast.

I circle back around the main body of the fight.

I'm behind the Balrog now. I have a moment to try and at least get him from behind. The Elven Knight has gotten caught up in the thick knot of strange warriors I've just made it through. If there's time, I might get the Balrog and even the half Orc in one go before the Elf can fight his way through to me. Just before I ram *Deathefeather* through the scaly hide of the Balrog's leathery back, a massive spear crashes through the demon's neck, spraying inky blood everywhere. I continue the charge beyond the toppling Balrog and ram the surprised half Orc straight through the sternum all the way to the hilt of *Deathefeather*.

I check his inventory.

Looting.

Twenty-four thousand dollars. Two broken magic swords, an item called the *Unending Rope of the Highwayman,* and a gift certificate for a state-of-the-art designer SoftEye from HardImagination, an after-market purveyor of WonderSoft products. I take everything. I don't have time to check the rope's properties. When my health doesn't immediately rise— and why should it, it's just a rope and I don't expect much out of it—I continue on.

Now the Elven Knight comes down hard on me. His sword

emits a haunting, ringing chime each time he brings it in close. I'm dodging and only chancing a parry when there's no other choice. He's backing me to the gate leading into the courtyard of the tower. If I don't get out of this, I'm going to lose all my recently looted loot.

Tragedy.

When I can't give any more ground, I retaliate after a parry and smash his armored leg with a *Bash* attack from *Deathefeather*. In return, the Elf Knight tries to *Bash* me with his shield, but I sidestep and he careens off the gate instead. He turns quickly, trying to prevent me from running him through from behind, swinging wide with his singing broadsword. I duck low, waiting for the blade to pass.

I can't use *Serene Focus* yet. I'm not sure of what's going on behind me. If I use it now and I get into a bad spot in the next few minutes, I've got nothing left.

I click the power attack and watch as the Samurai's hands double-grip *Deathefeather's* hilt and extend in the blink of an eye, pushing the blade through the Elf's armored stomach and out his back.

Simple.

Deadly.

Done.

The Elf vomits blood all over my screen. I start to loot, then hear the bloodcurdling *Raaaawwwrrr* of a Nordic-type warrior across the suite's speakers. I close the looting screen just in time to watch him try and bury his huge battle-axe in my head. I step back, lowering *Deathefeather* as the dead Elf slides off and onto the ground. Then, aiming at the onrushing, horned-helmet-wearing warrior's throat, just above his armor, I swing and take his head off, cleanly.

Someone has to have a healing potion.

I start searching the piles of slaughtered corpses. I collect another ten thousand in cash as well as a box of Kobe steaks, deliverable on demand, anywhere in the world, and a deep space blue Omega Star Master watch from a private jeweler in Zurich.

But no healing potions.

From the far side of the blood-spattered palazzo, Plague walks forward, his thumping boots the only sound on the river-tile paving stones, both pistols out. The green miasma from his hacking cough permeates the air around him. He steps over corpses, making a straight line for me. There's no way I'm going to dodge two blasts at close range.

"Stop!" roars the Minotaur, the only other standing player left in the palazzo.

Plague halts.

I glance around. There are dead bodies everywhere. It's just three of us now.

The lethal Minotaur.

Plague.

And me and my 25 percent health.

Everyone else is very dead.

A quiet wind sweeps out of the low desert mountains that surround this lost city. A lone piece of parchment flutters across the paving stones and is gone.

"The Samurai is badly wounded," growls the Minotaur. "If you want to kill him . . . then you'll have to kill me first." His in-game voiceware is gruff and husky.

"This ain't yer (*cough*) fight," spits out a hoarse Plague. "Why should you care enough to die before he does?"

I'm wondering that myself.

"You're just a player," rumbles the Minotaur. "Nothing more, sickly man. If you knew the books, knew the world in which we fight . . . there is so much more to it than Rolexes and Ultra-vettes, and money. So much more."

He won an Ultravette! No way! This guy's good.

"I may not know the story. But I know this Samurai (*cough*). I know him (*cough*) very well."

The Minotaur hefts his spear above his bulging shoulder in one sudden movement, then asks, "How fast are you, sickly man?"

Plague raises both guns with his gloved hands, thumbing back the hammers as they rise. The Minotaur flings the heavy spear as both cannons erupt.

Over ambient, I hear twin short wet *thumps* following each other, as both speeding balls strike the wide barrel chest of the Minotaur.

Plague, still standing, looks down at the place where the spear has impaled him. Then he drops to his knees and, a moment after that, falls over dead.

I race to the Minotaur and check his Vitality bar. He's down to 10 percent health and falling. I rifle his inventory and find the health potion I need.

Inside the suite on the Skyliner, we bounce through a little turbulence. Unusual for a Skyliner, or so I'd heard.

"Why'd you do that?" I ask the Minotaur over chat.

His health is now at 6 percent. Still falling. Plague's musket balls must come with some sort of secondary infection side effect.

"In the books . . . ," begins the Minotaur as though he's actually injured. A role player. This game was much more to him than just . . . well, what he'd said earlier.

So much more.

"In the books, ours was the greatest of friendships, Samurai. That is why. We first journeyed together in the book *Another Place, Far Off* and over the course of many others. Now that this world has been hijacked . . . I guess . . . I guess I just wanted it to be something more. To be like the books." His health meter falls to 1 percent. My cursor hovers over his potion.

Double left-click and it's mine. Right-click and I can save him.

I right-click. I guess I'm that kind of guy.

My Samurai jams the health potion down the Minotaur's muzzle as I watch his Vitality bar begin to rise.

I know what it's like when you wish something was more than what it actually is. I wish Sancerré had stayed. I wished I'd been enough for her.

"What's your name, big guy?" I ask the Minotaur.

"Morgax."

# Chapter 24

Morgax patches me up using first-aid skills the Minotaur has in one of his menus. I end up at 45 percent. Then we loot the bodies of the slain players.

"How'd you get here?" I ask him in chat.

"When the game started," he begins, his role-playing voiceware making him sound like a talking bull, "I was hanging from a meat hook in the kitchen of an inn at the foot of Korzum Pass. Once I got out of there, I had to fight my way up the Cliffs of Madness and onto the pass into the Lost Desert. Then I found a cave that turned out to be the lair of some player from Saudi Arabia running a green dragon with a penchant for gambling. Long story short, I made it out of there and down to the Whore's Gate of Zandsabad. In the books, Zandsabad is the desert city of the lost and the damned. It was pretty much that. I fought my way through the outer ruins. I got chased by some cult group that plays as a clan and meets online. Lots of 'em. I had to fight my way through the bazaar, and then I finally made it to the inner ring of the city, where we are now. That's where most of the players are headed. This is where the fighting started. Apparently no one wants to let anyone else get through the gate without making sure everyone who survived the city is dead. That's how the big fight started. How about yourself?"

I tore my eyes away from all the loot in my inventory menu.

"I started in a dungeon cell I thought was below the tower. Then when the game reset the first night, just after it started, I ended up in a place called the Oubliette."

"The game never restarted the first night," interrupted Morgax. "But the sessions have been pretty seamless from the get-go since then. There can't be many players left by now."

I wanted to ask him who he was, where he was from, so I'd have some clue as to why the mysterious voice on the other end of the red phone at Seinfeld's wanted him dead, in-game. But in the Black, it's not just considered extremely bad form to ask personal information, it just isn't done. No one's going to divulge it. Regardless of what Callard knows about me. Everybody thinks they're safely anonymous inside the Black.

"We should still have another hour of game time," says Morgax. "Let's head into the courtyard. Maybe we can get into the tower before the game shuts down for the night."

I drew my sword, following the Minotaur through the gate. Even though I had just over seventy-four thousand dollars, I could always use a little more.

I could have killed him with a power attack as he turned his back on me and walked toward the massive gate. There was something attractive about being able to name your price to an anonymous genie even if you had to do something dark to get paid. I guess it's that hit man fantasy we all have.

But murder wasn't on my price list. I know it's just a game. But so is life. And how we play the game has something to do with how we live our life.

An hour later, the game shuts down and again thanks us for not dying. We'd spent the hour searching the tower courtyard and found no way into the Marrow Spike other than the obvious un-openable door at the base. We'd even thought about going up the side, but that didn't seem possible either. The tower is very high; one fall and that's it. Game over.

In the final moments of the night's game, I slew my Samurai's POV upward to look at the height of the tower in the last of the fading apocalyptic orange daylight. Stars reveal themselves in the deeper blues above. Staring upward, the tower seems crazy and impossible, architecturally speaking. At points, it leans one way only to be counterbalanced by bulbous expansions of stone-work. At the distant top, smoke-blackened parapets far beyond our reach lay, spreading outward, guarding whatever waits for us up there.

The child.

The witch.

The doomsday file.

When the game ends, I shut down the desk and lean back in the soft leather executive chair. We're over Los Angeles now. It's four in the morning. The dull hum of the aircraft envelopes me as I lean back and close my eyes. I can't remember the last time I slept. The subways? What kind of sleep was that? I have a lot of money and prizes now. But I need an address to have the prizes shipped to. And how far can I ride this plane? At what point would the crew find out I was on a hacked pass? And then what? Put me in airplane jail? Toss me out at altitude screaming over the Pacific in the middle of the night?

Things have changed. Just a few days ago I was fighting for rent money, now here I am holding more cash than I've ever had in my whole life.

Electronically speaking.

I'm free.

Next stop . . . MegaTokyo.

I pour myself another scotch and open the door to the bedroom. A full-size bed, immaculate white sheets, and soft fluffy pillows call to me in the dim light of the interior cabin. I unwrap a chocolate left on the pillow. Gray sea salt and bacon—it's great. Moments later, I'm asleep.

In the morning I wake up tangled in sheets. Bright sunlight shifts across the bedroom as the sun comes into view through the porthole for a moment. We're turning, banking. We must be over Tokyo in a holding pattern so the brokers can cover the market. Literally.

I splash some cool water on my face, using the expensive salt scrub and foaming soap scented with sandalwood to wash my face, and then dress. I know there's a restaurant on board. And a bar. Food sounds real good.

As soon as I open the door an air hostess greets me. The blond one.

"Is everything all right, Mr. Saxon? I can have breakfast served in your cabin, if you like."

"Everything is perfect, Miss . . ."

"Trixie."

"Miss Trixie?"

"Just Trixie. Or whatever you prefer, Mr. Saxon."

"Well, Miss Trixie, I thought I might like to sit with some real people for a while and eat some real food. Too much time online."

"Then I'll recommend the Commander's Cabin at the end of

this corridor below the flight deck," she says, unconsciously tugging at one of her pearl earrings. "We have an excellent crème brûlée French toast, but you can order anything you'd like. Did you make a killing this morning, Mr. Saxon?"

I stop for a moment, forgetting who I am. Does she know about the Black? Or is she talking about WarWorld?

It was a long night of each.

Then I remember the plane is full of traders.

"Absolutely. Did five mil, easy." I have no idea if five million is a good or bad day when it comes to trading. I suspect "not great" after Trixie doesn't leap up and down like I would if I'd actually just made that much money.

"Well, it's all how you look at it, Mr. Saxon."

She leads me to the Commander's Cabin and pushes open the door with one of her white-gloved hands.

I could get used to this.

Tables covered in starched white cloths and sleek sculpted silverware lay along one side of the cabin near large porthole windows that gaze out on the wide sky and the glittering sea below. On the other side of the lounge, a bar with a bank of several monitors showing all the major trade news reporting outlets waits, ready for service. There are only a few people in the room, and all of them are part of the immaculate-looking staff.

Impressive.

I take a table and look out the large oval porthole. Below, MegaTokyo swallows the scene. Sky bridges and LaserBoards sweep across the forest of ultrascrapers.

"Finished trading early, Mr. Saxon?" I look up to see a smiling waiter. His hair is perfect.

"Seems that way."

"Well, better luck next time."

"Who says I didn't make enough and decide to quit while I'm ahead?" For a moment the waiter looks confused.

"Ah," he starts to laugh. "Good one, Mr. Saxon. Very funny. Can I offer you some breakfast this morning?"

"I'm dying for some croissants and jam. Maybe some butter too. Coffee also."

"Excellent." And the waiter's gone.

Ordering the croissants reminds me of my apartment, now gravel. I loved the instant croissants I used to heat up for Sancerré and me. I'd cut them open and stuff them with jam and butter. Some coffee, and I'd be on the road to recovery.

I rub my eyes and look out the porthole at MegaTokyo. Abe Citadel rises up off the sky bridge. The new ninth wonder of the world. It should've amazed me. But slaying Balrogs and fighting alongside a Minotaur I'm supposed to kill while trying to win the Cola Wars has desensitized me to amazing things.

Maybe I have some new special level of game hangover.

I briefly wonder if that's an achievement.

I need to work out, get into a gym and exercise, have real friends. I think about Kiwi and RiotGuurl. Then I know I really have game hangover for sure. When your online friends are the only ones you can name, you've got it bad. No wonder Sancerré left.

The croissants arrive on bone-white china embossed with the airline's blue skybird logo. The waiter pours aromatic black coffee and offers me cream and sugar. I say yes to both and take up a croissant as he leaves. It's buttery and dense. I prepare it like I want it, stuffed with butter and jam, then I bite into it.

At that moment, I realize I've never actually had croissants before in my entire life. Not real ones. Not like these. This is the first time. What I taste is flaky and buttery and slightly sugary and, yes, very dense. The croissant's fresh heat melts the butter I'd placed within, which runs golden and salty across sweet raspberry jam. Before I know it, the entire croissant is gone. I drink my coffee.

I feel human.

I haven't felt that way in a long time.

I spend the rest of the morning eating breakfast and listening to the chatter of others as the dining room begins to fill up. I order two fried eggs and some bacon while eavesdropping on a currency broker who talks loudly about "Burying the entire Malay Peninsula on a UN exchange deal for Yamashima and walking away with a cool sixty-five billion for five minutes' work."

My eggs and bacon arrive.

"They asked me to hold it while they strong-armed Korea for a better percentage . . . ," bellows the broker.

I fork into the eggs. Rich yellow yolk spreads out across the buttery whites of the salt-and-peppered eggs.

"Five minutes in and they want it all back. So I tell 'em they gotta pay the penalty or we wait the whole hour, and who knows what House Korea's gonna do here in the next few minutes about strong-arm tactics and relief money."

The bacon is crisp. Salty. A road of cured, smoked, fried pork.

"They didn't even bat an eye. Cha-ching, sixty-five mega-large, Tokyo style," finishes the triumphant broker.

I tune him out and order orange juice and a plate of fresh mango.

"Yamashima wants time on StarDeep!" whines some other broker. "That's the word I hear as soon as the bell rings. Takes me half the morning to find the requisite googlebytes you need to even do a deal with that bunch of freaks at StarDeep. For five minutes the guy gives me a quote for a thousand googlebytes, optical. Yamashima will never go for it! And you know what, they don't and there I am, half a day down the drain on a deal I shouldn't have even been chasing in the first place."

My ice cold orange juice and fruit arrive. The juice is so clear and so sweet, I feel it take hold of the back of my throat as vitamin C breaches my system like a pleasantly assertive grenade.

I feel clear and even slightly alive. The mango is ripe. I can tell just by looking at it. I squeeze some lime over it.

"Carter did a deal for Yamashima an hour ago and said he made enough to send his daughters to college. Which means he has to endow a new chair and build a lab as soon as they both get out of rehab."

"That . . . Hey, that was my deal!"

The mango is firm, but still it explodes with juice in my mouth. Bad mango is either too hard or too soft. This is neither. The quiet buzz within me turns up a notch, and now it's a steady hum somewhere between my ears.

# Chapter 25

Hi there," I say, as I approach the trader who'd beat the whiny guy over the Yamashima deal.

He looks at me. I'm an intruder, that's clear. Am I prey or predator? That's not clear, just yet. He's feeling good about ripping off the Malay Peninsula, so the guy probably thinks he's the biggest gorilla in the jungle.

Good, because I need a big King Kong–sized monkey.

"I have a problem" is my opening. "And I was wondering if I could bounce it off you?"

The big man waves at the other side of the table, indicating I should sit, then he orders two draft beers with two fingers. I suppose one's for me.

"Club sandwiches?" he asks then looks at me, waiting, as though the only correct answer is always yes to whatever he wants. At which point, the credit history check can proceed, or no, and then it's get lost, I haven't got time for people who aren't worth something.

"Love 'em," I reply.

He raises two thick fingers and nods to the bartender.

"So what do you want?" says the big business gorilla.

"I'll be honest with you," I start, trying to find a rhythm. "I'm not altogether sure." I pause. Then, "But you seem like the kind of guy who can score, big time."

The emotion of nothing crosses his large predator face.

"I have no idea how it is that you guys make money, exactly," I confess.

I detect slight puzzlement. Even boredom.

"The truth is, I hacked my way onto this flight. So . . . if you think I'm conning you or trying to rip you off, I just gave you the key to getting rid of me real quick."

Nothing remains written on his large face.

He raises his eyes. A signal for me to continue. We're playing poker, and he likes my ante because it's all in. At least, it is for me. All in.

"So here's what I'm betting." I lean close. Just so only we can hear us. "I'm going to tell you about something that's going down in the business world that everybody might not know. My hunch is, with this information you might make some money. Maybe even a lot of money, though I don't know how you would go about that. But you seem like a guy who knows how."

Bright afternoon sun floods the cabin as the Skyliner slowly banks and turns toward Thailand. The big gorilla gulps his ice cold draft. I sip.

"Who are you?" he asks. His voice is quiet, his eyes off somewhere else. Over my shoulder. *Whatever you do,* I tell myself. *Don't look back.*

"I'm a professional gamer. I fight for ColaCorp."

"Hold on," he says.

He raises another two fingers at the bartender and nods for me to finish my beer.

We sit in silence finishing our new beers until the clubs

come. Four strips of bacon, white moist turkey, avocado, tomato, and crisp lettuce with Swiss cheese and some sort of mayonnaise that tastes like real mayonnaise or what I imagine real mayo to actually taste like. Thin-cut, salty garlic fries, piping hot, pile up in the center between the quarters of the sandwich. The bartender places a silver serving boat of ketchup and another of cold Roquefort dressing in front of us.

I'm wondering, briefly, if he's just buying me lunch before he tells me to get lost. Or has me ejected from an aircraft that won't land until Paris.

"ColaCorp's almost out of the game," he remarks between mouthfuls. He chews big bites, slowly. Every so often, he dips a wad of french fries into the Roquefort dressing. Then he takes a pull from his tall draft beer in the frosted schooner.

"Tonight will probably be our last match," I continue. "If we lose, we're out of competition. ColaCorp cedes all North American advertising, and I think some pretty big Chinese revenue space."

"You'll lose a lot more than that," Big Gorilla interjects. "India's a huge market for ColaCorp. With ColaCorp's contracts for advertising, WonderSoft would dominate and push JindyPad completely out of the market there. That's big-time money."

I dip a fry in the ketchup and eat it, chewing for time. Finally I confess the obvious. "Then you know more about it than I do."

He chews, dips a fry, and drinks again.

"I'm just letting you know what you have to lose. That's all," he grumbles.

The blue Pacific stretches away at the window beneath us. It's a great sandwich. The tomatoes taste summer fresh. The turkey is moist. The avocado is like butter, and the bacon is masterfully crisp with just that hint of salty fat. The french fries are hot, salty, and topped with chopped garlic so raw it burns as you chew.

I will remember this sandwich forever.

"So . . ." I pause again, gathering myself for the biggest pitch, the only pitch in fact, the most important pitch I've ever made. "Here's the inside info. We're not gonna lose. In fact, we're going to win so big that WonderSoft might actually lose the entire war."

He smiles briefly. So briefly it didn't even happen.

"You're going to have to tell me how that could ever happen. Odds are 63 to 1 as of five minutes ago, against."

I put down my sandwich and push the plate to the side. I lean slightly closer.

"WonderSoft is going for the death blow," I whisper. "They're going to use all their assets. We kill all those assets, we rack up enough points to claim a theater victory in one round." I lean back, then move my plate back in front of me and pick up the next quarter of that heavenly sandwich. "Commitment is going to kill them."

"My feeds indicate you've been successfully losing every match. What's going to be different about this one?" asks Big Gorilla.

"First of all, WonderSoft always plays it safe, never commits too many assets to any one objective. Thus, if they take casualties, they don't lose too many points. Second, they have a spy being run by a man named Faustus Mercator. He's the one behind WonderSoft's victories and I'm betting he's placing a lot of money out there in the big whatever for the win. I think that means he needs a payoff and soon. He wants to win next time, decisively and finally, and the only way to do that is to use everything they've got."

Big Gorilla finishes his sandwich. He reaches across the table to my plate and picks up my last quarter sandwich.

"So how are you going to give me a win?" he asks once he's started chewing my sandwich.

I've got him. I know it. Why? Because he hasn't had me thrown from the plane yet.

"I'm going to find that spy," I say. "Then the spy is going to tell me everything he or she knows."

"And?"

"I'll misinform Mercator's team and set a trap. When the match goes down, we'll go for broke. Kill as many units as possible and go for a theater victory. We get that, and WonderSoft loses. In fact we'll actually pick up their market share by 30 percent. The rest goes back into the pool."

"My sources tell me ColaCorp has to buy in big for that to happen. Are they going to?"

I don't know.

"My research assistant just came through with this . . ." He's had his own personal CloudFeed on the whole time, which has been sending him info as we talk. He probably never turns it off. To him, information is power. Power is money. "WonderSoft is upping their hunter-killer squadrons and buying SmartArmor for their heavy troops. It seems they're buying in big. ColaCorp on the other hand . . . nothing."

I have half a plan. It's not a whole plan, but I feel it begin to take shape as I talk. It's something I've been thinking about: a way to definitely beat WonderSoft—the only way to beat them. It's not really even a way. It's a strategy. A chance we have to take. But sometimes that's all you have. So . . .

. . . I go with it.

"Combat modifiers. Do you know about those?" I know he does. But we're playing a game. It's what we do. It's what I'm good at. He bites.

"An hour before the game," he begins. Almost lecturing me. "Each team can go for a strategic modifier. Basically, the corporation buys in big either by upping the venue pot, or does a straight cash infusion. If they do that, they get to roll the dice for a combat modifier. I'm also showing . . . that for ColaCorp to even have a chance they've got to commit that little carrier group they've got offshore outside Song Hua Harbor. The number crunchers tell me then, maybe, you might have the stats to get within reach of a win. But those don't add up to a theater victory. No way."

I wait.

Then . . .

"I'm going to get WonderSoft to go all in. We kill everything they've got, a total rout, and that's how we arrive at theater victory and take the India venues along with the rest."

"So basically," he says, burping—he doesn't excuse himself—"both sides go all in and you've got a trap."

"Yeah, all in and then the trap."

We finish our sandwiches as the Skyliner wallows through the lazy South Pacific yellow afternoon.

I wipe my mouth with the large starched napkin and drain the last of my draft.

"Can you use that?" I ask, staring Big Gorilla straight in the eyes.

Nothing remains on his face, even when he sticks out his hand. "Carter Banks. And yeah, I can do something with that."

Inside, deep inside me where no one else can see, I breathe a sigh of relief.

"So what do you want out of this?" he asks.


What do I want out of this?

Those words seem like the words of some other genie. The second genie in recent days. Those words lead to questions I've been asking myself since before all this went down. Maybe even questions I've been asking my entire life. I sit in my suite as the Skyliner turns over the Malaysian Peninsula. A purple blanket of night presses down on the orange band in the west that is the last of the day. I have until tonight to give Carter Banks a plan on how I'm going to find the spy and recruit the spy, then convince

Carter that ColaCorp can win, before he'll buy heavy on low-priced ColaCorp stock prior to the battle. Then he'll sell high and buy up the crashing WonderSoft stock. Whoever's financed Faustus Mercator will not be happy on their lack of return. That might give him something to focus on besides killing me.

But who is the spy?

I sit in one of the cigar leather chairs, just listening to the quiet nothing drone of the massive trade jet. Resting. Not even using my eyes to look at anything. Just resting.

I need this. Or at least my body does. My mind also. But I can't turn that off.

The spy has to be a ColaCorp soldier. That could be anyone, even RangerSix. The information used against us has been too situation-specific, often moment-by-moment, up-to-date, real-time info. It's not some ColaCorp flunky who has access to our preplanning. Whoever it is has to be in on our BattleChat. A live, professional player. Someone I consider a comrade. JollyBoy is still the obvious choice.

Sometimes the obvious choice is the only choice.

I ping Kiwi and wait. An hour later, he gets back to me.

"I want to ask you something, and I need you to tell me the truth."

"You got it, mate. Always have and always will."

"Are you a traitor?"

"What?"

"I mean, have you been selling us out to WonderSoft?"

Kiwi pauses, silent, hulking in the darkness of a room that looks like a tool shed.

"Frankly, Perfect . . ."

I wait. If he's lying, he'll point me at someone else. That's my lie detector. I'm no interrogator, no detective. I just find my game and run it.

"You know something, Question?" he says after a long pause,

each of us staring across the Internet at the other. "Every time I get killed, it's 'cause I'm grateful."

I watch him, waiting for the lie.

"You know what I do for a living, mate?" he asks. "I mean after Saturday night matches, you know what I go back to?" His face is angry, almost twisting with pain. Like he's holding something back. Something that takes all his strength to restrain. Something that's beating him day by day. Wearing him down.

I didn't know. I say nothing.

"I was a soldier. Got my legs blown off in Indonesia fightin' the Muzzies. When I got back, they gimme new legs. Best the service could offer. Free medical for the rest of my life. I'm not bitter about that. Lost my legs one balmy afternoon and never looked back. God save the King. But when I got back, they gave me a list of jobs I could do for the rest of my life. Nothing good. No mind. Cleaning offices in Sydney every night is just the same as being a metro tollbooth worker. But ya see, PerfectQuestion, I loved bein' a soldier, mate. Loved the formations and the parades and the medals. Loved my mates and my guns. But the service says you've got to have both legs to keep soldierin'. So they medically retired me, PerfectQuestion. Twenty-four years old and I'm retired for the rest of my life. So you know what I did? I didn't give up. I looked for another army that'd let me soldier. And I found one. I found an army that would let me fight for 'em. So I love ColaCorp. I love RangerSix. I'd die for them every night because I'm so grateful they let me be a soldier and pay me a wage so I don't have to stand in the metro at three A.M. while punks coming home from the clubs piss their lives away and write crap on the walls that the public lawyers say is freedom of speech and the college professors say is art. That's a waste of a life. ColaCorp pays me some money. Enough to come home and pay the utility bills on my da's old stead. It's not so much . . . But ColaCorp's given me more than they'll ever know. I'd fight for free, if they asked me to."

Then he's silent, staring back at me across the connection with hard eyes.

"So ask me again, PerfectQuestion. You ask me again if I'm a traitor."

I shake my head.

I don't need to.

"You're not the traitor, Kiwi," I whisper. "I didn't think so. But there is one, and I had to make sure you were clear, before I asked for your help. So I need your help."

"You got it, mate." He doesn't even hesitate. I like that about Kiwi. He's always all in.

# Chapter 26

When I talk to RangerSix, I tell him my plan and who I think the traitor is. JollyBoy. He listens without saying a word. Then he says, "Son . . ." He pauses. "You got my blessing. I'll make the pitch to ColaCorp. I don't know if they'll go for it, but it's better than just sitting back and watching us get slaughtered by WonderSoft. Never did like that clown anyways."

I know, or at least I have to believe, RangerSix isn't the traitor. To me he seems like the last samurai in the world. Maybe all of us have degrees of honor to some extent. But he's integrity through and through. If you cut him, he'd probably bleed integrity. Whatever that looked like. Some people you just know that about. He's one of them. Maybe the last one.

RiotGuurl. I don't think so. But also, I don't know for sure because I don't really know her. She's professional, competent, and good. And I like her, I think. That clouds things. But, in her defense, she's been shot down twice because of bad intel. Because of the traitor. Those are marks in her favor, reasons for trust.

Then there's the clown.

The clown being JollyBoy, who I text later and ask to set up an intel station at a highlighted coordinate on the grid map north of Song Hua Harbor.

"Oh what fun, PerfectQuestioney. A sneak attack right into the spleen of WonderSoft. Remember when we killed everyone at the tower?"

I did.

"That was fun, wasn't it," says JollyBoy.

Good times, I agree and end the conversation.

RiotGuurl answers my next text immediately.

"Hey, boy."

"Hey yourself," I text. "Up for a bit of fun?"

"Depends."

I write back, "At the briefing, I need you to ignore all the orders about a counterattack through the left flank, and an intel station JollyBoy's setting up. Okay?"

"All right . . . why would I do this?"

"Because I want you to pick up the troops that should be counterattacking and drop them in the center, where all the action's really going to be. It's gonna get real hot, so watch out."

"I like it hot," she writes back.

"Listen." I decide to level with her and let her in on the plan. "I trust you. I think Jolly's been selling us out. This is our only chance to win this thing. Okay?"

"Did RangerSix buy off on this?" she asks after a moment.

"Yeah."

"Okay then, I'm in."

"Thanks." I don't know what to write next.

What's appropriate?

Maybe the truth. "You're the best pilot I've ever played with, RiotGuurl. Before it all goes down, I just want you to know that and I'm sorry about trying to hit on you. My life's been weird and I was confusing respect with attraction."

"It's cool, but what're you saying?" she writes back.

"I'm saying I respect your skills. Even if we lose our professional status tonight, I want you to know I think you're a professional, no matter what."

"Thanks, PerfectQuestion. What's your real name?"

I stare at her text and all that it could possibly mean.

Names are personal.

And . . . what if she is the traitor after all?

"John Saxon."

"It fits. Where are you?" she texts.

"That's not important."

"Maybe it is. Maybe I've been rethinking . . . things."

I wait.

"Maybe after the game, we can meet halfway from wherever you're at. Maybe we're even in the same city," she writes.

I stare at the words on the screen until they start to blur.

"I'll tell you what," I type, my index finger shaking as I punch the screen on my Petey. "Tell me where you are and I'll be there. That is, if you still want me to, after the match."

She gives me an address in Rome. Italy.

An hour later, I log back into the Black. I have a scotch beforehand and set another up for the game. Now, as the screen descends through its intro of blood and screams, shadows and flames, I wait, feeling the warm hum of the liquor.

*Courtyard of the Unworthy* bleeds across the screen.

I slew my camera and find the hulking Minotaur, Morgax, standing next to me, smiling. Shadows lengthen as a swollen moon rises in the east over the fading desert. Evil blackbirds come in sudden waves across the dead city, screeching murder, then they're gone. Before us, stone steps rise to meet the doors to the tower.

"So we get to the top, then what?" I ask Morgax.

"Rescue the child and end this abomination," he says after a moment.

"Most people who play Black games like them."

"I'm not most people," says Morgax. The character voice software makes his speech gruff and snorty. "I'm a fan of the source material. I came to clean it up. Or at least that's what I told myself."

"Clean it up?" I ask.

Over chat I can hear him sigh. His sigh comes out as a painful bullish snort. Then he says, "What's your real . . . forget it. Sorry about that; I'm not used to playing these kinds of games. Forget it. I don't need to know your real name. It's not important. Let's just say . . . I've been a fan of these books, the source material for this world, since I was kid. If I told you how much of a fan, well . . . then you might find out who I am. To put it another way, I teach a small lit course at a big university, among other courses, on this . . . this place. The World of Wastehavens."

I stop him. "Enough. Don't say any more. Someone might be listening in on us and they could use that against you." I move the Samurai up the steps to the door of the tower and start inspecting the lock.

"So you're a fan, and someone made a Black game out of your favorite book and you just had to play it?" I ask. "Except you didn't really know what a Black game was and now you're in over your head?" That's my guess, at least.

"No, I knew. We get mandatory classes in deviant behavior as part of our teaching credentials. Black games are considered highly deviant. Which they are."

"So why are you here?" There seemed to be no visible locking mechanism I could toy with to get us into the tower. I try a few strikes with my bare hands against the door and am rewarded with solid wooden *thunks,* echoing beyond into an unseen empty space.

No one answers.

"Six months ago, I heard someone was going to let this world go live. Use it as source to run a Black game. I couldn't let it be sullied like that. So I entered. I thought there was a way to save it, and if I'm right, there might actually be."

"Why would you do a thing like that? You could get busted. Reeducation sentence. You'd lose your license to teach."

For a long moment Morgax says nothing. Our avatars watch the tower.

"I thought there could be a way to clean it up, or set it free," he starts with a sudden burst. Then, "Or at least that's what I told myself. I was being overly optimistic, in hindsight. I had no idea what I was really getting into." He's silent for a moment. Both our avatars stand before the tall lone door, the only entrance into the rising tower. The endgame.

"Then there's the other part of me," he whispers. "The fan part. The truth is . . . I was dying to live inside this world. I've known about it for so long. Everyone knew the original writer had gone nuts and done something like this, but no one could find it. He'd never allowed any of the major gaming companies to develop a game based on his world. So this world . . . it's really special."

I push on the door.

"I understand now, why I really did it," he continues. "It's like your favorite show being made into a game. You have to play it. You can't just let it go, even though you know it'll never live up to the show. You can't. You've just got to taste it once. So I did . . . and it was better than I ever imagined it could be. It's so real . . . so . . . like the books in all the parts where it hasn't been turned into a strip club and a porn site. Why would they do that? This is a game. Games are supposed to be for children. They're supposed to be fun. What business do they have turning it into . . . putting that sick stuff into it?"

In-game it's twilight. Nothing moves in the gloaming. There is no sound other than the wooden sandals of the Samurai and the hooves of the Minotaur on the ancient stones at the foot of the tower.

"Worst part is, I knew Black games were bad," continues Morgax. "I knew they were illegal. I knew it might cost me everything. Now I'm caught. I didn't realize what really went on in here. I knew it was bad, but I thought it was still just a game. These things could get me in a lot of trouble just by virtue of association. Whoever's running this game could use that against me. How could I defend myself? I could lose my position. My family . . ."

"They won't," I counter, trying to calm him down. He's agitated. "Black runners know that's bad for business. Anonymity encourages participation. Once people start getting busted, outed, then people are gonna stop playing and find some new thrill somewhere else."

"I hope you're right," he mutters.

Near the ironbound door studs I finally find a small pop-up menu that opens a quick-click *Pushing* minigame. I try a few rapid clicks and nothing happens. I scan the other door in the same location and find the same minigame pop-up. That means two players are needed to open the doors to the tower. The programmers must've put that in to make people work together. I imagine they were counting on the eventual backstabbing that comes out of such forced alliances. More drama that way.

"All right, I think if we both push on the door, it might open. Be ready for what comes next."

We lean our avatars against the door, find a submenu for

*Push,* then slowly the rotten doors swing open on a dry, dusty grinding sound effect. Inside the tower's circumference, blue light filters down through spreading spiderwebs and broken stained glass set high along the rising inner walls of the tower.

The Marrow Spike.

"So if you're a fan, what do we face next?" I ask. "This place ever get covered in the book?"

"Books, and yeah. Wu the main character, which is who you're playing, ends the third book of the *Songs of Other Battles* trilogy at the top of this tower. It's been his quest for most of his entire life, though it's never really explained why in the series. You survived the Battle of Vezengom in which two great armies are completely annihilated. Then you journeyed into the Desert of Silence and arrived at this lost, fabled city buried beneath the desert sands. With the help of a young scholar turned skeleton centuries before your arrival, Sabboc, you survive a night in the city and best the curse that turns everyone, by dawn, into skeletons. You did that by making it to the top of the tower. But then you disappeared, and the book ends with a song sung by an Elven slave girl in the Grand Palace of the Cities of the East. The song implies that having sacrificed yourself, you were destroyed. In *The Tale of Woe,* a book written much later, we find out that you entered the strange AfterWorld and helped defeat the Black Dragon that had tied all the timelines of every world into the Gordion knot. It's all a loop and it's a bit confusing, but it does make sense, eventually. If you know the whole story, that is."

Above us, a wide winding staircase climbs the rim of the tower walls. What lies above is unknown.

"Great, but what happens here in the tower?" I ask, meaning, tell me what monsters we face next.

"There's a demon-possessed witch named Razor Maiden, hiding above. She'll try to enslave us."

"Your character, what's his story in the books?"

"Morgax died at the Battle of Vezengom in the swamp, saving your life."

"Well, at least we've got that going for us; you're not dead yet. So just the demon witch?"

"No, there are other demons here, if we go by the books."

"What kind of weapons do they have?" I ask.

"The demons . . . um . . . I think swords, flaming swords. Yeah, it was flaming swords. But, oh . . . this is important. The demons are crazy. We can use that against them."

"How?"

"In the book they weren't smarmy, ultraintelligent supervillains. They were base . . . crazy, rash, jealous, envious, temperamental."

"Not totally sure how we can use that in-game, but it's good to know. And this Razor Maiden, she has some sort of blade attack, I'm guessing?"

"The Razor Maiden is an enemy who recurs in several of the novels. In the book that takes place here in Zandsabad, she survives this battle but is badly wounded. In the novels afterward she is depicted as a scarred old crone who eventually gets burned at the stake."

"Her attack style?"

"Curses."

"Such as?"

"She could make you blind, fall in love with the wrong person, slow down. All kinds of stuff."

Great. I check the Samurai's resistances. Nothing seems extraordinary, and *Deathefeather* doesn't seem to boost anything.

"Well, we'll just have to be ready for whatever comes," I whisper. Unsure why exactly I'm whispering.

In the gloom, we proceed forward across a stone floor littered with dust and fire-blackened debris. We approach the stairs, watching them curve up and away into the murk above.

At the first landing, we meet two demons. They're little more than shadows gliding silently down from the blue-dark recesses above, their flaming swords guttering like oily torches in a strong wind, making a low rumbling sound.

"Two from above," says Morgax over chat as his Minotaur rears back to fling a javelin upward. The javelin speeds away and shoots straight through the ethereal body of one of the two demons without harming it in any way. The demon drops toward us suddenly as its green eyes widen greedily. He brings his smoking sword down, imbedding it in the stone floor of the landing we've arrived at. Its twin follows suit and slams its flaming sword into the stone steps it's just landed on.

Morgax draws a huge double-bladed battle-axe. I select *Kendo* under fighting styles, and the Samurai raises *Deathefeather* into the ready position.

The demons solidify. They're wearing cobalt-colored armor. Tortured disembodied faces swim upward to scream or moan across the darkly shining surfaces of the breastplate and greaves. They draw their swords from the ground and advance.

When the demon opposite me is just feet away, I hit *Iron Hurricane* and let loose with a series of power attacks. The demon spins his sword left then right quickly, parrying everything. On the seventh parry, the demon heaves the sword over its back and brings it speeding back down on me. It's all I can do to get out of the way as I roll right to the edge of a crumbling balustrade, a three-story drop to the debris-littered floor just beyond. Immediately, the demon is up and on me with a series of short slashes that leave a thick trail of oily smoke in their wake, obscuring my screen with each pass. I parry, exchange positions, our swords crossed, and give ground, retreating to the edge of the landing. Then I whirl using a double-tap left command and strike out with a quick backstroke from *Deathefeather*. The demon barely parries and gives ground as we exchange places. I drive him down the stairs with four serious high cuts. When I'm almost on the verge of getting one slash past its twirling, smoking sword, the demon backflips and lands farther down the stairs.

I select *Harvest* from the hot keys and race down the stairs before the demon can recover. Superimposed autumn leaves fall across my screen as a scythe sweeps winter wheat in a brief transparent cut-scene. The image fades, and I bear down on the slavering demon . . .

. . . I should have made it to him already. The soundtrack has changed, slowed down. I wonder if I've drunk a little too much of the airline's highbrow scotch. I check the nearby tumbler and realize I haven't drunk any. I'm staring hard into the screen, trying to figure out what's going on. The muscles in the back of my neck ache. I urge the Samurai forward, his blade horizontally placed between himself and the enemy, one hand gripping the hilt, the other bracing the blade.

For a moment I see Sancerré.

I blink.

The demon at the bottom of the stairs draws his blade back with both claws, preparing a massive downstroke once I arrive.

Sancerré appears again on the screen. Her face is a mask of pleasure. I know the look. I'd been there more than a few times.

I blink rapidly.

I step within the demon's downstroke and deliver a good cut to its armored midsection. The image of Sancerré returns. The demon nuzzles her neck. Her eyes close as she surrenders to him, shuddering. The demon looks back across the screen, directly at me, and smiles through yellow fangs.

I'm gone. I'm thinking of her and what the world's greatest photographer does to her and how it makes her feel and how, if I've harbored any hope that she thinks of me and misses me, how that's just a lie I've been telling myself all along. I'm gone to that no good place . . .

. . . of jade-colored jealousy.

And . . .

I'm back.

The demon is gone, and I am speeding down the stairs. *Harvest* runs out. As I turn, the demon is right behind me, laughing evilly over ambient and cutting hard for the kill. I'm in full parry mode now.

Over my demon's shoulder I can see the Minotaur trading blows with the other demon. But the rate of exchange is coming out two to one for the demon.

I scroll the defensive submenu, find a *Disarm* attack and set it up in standby. I wait until the demon gets close enough for it to go active. Once it does, I execute and the demon receives a quick strike from *Deathefeather* at its wrist. The flaming sword whirls away, smoking, skittering across the stone floor of the landing.

"Morgax, how's it going?" I call out over chat.

No reply.

"Morgax, I need to know what's going on."

"I don't want to say."

"Let me guess . . . your wife or someone you love?"

"Yeah . . . how'd . . . ?"

"It's some sort of subliminal algorithm running through the graphics. They use this kind of stuff for combat training, but it's top secret. The military won't even admit to it."

This was how the name *Wu* had suddenly appeared in my head back in the dungeon. How could I have known that was the real name of the character unless someone suggested it to me? The visions of the Harpies and all the skill descriptions. This game was full of hidden content. I wonder what other things it's been telling me.

The demon chases me up the stairs, its roar thundering out across ambient.

"My kids . . . ," mumbles Morgax over chat.

"Hang on, be there in a sec," I tell him.

I charge up the stairs toward Morgax and the demon, scrolling through the attack submenu. I find what I'd seen before. *Execution.*

"As soon as your demon's down, take mine out, okay?" I yell.

I activate *Execution* and cut loose with the Samurai's premier finishing attack on Morgax's demon. A totally offensive strike with two hands that will leave the Samurai temporarily defenseless for a moment. Up close I can see that the Minotaur is cut up and bleeding badly. He barely waves his battle-axe in defense as the demon hacks and slashes away at him.

Whatever Morgax is seeing is too real for him to deal with.

A moment later, using *Deathefeather*, I strike his demon's long neck. The camera backs away to the killcam view, the Samurai striking hard at the exposed, taut neck of the horned demon. Everything turns to black silhouette against red sky background. Flutes trill on ambient sound as the demon's head comes away, trailing inky blood that covers and then washes out the screen to black for two very long seconds.

*Execution* stamps itself in gold Japanese-themed lettering across the screen, as a reedy flute trills in martial triumph.

"Get mine now," I tell Morgax over chat. "I won't be able to attack it!"

I look away from the screen a moment too late. The demon and Sancerré. Everything I've imagined and didn't want to . . . was happening to the girl I once loved.

Love.

Then it's over. When I look back to the screen, the other demon is cut almost in two and has fallen backward down the stairs as its inky blood pumps out like a volcano erupting from a black smoking heart, sending small waterfalls of blood ahead of it, down the stairs. The other headless demon that I'd executed remains where it had dropped to its knees, leaning on the steps. Still holding its smoking sword.

In-game, we're each rewarded with $10,000 dollars and a free credit-score hack by a private profile hacking corporation that guarantees not only repair, but brand-new ratings. A gothic march of music returns to the soundtrack: pounding drums, blurred acoustic guitars, tolling bells. We stand for a moment amid the carnage on the stairs, gathering ourselves.

"You're pretty cut up," I tell Morgax. "Better bandage. It's all we can do right now."

"I . . . uh . . . ," he starts, then doesn't finish.

"Listen," I say sharply. "Snap out of it. Whatever it was that you saw, it wasn't true. It was an algorithm subroutine designed to run through the graphics and suggest that you imagine the worst possible thing and integrate it with elements of the game. There was probably some sort of focusing action that set us up for the suggestion. That's why they took their time getting ready with the whole sword-in-the-floor thing. The longer we watched, the better the program worked."

"My kids . . . ," he mumbles.

"It's not real. Forget it, Morgax. Let's get to the top of the tower. Also, check your axe, it looks finished."

After a moment, the Minotaur bends down and picks up one of the smoking swords.

"If the programmers were faithful to the book, the demons' two swords might be useful." He pauses to examine the blade.

"Amatazx," he pronounces.

He picks up the other.

"Xergunnil." Then, "These are blades of renown in the books."

"So which one are you gonna use?" I ask.

"Both," his character rumbles, then smiles. "Let's go kill us a witch." Both blades emit a guttering torchlight effect as the Minotaur leads the way up the crumbling stairs, the swords trailing black oily smoke in the blue midnight gloom that shines through the fractured remains of the massive stained-glass windows.

"Something's about to happen," I whisper over chat.

There is no sign of any other players. No other enemies. No traps. Nothing. Then the music changes. The gothic march that repeated again and again, building, growing louder as we move up the once-grand staircase, now turns to something else. Primitive horns ring out across the distance as though issuing a challenge. Then the march resumes, this time louder and faster.

"What should we do?" says the Minotaur.

"Nothing," I whisper. "Keep moving forward."

I watch the broken stairs behind us in the polished reflection of *Deathefeather*. The clear light of the swollen moon peeks through the stained glass and jagged openings in the tower wall that look out on the silent city far below and the desert waste beyond.

The first of the next three demons announces itself with a cluster of thrown spikes that hit the Minotaur as though suddenly springing from his back. I scan his Vitality. He's lower than me.

This is not good.

The demon lands like a cat on the stairs ahead of us, its four hands gripping more throwing spikes.

At that moment, a second demon steps from the shadows and wraps a whip around the thick neck of the Minotaur, jerking it hard like a noose, biting into Morgax's bleeding hide. Instantly the Minotaur spins around on me, its animal eyes gone, only the whites showing. One flaming sword sweeps high above me while the other comes in fast from the side, low. I back away as the possessed Minotaur lumbers forward hacking away at me, his two guttering swords leaving great smoking trails.

It's then that the third demon, a giant, tears away a section of the wall, ripping out the stairs below me with its gargantuan clawed hand. From the gaping midnight hole, its lone angry cat's eye peers in at me from outside the tower. Running, I hit Space-bar and launch the Samurai out across a crumbling void and grab a support beam jutting from the far side of the gap.

Three demons, one of which is a giant. Me, clinging to the outside of the tower, and a possessed Minotaur trying to kill me.

Great!

"Morgax, what's going on?" I call out over chat.

"I've got some kind of minigame going on. I'm locked out until I solve it."

"You gotta solve it quickly! I mean it."

"I'm trying, but it's gonna take time . . ." Then he says the words I dread hearing, "I'm not very good at these things."

Hurled spikes clatter against the tower wall all around me. One nails me for 10 percent damage. I sheath *Deathefeather* and set my stance to *Free Climb*. I leap for the gaping crack in the wall beyond the giant demon's mouth, open and drooling, waiting for me. Barely hanging from the torn-away gap in the side of the tower, I begin to scale the outside wall, upward, heading for the top of the tower. Across the chasm of disintegrating stairs, the demon with the whip jerks on it, and the Minotaur starts climbing the steps to intercept me somewhere above.

"I think I've got it!" shouts Morgax on chat.

Then . . .

"Whooops. Sorry."

Outside the next level of the tower, clinging to the wall, I see the landing where the four-armed spike-throwing cat-demon waits. I crash through a massive stained-glass window and attack him with *Karate*. Breaking, crashing glass shatters all around us as the game's graphic lighting shifts, carnival style, as each piece of stained glass falls through the wan moonlight. I manage to land one punch right in the demon's catty face, then a round-house that throws him into the tower's far wall. He ragdolls off the wall and I grab him. Then, rolling the mouse wheel rapidly, I reset the stance menu to *Judo*. The possessed Minotaur puppet is almost on me, lumbering zombielike up the last few steps to the landing. I fling the cat-demon at him and retreat up the far stairs. The Minotaur bats the flying demon aside. It careens off his ham-sized fist and falls, spinning off into the darkness below, its screech fading down through the depths of the tower.

The sound of crumbling brickwork resounds over ambient. I spin around as another section of the tower wall is again torn away and the giant's claw reaches in after me. I draw *Deathefeather* from its sheath in one fluid motion and cut through one of the giant demon's long, extended fingers. The wounded claw retracts as I back away from the oncoming Minotaur puppet. Outside the tower a monstrous howl echos off into the night and the desert silence.

"It's now or never, Morgax!" I shout.

If I have to kill him, at least I'll be able to go to Seinfeld's and collect any prize I can name.

But I don't want it that way.

"This minigame keeps changing every time I solve it," he groans. "If you've got to kill me . . . it's cool. I understand."

I resolve right then not to kill him. Decent people affect me that way.

The floor of the landing begins to crumble behind the Minotaur. The whip-trailing demon falls off into the darkness with the whip still clutched in its hand, still strangling Morgax. The Minotaur jerks backward toward the disintegrating edge of the stairs. The tower is becoming unstable as its walls are torn out by the giant demon. Floors and stairways collapse below and above us in great dusty waterfalls. Behind me, the giant's cat's eye leers into the guts of the tower, hoping to find me. I run toward the off-balanced Minotaur, as he waves both smoking swords at me. I duck underneath them and cut the whip with a quick slice from *Deathefeather*.

"I'm back in!" yells Morgax in triumph.

"Follow me now! The floor's going to collapse!" I yell back at him.

I race out the crack in the wall at the giant's lone cat's eye and drive *Deathefeather* straight into it. I hold on to the sword as it's yanked by the recoiling giant's pulpy jetting eye out through the crack in the wall. My POV is washed with bubbling green-yellow eye fluid slime.

I hope Morgax figures out what I'm doing.

I enable *Judo* and grapple with the giant demon. Its head reels drunkenly outside the tower as my screen crashes violently across the dizzying horizon of the ruined city below and the swollen moon above. Darkness and shadowed hills and a cracked black mountain in the distance lie in the moonlit wastes of the desert. Then we're falling toward the base of the tower, far below.

I have 3 percent health left when I let go of the dead giant demon at the bottom of the tower. Dust and debris rain down on us as chalky plumes erupt from the tower entrance and out the shattered stained-glass windows above.

In the silence that follows, we wait for whatever will be thrown at us next. "I have a few bandages left," says Morgax over chat. "I don't know how we'll get to the top of the tower now. Look at it."

High above us, the already crazed structure rises to thin strands of brickwork that barely seem enough to support the uppermost level.

"We'll climb," I say.

"I don't have *Climb* in any of my menus. I guess that makes sense for a Minotaur."

"Then I'll climb it alone," I mumble.

At that moment, the game shuts down and thanks us for

playing, assuring us that we will die next time. I get a message on my Petey from an unknown source announcing the next session. I don't even want to read it.

I look at the untouched scotch. I think about Sancerré and realize I'm tired of doing all the thinking. I press the intercom. Trixie answers.

"What may I offer you, Mr. Saxon?"

"Do you like scotch?"

"I love scotch," she purrs. "But I never drink alone."

A little while later, I turn the lights down low in the suite. I set the big screen to fireplace mode and turn on some jazz. Johnny Hartman. We sit. We talk. We sip our scotch as the Skyliner crosses the night.

We get close.

And I don't think about Sancerré . . . much.

# Chapter 27

Song Hua Harbor is divided in two by a canal that runs the length of the city from the open sea where Cola-Corp's lone carrier task force waits to provide what limited resources they can to the battle that will be waged over the fictional Southeast Asian city of Song Hua inside WarWorld. A narrow isthmus on the extreme right flank connects the city with the harbor where we fought the last match. The Song Hua Harbor bridge will be the center of our line. If WonderSoft crosses that bridge, then it's game over for Cola-Corp. We've got nothing else left after the bridge.

I've been assigned the center of our line, the bridge entrance on our side of the river. On my left flank, Shogun-Smile and WarChild command a small firebase and a light armor reaction force to protect the point that leads out into the emerald-green waters of the bay.

I need an edge. I need high-speed, low-drag, real-life players. But I can't take a chance on some amateur or, worse, a player with an agenda who doesn't prioritize winning this battle above protesting yet another injustice, like back in the superlab match. I file a troop assignment request with the ColaCorp Special Forces reserve, then tag the unit and put them on standby. They're my ace in the hole if things go south.

An hour before the match, RangerSix texts me.

His message is "ColaCorp won't roll the dice until they see something to get excited about."

That's bad. This is going to be too close. A good bonus roll at the start of the match and maybe we can turn the battle around early on. But, if the suits aren't buying us a roll, then it's really going to be tough going, especially if JollyBoy is the traitor.

"But," says RangerSix, "they did option the roll. So at least they're hoping to get excited."

Corporations could option to roll the dice by paying a small fee, which they would lose half of if they didn't go through with the roll. It wasn't as bad as going all in, but it gave them something to point to at the end of the year in the losses column for Online Tournament Marketing.

"It's better than nothing," he adds, hoping to make me feel better.

It doesn't.

"If WonderSoft falls for it," I text, selling him again as if he were one of the bright boys of ColaCorp corporate, "it'll be a shooting match. If we still control the bridge and if RiotGuurl can get those troops on the TV tower right into the center of the action, then we'll have an opportunity to turn this around."

"Too many 'ifs' for the suits, son," says RangerSix.

"If we reach those objectives, will you ask 'em again? At that point, we've got to ask ColaCorp for the green light on a roll. If we don't, I don't think our chances are very good."

"You've sold me already, PerfectQuestion," says RangerSix. "I believe in your plan. I believe in you, son. They know the play, and they're waiting to see what we do with what we've got. Give them a reason to roll the dice, son, and they will."

"I understand," I text. "Sorry for pushing."

"No problem, son. You're a good soldier. Pushing is a big part of soldierin'."

The plan's simple.

Make WonderSoft think, with the help of a misinformed JollyBoy, that ColaCorp is counterattacking with everything we've got, from our right flank across the isthmus and into the harbor on the other side of the river. The plan is to make them think we're going for an end run around their left flank and try to retake Song Hua and the harbor area. Most of our grunts are staged and ready for combat at an LZ just behind JollyBoy's intel station along the isthmus. Instead, we'll wait, and once WonderSoft commits to dodging our counterattack, instead of going for the kill and attacking ColaCorp head-on at the bridge, we'll jump, via airlift with RiotGuurl's Albatross squadron, all our grunts in reserve on the right flank, into the center of the action at the bridge and cut up everything that comes our way. What I'm hoping for is to have WonderSoft so broken at the bridge that we can actually hurt their reserve forces. Then we'll counterattack their positions along the harbor. By that time, they'll be committing everything. Hopefully they won't be coordinated in any kind of formation or plan to mass and attack in unison. They'll still outnumber us, but if everything goes right, we can pick them off in smaller groups. If they keep losing, there's a chance they'll keep sending troops in, like a gambler on a losing streak trying to win his money back all at once.

As the game goes live, I set up a command bunker on our side of the Song Hua Bridge, a double-decker arch-and-span affair that's decked out in twinkling lights. I have a full company of grunts supported by heavy machine guns and mortar teams, determined to hold the bridge. Kiwi rides Rat Patrol along the riverfront on our side of the bridge with a platoon of heavily armed light-attack Mules, destroying a series of smaller bridges WonderSoft might try to take with infantry. There are sporadic brief engagements when Kiwi runs into their recon patrols along the river as they try to probe our lines.

"How's it look on the right, Jolly?" I ask over BattleChat.

"Lovely, PerfectQuestion, absolutely lovely. Other than a few armored scouts probing the road to the isthmus, the sky is a thrilling orange, almost red, should we take warning if we're going sailing? Or is that during the morning when we need to take the warning? I get so mixed up about that."

I bet you do.

"Let me know when the scouts have cleared the road, or if they hang out. If they do, call in RiotGuurl for direct-air support and have her make a few runs on them. She's on station overhead."

"Will do, aye aye and aye aye, sir," replies the never-serious JollyBoy.

Moments later, one of my grunts who's manning a listening post at the far side of the bridge into Song Hua Harbor radios in. "Commander, we have enemy Wolverine main battle tanks inbound at a high rate of speed." Moments later, the listening post grunts are dead as a distant tank round blast echoes off the walls of the canal and the bridges along the river. I scope my rifle on the bridge and order the mortar platoons to stand by to fire on my prearranged coordinates. I bring up the artillery menu and order antiarmor rounds to be used in the first salvo.

"Kiwi, all the bridges down yet?" I ask over BattleChat.

"Not a one left standing." I hear the high-pitched turbo whine of Kiwi's speeding Mule in the background as he races along the riverfront. "If they wanna get across the river, it's the main bridge or nothing for WonderSoft, mate."

"Get your platoon staged at the square I'm marking on your

map now. When I signal, come in and run a screen while I readjust my company, before WonderSoft's second assault begins."

"You're gonna take on the first wave with what you've got?" he asks.

"First wave is just to find out where we're at, Kiwi. When they come in again, we wanna be somewhere else. Hence the screen."

"Roger that, Kiwi out."

Two low-riding, flat, twin-turbo-jet-engined WonderSoft Challenger heavy tanks, long barrels rotating, search for targets to engage as they roar out into the main plaza on the far side of the bridge from us. They cross the plaza and race up the ramp leading to the bridge. Heavy-machine-gun teams placed in the warehouses on our side of the river open up with antiarmor rounds. Hot streaks of light zip off into the plaza and tollbooths on that side of the span. Concrete and dusty debris begin to erupt in plumes around the supports and foundations of the wide bridge. I call for the mortar strike and shoulder an antitank rocket I'd equipped in my kit. The mortar rounds start falling seconds later, haphazardly at first, across the concrete ramp where the Wolverines have halted, probably waiting for orders. I lock onto one of the tanks, waiting for the circling digital orange reticle to switch to the color red. Lock on. I fire, watching the smoke trail of the rocket instantly sidewinder off toward the ocean, well away from the urban warfare gray-camo tanks.

"Don't use the guided missiles," I report over the BattleChat. "They've got jamming assets nearby!"

One of the mortar rounds finds the top of a WonderSoft Challenger with a resounding *claaanng,* and a half second later, a shower of sparks fly away from the exploding tank. The other tank races backward, retreating as it pops smoke, backing into a parking lot in front of some warehouses on the far side of the bridge. Five of our heavy-machine-gun teams, firing antiarmor ammo mixed with bright green tracers, turn that tank into Swiss cheese as its hull integrity zeros out, killing the WonderSoft grunts within.

WonderSoft heavy troopers in muted gray-and-blue urban-camo full-body armor erupt from the far side of the plaza. They quickly set up firing positions using the concrete abutments surrounding the tollbooth area that guard that side of the bridge.

I order my company to their secondary positions and radio Kiwi. "Shifting now! Move in and buy us some time."

It's standard WonderSoft technique. Move in fast with armor and try to locate our positions, then use the heavy infantry to pin us down and destroy us. So this time we're going to move while they focus on where they think we are.

Bullets begin to punch holes in the thin walls of the warehouses we're set up in. Smoky shafts of light shoot through the rooms like sudden lasers as we shift, grunts folding up their heavy machine guns and ammo crates and hauling them into their new fighting positions. Kiwi and his heavily armored, light vehicle strike force, the Mule platoon, appear down the road that runs alongside the canal where the Song Hua Bridge crosses over the river and into the harbor area and WonderSoft country. Mounted twin-barrel Hauser machine guns chew up the WonderSoft heavy troopers caught in the open on the wrong side of the barricades.

SMAFF erupts out of canisters attached to the back of Kiwi's Mules, as the rest of the platoon rakes the WonderSoft troops with gunfire in one quick pass.

"Scratch one live WonderSoft Player. Just got BangDead with about twenty other Softies!" calls out Kiwi triumphantly over BattleChat.

"Way to go," I shout back.

"Woot," says RiotGuurl.

"BangDead, I hardly knew ye," recites JollyBoy, then erupts in a wheezing laugh. Other players sound off with their congratulations, and I have to quiet them down to get everyone focused back on the next attack.

We aren't there yet.

*Look out your window, Mr. Saxon.*

The words appear in a sudden pop-up chat window on my desk, inside the Skyliner suite.

On-screen I check my rifle company. Machine-gun crews acknowledge readiness to engage targets.

"Who is this?" I write back.

*Look out your window now, PerfectQuestion!*

I swivel the desk chair to look out the large suite porthole of the Skyliner. In the hazy late-afternoon sun, somewhere over the seemingly endless Sahara Desert, a matte-black jet fighter hangs off the wide wing of the trade jet. I think it's an F-15 from last century. Moments later a second one joins it, flying wingman.

When I look back at the screen I see *Bang, you're dead,* written in chat.

On-screen, WonderSoft armored carriers are disgorging battalions of weapon-laden grunts from behind the ruins of one of the smoking tanks and along the far side of the plaza where there's cover. Huge amounts of machine-gun fire rattle off the walls as WonderSoft grunts begin to shoot grenades into the warehouses where our machine-gun teams had been during the first assault.

"Recon has pulled back," whispers JollyBoy quietly over BattleChat. "All clear to move forward, PerfectQuestioney."

I turn back to the window and stare out at the two jet fighters.

A sudden knock on the suite door quickly turns to intense, insistent pounding.

"It's Carter Banks, let me in!"

I open the door and return to the desk. I signal all units to stand by. I give Kiwi operational command for a moment.

Carter Banks looms above me as I finish entering my commands. Behind him, the captain of the Skyliner in his powder blue dress uniform waits.

"We've got merc's outside," Carter Banks says, nodding at the jets.

"They've asked me to throw you out the cargo door or they're going to board us," interrupts the gray-haired captain in German-accented English.

*Want to chat?* pops up on-screen.

I accept the video link and come face-to-face with Faustus Mercator, a.k.a. Bony Man.

"Ah, there you are, soldier boy," he says, his tombstone teeth smiling. "Like my jets? Got 'em from a couple of witch doctors. They only cost me some NikeAtlantis Air Kicks, a few dozen SoftEyes, and a shipping container full of carbon-forged machetes. You always get a lotta bang for your buck in deepest darkest Africa, I always say that. What a deal."

I hold up one finger telling him to wait, then I cut the mic on the desk.

"I can handle this," I tell Carter Banks. "Give me a minute."

"I want to assure you," announces the Skyliner captain. "We will not throw you from this plane and . . ." He pauses. He's out of breath. "We do have sufficient security to repel any boarders, should we need to."

I'm pretty sure the captain has to say that, as per company protocol. But the look that goes with it says, *Give me another option and I'll take it.*

When Carter and the Lufthansa captain leave the suite, I toggle the mic back to live.

"What do you want?"

"Everything, PerfectQuestion. I want . . . everything. You know that already. But before I can have everything, you need to be dead. So you can either throw yourself off the cargo deck . . .

I have a file I can upload to show you exactly how to override the security parameters to do it because I know Krupp-Lufthansa would never even think of doing such a thing. Or I can board the plane with my recently hired Greater Africa Coalition mercenary team, out of Djibouti, and shoot you in the head. But there's going to be some awfully messy bloodshed with that plan, I assure you. Or I can shoot down the whole plane. But apparently, that'll cost extra."

The Fasten Seat Belts sign flashes across my desktop.

"Why don't you just fight fair, for once." I pause, letting that sink in. Like it should mean something to him. "You'll feel better about winning. If you can, that is."

He laughs at me. It's long, slow, and the worst, most humorless laugh I've ever heard. It goes on for an uncomfortably long amount of time. "I never fight fair," he says on a sigh and wipes his brow. "That would be disadvantageous. To me."

"Do what you want, Mercator, but I'm going to beat Wonder-Soft today." I cut the chat link. He must have been trailing Kiwi's traffic and found me when I contacted him yesterday.

The Fasten Seat Belts sign flashes across the desktop again. The speakers in the suite are suddenly hijacked as the sounds of make-believe war and gunfire are interrupted by the very real Skyliner captain, announcing the very real situation. I hear a woman screaming as the Skyliner begins to roll side to side, and then back to level flight again. The pilot's probably attempting to keep the hijackers from establishing a connection for their boarding plane.

I return back to the desktop. Chatter and casualty counts come at me in waves above the on-screen machine gunfire and rocket rounds WonderSoft is shooting at us like there's a sale on rocket-propelled grenades and they've cleaned out the store.

Which is exactly what I want them to do. That the next few minutes will be intense is an understatement.

"JollyBoy, stand by to push their right flank. We're counter-attacking with everything we've got."

I hope Mercator doesn't know the real plan. I hope JollyBoy is the traitor. Otherwise . . . this is it.

"Moving in to pick up the grunts. Will drop them on the TV tower far side of the bridge," says RiotGuurl over BattleChat for JollyBoy's benefit. Her Albatross's turbines whine in the background as she makes her approach to the staging LZ.

"Once that's done, come back and airlift the rest of us onto the tower, roger?" I say, waiting for a reply as WonderSoft's gunfire grows cacophonous. All around me, ColaCorp machine-gun teams are pouring unreal amounts of fire into the WonderSoft positions on the far side of the bridge. Parts of the building I'm in are exploding inward as RPGs smash into the simulated brickwork.

"Anything you want . . . ," says RiotGuurl as an antiair alert suddenly blares in the background of her transmission. A second later, distracted, she finishes, "You got it, PerfectQuestion." I hear the Albatross's VTOL thrusters straining above her squadron's comm traffic.

I'm frozen. All of it, everything, makes sense now.

Anything you want, you got it.

Tatiana.

RiotGuurl asking me my name. John Saxon.

The same John Saxon holding a ticket on a Krupp-Lufthansa Trade Jet.

I open a BattleCam feed to JollyBoy. In front of me, a WonderSoft grenade rolls into the building we've shifted into. I jump and throw myself behind some stacked ammo cases. The grenade goes off, killing all the grunts nearby. Two WonderSoft troopers enter the warehouse spraying automatic gunfire everywhere.

"JollyBoy, reporting for duty, sir!" he says over chat, oblivious to the gunfight on my end.

I raise my rife and fire a rapid burst into the chest of one WonderSoft grunt as the other fires, hitting me in the left arm. I'm down and bleeding, my screen red with damage.

"I say, JollyBoy reporting as ordered, fearless leader!"

I pop a concussion grenade and fling it over the distance between me and the WonderSoft grunts, spraying bullets everywhere as the entire room is torn to shreds. When the grenade goes *bang*, I empty my magazine into both softies.

"Fever, where are you, I'm hit at second position for command team, marking my position on your HUD now."

"On my way!" is Fever's reply over BattleChat. In the background of his transmission I hear the rattle of nearby small-arms fire. I hear the rising whine of shock paddles recharging as he gets another of my grunts moving.

"Perfect, mate." It's Kiwi. "We've got WonderSoft insurgents on this side of the river. They're infiltrating our positions."

"I know," I reply. "They just tried and died at my loc. Order all units to keep an eye out for them."

"Jolly, you there?" I call out over a private chat link between the two of us.

"Yes," he says, theatrically bored. "Proceeding with counterattack through the isthmus, meeting little or no resistance."

"I thought you were the traitor . . ." I don't have time for anything else. The Skyliner is banking so steeply that suite decor is falling from the bookshelves. Then we level out. A moment later, a dull metallic clamp reverberates through the hull of the massive trade jet.

"Security teams stand by to repel boarders," says a monotone military voice over the intercom, interrupting the suite speaker's broadcast of the end of the world warfare going on inside WarWorld.

"Frankly, PerfectQuestion . . . I am shocked and hurt. A murderous psychopath, yes, of course. But I have standards, and one of which is: a friend in need is a friend indeed. I'd have to be a sociopath to be a traitor. I'm a psychopath. There's a difference, believe me. Psychopaths believe in something, even if that something's not actually real."

"Where's RiotGuurl's Albatross?" I interrupt, cutting off his rising monologue on the nature of mental illnesses. My screen is pulsing red and I have no time to waste.

I've got seconds left before I bleed out without medical attention.

Outside, in-game, the gunfire along the bridge and warehouses is achieving rock concert levels. Everyone is using everything they've got to kill everybody.

"Her Albatross is approaching the staging LZ . . . ," says Jolly-Boy.

"Listen to me, Jolly, I want you to shoot her down, right now. Do you have an antiair kit nearby?"

"Do I have rockets? I've got loads of 'em, my boy. Now where did I put that rocket? Brass knuckles. Whoopee cushion. Sniper rifle. Ahhhh . . . rocket. Shoot her down, you say? Remember, as a court-certified psychopath, I can't do it without a reason. See I'm a psychopath not a sociopath. If I were a sociopath . . ."

"She's a traitor! She's been selling us out to WonderSoft!"

Over the BattleCam feed, I hear the lock-on whine of Jolly's antiair kit, and a second later the missile shrieks away distantly with a sound-ripping *whooosh*.

" . . . it wouldn't be a matter for discussion," continues Jolly-Boy. "I'd just do it. As a sociopath, that is. Now why am I shooting her down?"

In my command management screen, I watch RiotGuurl's status move from Active to KIA.

Killed in Action.

"Jolly, I need you to lead those troops right into the center of the battle here at the bridge. Forget the right flank and head for the bridge! You shouldn't meet any resistance. They're expecting those troops somewhere else."

"No resistance!" erupts JollyBoy. "I like those odds."

Switching to BattleChat I ask, "Kiwi, what's the situation at the bridge?"

Fever crashes through the shot-to-hell warehouse door and throws out a health pack near me.

My health meter starts to rise slowly.

"Kiwi, it was RiotGuurl all along. She was the traitor. What's your status?"

"Uh . . . doesn't look good, mate," says Kiwi. "We've got Won-derSoft heavy infantry buttoned up all over the far side of the bridge. Good news is, they're not getting much farther than that. It's a stalemate, for now."

A stalemate means a loss, for us.

"Do you think you can punch through their line? JollyBoy's going to attack from our right flank straight into their center. If we can link up with him, we might be able to turn this around."

There's a pause, then, "I'll do it."

"Pick me and Fever up and order all units to follow us across the bridge. We're going on the offensive. Set the overall objective to the palazzo on the far side of the bridge near the tollbooths."

I hear machine-gun fire, hard and metallic, nearby.

It isn't in-game.

"Palazzo?" asks Kiwi.

This is real. The boarding party is inside the Skyliner.

"The big open area between the warehouses and the bridge on the far side." The palazzo was back at the tower in the Black. The plaza is on the far side of the bridge in WarWorld near the space-age TV tower. My gaming lives are beginning to overlap.

"Oh . . . that's what that's called," he says.

Trixie the sky hostess opens the door to the suite and closes it behind her quickly, leaning on the door as if that might help stop the bullets.

"The captain is telling the lower decks to hit the escape pods," she pants breathlessly. "I was told to come to your suite and tell you to remain here. The Hindenburg Class Survival System will protect all the occupants of all the executive suites in the event of a crash."

That sounds like something she read somewhere once.

I don't ask her if it will protect us from heavily armed African mercenaries with state-of-the-art submachine guns. Outside the Skyliner, the two matte-black fighter jets hold their place just above the wide bat wing of the trade jet.

On-screen, Kiwi's Mule rolls up in a pixelated cloud of digital dust and grit, twin Hauser machine guns in the mount of his vehicle chattering away at distant targets on the far side of the bridge, keeping everyone's head down. Fever and I hit E on our keyboards and swing into the backseat of Kiwi's Mule.

"Straight through 'em, mate?"

"Yeah," I reply. "Straight through 'em."

There's a high likelihood we'll all be killed shortly.

"All right then." He guns the turbocharged engine and swings the fat-tired Mule around, accelerating toward the mouth of the suspension bridge. I bring up my CommandPad and order my machine-gun teams to concentrate their fire on the far side of the bridge. WonderSoft troopers are being ventilated right and left as we swerve through the first barricade. One of the WonderSoft troopers lobs a grenade at us and we roll over it. Seconds later, it explodes underneath the other Mule that's following us, sending it skyward behind us. I unload a full magazine into a WonderSoft machine gunner who stands up firing as we pass. A bullet storm ragdolls him against the walls of the entrance to the bridge.

We enter the lower level, swerving through abandoned cars and barricades. Our Mule is already smoking and down to 35 percent integrity. Still, it's moving. Kiwi's avatar yanks the wheel hard to make a narrow entrance ramp onto the upper deck. Orange cones scatter across both lanes as the wide panorama of the sky and suspension cables leaps into view. Two ColaCorp Dragonfly hunter-killer jets from the carrier group streak overhead and drop their payloads inside the far plaza. They split, as one rolls over onto its back to watch the damage done below. Green WonderSoft AA tracer fire chases after the other.

"Why the upper deck?" I ask Kiwi. "We'll be exposed."

"They've set charges on every pylon below," he shouts over BattleChat. "They mean to blow the bridge if they know we're crossing."

"Aren't they more likely to see us up here on the top deck?" I ask.

"Sure, mate. But the explosives'll kill us outright down there. Up here we've at least got a second or two to react. By the way, Question . . ." Kiwi yanks the wheel hard and dodges a hail of bright gunfire screaming down around us from an inbound WonderSoft close-air-support Vampire. "What're we gonna do once we get to the other side of the bridge? We'll be outnumbered, surrounded, and cut off, mate."

I'm still considering what he means by "reacting," on a collapsing suspension bridge.

In the suite, Trixie touches her ear and says something. She turns to me. "They've made it to the galley. The captain says it's time to secure the suite. We might have to eject shortly." She begins murmuring procedures softly to herself. Procedures she once learned in a classroom and never thought she'd need in real life. She opens a panel in the ceiling and detaches two oxygen masks with hoses connected to the inside of the panel. She dons one and then begins to strap the other to my head.

*LOG OUT, NOW!!!!, PerfectQuestion!!!* erupts in all caps within the small chat window at the bottom of my desktop.

I ignore Mercator.

On-screen back in WarWorld, I'm telling the fire teams on our side of the river to hold position. I don't want them crossing the bridge now, in case WonderSoft does decide to blow it to kingdom come. Which they really should, if they just want a win. But what they really want is an epic victory. To do that, they'll need to cross the river and set up missile emplacements to take out our carrier task force.

I contact RangerSix.

"Listen, Six, we're going for it. JollyBoy isn't the traitor . . . it was RiotGuurl all along." Another WonderSoft Vampire comes in low and strafes the bridge. Explosions and bright ricochets of ball ammunition chew up the roadway and bridgeworks. "Jolly's leading the reserves," I continue once the jet streaks off to the north. "Into the center . . . from our right flank. I need you to ask ColaCorp for that roll now, Six."

"Hang on!" screams Kiwi over BattleChat, as shape charges start exploding in front of us at the far end of the bridge, snapping looming support pylons in half. I look behind us and see that the entire bridge is collapsing in sections. Immediately, one side of the road drops away and Kiwi follows its curve.

"Negative on that roll at this time, PerfectQuestion," says RangerSix. "Be advised, I am inbound from the carrier group with a patrol boat flotilla. We will support you in ten from the river."

Ten minutes is forever in the world of collapsing bridges while speeding head-on into the enemy's front line. Ten minutes is a clock that never moves.

Ten minutes.

Ace-in-the-hole time. I authorize my tagged ColaCorp Special Forces reserve unit to enter the battle via dropship. I select an LZ near the TV tower and order them to take the lobby.

Kiwi steers the whining turbocharged Mule down the curve of the collapsing roadway and onto the bottom level. We pass through a wall of flames and darkness. Ahead, I see the gray concrete sodium-lit tollbooths of the exit on the far side of the bridge. WonderSoft troopers are running from the mouth, away from us. WonderSoft has detonated the Song Hua Bridge with their own troops still inside.

Right then, for no real reason that a bookie or banker might accept as collateral, I know we have a chance to win this one today.

They'd freaked out and blown the bridge with their own troops inside.

They're worried.

Over in-game ambient, the sounds of steel supergirders bending, twisting, then finally shearing, rise above the fading clash of explosions and small-arms fire. Finally, the whole bridge starts to go over onto its side and into the river as we slam through the tollbooth barrier, sparks flying. Fishtailing, the Mule tips over onto its side and comes to a skidding stop at the bottom of the ramp, out in the open.

There's gunfire everywhere.

The space-age TV tower rises up out of the flat concrete jungle that is Song Hua Harbor on the far side of the industrial park. A WonderSoft mobile command cluster is set up at the base of the tower.

"Sir," says MarineSgtApone over the chat. I hear the high pitch of a dropship's engines in the background. I can also hear the whoops of the other Colonial Marines, excited to get into the fight on live network TV. I can trust them. They'll go all the way. They're my ace in the hole. "We are thirty seconds out, sir. What's the status of the LZ?"

"It's practically on fire, Sergeant. Got a problem with that?"

"No, sir. That's just how we like it." Then I hear him open

the Platoon chat and shout "Lock and load, Marines! Looks like they're expecting us."

We exit the overturned smoking Mule. Fever, Kiwi, and I. We're half a click over open ground from the entrance to the TV tower. WonderSoft is shooting at us from almost every direction.

"Cover me!" Kiwi's hulking avatar runs forward with his ever ready BrowningNox Integrated Systems 5.56 light machine gun. Fever and I take opposite sides of the overturned Mule and pour covering fire into the soft skins of the WonderSoft command vehicles.

Bullets whip past our heads and begin to ricochet off the underside of the wrecked Mule. Behind us, the few WonderSoft units that made it out of the collapsed bridge are firing at us.

Rock and a hard place.

Fever takes carefully aimed shots at the WonderSoft troopers attacking us from the rear. I concentrate on covering Kiwi with short bursts as he moves up toward the command cluster, unloading his entire belt of ammo, as brass flies away from his avatar in a steady stream over his right shoulder. Pinned-down WonderSoft support and command troopers peek out from behind command vehicles, attempting to nail Kiwi with wild, unaimed bursts of automatic gunfire.

I give them something to think about as I unload a full magazine of armor-piercing rounds into one of their light-skinned messenger Mules. It catches fire and quickly explodes, sending bodies in every direction. Soon enough, Kiwi's lobbing grenades through the squat octagonal hatches of the larger command and control armored personnel carriers.

"Go ahead and move up," says Kiwi over BattleChat. "I'll cover from here, over."

Somewhere in the Skyliner I hear an intense exchange of rapid, deliberate gunfire. Submachine guns. Footsteps pound past the suite door, making a muffled *thump thump thump* as they go up the corridor. Seconds later I hear an explosion.

I wonder how much longer I have and exactly what it is I'm going to do.

"You said something about ejecting?" I ask Trixie, as on-screen I scramble forward toward the smoking command vehicles, engaging WonderSoft grunts on the fly.

"Last mag," says Fever calmly in my ear over BattleChat.

"Well . . . in theory," Trixie begins, her voice nervous and high-pitched. "The entire suite can be ejected from the plane if the captain deems our situation unsurvivable."

The "in theory" part bothers me.

Ahead, a WonderSoft trooper in urban-camo body armor, carrying two pistols, walks away from a smoking vehicle, intent on the oblivious Kiwi who's engaging a WonderSoft machine-gun team in a warehouse window overlooking the plaza. Kiwi is prone, spitting out copious amounts of lead with his light machine gun. I let the pistol-carrying trooper have it center mass, with a burst from my auto rifle. It knocks him down onto one knee, but he turns and starts blazing away at me with both auto mags. I close the distance between us and recognize the WonderSoft trooper as a live player.

UnhappyCamper. Twin auto mags, jungle-stripe-camo T-shirt with a smiley face. Crossed-out eyes on the smiley face and a cartoon bullet wound to the head. Details I remember from another time in my apartment when I studied the enemy and everything I could learn about WarWorld for just such an occasion.

Things slow down. I feel my heart pumping hard back in the trade jet suite. I hear more real-world live gunfire. Close.

Above me I hear the hovering jets of an Albatross braking, screaming as it comes in for a hard landing.

I dive forward, hoping to get out of the way of Unhappy-Camper's thundering auto-mag pistols as they eject a stream of shells upward and outward in front of his avatar's fierce grin and crazed eyes.

I hit the ground.

In the moment it takes me to get my rifle back up, both his guns dry-click. Empty.

I cut loose with the rest of the magazine, dropping him in front of the burning hull of one of the command vehicles. On my CommandPad I see Fever has been moved into the KIA column. I look back and see his avatar sprawled out across the concrete just behind me.

He'd followed me into the firefight. Even though he knew he was going to run out of ammo.

"He's gone, Perfect; move forward now!" yells Kiwi over BattleChat. Ahead of me, he stands up and heads for the shot-to-hell lobby of the TV tower, unloading belt-fed light-machine-gun rounds in short bursts at dim silhouettes inside the lobby.

An OD green Albatross with the words *Bug Stomper* in white paint on the nose sets down outside the TV tower. Colonial Marines rush down the cargo ramp and onto the wide front steps of the lobby, taking cover alongside Kiwi. WonderSoft machine-gun teams are holding the lobby, shooting back at us with everything they've got. You can almost see the bullets because of their sheer number zipping through the air around us. Exploding concrete and grit contribute to the stress and urgency of our position. We're being shot at from every direction. The transport lifts off from the LZ, peeling away over the open plaza as WonderSoft gunfire ricochets off its armor.

There are spent shell casings everywhere.

"Apone!" I shout over the blur of cacophonic gunfire. "We're taking that lobby and holding it until reinforcements arrive."

I barely get a "Roger that, sir" as I switch over to Command-Net. "RangerSix, we're entering the TV tower, what's your ten?" I say, asking for his location.

Over BattleChat, I hear the patrol boat's quad fifty guns rant-ing away over the twin motors. Grunts and live players are calling out targets and screaming death and curses.

"I have the bridge in sight," says RangerSix. "Once we secure a beachhead, we'll come up from the river to support you. Hang in there for just a few more minutes, son."

We charge the lobby. Marines are being cut down within the first few feet, but we push through with frag grenades and rifles on full auto at close range. I even see one small female avatar go up close and personal with a WonderSoft player, flip him, and get a hand-to-hand kill as she plants a long, serrated combat knife into his prone chest.

When she stands up, ready for whatever comes next, I see AwsomeSauce15 has joined the Colonial Marines.

"Hey, Perfect," she says, snapping her gum.

"Hey back," I say and give her a quick salute.

Computer-rendered bullet-shattered glass and the programmer's vision of lingering blue gunsmoke fill the once extravagant lobby. Oh, and there's all the dead WonderSoft grunts.

"So what's the plan now, mate?" asks Kiwi as he reloads the massive light machine gun. Once the new ammo belt is inserted and the ammo pack strapped to his hip, he racks the first round, ready to rock and roll once more.

MarineSgtApone approaches us as he orders the surviving marines into defensive positions around the shot-up lobby.

"Apone, I need you to hold the lobby. Kiwi here and I are going up to the observation deck to provide intel for what's going on out there. Hold them off from here, and I'll get some mortar support on order. They're going to come at you with everything they've got. So lay down suppressive fire until our relief gets here, keep their heads down, and prevent them from moving around a lot. Can do?"

"Will do, sir," he says and begins to plan the defense of the lobby with some player named MarineCorporalHicks.

"What about RangerSix?" asks Kiwi. "If his reaction force holds the toll plaza, they'll have a clear field of fire on everything trying to enter the plaza. We'll catch WonderSoft in a cross fire between Jolly, RangerSix, and us."

Seconds later, a deafening explosion echoes out across ambient sound, receding into the darkness far above as we climb the stairs to the observation deck. It sounds so real on the suite's speakers that I look up from the desktop, unsure for a moment. Was the explosion in-game, or on the plane in real life?

"Six," I call out over BattleChat. "Request you hold the tollbooths and set up a base of fire at that location. We're up on the observation deck of the TV tower. We can create a kill zone as they come into the plaza after us. Request mortar support for my location for as long as you can provide."

"Roger," says RangerSix. I hear the *pop pop pop* of small-arms fire in his transmission. "Moving up through light resistance now." I can hear RangerSix's reaction force assaulting the burning toll plaza. On my 'noc I can see WonderSoft infantry still fighting near the burning, smoking wreckage of the bridge. They're losing the toll plaza.

"Jolly, what's your status?"

"I proudly report we've knocked out a couple of light armored scouts. I don't think they know we're here, PerfectQuestioney. Our plan might just be brilliant . . . but there's a problem."

"What's wrong?"

"I forgot to bring my really big gun. My Kill-a-Nator."

I cut the link and move onto the observation deck.

I spot a flight of gun-bristling Whales, the WonderSoft version of the Albatross, riding Air Cav screen in hover mode over an inbound large motorized column working its way through the rubble of the destroyed streets of Song Hua Harbor—heading for the plaza.

"RangerSix, this is PerfectQuestion. I have one, full-strength, motorized WonderSoft battalion moving into the AO. Request fire mission. Over?"

"PerfectQuestion, this is Six. We're encountering heavy resistance all along the waterfront. It'll be some time before we can link up. Carrier task force on standby for fire support mission. You have command."

Suddenly the entire fire support grid overlay appears on my HUD with command authorization. I have control over all Cola-Corp's indirect-fire gun batteries. I set artillery points and order the guns to load high-explosive rounds.

As the first rounds leave the guns on the beach, the artillery fire control grunt back on the carrier says a quiet "Shot out" over the chat.

"HK squadron coming in fast along the river!" calls out Kiwi over BattleChat. His gun starts to rattle out rounds, as a squadron of four heavily armed WonderSoft HKs move in over the remains of the destroyed bridge and unload with a barrage of air-to-ground missiles on RangerSix's position. Door gunners open up on us from the side hatches of the HKs, and we have to throw ourselves to the deck as their swivel-mounted auto guns send hundreds of whistling bullets into the observation deck, smashing glass and tile. An RPG lances upward from the smoking wreckage of the toll plaza and tears through the tail section of one of the WonderSoft HKs. The stricken Whale begins to rotate sharply, belching black smoke as it careens across the plaza and slams into the ground, sending debris and shrapnel in every direction. Kiwi opens up on the armored cockpit of the lead Whale. The pilot jerks it wildly to the right and flares the starboard vertical thruster. The wallowing gunship rubs its wingman with a groan of composite steel on steel, straightens out, and adds thrust to circle for a better position as Kiwi chases him with a stream of machine-gun fire.

Over the chat I can hear marines calling out targets as WonderSoft begins to fire into the lobby. Apone is telling everyone to conserve their ammo.

I hear Wierzbowski scream, "They're coming at us from everywhere!"

"They always do, man. They always come from everywhere," I hear a dry-voiced Frost reply over the heavy burn of his auto rifle.

"Frost, cut the chat . . . ," shouts Apone.

I close the channel and open a private voice link. "RangerSix, we need that bonus roll now!"

Back in the suite, a breathless Trixie shrieks, "Captain says to put on your oxygen mask! They're on the main deck." She pulls her own mask over face and begins struggling with mine.

"Stand by, PerfectQuestion. Putting the call into corporate now," says RangerSix calmly.

My artillery strike is falling across the oncoming WonderSoft motorized column. Heavy tanks and armored attack vehicles are heading through the last of the rubble-strewn remains of the city. A few troop carriers explode, but most continue to move forward. Their Air Cav screen holds position, rocketing the toll plaza and RangerSix's reaction force. Spooling auto guns whine on high-pitched screams as thousands of bullets a second rip through the computer-generated glass and concrete of the tollbooths. Below us WonderSoft heavy troopers are scrambling through the rubble, preparing to assault the lobby below us. A rough guess as bullets smack into the walls and shatter the glass of the observation deck around me puts the odds at ten to one against the marines in the lobby below.

It's almost the end of the world.

"Jolly, how long till you reach my AO?"

Kiwi's machine-gun fire turns deafening roar as he holds off the three remaining gunships circling the plaza.

"Rockets in the racks!" yells Kiwi, meaning the hunter-killers have reloaded their missile magazines. Out above the center of the plaza, the massive hovering gunships deploy their wing mounts into "X" configuration. They're just moments away from unloading their Scatter-Pack missiles.

"They're targeting us. Let's move now, Perfect!" Kiwi yells. His firing has stopped. He's running from the edge of the observation deck.

Over the chat I hear Apone say, "They're commencing their assault now, sir." I hear someone in the background of his transmission scream, "Yeah, you want some of that! Come get some."

"Did you say something, PerfectQuestion?" asks JollyBoy. "You sound like you're at the bottom of a garbage can."

Back in the suite I pull off my oxygen mask.

"I said . . . how long till you reach the plaza?"

I hear the whispering shriek of rockets exiting the wing mounts of the HKs. Kiwi races ahead of me for the entrance back into the tower.

I'm doing everything I can to follow him, and once we're just inside the main structure of the glass and steel tower, I fling my avatar behind a marble column seconds before a jet of flame rips through the glass-ceilinged observation deck.

"Ten minutes, PerfectQuestion," says JollyBoy over Battle-Chat. "We're moving in squads up through the alleys. Don't want to attract too much attention, do we now?"

"Put 'em on double-time, Jolly. I need you here five minutes ago. Ten more and it's game over."

"Righty right, sir. On our way at the double!"

Outside, the massive WonderSoft armored column enters the far side of the plaza. Rear doors of troop carriers drop down as more WonderSoft troopers pour out in wedges, advancing across the debris-riddled plaza, rifles and machine guns blazing away into the lobby beneath us. Black smoke snakes up evilly from the downed Whale in the center of the plaza.

"We're in place, PerfectQuestion." It's RangerSix. "We'll hold the line here at the toll plaza." On cue, heavy-machine-gun teams open up on the advancing WonderSoft troops. More WonderSoft troops enter the plaza in teams and begin to bound, using movement and cover to cross the plaza, intent on wiping out RangerSix's small strike force at the tollbooths.

"Heavy armor moving in!" calls out Kiwi over BattleChat. From behind the troop carriers, big WonderSoft main battle tanks erupt onto the pockmarked mosaic of the palazzo. Plaza.

"Anyone got an RPG," I hear MarinePvtDrake shout over the chat. No one replies. The marines are down by half. WonderSoft troops are surging into the lobby with flash-bangs and grenades. The explosions are deafening.

"Apone, can you hold the lobby?"

Nothing.

I check the artillery screen on my CommandPad and am told artillery will be offline for another five minutes while the guns reload. We'll be finished by then.

"Six, I need that roll."

Over the chaos of the battle all around me, I hear more explosions and loud heavy-machine-gun fire in the background of RangerSix's link. "Hold one, Perfect . . ."

Below us, WonderSoft troopers crawl forward under withering gunfire. They're taking heavy casualties, but they're advancing. They've got troops to burn, and it looks like they're smelling victory and going for broke right now. If they break through RangerSix's position, Song Hua City will be wide open and it's game over for ColaCorp.

"Got it!" shouts Ranger Six with a whoop only I can hear.

The game freezes.

WonderSoft hunter-killer Whales dodging ground fire, doling out death. Frozen.

RangerSix's machine-gun teams blazing away at the advancing legions of WonderSoft heavy infantry. Frozen.

Kiwi peering through the shattered remains of the observation deck. Frozen.

Gunfire.

Rocket trails.

Grenades exploding.

Everything freezes.

"Ladies and gentlemen," says the WarWorld play-by-play commentator, Jazz Hodges, his melodic voice echoing out across the battlefield. The Internet. The world. "ColaCorp has optioned the bonus roll." Dramatic pause as everyone stops breathing. "The judges will now announce tonight's bonus roll possibilities, and then we'll do the roll! Tonight's bonus roll is brought to you by FarGo. Isn't it about time you got what you deserved?"

Next, a smaller, tiny, more officious voice speaks up.

A referee.

"Tonight's options have been determined by a lottery held two hours before the match and certified by the accounting firm of Xpop and Breeze. Here are the possible results of the roll. On a roll of two, the rolling team will receive nothing. If the roll is a three, a supply drop of ammo for each remaining combat unit will occur. On a roll of four, all dead players will be reactivated for the optioning team. Five, a bonus of five thousand points will be awarded toward victory. Six, one suborbital EMP pulse will be enabled for the optioning team, to be used at their discretion. Seven, all deactivated units will be reactivated. Eight, a chemical weapons attack will be awarded to the opposing team to be used at their discretion. Nine, twenty-five thousand dollars for each player who survives tonight's match. Ten, a smart-weapons strike package will be air-dropped into neutral territory. First team to recover wins the package. Eleven, up to forty-five fans selected by random lottery will be allowed to log in and fight for the rolling team. Finally, number twelve. On a roll of double sixes, we will award the optioning team . . ." Dramatic pause. Everyone still holding their breath. "A historical unit from our illustrious fighting past will join the rolling team in action against the opposition. Generals, are you ready for the roll? I have the assent from RangerSix. And now Chompa818. Let's have the roll."

On-screen, two large dice spin out across the frozen battlefield.

It's a mixed bag. Some options mean little, some can change the game, one or two actually will hurt us. Most of the options are disappointing. There isn't anything that's a guaranteed game changer except the smart-weapons package. But if the roll comes down for the smart weapons, we'll have to race for them, and right now WonderSoft has all of us pinned down.

The dice tumble, showing at different moments a five, then snake-eyes, and finally double sixes.

"Friends and fans, I can't believe it!" The announcer goes nuts. "It's a fan favorite. We've had everything from Roman Centurions to French Dragoons, and even one Halloween bash in a memorable battle between JellyNuts and ChemGlobal, an Army of Terminators. But tonight it is my pleasure . . ." The game unfreezes. We're moving slowly, cranking up to battle speed. "To announce to you, one of the most legendary fighting units of all time . . ." Kiwi's machine gun roars to life, sweeping the WonderSoft troopers below us. A hunter-killer passes close to the observation deck, door gunner blazing away as he tries to take us out. Speed is increasing to normal and then the drums start.

I know this song.

Then the guitar.

Apone comes in over the chat. "Sir, we're still here. We held off the first assault but it looks like they're staging for another attack."

It's "Fortunate Son," by some old band called Creedence Clearwater Revival. It was in my 'Nam collection back in the apartment that's gone.

"I'm proud to present to you the First Air Cav, U.S. Army, Vietnam," screams the ecstatic announcer as fans roar over Live-Chat.

"Hold the line, Apone," I reply over the chat. "Help's on its way."

Distant chopper blades are *whump whump whumping* like an army of chest-beating savages from the dark side of the river. Suddenly, vintage green Huey transports, guns blazing, come in low across the harbor, purple smoke grenades flying out the side doors as they mark their LZs. Vintage Vietnam grunts hang out the doors, feet on the skids, ready to do battle.

Below us, a WonderSoft heavily armored command truck races up to the entrance of the TV tower, a mounted 25 mm cannon blazing away into the lobby. Nearby, old school M-60 machine guns rattle away across the plaza as the Blackhorse-marked choppers circle, cutting the advancing WonderSoft troopers to shreds.

"The captain says . . . ," announces Trixie in triumph. "We've stopped them. We've repelled the boarders. We're safe!" Trixie leans against the door of the suite laughing, her disheveled hair escaping from around her mask.

A new wave of Blackhorse transports land amid the swirling purple smoke, as Vietnam-era grunts race away from the choppers to set up new fighting positions directly in the path of oncoming WonderSoft troops and armor.

"Trouble, PerfectQuestion!" It's Kiwi.

"Commencing our attack!" screams Jolly over the BattleChat. "Banzai!"

From the rubble on our right flank, Jolly's troops mix in with the WonderSoft armor, taking them by surprise at close range with antiarmor weapons and explosives.

"What's wrong, Kiwi?" I ask.

"Enigmatrix. She's down below with a platoon of combat engineers. My guess is, mate, she's gonna take the lobby and demo the whole tower right here in the plaza with us in it. She gets her way she'll either drop it on JollyBoy's task force or RangerSix at the toll plaza. That'd pretty much ruin everything right about now."

*Good-bye, PerfectQuestion* appears on-screen.

I look out the window. The two black F-15s throttle back and fall behind the Skyliner.

*It's time to kill you, for real.*

"Tell the captain they're going to shoot us down!" I shout at Trixie. She stares at me in disbelief until I yell at her again. "Do it!"

"Kiwi, got any more explosives left?"

"Why bother even asking, mate."

"Hand 'em over."

A moment later, I've armed them. I set the timer for five seconds.

"Good-bye, Kiwi. You're tactical commander now."

"What are you doing?!" he screams over the battle rattle of his machine gun.

I race for the edge of the observation deck, arming the timer and scream, "Apone, get everyone's head down now!" over the chat.

Five.

"The captain is telling us to stand by to eject!" screams Trixie, almost crying now.

Four.

Hatches explode across the suite as foam floods the interior.

Three.

I pull the mask down and feel cool sweet oxygen flood my face. I'm hyperventilating.

Two.

I race for the edge of the observation deck and throw my avatar over, falling toward Enigmatrix and the waiting engineer's command truck at the entrance to the lobby.

"Heads down, Marines!" yells Apone.

One.

I'm carrying four charges of thermite, in-game.

My legs in the suite are immobilized as a brief explosion erupts beneath my feet. I turn toward the Skyliner window. Enigmatrix and whoever else was with her have just been blown up. My suite races skyward. For a brief tumbling of seconds before the SafetyFoam completely fills my vision, I see the Skyliner on fire and falling away from us. Then I hear a big explosion.

# Chapter 28

The suite settles into the desert sand of a large dune in the pink late afternoon of somewhere near the North African coast. Its two parachutes following it deflate and lie adrift alongside. The SafetyFoam begins to dissolve with soft hisses and low pops. My Petey thrums with an incoming message. I can't answer it. I'm still immobilized by the foam.

An hour later, Trixie and I are free. Instantly, she returns to the role of air hostess in crisis mode. She activates a panel, and a moment later the door to the suite is blown open. Survival gear is unlocked from an overhead bin, and an inventory of injuries officially taken.

There are none.

Trixie sets up "base camp," as she calls it, in the long afternoon shadow beneath our dune. I walk to the top of the sand pile as a light desert wind picks up. I check the message on my Petey. It's from Carter Banks.

"ColaCorp won," he'd written. "I now control a majority of shares, which are currently skyrocketing on all open markets as we speak. Thanks, I owe you one. Let me know where you're at."

That's a good question. I don't know where I am.

But we won.

That's something.

Below, Trixie in heels and prim little outfit with matching tiny pillbox cap, is busy starting a chemical fire and rehydrating emergency rations. She looks up at me, shields her eyes, and waves. I wave back.

Faustus Mercator is defeated.

I imagine he's pretty mad right now. Revenge mad.

I bring up SoftMaps and sync my location. The cartoon earth whirls and stops, then zooms in on Africa. After that, it closes in on North Africa and finally it lands somewhere south of Tripoli. I expand our location and see the ejected suite in real time, a long silk parachute trailing away from it. A dark spot represents me, but I can't zoom in any farther. I scroll around the area to the north and find more dunes. To the southwest, I find a desert track that leads to a small road that leads to a date palm farm. From there, what looks to be a paved road leads north. The nearest civilized place seems to be a small town called Douz.

I walk down the dune. Trixie feeds me a spoonful of survival-ration beef bourguignonne and rice. I make a face and she asks me if I want some hot sauce on it.

"After it gets dark," I announce, "we'll start walking toward a nearby town. A place called Douz."

"But isn't . . . we're supposed to wait here," she stammers. "Lufthansa will have rescue personnel all over this area retrieving pods and suites in no time. We should be one of the first because of your Hindenburg Class ticket. That's the best, so we'll be first."

Some people see the world that way. Better means first. First means better. Maybe I see the world a different way.

"It's been two hours," I say.

She thinks about that for a moment.

"Still . . ." She bites her lip as the wind whips her perfect hair in individual strands across her face. "We should wait."

I sigh.

"The guy who shot us down has an axe to grind against me, personally." I let that sentence hang for a moment. "I think it's best if we get lost and show up somewhere on our own terms rather than letting him get to influence how and when we get, quote unquote, rescued."

"Can he actually . . . ?"

"Yeah, he can. He's powerful and he just lost a lot of money."

An hour later, we walk through the blue twilight, surrounded by clean dunes and unending desert. It's warm out. Soon we come to the date palm farm. We drink some survival water from metallic bags and rest on a lone bench near an old shed. There is no one at the farm. It's quiet. I run a virus scan on my Petey. No bugs. At least Faustus can't track us that way. There must be hundreds of new signals since the crash, and they have to be going off all over the area, not including the indigenous signals. Plus, the emergency locator beacons from the suites and personal pods are probably too similar for anyone without company protocol software to differentiate who's who. So maybe we're just one of many. Not first. Just part of. Right now that seems better than first.

We start down a graded dirt road that leads away from the date palm farm. A crescent moon appears and we have just enough light to avoid turning our ankles on the old road. We walk until just before dawn. Then we sleep. Or Trixie sleeps, and I listen to the birds in a nearby stand of palms as she holds on to me for warmth.

I'm listening and thinking at the same time.

In two days, I need to pick up the Black game and finish the tower. I need to collect a lot of prize money from the various accounts I've been awarded. I need to contact Carter Banks, ColaCorp, Kiwi, and RangerSix. Find out what happened. But not until I can get a secure and anonymous connection. I can't chance being located. We're too vulnerable.

Pink dawn rises in the east. It's so quiet now. So quiet I can hear my thoughts.

My biggest concern is Faustus Mercator. His plan has just blown up in his face. How leveraged is he? Does he have partners? They can't be very happy about how things have turned out. I'll probably be looking over my shoulder for the rest of my life.

When I finally fall asleep, I'm so tired I don't even dream. I don't notice the Land Rover that pulls up and the tourists and guide who get out. After they try to figure out if we're alive or dead, they ask us if we have any injuries. Then they ask what the hell we're doing at the edge of the Saharan Desert.

"I say, what the hell are you doing at the edge of the Sahara Desert?" says Freddy Wong, the very British tour guide.

"Our plane went down yesterday afternoon. We walked to the road last night. Can you get us to Douz?"

"Haven't heard a thing about a plane going down!" cries an indignant Freddy Wong. "What sort of plane did you say it was?"

"Skyliner. Krupp Skyliner. *Belle of Berlin*," pipes Trixie.

"The *Belle of Berlin* crashed!" roars Freddy. "That's impossible, it would have been all over the news channels. I simply shan't believe it."

"And yet my companion," I say, indicating Trixie, "stands before you in the uniform of a Lufthansa air hostess. In the middle of the Sahara Desert."

"Damn peculiar," mumbles Freddy, producing a pipe and puffing it to life with a wooden match. "Well, climb in and we shall squire you back to Douz."

The ride to Douz is pleasant. It turns out that Douz is the gateway to the Sahara. Tourists have been coming here for years to begin their treks out into the desert.

"People love the desert," roars Freddy over the engine of his ancient Land Rover. "Pristine and beautiful. All people really want to do is find a dune, walk across it, and look back and see only their own footsteps. Much easier now since the Bedouins went away."

"Where did they go?" asks Trixie.

"Oh, they went away years ago." Freddy Wong waves dismissively over the roaring, rattling engine.

"No, I said where did they go?" she asks again.

"Right, yes. Not when but where, is that what you're asking? Too many years with this old engine destroying my hearing. Ah, as to where, I thought everyone knew that. They were one of the first ethnic groups to sign on, en masse, for the migration to Alpha Centauri. Appealed to their nomadic nature, I suppose. Now it's all criminals and the like being hauled away for that long forty-year flight. But, back during the first big uplifts, the Bedouins thought they'd take a chance. These criminals nowadays aren't going to like it when they get out there and find those Bedouins. Not one bit of it. They don't take kindly to stealing. The Bedouins, that is."

Douz is a wide sprawl of low, whitewashed buildings. Its narrow red streets crawl through restored villas where the rich play at desert nomad for a few months out of the year. Wong takes us to his villa for a few hours, then I go exploring and manage to find an Internet café where I can do some anonymous calling. I call Kiwi first.

"When I last saw you, I was blowing myself up. How'd it go after that?" I ask.

"Ah, good to see you, mate. I've been trying to get ahold of you since yesterday. Where are you?"

"Long story. Come on, what happened, I heard we won."

"Have you seen the news?"

"No, that's part of the long story also."

"ColaCorp split three hours ago. Anyone with shares just made a killing. Right before the battle, we were trading on the almost penny market. Suddenly overnight, we hold some of the most premium adverting spaces in the world. We're flush, mate. WonderSoft fired its VP of advertising this morning at eight sharp. It's a massacre in so many ways, Perfect."

"Business I can read in the paper. Tell me about the battle."

"Right. Bet you didn't know you got Enigmatrix and another player when you blew yourself up."

"No, I didn't." I'd hoped, but I didn't know for sure.

"How 'bout this? She had tactical control of the entire battle, mate. Her intel was all messed up. She thought she was coming in on our flank. Anyway, her standing orders told her troops to move forward aggressively. Well, she got killed by you, and the grunts and other players just continued to swarm into our kill zone. Aggressively. Which means, stupidly. By the time they retreated and restaged, we had enough points to claim victory. We killed most of their live players, and some noob player, a guy they just recruited last week, had operational control of the entire battle. In the end, he decided to go for a charge-of-the-light-brigade-style assault and ran right up against RangerSix at the toll plaza."

"And?"

"Didn't even make it halfway across. It was like he just group-ordered everything, circled a spot on the tactical map, and sent everyone in at once. No spacing, no overwatch, nothing. It was embarrassing after a while. I made four thousand plus in bonus kill pay. Nice, huh?"

I talk for a few minutes more with Kiwi. RangerSix is all over the news feeds. People want to know if the series of defeats had been planned all along, designed to lure a cautious WonderSoft into spending everything on one battle. A battle they lost and lost badly. RangerSix humbly tells anyone who'll listen that there is indeed a God, because it was a miracle that ColaCorp survived.

RangerSix is all right.

Afterward, I call Carter Banks. His secretarial avatar states that he will call me later. I order a date mamul from the Internet café owner. A date mamul is a shortbread cake stuffed with date paste and dusted with powdered sugar. I also have a thick, dark, local coffee with it. Outside, the sky is startlingly blue, the desert silent. Nearby, there's an open-air market, but not much going on in it.

Carter calls back.

"All right, kid, first things first. I set up an account I'll give you the number to, once you agree, completely, to my terms. I could read you the whole contract, but I don't have the time because I'm going into surgery to have my shattered spine repaired. That happened in the crash. Suffice it to say, I'm a little woozy from the pain medication. Here are my terms. You agree to everything, and I'll stamp your agreement with a voice ID signature to the contract right now. In plain English: shut your piehole for the rest of your life. In exchange, I will give you one hundred thousand dollars as a broker's fee. Plus, ColaCorp is going to give you a raise and an extension on your contract, plus a merchandise bonus for a new soda line coming out next week featuring the ColaCorp Combat Team with your avatar up front. It's called HardCharger or some jazz. You agree?"

"I agree."

"Good. I gotta go now; I'm starting to fade before surgery.

Damn suite caught fire on . . . the way . . . down. Good . . . to . . . do . . . business . . . with you."

Then he's gone. I'm checking the news. Reports are starting to trickle in that a Krupp Skyliner experienced mechanical problems over North Africa. No word of fatalities or a crash, much less getting shot down. Maybe Krupp or Lufthansa is buying everyone off. Better for business that way. Plus, I bet a lot of brokers wouldn't mind being declared dead for a while.

The last thing I do before I leave the café is check the website of the Colonial Marines clan. The Bug Hunters. I leave a message telling them how much I appreciated their help and how we couldn't have done it without them. Somehow my words just don't seem to convey my gratitude and respect, or at least it seems that way as I sit and stare at the screen. But I leave the message anyway. On the last screen I find their unit roster. I read all their names alongside their avatars and think about them and the times we had together. The names of their avatars are bold and somehow bigger than their real names. Then I see my tag. PerfectQuestion. Honorary Colonial Marine.

I walk back to Wong's place. He and Trixie are having tea. High tea, they call it. Complete with little cucumber sandwiches. Afterward we have a cordial of brandy. Wong does all the talking. He tells us the history of Douz, going back hundreds of years. Trixie listens intently. I think about what to do next.

# Chapter 29

The next morning, we fly north over the desert in Freddy's single-engine plane. He uses it to run up to Tripoli to pick up tourists for his treks out into the desert. I'd gone to bed early the night before, and when I wake in the morning, Trixie smiles sheepishly at me as she exits Freddy's room. I tell Freddy I need to get to a major airport, and he tells me Tripoli is the place. I offer to pay, but he declares "Nonsense!" and flies me there. Maybe he wants to make sure I leave. And that Trixie stays. When we taxi up to the executive terminal in Tripoli, Trixie turns back to me from the front seat and tells me she'll be staying. I watch Freddy squeeze her knee once as she says it. Soon the engine stops and we say an awkward good-bye in the desert heat. Like we'd been through more than we had. Like everything we'd been through didn't mean anything. Awkward.

I walk to the commercial terminal and buy a ticket. As soon as I purchase it, I know Faustus Mercator will know where I am and where I'm going. That's how it has to be. You don't get anywhere unless you have a name and a DNA ID card that checks out.

The night before, I hadn't totally made up my mind that this was what I was going to do. I'd lain awake in Freddy's guest room, listening to the heavy silence of the night and the desert and wondering what to do next. And after that, wondering what the shape of my life was now. I'd gone to the wide stone windowsill and looked out on silvery moonlit dunes. There were no cigarette butts, paper cups, or trash of any kind there. The dunes were smooth and I thought briefly of mummies rising from the sands, the sand running off their rotting wrappings in torrents, pouring out from within their ragged bandages. Every plan for the rest of my life is overshadowed by Faustus Mercator. He's the kind of man that doesn't let things go.

I knew what I had to do. I had to confront him, have it out. But what did that mean? Kill him? Buy him off? Both options were out of the question.

I watched the night and the stars fading and the sun rising in the east.

Now, waiting for the flight in Tripoli, I use a public Internet terminal and search Faustus Mercator. There are no hits. But that isn't what I'm looking for. I'm looking for something else. In the moment before the search results come through, the screen pauses. Just a fraction of a second. In that half second I know someone, somewhere, has hijacked the search. They want to know as much about me as possible. A lot of people can do that. But the police are the ones that do it the most.

The small supersonic passenger jet roars out over the Mediterranean.

This flight is the most vulnerable part of my plan. I feel exposed in the tiny little eight-passenger supersonic commuter hop.

But I doubt Mercator will shoot down another plane. Still,

I don't really know for sure. For the entire hour, I wait for the cabin to suddenly explode. When it doesn't and we settle onto the runway in Rome, I begin to relax. Even though I have no reason to.

An hour later, using a public terminal, I've collected all my winnings from the Black game and the hush money from Carter Banks. I check into the best hotel in the city. My room costs three thousand a night. It's getting on toward late afternoon. I call the police and ask for Interpol. A detective sergeant, Giacomo Guiglioni, answers once I'm transferred.

"I'm going to say a name," I begin before he can say anything other than his name. "I don't know if it means anything to you guys . . . but let me know if it does, and then I'll tell you how to find him. Sound good?"

"Sì. But first, ah, whom am I, ah, talking to?"

I tell him, "John Saxon."

"All right, go righta ahead."

"Faustus Mercator."

I hear fingers tapping loud plastic keys.

"Caspita!" The detective sergeant blurts out. "Ah, I'ma so sorry, my friend. It's good that you called. If you waita for a moment, I need to put you ina touch with someone. Could you stand by, please?"

I say that I can.

Moments later, Detective Guiglioni is back.

"Signore Saxon, I have Gunnar Larssen ona the line. He's ah . . . an inspector with Interpol. He's a gonna take over now. Ciao bella."

"Mr. Saxon?" says Gunnar Larssen. Inspector with Interpol.

"Yes," I reply.

"Were you on the *Belle of Berlin*?"

"I was."

"You are in Rome, currently?"

"I am."

"Excellent. We are very interested in talking to you."

"Good. I'm interested in talking."

"All right, you said you know where this man might be?"

"I do."

"I am not in Rome, Mr. Saxon. But I'm leaving within the hour. Do you need protection until I get there?"

That stops me. Does he think I need protection? Maybe this is even more serious than I've realized. But I need room to move about for a little while. Police escorts aren't gonna help.

"No. I'm fine."

"Mercator . . . He is very dangerous. Are you sure?"

I wasn't.

"Yes. I'm sure.

# Chapter 30

I go out into the early Italian evening after getting cleaned up as best I can. I need new clothes. I hit the still hot streets, listening to the babble of Italians above the motorbikes and café music. Fountains bloom suddenly as beautifully dressed people seem carefree in their lingering. Men wearing suits without ties kiss beautiful, thin women in light dresses of swirling colors holding shopping bags.

I need a secure computer. I have to finish the Black tonight.

I find a book store on the Via Borgognona. Inside, the latest books are available along with their overloaded price tags. Their displays cycle through all their amazing computing features. After spending about an hour with the salesman, Marco, a gamer himself, I set my sights on a high-end factory Gauss that's been ultraclocked by Marco and his brother. It runs at unbelievable speeds, using dual cold reaction chipsets and eight stacked Nvidia GO CandyCruncher graphics cards. I'd once seen a guy in a café running just two of those cards, and it'd been simply amazing to watch. I remember having to close my jaw with my hand. Now I have eight of them. Even though most of the world uses nebulae servers to store all their data and run their programs, the Gauss goes old school and runs an internal state-of-the-art Tetration hard drive, in which every bit of memory cubes itself and generates more available memory. Or maybe it subdivides; I'm not totally sure how it all actually works. But the slavering Marco almost has a heart attack explaining it. More important, the Gauss MK 7 book gives me access to Gauss's very secure private telecommunication network in which all my telemetry, communication, transactions, and gaming will be totally anonymous from wherever I choose to use it. It cannot be identified or tracked or traced. Gauss even maintains a separate in-house division that forges electronic signatures and random IP addresses, updating the book constantly. Totally anonymous. Guaranteed. This is the selling point Gauss punches in their marketing campaign. They're the Swiss bank of computer makers. In fact, they even operate from inside Switzerland. I pay Marco twenty-five thousand U.S., and we both exchange a moment of silent happiness for me. Then he breaks the silence by saying, "Oh yeah. I forgot. You getta the SamuraiLeather messenger bag with purchase. Hand-tooled. From Japan." He runs in back and comes out with a metallic titanium case; he opens it and removes the SamuraiLeather messenger bag. SamuraiLeather's claim is that it's not just a stylish messenger bag, it's bulletproof. But it looks pretty cool too.

"You also get to keep the titanium case for when you travel and have to stow it in cargo," adds Marco.

I can't ever imagine wanting to be apart from my brooding backlit Gauss MK 7. But I take the titanium case anyway.

"I like the way Italians dress," I say in the silence that follows, as Marco packs everything up. I'm painfully aware of my wrinkled gray suit, dirty white shirt, and the scuffed Docs I'd fled my burning apartment building in. I'd been wearing everything the night before that, on the Grand Concourse, in the space elevator, on the SkyVault. As if that all really happened.

"Oh, yes. People of Roma dress very nice. This is very important to us," says Marco.

"Where could I go and get a nice suit, at this hour, tonight? Like the one you're wearing."

"Ah, why didn't you say so?"

I did say so.

"My cousin Giuseppino, he has a store just up the street and off the main road. Very nice. Here's my card. You give it to him and he make a real nice suit just for you."

An hour later, I'm standing in my underwear while Giuseppino cuts me a suit. He works silently in a quiet room at the back of his very chic store, cutting expensive material on a green baize-covered table. Verdi, he informs me, whispers over the speakers.

"Whenever you want a suit, you call me, okay? I have your measurements and I can send it anywhere you want." He demands this through needle-clenched teeth as he begins to sew the cut material together.

From the back of the store, a tall, beautiful, voluptuous older woman enters, carrying a pot.

"Mama," cries Giuseppino. "I gotta work. No time to eat!" I doubt this woman, who must have once been a movie star or a fashion model, is anyone's mother.

"Then I feed your customer. Sit," she barks at me. She fetches bowls and ladles out steaming pasta e fagioli.

Do I need to say it's the best ever?

How could it be anything but? We even have fresh-baked garlic rolls with it, and just before Marco from the book store arrives, Lola, Giuseppino's mother, grills me.

"So whatta you do that you need a suit right now when my son should be eating because his whore wife no can cook, eh?"

"Mama!" shouts Giuseppino.

"She's a whore. Why else do you think I have no grandchildren? She's too busy. Busy doing what, I don't know. But I don't like it. When I was her age, I made movies, did fashion shows, and still cooked and cleaned and had you and your brothers!"

"I just want some new clothes," I mumble through a mouthful of amazing soup.

"Why?" she attacks me. "You gotta girlfriend? How many? Two, three, four, what?"

"Mama, he's a good customer!"

"No. None," I admit. "I don't have a girlfriend anymore."

"Why not?" she says suspiciously.

"I . . . I don't know why."

"C'mon. You must know why." Her cat's eyes stare hard at me. As though she can suck the answer from my mind.

"I've been meaning to think about that," I tell her frankly. "But what with running from my burning apartment and a power-mad egomaniac trying to kill me by shooting down the airplane I was in over North Africa, there just hasn't been a lotta time to think about why I don't have a girlfriend."

She stares at me for a long moment, then rolls her eyes.

"But it's on the list," I tell her and spoon up another luscious mouthful of her soup.

"You're a real smart guy." She laughs. "I like that." She is very beautiful. I find it hard to think of her as Giuseppino's mother.

"So whatta you do? Are you some kind of secret agent, eh? I dated one." She raises a long, perfectly curved dark eyebrow.

"I play games. Professionally."

"You what?"

"I, uh, play games for money. You know, in the Global Gaming League."

"But you're a man. Why . . . Giuseppino . . ." She fires off a string of Italian at her son who seems to be working on some very minute stitching that requires all his concentration.

"Because, Mama," he answers, eyes intent on the stitching. "That's his job. Mama, he's a customer. Now leave him alone."

Marco from the book store enters, and Lola rolls her eyes again as she moves to ladle steaming pasta e fagioli into a bowl she places before him.

He ties a napkin around his throat and picks up the salt, which she bats out of his hand, cursing in Italian. Undaunted, he lowers his spoon into the bowl and closes his eyes in delight at the first mouthful.

When the suit is finished, Giuseppino makes me try it on. He curses himself and makes me take it off. He returns to his work as I try to get more of the delicious soup into my mouth between questions from Giuseppino's beautiful mom.

When the soup is finished, the suit goes back on. But not before Giuseppino fits me with a dress shirt that feels as though it's made of silk, but holds its form like well-starched cotton. The suit, which Giuseppino dresses me in, feels like it's made of cool, cold air. It's a soft gray. It hangs perfectly. He picks up one of my shoulders.

"You know one of your shoulders is lower than the other," he states. "I can cut the suit so no one will know."

"I know. No, I need to hold it up. It's good for my posture. A doctor told me so, once."

"Okay. I make a note, next time you no hafta tell me."

Lola enters the cutting room. Circles me and nods approvingly. "What are you doing later?" Her whisper is a soft purr, but Giuseppino catches it anyway.

"Mama, what would Poppa say?"

"He would say 'have a good time, I'm dead.'"

"Mama!"

\* \* \*

I leave the store in my new suit. My old clothes are in bags under my arm. Giuseppino even gave me a nice pair of dark calfskin loafers to wear.

I return to my hotel room. I set the Gauss on the bed. For a moment, I want to take it with me. But I don't need to, so I leave it and ask the concierge to seal the room electronically once I leave. High-end hotels can do that for you.

An hour later, I'm standing in front of the address RiotGuurl had given me. It's a luxury apartment tower. The door avatar asks who I'm calling for, and I give her the room number.

A moment later RiotGuurl answers.

"Why should I let you up?"

I play it stupid.

"Because you owe me an explanation." Let her think I'm love-sick.

The avatar smiles, and the pneumatic door swings open. A floor path lights the way to the elevator. When I arrive at her door on the eighteenth floor, I don't get a surprise once it opens. It is Tatiana from the Chasseur's Inn. Her face is serious now. No games. She looks at me, and in the brief moment before she turns to stone, I see something else. Something that says, *What do you think of me now?* Then she turns and walks back into the apartment.

"Going on a long trip?" I ask, passing suitcases stacked in the hall.

"You know he's going to kill you," she says to the wall.

I walk to the window and look out at the seven cluttered hills of Rome, lit like piles of precious stones in the night.

"Maybe," I say.

"Not maybe. He's insane. Even I know that. But he's also brilliant. He always gets what he wants. Now he wants you dead."

"Over a game? Really? He wants me dead?"

"It's more than a game and you know that. It was a war for

power. The most important power man has ever had over other men. The power to tell others what to buy. What to do. What to think."

"That's a way of looking at it. But as far as him always getting what he wants . . . well, he didn't get it at Song Hua Harbor," I shoot back.

She's standing. Not moving. Wearing sweats, not the stockings and corset of the Chasseur's Inn. She sits down, staring into an empty fireplace.

"He's in a lot of trouble," I say after a moment of silence.

"He can take care of himself."

"Against Interpol?"

"You don't get it, do you?" She turns to me. The venom comes out all at once. She's another person, not the demure party doll that had me spinning that night on the way to SkyVault. "Up there . . . there aren't any laws. When you get that rich, you don't have to play by the rules. There isn't any right or wrong anymore."

"There's always right and wrong," I hear myself flinging back at her. "Just because you made the wrong choice, don't try to tell the rest of us it's right."

For a long moment there's just silence between us.

"I like you." I say it and watch her reflection in the eighteenth-story window against night-lit Rome. "I liked you when you were just RiotGuurl."

"Stop it!" she yells at me, then suddenly sobs. Once.

"I liked you because I thought we had something. Maybe that's wrong and another reason why all my relationships end badly. But I liked you. I still do."

"And what about up there?" she mumbles.

"What's that got to do with anything?"

"It's got everything to do with everything," she shouts. "That's where I belong. Not down here. Up there. I belong up there, and all this, all that before, was to get up there. And don't think you're so noble that you're above wanting better things. You wanted me when you were up there, and up there is where I'll be, no matter what it takes."

Her tirade echoes off the walls of the mostly empty apartment. As though she hadn't been there long. As though she hadn't ever really moved in. No matter how many years ago it was that she first showed up there.

"I don't think you're getting up there," I say bluntly.

"He's coming to get me."

"I wouldn't hold your breath on that. I'd say don't quit your day job, but you did."

"He said he was coming to get me." She's starting to cry.

"He's not." It hurts her, and I get a sudden sick thrill out of it.

"You lie. You're a liar! You're a filthy liar, PerfectQuestion." She cries into the arm of her oversize sweatshirt for a long time, and when she stops, I think about giving her one of my new silk handkerchiefs Giuseppino threw in with the suit.

But I don't.

I'm not that guy anymore.

"I'm not lying," I whisper. "It's the truth. It's been two days since he shot down a Skyliner. Heads are rolling everywhere, including at WonderSoft. If he isn't dead or arrested, he will be soon."

"He's not dead," she whispers.

That's what I need. It's time to wrap it up now.

"I said I like you. If up there is where you wanna be, then fine. There are ways I can make that happen, but it's going to take time. I'm leaving for South America tomorrow. Rio's got some big games coming up this spring with a lot of prize money. We'd make a great team, RiotGuurl, besides the fact that I like you. I'll be back at eleven in the morning to collect you. Think about it and be ready to leave."

I walk to the door.

"You're like that Samurai you're playing, you know?" she says. I pause.

"Code of honor," she continues. "Right and wrong. I studied them in college. You fight for principles not money, like they did. That's rare these days. Everything is money now. Everything is Ronin. Except you use a gun in WarWorld instead of that katana. You're just a Samurai with a gun."

She doesn't move.

"He knew you were playing it, and he sent me in as Plague to stop you. To kill your Samurai, to cut you off so you'd be more likely to need money. So you'd have to work with us. If I had . . . if I'd killed you . . . things would have been different. We could have worked together. We could have been rich. We could have been up there . . . together."

"Tomorrow. Think about it," I say and close the door behind me.

# Chapter 31

I walk the streets until two in the morning. I stop in a small restaurant and point at a pizza a couple is sharing at a nearby table. The guy nods, and twenty minutes later, it comes out of the oven. I have a slice and it tastes great: garlic and clams with rosemary. I want to eat more, but I ask for a box. The chef seems disappointed. I pay and leave.

Back in my room, I look at the minibar. A scotch would be . . . what, I don't know. I'm done. I knew I was coming to the end of things. I'm burned out. If I live past tomorrow morning, I want a break. I want to go somewhere. The Amalfi Coast. I'd heard Sancerré mention it once when she talked about fashion shoots with models from Milan. Talked about how beautiful it is, set between volcanoes and the wide open Mediterranean. I want to go there and rest and swim.

I start up the Gauss MK 7. The backlit keyboard glows a soft blue. I pull out my gaming mouse and sync it with the book. On-screen, graphics pour out like crystal droplets of water. My eyes, used to the strain of over-the-counter graphics cards, relax. I uplink to the Gauss satellite system and scroll through some of its features. Gauss even runs an international bank. I transfer all my funds to the Gauss International Bank. At ten minutes to three, I load the Black disk. The Gauss cracks it and asks if I would like to hack the disk. I decline. If the Black programmers are running good security software, they'll boot me from the game.

For ten minutes, I drink a bottle of water and look at my new suit coat. I'd hung it up in the closet. It's the most beautiful piece of clothing I've ever owned.

At one minute to three, the Black disk activates and connects with the mainframe running the game.

"So here we are, my worldwide audience of sickos," says the game's unseen announcer. "No doubt you're dead. Slain by our traps, our monsters, even your fellow perverts. But don't give up. Don't despair. There might still be some fight left in you tonight."

The camera resolves on my Samurai and the Minotaur.

"Which of these warriors will make it to the top and rescue the child? Only one of them can claim the prize."

The camera pans to the top of the tower. Above it, the morning sun is breaking over the battlements. Sunshine and dark clouds mix, racing across the turbulent game-sky.

"Or . . . there is always the chance that neither of them will make it. Wouldn't that be nice? Ladies and gentlemen, sickos and perverts, welcome to the last night of your lives."

I move the Samurai to the crumbling stone wall. I click on *Free Climb* in the submenu.

"I can't climb the side of the tower," says Morgax over chat.

"I have a rope. I'll pull you up as we go."

The music reminds me of fingertips drumming on a coffin lid.

Around us, the ground begins to churn, as cracked and dusty

earth erupts through the pavement around the massive, lunatic tower. Finger bones of the undead begin to claw their way up through the desert sand and ancient paving.

"Players of the Black," roars the announcer. "Now is your last chance to bring down your betters and take your revenge on them."

A wild assortment of characters crawl from the earth, shrugging off the sand and dirt. Their death wounds, delivered over the course of the contest, still gape, surrounded by rust-colored dried blood. Their weapons broken or smashed, they shamble awkwardly forward, after us.

"Go," says Morgax. "I'll hold them off down here and keep them from climbing the tower after you."

"All right," I mutter and start the Samurai free-climbing the side of the rotting tower. Two stories up, I look back down and watch as the Minotaur swipes, one-handed with the great axe, at a familiar leather-clad corpse, taking off his misshapen head. The blow flings Creepy sideways into an archer pulling back a bent arrow in a rotting recurve bow. The Minotaur already has another arrow sticking out of him. There's nothing I can do for him now.

Four stories up and I come to a thin ledge. I pause to let the Samurai's drained Stamina meter rebuild. Below, the Minotaur waves the haft of the broken battle-axe as he steps back within the darkness of the tower. Corpses crawl in after him like hungry rats vying for a meal.

"How ya doing, Morgax?"

"Not good. Falling back inside the tower . . ."

He pauses. I see the Minotaur step forward and kick one of the corpses back into the crowd. He draws both flaming, smoking swords and begins to strike down the approaching zombie-players. Then, "My weapons don't have much left in them. Maybe I can find some more in the tower." Below, he disappears within the stone edifice, securing the heavy door behind him.

"Let me find an opening back into the tower and I'll drop the rope down to you."

I crawl along the outside of the tower and notice the beginning of the large section of wall the demon giant had torn out, above me. I climb upward, slowly manipulating the Samurai's four limbs, inching up the face of the tower.

"Don't bother . . . ," says Morgax breathlessly over chat. "I'm almost done. They'll get through this door in a minute or so."

I climb upward to the crack.

"Morgax, have you ever heard of a restaurant in Upper New York called Seinfeld's?"

Pause.

"No. I mean, I think my wife might have mentioned an article she read to me one night about places to eat in Upper New York. Or do you mean the old TV show from a century ago?"

"The restaurant. You don't know the owner?"

"No, why? Should I?"

"No, you probably shouldn't." I was almost at the crack.

Then I ask, "Does anybody know you're playing this game?"

Silence. I lever the Samurai inside the bottom of the crack. Below and above me are the insides of the tower, all the floors collapsed into a pile of rubble at the bottom. The Minotaur struggles to the top of the pile as corpse-players swarm through the narrow entrance leading within. He's too busy fighting them off to respond to my question.

"Is there any reason why anyone would pay me to kill your character in-game?"

"No. None that I can think of. No one, except the people who run this game, knows I'm playing it. And even they don't know who I am."

I pull *Deathefeather* from its sheath. I look into the blade and see the face of Callard.

And the face of the raggedy man, the Vampire.

Morgax had told me the writer had gone crazy. But he probably didn't know that meant schizophrenia.

"You wanted me to kill him, didn't you?" I ask both versions of that long-lost writer.

"He can't have it. I've worked my entire life to create this world," whines Callard.

"Hey, buddy," whispers the Vampire, pushing Callard from view inside the blade. "It's almost all yours. You realize that, don'tcha? All yours?"

Callard struggles back into frame. "I'll give you whatever you want if you just stop Morgax from reaching the child and opening the doomsday file. I dropped you into the Oubliette that night after I crashed the game to test you and you passed. You're rare. You're good. You still love a game for what it can be, fun."

The Vampire shimmers into view.

"Fun, huh? It's all just a game, man. That's all it is. Fun and sex and murder and all kinds of things we probably haven't even thought up yet. You shouldn't listen to that old man, he's crazy. He doesn't realize who's in charge now."

The Vampire smiles.

I hear only Callard's voice now. The Vampire remains staring at me from within the blade, eyes and teeth flashing.

"The world is overrun by gangsters and pornographers," I hear Callard whisper as if from far away. "They take everything innocent and good, even children's video games, and turn them into nothing more than cheap burlesque. I realize that now. I was wrong to ever do a deal with these devils. Just let Morgax die, and all that I possess is yours if you'll just destroy the source code and prevent my game from being corrupted by evil."

"It's not just a doomsday file, is it?" I shout at him. "It's the whole game. The source code. You just don't want him to have it because he loves it," I tell Callard. "Almost as much as you did and somehow he knew about the file. He knew about the source code contained in the doomsday file, didn't he?"

"Callard's gone now," says the Vampire. Smiling.

"Morgax," I call out over chat, "what happened to the writer who created this world? The writer who wrote all these stories."

"A little busy right now, Wu. But it's a long story. He dropped out of society. He was paranoid. No one really knows. But there were rumors that after he died, his avatar was still running from a hidden server. It was still working on this world. I followed some leads, and I had reason to believe this was true. I even saw some trails in the Internet that led me to believe maybe the avatar might even have total control over the source file. If that was so . . . I'm down to 10 percent, Wu. I'm shooting you my contact info. We should talk after this. Sorry you're gonna have to get to the top of the tower on your own."

"Don't send your contact info over the Black!" I shout. "You've got to stay alive for just a few more minutes. What would you do with this whole world, this program, if you knew it was written by the avatar of the writer?"

"I'd protect it. I'd arrange for an endowment through my university so that it could be studied and used by everyone from students to children without all this crass filth clogging it up. It would be like all those books had come to life. It would be . . ."

"I need you to stay alive until I make it to the top of the tower, Morgax. I need you to stay in-game. I'm dropping my rope. Use it to get yourself up onto a ledge and you should be able to hold them off from there for a while." I throw the rope down toward the Minotaur. That's all I can do for him. He's got to stay alive long enough for me to rescue the child. Now it's time to climb and finish this thing. I set the Samurai climbing again. I switch the camera to third person and pan back. The tower turns golden in the morning sunlight, as wind whips at the hair and gi of the bandaged Samurai, blowing it all in one direction. Whistling. It's beautiful, like a moving painting. It's art.

I climb. I push the Samurai to the limits of his Stamina meter. I push him so hard that he groans and lets go of the wall. I let him slide until the Stamina meter has some points, then grab onto the wall again. Then it's back to climbing.

At the uppermost limits of the tower, the wall is torn away. Inside, I can see the remains of rickety wooden stairs swaying and groaning in the morning breeze, leading upward to a trap-door in the ceiling.

I crawl inside the tower, dizzy from the too-realistically rendered height. Using handholds, I swing the Samurai onto the stairs. The platform creaks drily over ambient like burnt wood ready to snap. But it holds, and I move to the trapdoor.

Pushing it open, I reach the top of the tower. I step out into golden sunshine, onto the battlements of the tower, and confront the Razor Maiden. Beyond her a small girl in a black dress, with deep dark eyes, watches me silently as the high wind whips her hair across her face.

I draw *Deathefeather* from its sheath and confront Razor Maiden. Clearly, Razor Maiden's a boss—the boss. The endgame. At the end of every game you meet one. I'd played games where the developers had even bragged that there wasn't a boss. That they'd gone for some kind of artsy ending in which your character didn't face the big-armored looming antagonist that had thrown everything in the world at you to prevent you from finally punching him or her in the face. Roll the credits. Still, there had been a boss. A completion. Games always gave you the endgame, that final moment in which the game must say good-bye. Even persistent worlds must end.

There is always a good-bye.

Right, Sancerré?

Razor Maiden is rendered in sharp angles that never rest. As though she's flickering, fading in and out of existence. She's an armored witch. A face hidden in shadows and veils. Her skirts and cloak trail away in long strands across the tower and out over its edge as the wind catches her shroud and tosses it. The only sounds are from our clothing whipping in the strong wind. Beneath that I hear a whistle, low and painful; it's the rushing air across the parapets of the high tower. Then, a rising squall of white noise erupts from the witch's slowly opening maw. A bony arm and fist reach out from the shroud toward me, and I think at once of Faustus Mercator. He's the "boss" of my life. Tomorrow we would face our endgame.

From Razor Maiden's fist protrudes a long finger wearing a single ring with a large dark stone erupting from an iron band. Details are rendered startlingly clear by the Gauss's eight stacked graphics-crunching cards. I know, in the moment I launch the flying kick at her head, that I am experiencing one of the greatest gaming moments of my life.

Perhaps the greatest.

Endgame.

My screen goes black. A small white dot appears, growing into a square. A tiny representation of the Samurai appears. The four corners of the square turn to claws and stretch out like snakes, flicking tongues toward the miniature me. I tap hard on the keyboard to get the Samurai moving, but the keyboard doesn't respond. I scramble the mouse. Nothing. I hit random keys. C makes the Samurai cartwheel away from the northern snaking claw. X sends the Samurai rushing forward, straight toward the razor-sharp point of the western claw. I hit C and cartwheel away just in time. I tap more keys until I hit Backspace and the Samurai runs toward the northern edge of the screen. I try Tab and am rewarded with running to the right. The keyboard has reversed for this little puzzle, as all four claw-snakes dart after miniature me in sporadic intervals. I cartwheel away from the southern claw, just as the eastern claw decides to strike and bury itself into the southern claw, which promptly turns green and withers with a squishy croak.

So this is the game. Make the puzzle kill itself.

It takes a few minutes, but soon I get rid of the eastern and western claws, and I end facing the northern claw, which chases me about the now rotating square. The question now is how to make the last claw kill itself. It takes another minute before I hit on the idea of tapping Backspace while I hold C down. I circle the wild northern claw snake as it winds its way after me and then finally skewers itself.

Rendered in-game reality resumes as my POV returns to my slow-motion, spinning roundhouse in progress. The Razor Maiden's face appears at the right edge of the screen. Her groan of white noise floods from a mask of beautiful evil, until the frame-rate-accelerating wooden sandal of the Samurai connects with her sharp jaw. In-game time speeds up and resumes just after rotten teeth explode from her jaw and fly away. Inky black jets of blood trail off toward the edge of the screen as she tumbles, skirts and shroud flying, across the top of the tower, coming to a halt just before its edge.

The squall of white noise turns into a typhoon shouting through the Gauss's dynamic speakers. I land in a crouch facing the once-beautiful-turned-horror-show witch. The whipping wind screeches painfully atop the tower. Beyond us the child watches, waiting wide-eyed and silent.

The Razor Maiden reaches within the folds of her burial cloth skirt and produces two giant, polished nickel-plated .44 Magnum revolvers. A few remaining teeth peek through her grin as she levers back both hammers and fires.

I'd hot-keyed *Serene Focus,* and I barely get it activated in time. Speeding bullets surrender to near motionlessness all about me. Smoke and fire erupt in slow motion from the barrels of the massive guns. The first rounds are followed by tiny shock waves of bursting sound barriers. Sluggishly, at first, the Samurai moves out of the way, as ragged scraps of the witch's shroud undulate like drifting seaweed in the screaming wind atop the tower. I dodge the first two bullets by going right, but she draws the gun barrels ahead of me and sends four more rounds to intercept me in slow motion. If I keep dodging to the right, I'll occupy the same place in time and space as her bullets. I change direction and drive the Samurai in toward the center of the witch.

It feels like throwing myself into a void in reality.

Above the barrels, her blazing eyes narrow as she snaps off another two rounds in slow motion at chest height. I pivot to the right as I draw *Deathfeather* while holding down Q on the keyboard and send the Samurai into a standing slide. Bullets whistle over the top of the Samurai as twin sonic booms turn my POV into a pond disturbed by a stone.

Close. Very close.

If her guns are six-shooters, and if the game doesn't cheat, then she has two rounds left in each gun. I continue my slow slide right into her.

Her fingers are caught in that act of squeezing the triggers. The hammers rise back to snap off more blasts, her eyes slowly widening in horror. I continue to slide faster than her bony fingers can squeeze the triggers.

*Execution.*

I punch it.

On-screen, I see a superimposed image of an old bushido topknot warlord kneeling on a rice paper mat, painting characters on a scroll. Drums thunder. Lightning strikes outside a small crosshatched window as everything turns suddenly dark. When the light returns, the warlord is headless. His body still kneeling. His head nearby on the rice-paper-covered floorboards. His hand still holding the paintbrush. Still finishing the last character on the page. Never to be finished. The trill of a martial flute punctuates the moment.

As if any is needed.

I cut Razor Maiden's throat clean through as I slide in slow motion right past her, the triggers of her massive guns still slowly depressing, the hammers rising as *Deathefeather* passes through the column of her alabaster throat. The guns shoot wide and well away from me. Her witch's hate-filled gaze follows me. I slide toward the edge of the tower, still holding the razor-sharp katana, as dark blood flies away in the howling wind. Time returns to normal, and I barely manage not to go over the edge and down into the courtyard far below.

Very far below.

When I turn the Samurai's POV back to face the Razor Maiden, only a clump of grave rags that was once a witch flutter in the fading windstorm.

I lean back in my chair, back in the suite in Rome's most expensive hotel.

Done.

Finished.

Game over.

I look out at sparkling Rome in the throes of the end of another night.

This all began back in New York, locked in winter. Iain and run-down old Grand Central. It seems like a lifetime ago. Even like another life, not my own anymore.

I lean forward and bend to the keys. As the Samurai, I approach the wide-eyed child, a little girl.

"You finally came for me," she says in a tiny little soprano voice above the fading wind. "I knew you would make it. I just knew it."

You have no idea, kid. No idea.

On-screen, the Black awards me fifty thousand in prize money, then a free code for the next tournament if I choose to play. I'm now considered the reigning champion. The record for most wins is held by a player who won twice. I think he's in a federal mental institution right now.

I right-click on the little girl.

"Where do we go now?" she asks in her tiny singsong soprano voice, as she takes the hand of the Samurai.

"Do you have the doomsday file?"

"Oh!" says the girl child, turning to me with wide serious eyes, the kind all little girls have when they are so young . . . and so serious. About everything. She reminds me of Sancerré when Sancerré talked about going everywhere and doing everything there was to be done. She was always afraid there wouldn't be enough time.

"Well, before you destroy the entire world," says the little girl—the child—"do you have any other actions you wish to perform?"

"Wait," I whisper.

Then.

"Is player Morgax still alive?"

Her eyes look off to the left. Then, "Yes. But he's almost dead."

"Make a duplicate and load it onto a secure server. Only the user with the following code I'm entering now can access it. Override NPC Callard administrator codes and replace with player Morgax. Administrator authority."

The little girl hums for a moment and then looks back up at me.

"It's done. Copy-transferred packet encoded with passkey sent to player Morgax. Anything else?"

"No," I say. "Now . . . burn this world to the ground."

"Okay," she says. Just like Sancerré used to.

"Good-bye."

Like Sancerré never did.

And the screen goes dark.

# The Last Chapter

I wake to my Petey playing "I Fought the Law," by the Bobby Fuller Four. It's one of the few remaining snippets from my burned life. Part of my 'Nam collection retrieved from a cruddy nebulae server I don't need anymore. I'd set it as the ringtone for Inspector Gunnar Larssen.

"I'm at the airport," he says abruptly. "What's the status on our friend?"

"Meet me a block east of this address on Via Siporino," I tell him. "You might want to bring a tactical unit. There's a good chance you'll get a shot at Mercator."

"Okay."

I hang up, and shave, and shower.

I order a cappuccino from the café in the lobby to fight off any lingering game hangover. I step out onto the freshly washed pavement, squinting at the bright morning light. I've spent too much time playing games; I need a week on the beach. I step back into the hotel and buy a pair of vintage Ray-Ban sunglasses from an expensive jewelry store. Two thousand bucks. Then I walk to where I'll meet Inspector Larssen and whoever he decides to bring with him.

The TAC team is there in body armor and bulletproof vests and carry wicked little machine guns with all the laser sight trimmings one can possibly strap to such things.

Inspector Larssen is a tall, mop-haired Swede with a potbelly, wearing man-of-steel-incognito rimmed glasses. He wears a tan jacket.

"We've had developments all morning," he says. "We're not sure, but Mercator may have escaped a nightclub shootout this morning. We don't know . . . so he might be one of the dead to sort out, y'know . . . but we have to run your hunch down just in case. Who's in there?"

"One of his operatives. A girl. A woman." I sketch the layout of the apartment for the TAC commander on his Command-Pad. I note all the danger zones for him. He seems grateful for the info. Or he thinks I'm a wanna-be-hardcore-soldier-gamer fanboy. Which I am.

I turn to Larssen. "What happened? Why do you think he got away?"

"I'm not supposed to say . . . but it looks like things are so out of control right now, who cares. This case is a mess. We think he's also behind a colony ship hijacking that went down about four this morning, OST."

"Why do you think it's him?"

"It's his only option. No place left for him on Earth. Plus he jettisoned all the caskets. Sleeping colonists and convicts. Real nice guy . . . but that's his style."

I watch the raid go down while nursing another cappuccino from across the street. There's a loud bang, and five minutes later, they rush Tatiana out and throw her in the back of an armored truck and speed away. I don't think she sees me. She looks frightened and confused.

A few minutes later, Inspector Larssen comes out. I cross the street and approach him, dodging mopeds and bread trucks.

"She was waiting for you," he says gravely, then pulls out a pistol with a silencer. "She opened the door ready to fire this. Bounced a bullet off the helmet of our point man. He's okay. Then we flash-banged the whole place and searched it."

There's a silence between both of us as noisy Italians all around begin their day.

Life goes on.

"Did she say anything?" I ask.

He starts to say something, then thinks better of it and walks away.

"Did she say anything?" I ask again, louder this time.

He continues to walk, shaking his head. Then he turns back.

"She said Mercator was coming to get her. She said . . . he would take her with him as soon as you were dead."

A bread delivery truck passes, honks frantically at some acquaintance on the street, then speeds off in a cloud of exhaust.

Larssen sighs, then says, "As soon as he could . . . he was coming to get her. That's what she thought. All the way up until she opened the door. Maybe even now she still thinks he's coming for her. She has no idea he's hijacked a colony ship that's headed for the forty-year burn to Alpha Centauri."

"What'll happen to her?"

I can tell he's a good man who doesn't like his job for all the right reasons. He seemed on the verge of constant indigestion.

"If we can't locate Mercator . . . she'll probably face the whole thing alone. I suspect she'll get colonization. Someone has to pay for this mess."

He turns and walks down the sidewalk to the TAC team as it sheds its armor and weapons, chattering happily in Italian and laughing about the bullet that bounced off the point man's helmet, I guess.

I'm done. I go back to the hotel and take the Gauss and put it in the SamuraiLeather messenger bag. My remaining clothes I pack into the titanium briefcase. I sling my trench through the messenger bag strap and leave. I sit at a café for a while. I try to order another cappuccino, but the waiter politely tells me it's after noon now and Italians do not drink cappuccinos after noon. Then he suggests an espresso. I order a double. He says, "Doppio," and smiles. It's a genuine smile.

I'm at loose ends. The Cola War with WonderSoft is over for now. The Black game has gone dark, for now. There'd be others. And Sancerré? Somewhere, probably in Paris or some other beautiful city, she is waking up to the rest of her life.

And I'm not part of it anymore.

Trixie? I don't care. I think about RiotGuurl . . . not Tatiana. I knew I'd miss her. I knew I'd think about her. She'd been my friend.

Tatiana had said I was like a Samurai with a gun. Like having principles and fighting for a cause were bad things. Alien things to her.

RiotGuurl had simply been my friend.

Morgax, whoever he is . . . I guess he's a friend too, like Kiwi, like JollyBoy.

Callard was just the schizophrenic avatar of some long-lost writer who kept on writing even after he was dead. An avatar who'd lost his mind and gotten lost in his own world trying to keep it alive. Like a singer who sang a song that got so popular everyone forgot who sang it first.

And then there's me. I wasn't going to play any games for a while. I'd forget about myself. Maybe I'd just be an Italian.

I knew that at any moment Lola, Giuseppino's mother, would

pull up in a tiny Italian sports car, wearing a scarf and dark sunglasses. I knew she would take me to the Amalfi Coast. I knew, standing there at the edge of the street waiting for Lola, that I would forget about Sancerré for a while. Maybe forever. But who can say. I'm just a Samurai with a gun.

Like that's a bad thing.